ChangelingPress.com

Kraken/Demon Duet

Harley Wylde

Kraken/Demon Duet

Harley Wylde

All rights reserved.
Copyright ©2021 Harley Wylde

ISBN: 9798715047250

Publisher:
Changeling Press LLC
315 N. Centre St.
Martinsburg, WV 25404
ChangelingPress.com

Printed in the U.S.A.

Editor: Crystal Esau
Cover Artist: Bryan Keller

The individual stories in this anthology have been previously released in E-Book format.

No part of this publication may be reproduced or shared by any electronic or mechanical means, including but not limited to reprinting, photocopying, or digital reproduction, without prior written permission from Changeling Press LLC.

This book contains sexually explicit scenes and adult language which some may find offensive and which is not appropriate for a young audience. Changeling Press books are for sale to adults, only, as defined by the laws of the country in which you made your purchase.

Table of Contents

Kraken (Hades Abyss MC 4, Mississippi Chapter)......4
- Chapter One..5
- Chapter Two 16
- Chapter Three..26
- Chapter Four..33
- Chapter Five 42
- Chapter Six...54
- Chapter Seven 66
- Chapter Eight...77
- Chapter Nine 84
- Chapter Ten 97
- Chapter Eleven..105
- Chapter Twelve 118
- Chapter Thirteen 127
- Chapter Fourteen 138
- Chapter Fifteen..147
- Epilogue 159

Demon (Devil's Fury MC 6)..165
- Prologue 166
- Chapter One..171
- Chapter Two 181
- Chapter Three...191
- Chapter Four...201
- Chapter Five 211
- Chapter Six..220
- Chapter Seven 232
- Chapter Eight..243
- Chapter Nine 255
- Chapter Ten 270
- Chapter Eleven...281
- Chapter Twelve 291
- Chapter Thirteen 304
- Chapter Fourteen 312
- Chapter Fifteen...322
- Epilogue 332
- Harley Wylde 338

Changeling Press E-Books 339

Kraken (Hades Abyss MC 4, Mississippi Chapter)
Harley Wylde

Phoebe -- I've spent the past year suffering at the hands of the Sadistic Saints. They've done vile things to me, made my life a living nightmare. My only bright spot is my daughter, Ember. Until another club arrives. Kraken is different from any man I've ever met. He's more than a decade older than me, but I don't care. He makes me feel so many things, and I never want it to end. He said he'd take me with him, claim me as his own. I know the Sadistic Saints will never let me go, but I'll risk it all to be with Kraken.

Kraken -- The Pres sent us to the Sadistic Saints for a deal, and I damn well knew shit would go sideways. Never counted on finding a single mom trapped in a life she never asked for. Taking her with me means war, but there's no fucking way I'll walk out of there without her. Phoebe is mine, so is her daughter, Ember, and I'll protect them with my life. I didn't become the Sergeant-at-Arms for my club by being a pushover. I'll spill as much blood as I deem necessary to protect my family, but no one will take them from me.

Chapter One

Phoebe

How had I ended up here? Figured it was much the same way most people landed in hell, or so I told myself nearly every day. I'd done something stupid. I scanned the interior of the clubhouse and wondered when I'd be able to slip away unnoticed. Being in the main room always made me uneasy. A bottle crashed against the wall and I winced as shards of glass went everywhere. It wouldn't be long before things were out of control. I skirted the room and made my way to the hall, looking over my shoulder as I scurried away. I didn't quite make it before a hand reached out and yanked me off my feet.

I yelped as I landed against a hard body. The patch in front of my eyes made me want to bolt, but I couldn't. I lifted my gaze to Deuce's, knowing there was no escape. Once he got his hands on me, he never let go until he was done. I could only hope he'd finish with me quickly.

"Where you going, whore?" he asked.

I swallowed hard. I wasn't a whore. Not really. They might have kept me against my will, forced me to be with them, but it wasn't by choice. I'd never willingly lie with any of them. Ever. "I need to check on Ember," I said.

He grunted and glanced away. The monster might use her against me, but at least I'd gotten to keep her. "Got some special company coming tonight. Be ready." He looked me over. "And change your fucking clothes."

I gave a quick nod and hurried away from him. I pushed open the door near the end of the hall and rushed inside. Ember lay quietly in her bed. I smoothed my hand over her, marveling at how I could love someone so much who'd been born from nights of pain and suffering, but I did. She was my angel, the only reason I kept going. "One day I'll save you from this place."

Just as soon as I figured out how the hell to save myself.

Remembering what Deuce said about company, I showered and shaved. I'd been told lots of times how beautiful my hair was, so I took the time to dry and curl it. The long, heavy black mass hung down my back nearly to my waist. Before Deuce kidnapped me, I'd never cared for makeup. I still didn't like it, but I wasn't given a choice of wearing it. The black eyeliner and mascara made me feel like I was putting on a mask, becoming someone else, and maybe for a few hours each night I did.

I ran the gloss over my lips and added a tinge of blush to my otherwise pale cheeks. The girl staring back me looked a far cry from the preacher's daughter I'd been in another life. I rubbed some scented lotion into my skin before getting dressed. I checked on Ember again, then curled up with a book in the corner chair to read until I was needed. Deuce would come find me, or send one of his lackeys. I wondered who was visiting this time.

Deuce never shared club business with any of the whores, and certainly not with me. I could only hope whatever club was coming, they wouldn't be as bad as the Sadistic Saints. There wasn't a line Deuce and his club wouldn't cross, which I'd learned the painful way. When my door slammed open, I jolted and glanced at Ember. Thankfully, she didn't wake.

"Come on, sweet cheeks. Time to do your thing." He leered at me as I stood. Should have known Deuce would send Joe. The Prospect made my skin crawl, even more so than Deuce himself.

I left my room with Joe's hand on my ass, and made my way to the main part of the clubhouse. I'd been right about the party getting out of control. Naked women paraded through the area, smashed bottles crunched under my feet, and smoke hung heavy in the air. I doubted they were smoking cigarettes, or at least not *only* that. Three men sat at the bar with colors from another club -- *Hades Abyss MC* was stitched on the rockers. I ran my hands down my short skirt and took a breath to steady my nerves. At least with Deuce and his crew, I knew what to expect. These guys were an unknown.

Then again, after surviving my first night here, I could live through anything.

"Get moving, whore," Joe said, shoving me from behind.

I stumbled and made my way over to the bar. Deuce had his head thrown back, laughing his ass off at something they said. His eyes lit with an unholy fire as he saw me approaching. The smirk on his lips made my stomach flip and knot. It never meant anything good.

"Here she is, boys. The best I have to offer. The three of you are welcome to take her to the playroom, or just have your fun with her out here," Deuce said. "The rest of us wouldn't mind watching."

I swallowed the knot in my throat and plastered a smile on my face. "Hi, I'm Phoebe."

"She'll treat you real good," Deuce said. The look he cast my way clearly said there would be hell to pay if I didn't. "She'll do anything you want."

The man closest to me turned and my breath caught at how striking he was. Handsome didn't seem to do him justice. Ink covered his arms and peeked from the neck of his shirt. His beard wasn't wild like Deuce's but trimmed neatly and the perfect length. I scanned his cut and saw his name: *Kraken -- Sgt at Arms*. He blocked the others from my view and I wondered if they were officers too.

"They're here for business," Deuce said. "Why don't you take them and show them all a good time?"

"No offense, but we don't like sharing," one of the others said. "If she's your best, let Kraken have her."

The biker stood and held out his hand. My palm slid against Kraken's rougher one and shivers raked my spine. I'd never met anyone who looked at me the way he did. I could drown in his gaze. He led me down the hall and my heart slammed against my ribs. He drew me to a stop in the middle of the hallway and I wondered if he wanted to start here. Wouldn't be the first time I'd been shoved to my knees or backed against the wall.

"Where's your room?" he asked.

My... No. No, no, no. We couldn't go in there. It felt like someone tightened their hand around my throat. My heart raced, and my knees nearly gave out.

"Not my room."

He looked down at me, pinning me in place with his gaze. "You got something to hide?"

"I..."

His grip tightened on my hand and my eyes went wide as I sucked in a breath. Pain shot through my wrist and up my arm. I whimpered and he loosened his hold, but dragged me farther down the hallway. He stopped in front of the last three doors, eyeing each one. I dug in my heels when he opened the one to my room.

"No, we can't... please!"

He yanked me into the room, but the moment he saw the crib in the corner, he froze. "What the fuck?"

"Please. I'll do whatever you want, but not in here. Not near my baby."

"Jesus fucking Christ. You look like a damn kid yourself and you have a baby? In a clubhouse?"

"You didn't care a minute ago how young I look," I said. I inwardly winced and wondered if he would hit me. Deuce had, and for much less. This guy was visiting the Sadistic Saints, and held rank in his club. Now wasn't the time for me to be mouthy.

"I don't fuck kids. I figured if you were out there on offer, you must be legal, but now I'm not so sure. Don't know a single damn club who lets a whore keep a kid in her room. Start talking, girl. How old are you? Why the hell are you here?"

I sucked in a breath, wondering if I could trust him. He hadn't tried to force himself on me, or demand I drop to my knees. It made him different from the men who'd come here before. I could be wrong. What if Deuce sent him here to gain my trust, see if I was loyal?

He moved in closer and tipped my chin up. "Baby girl, talk to me. You aren't like the others, are you? Girls like you, especially with little babies, don't live like this. You're a pretty little thing, look sweet as sugar."

I licked my lips and glanced away. "If Deuce walks by or sends someone else and they don't hear us having sex, it won't end well for me. Just… tell me what you like. I'll do whatever you want."

"You want to have sex?" he asked.

I gave a slight nod.

"Really? Want a good hard fucking?" He moved in closer, pressing against me.

I swallowed hard and waited. He reached for me, sliding his hand up under my skirt, wedging it between my thighs. He stroked my panties and I tried not to lock up or run.

"You're not wet. Makes me think you don't want me after all."

"No! I… I'm sorry, I'll do better."

He backed me against the wall. "Again, start talking, pretty girl. Why are you here? Because I wasn't patched in yesterday. You're no fucking club whore."

A tear slipped down my cheek and I took a shuddering breath. I wanted to tell him the truth, but I didn't dare. If Deuce heard me, if he knew I'd talked, I'd be good as dead, and my sweet baby… I didn't want to think of what would happen to Ember.

Kraken ran his fingers over my cheeks, wiping away the tears. "You don't have to talk, baby. I can see you're scared. Just shake your head yes or no. Are you here because you want to be?"

I frantically shook my head no.

His gaze strayed to the crib, then back to me. "You have that baby willingly?"

I hesitated, not quite sure how to answer. Had I wanted to have a baby under these circumstances? No, I hadn't. But I'd ended up pregnant, and I loved Ember. I couldn't imagine my life without her now. Just because she'd been conceived out of pain and hate, it didn't mean I would ever toss her away, or endanger her life.

"Honey." He dropped his voice to a near whisper. "Did they hurt you? Did they rape you? Be honest with me, angel."

"Y-yes," I said softly.

"Who?" he asked. "Give me a name and I'll make them pay."

Tears blurred my vision and I swallowed hard. "All of them."

His body went tight and I could practically feel the rage rolling through him. Kraken cocked his head to the side as loud steps came down the hallway. I heard the doorknob rattle. The big biker muttered a *sorry* just seconds before his lips closed over mine. Heat engulfed me and I felt my nipples go tight. Kraken thrust his tongue into my mouth, and I couldn't hold back my moan as he kissed me hard and deep. I reached up, placing my hands on his shoulders and held on.

Someone snickered and I tensed, but Kraken threaded his fingers into my hair, holding me still. He ravaged my mouth, taking what he wanted. In the past, someone taking control would have scared me. After all I'd suffered at the hands of Deuce and the others, it should have made me want to run. Instead, I leaned into him. He was big, strong… in charge. But unlike Deuce and the other Sadistic Saints, his strength gave me comfort.

"Damn, guess the bitch does like getting fucked," someone said.

Kraken growled and pulled away, casting a glare their way. "Get the fuck out. Deuce said she was mine, and I'm taking her."

"Enjoy her while you can. She'll be back under the rest of us by tomorrow."

"Not if I decide to keep her," Kraken said. My eyes widened, knowing he'd just crossed a dangerous line. I didn't understand why he'd said it. I wasn't anything special.

"No, Deuce said the little whore could show you a good time. He didn't say a damn thing about you keeping her. That bitch isn't going anywhere."

Kraken stalked toward them. I tried to focus on something other than my raging hormones and racing heart, and I realized he was holding onto Deuce's VP, Leviathan. The man's feet dangled off the floor. It was obvious Kraken was powerful, but he didn't look big enough to manhandle someone like Leviathan.

"Kraken, he's the VP," I said. "And he's right. I'm only here for your amusement, nothing more. I'm a place to put your dick. A toy."

He slammed Leviathan into the doorframe before turning toward me. This time, his anger was directed at me, and I really wanted to bolt from the room. He gripped my arms and pinned me to the wall. "You're not a fucking toy, or a place for someone to put their dick."

"Kraken, please… you don't understand."

"If you're not going to play with the little whore, she can go service someone else. Lots of someone elses." Leviathan smirked. "It was more fun when she screamed and fought back, but breaking her was rather exciting."

"Leave us," Kraken said. "Deuce gave her to me for the night. I won't be leaving this room until morning, and neither will she."

"Enjoy your time, Phoebe. Tomorrow night, Deuce has special plans for you."

Leviathan left and slammed the door behind him. I couldn't stop the tremors, making me shake in Kraken's hold. Tears slipped down my cheeks as I thought about what Deuce would do to me. Since Kraken attacked Leviathan, they'd take it out on me. A quick glance at Ember showed she still slept. I didn't know how, but I was thankful.

"Baby girl, we need to talk, and I need you to tell me everything. I can help you, but only if you're honest."

"You can't. No one can save me. What you did right now was dangerous. What if Deuce takes it out on your club? Or on you?"

He caressed my jaw and pressed his lips to mine in the softest kiss I'd ever had. "I can, and I will save you. I can't explain the way I'm feeling right now, or why I did what I did. My club will back me up. I have no doubts when it comes to their loyalty or support, and they don't doubt mine either. Now, start from the beginning."

He led me to the bed and I sat on the edge. My story tumbled out of me. His fists clenched tighter with every word. "My father was a preacher in a small town. He never let me have any fun. I thought it was unfair, but I should have listened. The one time I snuck out at night, Deuce found me. I was seventeen and just trying to be a normal teenager. I'd never snuck out before, but it seemed easy. I just walked right out the door without anyone noticing. He grabbed me off the street and brought me to this clubhouse."

My fingers knotted in my lap, the words stuck in my throat. I struggled to get out the rest. I'd never voiced what happened. There'd been no one to tell. Even if the opportunity had presented itself, it never would have mattered. The moment Deuce knew I'd told, I'd have been punished.

"What happened when he brought you here?" Kraken asked.

"They ripped my clothes, held me down, and…" I swallowed hard. "It lasted all night. I thought I was going to die. There was so much blood. I'd been a virgin, saving myself for the right guy. The pain was unbearable. When they were finished, they threw me into this room and locked the door. Deuce and

Leviathan came to me throughout the day, every day for a week or more. They took turns, breaking me. When I stopped fighting, they left me alone. I was... broken. They had some guy come check me over, patch me up. I'd barely healed before they made me start servicing the club and their guests."

"I'm going to fucking kill them," Kraken said, his voice nearly a growl.

I glanced at the crib again. "Ember was the result of either my first night here or the days following. I have no idea who her father is."

Kraken took a breath. I felt the coiled tension in his body. I'd never met anyone like him before. The only bikers I'd been around were cruel, like Deuce. But Kraken, despite the fact he was the Sergeant-at-Arms, seemed like he was a kind man.

"You said you were seventeen when they took you. How old are you now, Phoebe?"

"I'll be nineteen in a few weeks."

"Fuck me. I'm old enough to be your dad." He winced. "I shouldn't have kissed you."

"It was nice," I said, reaching up to touch my lips. "No one's ever kissed me like that. I'd never enjoyed being with a man... until you."

"Baby girl, you don't know what you're saying."

"You can't save me, Kraken. They'll never let me go. At least I had one brief moment where I didn't feel like the whore they've made me." I gave him a sad smile. "I know they'll kill me one night. It's not a matter of if but when."

"Breakin' my heart, little girl." He shook his head. "You're not a whore. You're a beautiful young woman who's suffered at the hands of monsters. There's a difference. You didn't choose this life, and I can't leave you here. I won't."

"Deuce said you came to make a deal with them. Whatever it is, he'll back out if you try to keep me, Kraken."

"You think I give a shit? My Pres would have my ass if I walked out of here, leaving you to this life. Those men out there *are* monsters, sweet girl. Pure fucking evil. Hades Abyss doesn't like dealing with bastards like them, but this deal was too good to pass up. At least, I'd thought so. When Titan hears about this, knows what they've done to you and probably countless others, he's going to be pissed as hell."

I licked my lips and wondered if I had the courage to ask for what I wanted. If I let him leave without at least trying, I'd never forgive myself. This was it. My one and only chance. I knew it deep in my gut.

"Kraken, I'm property of the Sadistic Saints, and they'll never let me leave. I have a favor to ask. You can say no, but... I liked it when you kissed me. Just once, I want to know what it's like to be with a man like you."

"Not a good idea, Phoebe."

His rejection hurt, but I tried to hide it.

"You're right. It was stupid. I don't even know if I'm clean. These guys, they take what they want and they don't care about anyone. It's better if you don't take things any further."

"Fucking hell," he muttered.

I sat patiently, waiting, unsure if his words translated to yes or no.

Chapter Two

Kraken

Coming here hadn't been my plan. I hadn't wanted to deal with the assholes from the beginning, but Titan had insisted. Nothing made sense. He never made deals with murderers and rapists, and it had been clear from the beginning the Sadistic Saints had no boundaries. Hell, I'd heard the rumors about them before I'd come here, but I'd hoped like hell it wasn't more. Wouldn't be the first time a club had been painted as a bunch of killers when they weren't. Now I knew different.

"Come here, pretty girl," I said softly, holding out my hand to Phoebe. There might be warning bells going off in my head, but I wasn't about to let her think she was unwanted.

I slid my hands around her waist, pulling her against me. She tipped her chin up, her gaze locking onto mine. Even after all she'd been through, there was an innocence she couldn't hide. They might have used her any way they wanted, but it didn't make her a whore like she said. They might call her one, but she was too angelic.

"We do this, it changes things," I said. "I'm not like them. I won't use you and walk away. Baby girl, you're emotionally damaged, and it's all kinds of wrong for me to even contemplate claiming you."

She shook her head. I reached up to grab a fistful of her hair to hold her still. She could deny it all she wanted, but it was true. If I took her, there was no fucking way I'd be able to walk out of here without her. As it was, I didn't like the thought of leaving her and the sweet baby in the hands of these fuckers.

"Yeah, angel, it does. I was going to try and get you out of here anyway, but we take this further than what we've done so far, and the rules change. I'll give you what you want, but you're going to give me something in return."

Her breath hitched. "What?"

"You. I want you. Not for an hour or a night. You'll leave here with me, and you'll be mine." I glanced at the baby. "Both of you."

Her mouth opened and shut. "No one does that. You can't just take one look at me and decide I'm yours. The world doesn't work like that."

"Yeah, I can." I smirked. "My club has a few old ladies in another chapter, but you'd be the only one in mine. Only other women who come around are like the ones out there on the main floor. You're not like them, baby girl. Not by a long shot. So I take you, I'm making you mine. Permanently."

I could see she was both tempted and scared as hell. I didn't know if she feared me, or the repercussions of what I'd asked of her. It would be stupid to think Deuce would let her walk out of here without any problems. There was a reason he'd taken her, kept her. The fact he hadn't ripped the baby away from her was enough to tell me there was something more going on. I just needed to find out what it was so I could exploit it.

"What's it going to be, baby? You going to be mine?"

"You'd take us away from here? Me and Ember?" she asked.

"Yeah, I would. We'd go to my home in Mississippi. I have a house at our compound. The two of you would be safe there. Protected."

She took a shuddering breath. "Okay. I'm completely crazy, but I'll go with you."

I pulled my phone from my pocket to text

Wizard. He wasn't just a damn good hacker, but he was also our club secretary. If anyone could find out the information I needed, it was him, and he could help smooth things over with the other officers when I came home with a woman without taking it to a vote.

"What's your name, Phoebe? Your full name, and Ember's."

"Phoebe Whitlow," she said. "And Ember Whitlow, but she's not... They had some woman come in when I gave birth to her. I had her in the bed here. She doesn't have a birth certificate or anything."

Not good. Not even a little. It would make it too damn easy for Deuce to make the kid disappear, and I wasn't about to let it happen on my watch. I sent the information to Wizard and let him know they were coming home with me.

Tell Titan and Boomer I'm calling in my favor. These two are mine.

I knew if we took it to a vote, chances were good they'd let me keep Phoebe and Ember, but I wasn't going to risk it. I put my phone on silent and set it on her bedside table, then slowly reached for her. She shivered, but the heat in her eyes told me it wasn't from fear. I slid my hands under the hem of shirt and felt her silky skin against my fingertips.

I was nearly two decades older than her, but if she didn't care, then neither did I. I wasn't about to walk out on her knowing she'd only experienced pain during sex, even if part of my brain was telling me to back the hell away. She licked her lower lip and I nearly groaned, wondering what it would feel like to have her lips around my cock. I wouldn't ask it of her, not right now. Maybe later. This moment was all about her. I wanted to give her pleasure.

She didn't stop me as I lifted her shirt, pulling it

all the way off. The lace cupping her breasts was sexy as fuck, the black standing out against her creamy skin. I reached for her skirt, unfastening it, then shoving it down her hips until it hit the floor at her feet. Phoebe stepped out of it and stood in front of me in nothing but her lacy underthings.

"So fucking beautiful," I said, skimming my fingers up her side.

"I want to see you," she said. "Please."

I shrugged off my cut tossing it onto a chair, then reached behind me and grabbed the collar of my shirt, yanking it over my head. It fell to the floor and her eyes went wide as she reached out to trace the ink on my chest. I was covered from my neck to my wrists. Her touch was light as she explored.

Gripping her hair in my fist, I tipped her head back. "We going to wake our daughter?"

"Our?" she asked.

"Told you, we do this it means I'm claiming you. If you're mine, she is too. Now, will we wake her? Do we need to go somewhere else?"

She shook her head. "Ember sleeps pretty heavily. Most of the time. I didn't want to do this in here earlier because I thought…"

"You thought I was like them. Thought I'd use you and throw you away."

She nodded.

I pressed my lips to hers, kissing her hard and deep. Her soft whimper, the way she melted against me, damn near made me lose control. I held on, not wanting to scare the shit out of her. This wasn't the type of woman you threw on the bed and fucked like a whore. The fucking Sadistic Saints might treat her badly, but I damn sure wouldn't. She'd suffered enough.

"Gonna make you feel good, baby girl."

"Kraken, I… I've never wanted anyone like this before, but I feel all hot and achy."

I cupped her cheek. "I do anything you don't like, or you want me to stop at any point, you say so."

"I need you, Kraken."

I wanted to tell her my real name, but not here. Not in what I was almost certain was enemy territory. I didn't trust the Sadistic Saints, and I sure as fuck didn't want them to know who I really was. It was a part of myself I'd share with her, after we were safe.

I popped the clasp on her bra, letting the sexy garment fall to the floor. Her breasts weren't overly large, but they were the perfect handful. I brushed a thumb across her nipple, the dusky peak tightening, and her eyes slid shut as her lips parted. It made me wonder if she'd ever had an orgasm. Obviously not by the hands of anyone here, but she might have given herself one. I rolled the hard tip between my fingers. Phoebe moaned and her nails bit into my shoulders.

"Kraken."

"That's it, baby. I want to hear you."

"Need more," she said.

I worked her panties down her hips until they fell to the floor, then I lifted her into my arms and placed her on the bed. Her eyes were dark with passion, and she looked so fucking beautiful it hurt. I dropped to my knees next to the bed, sliding my hands up her thighs. I tugged her closer and spread her open.

"Anyone ever licked this pretty pussy?" I asked.

"N-no."

I stroked the soft lips. "They make you shave?"

"Yes, but I kind of like it."

As long as it was her choice, it was fine by me. I leaned forward and lapped at her, gathering her essence on my tongue. Her hips bucked as I brushed over her clit. The sounds she made were almost enough to have me coming in my pants, but I tightened the reins on my control. This was about her, not me. I worked her clit with my tongue and thrust a finger into her tight pussy.

"Oh, God! Kraken! I... I..." She screamed as she came. I added a second finger, driving them in harder and faster. Her orgasm stretched into a second one, then a third.

She trembled as I withdrew my fingers. I kissed her pubic bone, then worked my way up her body. I sucked on her nipples, and gently bit the side of her neck. While I ravaged her body with my mouth, I unfastened my belt and pants, shoving at them with one hand. As much as I didn't want to pull away from her, I stood up long enough to remove my boots and the rest of my clothes.

I wanted to take her bare, but I'd wait until she'd been tested. I took a condom from my wallet and rolled it down my shaft before I settled between her legs. My cock twitched as I thrust forward, easing my way into her tight pussy. I couldn't hold back my groan. Fuck, but she was incredible.

"So perfect, baby girl. You feel like heaven."

I braced my weight on one elbow and gripped her hip with my other hand. I stroked in and out of her, long and deep. Her legs came around my waist as I rocked into her. With her gaze fastened on mine, I fucked her harder. I'd always been a bastard and taken what I wanted with women, but Phoebe wasn't just any woman. She was *my* woman.

"Come for me, baby."

I ground against her on the next thrust and felt her pussy clench down. She called out my name, her body going tight. I pounded into her, my balls drawing up, then my cum shot into the condom. Christ! My dick was still hard, but I pulled out and removed the latex. I tied it off before putting it in the trashcan beside her bed.

Phoebe scurried under the covers and I settled next to her. I drew her into my arms and kissed the top of her head. A quick glance at the crib was enough to tell me Ember still slept soundly.

"I never knew it could be so amazing," Phoebe said softly.

"Hasn't been before. You're something special, baby girl."

"I'm not special, Kraken, but you make me feel like I am. Thank you."

My heart hurt hearing those words. I ran my hand down her back, hating everything she'd suffered. At the same time, if the Sadistic Saints hadn't kidnapped her, I'd likely have never met Phoebe. As selfish as it was, I didn't like the idea of never knowing her. If only I'd been here the day she'd arrived. I could have saved her, or at least tried. She'd have been too young, but I knew the pull I felt toward her would have been there even then. I'd have kept watch over her, and maybe one day I'd have made her mine.

"We're leaving in the morning," I said. "I'm not fool enough to think Deuce would let you walk out of here. Not without wanting some sort of payment in return."

"Whatever he wants, he'll only use it for evil. You can't give in to his demands, Kraken. I'd rather stay here and know other people aren't suffering. Just… promise you'll take Ember with you." She curled tighter against me. "You said she was yours now. Keep her safe."

I rolled her under me and smoothed my thumb against her cheek. "Baby, I'm not leaving you here. These men are monsters. You think you're broken now? They aren't done yet. They'll completely destroy you. I can't let that happen. I don't know how you've held on this long, but I'm fucking grateful."

My phone lit up on the bedside table. I reached for it, clicking on the text from Wizard.

Call me.

Well, fuck. I sat up and leaned against the headboard. I dialed Wizard and he answered immediately, foregoing his usual greeting.

"What the fuck did you get mixed up in?" he asked.

"I take it you found something."

"Phoebe Whitlow isn't a missing person. Her family never looked for her. As for the daughter, Ember, there's no record of her. She doesn't exist."

"She's in a crib a few feet from me, asswipe. She exists."

"Easy, Kraken. I'm just telling you what I've found. Phoebe's father is a minister. The girl in bed with you is a preacher's daughter, but the family spun some story about her going to live with family out of state."

I looked over at Phoebe. "If she was snatched off the street, why would they say she'd left voluntarily?"

"Don't know, but we need to find out."

"Hold on," I said, pressing the phone to my chest. I turned to Phoebe. "Is there a reason your family wouldn't have looked for you?"

"I don't know, unless Deuce threatened them or something. It never occurred to me he might know where I lived. I wasn't near the house when he grabbed me. Are my parents okay? My little sister?"

I put the phone back to my ear. "The parents and sister okay?"

"Fine far as I can tell. Wait. There's something else... The day after your woman's family claimed she'd left to stay with relatives, her parents made a rather large deposit. Cash. Now where would a small-town preacher get several hundred thousand?" Wizard asked. "It's not like the guy is some big-wig televangelist raking in millions."

My gut clenched. He was right. There was no way Phoebe's father would get his hands on that much money, unless it was a payout from a family member passing, or a pay*off* when his eldest daughter was brought here. They knew. Those sorry motherfuckers knew their daughter was with these bastards, and they'd sold her. Maybe not intentionally, but the end result was the same.

"Kraken, I don't have to tell you how this looks," Wizard said.

"No, you don't. I think we know what happened, or at least partly. I won't rest until I know for sure. They might be her family, but if they abandoned her when she needed them most, I will fucking end them."

Phoebe tensed next to me, and I curved my arm around her so she wouldn't bolt. I disconnected the call. I didn't know what part Phoebe's parents had played in her abduction, but she needed to know they'd stabbed her in the back. If I'd known the turn the conversation would take, I'd have stuck with text so she wouldn't overhear.

"Baby girl, we need to talk."

"No." She shook her head. "My parents wouldn't do that. They couldn't know where I am. They'd never..."

"Phoebe, honey, your parents deposited several

hundred thousand in cash after Deuce took you. Where would they have gotten the money?"

She seemed to deflate, anguish twisting her face as she crumpled against me. I held her, murmuring words of comfort. She'd been here for roughly a year, thinking her family loved her, missed her. Only to find out they might have very well sold her out to the evil bastards who had raped and hurt her.

"We can keep digging," I said. "Find out the truth. If they plotted with Deuce for all this to happen to you... Do you want to know?"

"I need to," Phoebe said. "All this time, I worried they would be scared, not knowing what happened to me. I don't understand, Kraken. Why? Why would they do this to me?"

"Don't know, baby, but Wizard will keep looking."

Whatever it took, I'd get the truth for her. She needed closure. I couldn't imagine her family selling her out. I might not know Phoebe, not really, but she was so damn sweet. How could someone throw her away? Give her to the demons who ran this club? We were leaving in the morning. I didn't give a shit what Deuce said. If they tried to stop us, I'd kill every fucking one of them.

Chapter Three

Phoebe

My family had a part in everything I'd suffered. Even if it happened after the fact, they'd accepted money when Deuce took me, raped me. They knew where I was, they knew who had me, and they had left me here. There was no other explanation for the money they deposited. My father hadn't even had the money to put a new roof on the church. It seemed his church was more important than my life. I stood next to Ember's crib, rubbing her back. My sweet little angel. I couldn't imagine ever selling her, or letting monsters keep her. What kind of people did that? Had they ever loved me?

I felt the heat of Kraken's body behind me a moment before he placed his hands on my waist. I leaned back, taking the comfort he so willingly gave. The sun filtered through my only window. Morning had come, which meant we would be leaving. Or rather, Kraken was leaving and planned to take us with him, but I didn't for a second think Deuce would let us go. He didn't seem to care about Ember, except for the leverage she gave him. He used her to control me.

"You ready, baby girl?" he asked. "Got everything packed?"

"Only Ember's stuff. I packed two changes of clothes but I don't want anything else. It's only a reminder of what I've endured at the hands of these bastards."

"Fair enough. I'll buy my girls all new stuff when we get home. I rode my bike here. The two of you going to be okay riding with Poison? He drove the truck parked outside, and I had him get a baby seat for Ember this morning. Brick is going to ride his Harley back. One of us will take the rear and the other will ride point."

"Kraken, what if..." He placed a hand over my mouth.

"No, baby. Don't even start. We're walking out of here. All of us. And we're doing it right the fuck now. Got me?"

I nodded. He let go and I reached into the crib, lifting Ember against me. I cradled her to my chest and followed Kraken to the door. He hefted the duffle filled with what little we were taking, and I saw one of his brothers in the hall. *Brick* was stitched on his cut. A tremor ran through me and I took a breath to steady myself. I slipped into the hallway behind Kraken and followed him to the main part of the clubhouse. I felt Brick's presence behind me. I didn't know where their third brother was, but I hoped he was safe.

The place looked deserted, which freaked me the hell out. I'd never seen it this cleared out before. There were a pair of motorcycle boots sticking out from under a table, and I realized one of the Sadistic Saints had passed out on the floor. My heart slammed against my ribs as we walked through the main area, and I hoped like hell the guy didn't wake up.

We made it outside and still my fear didn't ease. Something was wrong. It was too quiet. Deuce always had someone watching the place, keeping an eye on me. Why didn't he now? He'd known I was with Kraken last night. Did he trust the Hades Abyss? If he did, was I making a mistake by going with them?

I saw their third club member in the truck waiting outside the doors. Kraken opened the rear door and stashed our duffle on the floorboard. He held out his hands. I passed him Ember and he eased her into the baby seat in back, fastening her in. Once he'd secured her in the seat, he shut the door and opened the front passenger side.

His arm curled around my waist and his lips pressed to mine. "Everything's going to be fine, baby girl. Poison will keep you safe. Brick is going with you, and I'm going to hang back a minute. Make sure you get away."

"What? No! Kraken, if they know you took us, they'll be furious. You can't say behind."

"Phoebe, I'll be fine. Now get in the truck, baby. Need to get you and Ember somewhere safe."

I hugged him tight, then followed his orders. Even if it scared the hell out of me, worrying I might be trusting the wrong people, I didn't like the thought of him remaining behind. After the night we'd shared, I already felt attached to him. More than I should have been.

"Be safe, Kraken. Come home to us," I said.

He kissed me one last time and shut the door, then patted the hood of the vehicle. Poison put it in reverse and backed out. He headed for the long drive leading to the road. The Sadistic Saints didn't have a fence or gate around their property. They didn't need one. Only an idiot would dare try to break into this place, or run from it. Until now, I'd been smart enough to stay put.

I turned in the seat and watched as Kraken got smaller and smaller. Brick zipped past us once he hit the main road and took the lead. I heard the engine rev on both the bike and truck, and soon we were rocketing down the highway. I kept an eye on the side-view mirror, but I didn't see a motorcycle closing in. I didn't see one at all.

"He'll be fine," Poison said. "Kraken isn't our Sergeant-at-Arms because he looks pretty. He earned it. No one stands a chance against him. And if those bastards think they'll keep his woman and kid from him, I have no doubt he'll kill them all."

I glanced his way. "You know Ember isn't really his, right?"

Poison shrugged. "Kraken claimed you, claimed her too. Makes her his daughter. Don't matter if he helped make her or not."

If only life were as simple as these guys made it seem. I knew better. And now, knowing my family had most likely benefited from all I'd been through didn't make me believe in rainbows and happiness. My own parents had essentially sold me. If they didn't want me, didn't care what happened to me, why would Kraken and the Hades Abyss? It wasn't like the guy loved me. We barely knew one another, even if he had given me the best night of my life.

We passed the sign for the town limits, but Poison and Brick didn't slow down. If anything, the truck seemed to pick up speed. After we drove through a third town and Kraken hadn't caught up to us, I started to worry even more. What if Deuce hurt him? I didn't know why the Sadistic Saints wanted me, or why they'd have paid my family so much. I didn't see Deuce being okay with me walking out on him. He'd made sure I knew I was less than nothing in his eyes. A place to put his dick, his little whore, but if he'd given away a lot of money to keep me, he'd want me to earn it back somehow. It's just how Deuce worked.

"I need to stop," I said, my hands clenching in my lap.

"No can do. Kraken would have my ass if I stopped for anything other than an emergency."

"If I pee on your truck seat, is it considered an

emergency? Because I need to go and I don't see a bathroom in here."

He cursed and flashed his lights at Brick. At the next off-ramp, they exited the highway and pulled over to a gas station. I glanced at Ember in the backseat, happily cooing to herself. She'd need a bottle soon, and probably could use a fresh diaper. I used the restroom, mixed some formula, and took Ember from the baby seat.

"I need something to lay her on so I can change her," I said. "I don't have one of those diaper mats or anything similar."

Brick cursed under his breath and pushed off from the truck where he'd been lounging. "Wait here. I'll see if this place has anything you can use."

He disappeared into the store and I pulled out the package of wipes and a clean diaper from the duffle. I didn't know how far it was to our destination, but I'd need more diapers before too long. Brick returned with a T-shirt.

"Best I can do. Once we're closer to home, we can stop for whatever baby shit you might need. Get your girl taken care of so we can hit the road. If the Sadistic Saints send anyone after you, and we're sitting here with our thumbs up our asses, Kraken will fucking end us."

I changed Ember and gave her the bottle. She really needed some cereal or baby food, but I wasn't about to ask for those things right now. This would do for the moment. Once I had her back in her seat, and buckled, Poison and Brick insisted we get back on the road and put more miles between us and the Sadistic Saints.

The fact Kraken never caught up to us worried me. If Poison and Brick were concerned, they hid it well. Despite their words of buying essentials for Ember along the way, we pulled through the gates of what I assumed was their compound and stopped in front of a large building. A man came down the steps, an air of power and authority clinging to him. As he drew closer, I saw his cut. *Titan -- President.*

"Take them to Kraken's house," Titan said. "I'll meet you there."

I hesitated only a moment before climbing back into the truck. I didn't know what I'd expected, but the cute two-story clapboard house wasn't it. White with black shutters and a red door, it looked like the perfect family home. Completely out of place at a biker compound.

I carried Ember inside and looked around. She squirmed in my arms and I put her on the floor. She took off crawling. The place was rather spotless for a bachelor's home. I hoped Kraken didn't plan for it to stay this clean with a baby in the house. Titan stood in the doorway, hands shoved into his pockets.

"Might want to check the fridge and cabinets. Make a grocery list, and one for other items you need. Kraken said you'd need clothes, but I'd rather wait and let him take you shopping when he gets here."

My heart nearly stopped. "When he gets here? So he's okay?"

Titan smirked. "Honey, it's going to take more than some Sadistic Saints to take him down. He'll be here sooner or later. Until then, I need to make sure you and the baby don't starve. So whatever you need, write it down."

I dug through the kitchen drawers and found a pad and pen. I took stock of the kitchen supplies and wrote down anything we might need, including baby food and cereal for Ember, more formula, and diapers.

I checked the bathrooms for other stuff, then added those to the list. By the time I'd finished, I had over twenty items and hoped Titan wouldn't balk. I didn't know who was paying for it, but I knew it wasn't me since I didn't have so much as a penny.

"I'll have a Prospect outside if you need something. His name is Sean," Titan said.

"We'll be fine. I, um, don't have a phone."

"Kraken will take care of it. You're safe here, Phoebe. Just don't leave the compound. Hell, don't leave the damn house unless you have someone with you. Got it?"

I nodded. He seemed nicer than Deuce, but if he was the President of the club, the man was a badass in his own right. I only hoped he wasn't evil like Deuce. I'd feel better once Kraken was with me. He might be a stranger still, but I felt safer with him than these other men.

After Titan left, I cuddled Ember and hoped we'd made the right choice. We were miles and miles from the only town we'd ever called home. Among strangers, locked behind a gate, with no way to call out for help. Wouldn't matter. There was no one in our lives to call. No one to come running if we got into trouble. It was just me and Ember, like it had been since the day she'd been born. And before I had her, I'd been alone.

"I hope your momma didn't just land us in more trouble," I muttered to her. "Let's hope these men are as nice as they seem."

Chapter Four

Kraken

Sending Phoebe and Ember with my brothers had been the right call. I'd known it the moment I handed her into the truck. I could have gotten on my bike and followed, but running wasn't my style. Instead, I'd grabbed a beer and sat at the bar, waiting for the Sadistic Saints to wake the hell up. So far, only their President had stumbled into the room.

Deuce ground his teeth and his eyes flashed with fury. "You're telling me the little bitch is gone?"

"Yep. Long gone." I smirked. "You miscalculated. I always take what I want, Deuce. And little Phoebe? Once I had a taste, there was no fucking way I was letting her go. So yeah, she's gone. Safely tucked away. Her and Ember."

"I paid for her. Broke her. The whore will do whatever she's told."

I tapped the bar. "About that payment. Did her family know you had her before or after you dropped the cash on their doorstep?"

"We gave the preacher a choice," Deuce said.

"What kind of choice?" I asked.

Deuce smiled. "He either gave up his daughter, or we would burn his church to the ground. Imagine my surprise when he gladly gave her up. Not without a little bit of a fight. He did ask for some money. Once we agreed on an amount, he let us know when and where to find her. She thought she'd been sneaky, slipping out of the house. They'd been watching and waiting. The moment she left I got a call."

When I finished with these fuckers, I should pay the good preacher a visit. I wondered if his church members knew what he'd done. Doubtful, since he'd spread the word she went to stay with family. I would expose him, take my pound of flesh, and then I'd send the asshole straight to hell.

"You'll have your men bring her back," Deuce said. "Now."

I rolled my neck, cracking it. "You seem to think I answer to you, Deuce."

He slammed his fist onto the bar top. "You're in my territory! My house. My rules."

"Let me tell you exactly how I feel about your rules." I turned to face him fully. "You're a pathetic excuse for a leader, Deuce, and your club is even worse. You're nothing but a bunch of murderers and rapists. Scum. It's clubs like this one that give all of us a bad name. If I were to wipe the lot of you from the face of the earth, they'd probably throw me a fucking parade. You have no authority over me, Deuce, because I'm not weak and pathetic like the rest of these men."

"You fucking..." Deuce stood so fast his stool toppled. He pulled a gun from the small of his back and pointed the barrel at my chest. "You can't talk to me like that. I'm the President!"

I knocked the gun from his hand and slammed my fist into his jaw. Fury ignited in me as I thought of all he'd done to Phoebe. I plowed my fists into his ribs, his face. I heard bones crunch and watched blood fly. He'd made the mistake of talking to me without an audience. Deuce fell to the floor and I leaned over him. I fisted his shirt and yanked him closer.

"Now, you're going to shut up and listen. The only reason you're the President is because your club is just as pathetic as you. There's no fucking way real men would ever follow you. Rapists. Pedophiles. Murderers. Those are the people who willingly let you lead. And since I can't trust you to leave Phoebe alone,

I'll have to make an example of you."

I hauled him on top of the bar and yanked the knife from my hip. I jabbed the blade between his ribs twice, then sliced it across his throat. As he gurgled and drowned on his own blood, I tore open his shirt and left a message for his club. My blade ripped through his skin as I sketched the words into his flesh.

She's mine!

I cleaned up and went out to my bike. Watching the clubhouse, I waited a moment. No one came for me. No shouts. Nothing. I shook my head. These sorry fuckers were so damn drunk and stoned, I could probably burn the place down with them inside. They hadn't even left a Prospect to stand watch. As tempting as it was to roast them in their beds, it wasn't my style. I'd give them a chance. One. If they failed and came for me or Phoebe, I'd take them out.

I pulled away from their clubhouse and hit the road toward home. Other than a stop for gas and to take a piss, I didn't take breaks. I wanted to get home to my girls, make sure they were all right, and get them settled into their new home. The look in Phoebe's eyes would haunt me for a while. She'd been scared and uncertain. I'd hated leaving her with Poison and Brick, but I'd needed to do this.

It was late when I pulled up to the gates. Morgan, a new Prospect, let me through. I bypassed the clubhouse and went straight to the house. By now, Phoebe was probably going out of her mind. I should have called. Talked to her. Reassured her everything would be okay.

Sean stood outside my house and gave me a nod as I parked my bike. I walked past him and inside. The door hadn't even shut before Phoebe rushed toward me. Her hair looked like she'd been running her fingers through it. Still, she was the most beautiful thing I'd ever seen.

"You're here," she said.

"Told you I'd catch up."

She folded her arms and tipped her chin up. "Catch up? Kraken, we've been here for half a day. Where were you? What happened?"

I pulled her to me, wrapping my arms around her. "Baby girl, there are some questions I'll never answer. Just know Deuce won't be coming for you, and if his club has even half a brain cell among the lot of them, they won't either. Damn near went to see your parents, but when I finished with Deuce, I just wanted to see you. Make sure you were all right."

"My parents? Why would you go see them?"

I pressed her cheek to my chest and held her. I didn't want any secrets between us, not as long as they weren't club business, but I also didn't want her scared of me. She'd lived with monsters long enough already. There might be darkness inside me, but I only let it out when someone needed to be punished. I never went after innocents.

"We'll talk later, baby. Right now, I want a shower and some food. I promise I'll tell you what I can. There are some things I'll never be able to share."

"But you won't lie to me, right?" she asked.

I cupped her cheek and pressed my lips to hers. "No, baby. I won't lie to you."

"All right. I'll go start the shower for you, then find something for you to eat while you get cleaned up."

I rubbed my hand over my beard. I hadn't had anyone take care of me before. It was nice. I watched her ass as she hurried down the hall, her hips swinging side to side. Despite being hungry and tired, my dick hardened. I wondered if she'd understood what it meant for me to claim her. She wouldn't be sleeping in a guest room. My woman belonged in my bed, under me, and screaming my name.

I followed, stripping off my clothes along the way. I tossed my cut onto the dresser along with my phone and dumped my boots in the closet. My clothes went into the hamper in the bathroom. Phoebe openly stared at me, and I saw her fingers twitch. I reached for her, tugging her closer.

"You can touch me, baby girl. You might be mine now, but I'm also yours." I took her hand and placed it on my chest. "You understand what I meant when I said I was claiming you?"

"You mentioned old ladies, but the Sadistic Saints only have whores."

"I'll have a property cut made for you. You're not a club whore, Phoebe, and you damn sure never will be. Any man touches you, I'll fucking kill him." She tensed but I held onto her. "Not trying to scare you. I'll do whatever it takes to keep you safe, or this club. You didn't ask how I knew Deuce wouldn't come for you."

"You killed him, didn't you?" she asked, her voice nearly a whisper.

"Beat the hell out of him first. I'm the Sergeant-at-Arms, baby. My hands are covered in blood. Doesn't make me like that shithead. I don't kill innocent people, and I would never hurt a woman. Well, maybe not *never*. There are some evil bitches out there, and if one of them hurt you or our kids, I'd end her. Someone betrays this club, won't matter their gender. I'll handle it."

She took a breath and seemed to be thinking it over. "You've never forced yourself on a woman, have you?"

I smirked at her. "Baby, do I look like I'd need to force anyone? They always fell at my feet."

She rolled her eyes. "I'm being serious, Kraken."

"And then there's that. Around the club, I'm Kraken. In enemy territory, I'm Kraken. Here in our home and it's just us? Call me Blake. No one's used that name in a long-ass time, and only you get the privilege of saying it now."

"Is it just you and me?" she asked. "Or will I have to share you with those other women? Is there even a reason for me to get tested? If you're just going to bring something home to me…"

I silenced her with a kiss. "Said I'd never do anything to hurt you. I won't fuck around behind your back. After I've showered and gotten some food, I'll call Bones and ask him to stop by when he's got a chance."

"Bones?" she asked.

"Club doctor." Something occurred to me. If they hadn't cared about getting Phoebe tested, and Ember had been born at the Sadistic Saints clubhouse…"Has Ember had any shots or anything?"

She shook her head.

"Right. Well, we'll get her taken care of too. Need to make sure both my girls are safe." I kissed her again. Tonight, I'd take my time exploring her body. As much as I wanted to strip her bare right this fucking minute, there were other things we needed to handle first. "Get out of here, Phoebe, before I can't hold back."

She headed for the door, but stopped, looking at me over her shoulder. "Thank you. For getting me out of there, and for saving my daughter. It's not her fault. I don't want her to know, ever. Not about Deuce, or how she was conceived. She's an innocent little girl."

"So are you, Phoebe." I held her gaze. "I said you were mine and so is she. No one will ever tell her different."

Tears misted her eyes and one rolled down her cheek. "You'll let her call you Daddy?"

Christ! She was killing me with this shit. I always said what I meant and meant what I said. Playing games wasn't my style. I knew there was only one way for her to accept this was real. I brushed past her to get my phone. Didn't matter what time it was. I dialed Wizard and put the call on speaker.

"I hope someone's dying because I'm balls-deep in --"

"Shut it, asshole. You're on speaker and Phoebe is right here."

Wizard cleared his throat. "Right. Sorry, Phoebe. What can I do for you, Kraken?"

"You said there's no record of Ember. I need a birth certificate, and you need to list me as her father. Understood?"

There was silence for a moment. "Right. Got it. Um... Since you seem to be taking a page from the Dixie Reapers, any other documents I need to create while I'm at it? Like say a marriage certificate?"

I glanced at Phoebe. Her lips parted and her eyes went wide. She'd frozen mid-step at his words. Other than shock, I couldn't read her expression. Did she want to be married to me? Would it make her feel safer in her position here? I'd already made a commitment to her by claiming her and Ember. In my world, it was more than marriage. Once we claimed a woman, there was no going back. It was 'til death do us part. Didn't need a piece of paper to say so, but maybe Phoebe needed it.

"Do it. I'll hand the phone to her so she can tell you any information you need like birth dates or whatever."

I handed the phone to Phoebe and she stared at me. "Are you sure? You don't have to marry me."

"I'll give you anything you need, baby girl. If you need us to be married, then Wizard can make it happen. I'm all in."

I pressed a kiss to her forehead and went back into the bathroom. I took my time in the shower, scrubbing better than usual. Even though I'd cleaned up before hitting the road, I didn't want to chance even a drop of Deuce's blood might be on me. I shouldn't have even touched her when I came in the door.

When I got out and dried off, I wrapped the towel around my waist. A smile curved my lips when I saw she'd laid out some clean clothes for me. With my new daughter in the house, I couldn't very well walk around naked. Looked like I'd need some sweats or something to wear around here, but if Phoebe thought I was sleeping with clothes on, she'd be in for a surprise.

I followed my nose to the kitchen and leaned against the doorway. Phoebe stood at the stove, stirring something. It had to be the most domestic thing I'd seen in for-fucking-ever. Probably since my mom died. I sat at the table as she plated some food. I hadn't asked her to wait on me, hadn't expected it, but I'd be lying if I said I didn't like it.

"You eating anything?" I asked.

"I had a bite earlier. I just warmed up the dinner I'd made. Hope it tastes okay."

I took a bite of the meatloaf and my mouth watered. Holy shit! It seemed my woman could cook! "It's great, baby girl."

She worried at her lower lip, her teeth nibbling at it. "About the phone call, with Wizard... He assured me you meant what you said. He's working on the papers for Ember and our marriage certificate. I don't understand how it all works, but he said if anyone goes looking, it will appear as if we're genuinely married. The state will recognize it, and will show you're Ember's father."

"How old is our little girl?" I asked.

"Six months."

I paused. "Six months. Then you were with the Sadistic Saints for more than a year."

"Ember was born a little early. I call her my miracle baby because I have no idea how she made it without being in a hospital. She was five weeks premature. But yes, I was with them a little over a year. I tried not to count. Not after the first few months. I gave up hope of ever escaping them. No point counting days or weeks."

"We'll get Bones to check her over, but I'm sure he can recommend a pediatrician for her. Anything she needs, she'll have."

"You say that a lot." She smiled faintly. "All we've needed was each other, and now we have so much more. I don't know what deal you had with Deuce, but I'm glad you were there."

"Me too, baby girl. Only wish I'd known about you sooner."

Chapter Five

Phoebe

I hadn't known what to expect of a man called Bones, but his easy manner went a long way to winning me over, and same for Ember. It never occurred to me an actual doctor would be part of a motorcycle club. I didn't know his story, and I might never hear it, but I was glad he was here right now. He'd checked me over, drawn some blood, and even taken saliva and urine samples. If there was anything wrong with me, he'd find out.

Ember had babbled to him. Watching him hold my little girl, it was clear he'd been smitten with her. She was such a sweetheart I didn't know how anyone could ever hate her. I might not know who her sperm donor had been, but I hoped growing up under Kraken's watchful eye, she'd never turn into a monster like the Sadistic Saints. She deserved love and happiness, and I felt she'd find it here.

He'd written down the name of a pediatrician in town, and said he'd give the man a heads-up about our situation. I only hoped they didn't try to take Ember from me. It hadn't been my fault she'd been born at the clubhouse, or hadn't received any sort of medical care since then. Would they think I'd neglected her?

Bones reached over and patted my hand. "Whatever you're worrying about, stop. Kraken won't let anything happen to either of you. The nightmare you were living is over. He'll take good care of you."

"The tests you're going to run... how long before we get the results?" I asked.

"A few days. No more than three, usually." Bones glanced toward the doorway, then lowered his voice. "If you've already been intimate with him, the damage has been done. Assuming you have anything.

Maybe you got lucky."

Lucky. I knew what he wasn't saying. I spent just over a year with the Sadistic Saints, and not once did they bother using a condom. It was surprising I hadn't ended up pregnant again already. Oh, God. What if I was? What if there was already another baby inside me? Kraken accepted Ember, but would he want a second baby who wasn't his?

Bile rose in my throat. This could all go so horribly wrong. What if I'd given something to Kraken? Panic welled inside me. What would his club think? Would they hate me? I dropped my gaze, shame overwhelming me. It was Deuce's fault. He'd done this. Because of him, I was dirty.

"Phoebe?"

I shook my head and backed away. My back hit the corner of the room and I sank, wrapping my arms around my knees. I'd told Kraken I could have something. He'd insisted it didn't matter. We hadn't discussed the possibility I could be carrying another baby by those men. Why had I listened to him? This man was being nice to me right now, but would he turn on me later? What would become of Ember then?

White noise filled my ears and I tried to make myself smaller, curling in. I felt large hands gripping me and I whimpered, my eyes closing tighter. I needed to leave. It would be better if I left Ember and ran. Without me, they might take good care of her. If they never knew of my past, they couldn't hold it against her. He'd only told one or two people, hadn't he? No, maybe more. But still, there was a chance the entire club didn't know yet. None of this was Ember's fault. She was innocent.

Someone picked me up. Kraken's scent surrounded me. I clung to him, even when I knew I should push him away. Tears soaked his shirt before I even realized I was crying. He eased me down onto the bed and crawled in next to me. Kraken pulled me against his chest, his arms banding around me.

"She okay?" Bones asked softly.

"Don't know. What the fuck did you say to her?" Kraken asked.

"She wanted to know when the results would come back on her lab work. Told her a few days."

"And?" Kraken asked. "I know there was more to it."

Bones sighed. "I told her if the two of you had been intimate, the damage was done already. I only meant it as a warning. More like, if you hadn't been together in an intimate way yet, it would be better to wait. I don't think she heard it the way I intended."

"You're a fucking idiot, Bones. Go check on Ember, then get the hell out of my house," Kraken said.

He smoothed his hand down my hair and murmured words of comfort. Slowly, I began to relax again. He hadn't thrown me out.

"Baby girl, talk to me. I can't make it better if I don't know what you're thinking."

"Your club will hate me," I said.

"For what?"

"If I have something and gave it to you, they'd hate me. Condoms aren't foolproof. And what if... what if I'm pregnant? They didn't use protection, Blake. I got pregnant with Ember right away."

"And you think it matters to me? It does in the sense I hate they hurt you, but do you think I'd be angry over a second baby? Care for them less than Ember? Are you worried I'll toss the lot of you out of here?"

"Something like that," I said. "I'm scared, Blake."

"I've got you, baby. No one is going to throw you out, or harm you." He kissed the top of my head. "I will kill to keep you safe, both of you. I'll keep telling you until it sinks in. Until you believe me. My brothers accept you, Phoebe. They're my family, which makes them *your* family now too."

"I'm sorry I'm such a mess," I said. "I don't know what happened. I was fine, mostly, but all of a sudden, this weight just pressed down on me and I got scared all this would disappear."

"All what?" Kraken asked.

"You. This house. Being… wanted. I know we're strangers, Blake, but I'm already getting attached to you."

"Not going anywhere, baby. And neither are you. We're a family, Phoebe. You, me, and Ember. My wife." He caressed me, his hands making me shiver. "My lover. The mother of my children."

"Children?" I asked.

He nuzzled me. "Once we get the all-clear, I'm doing my damnedest to put a baby in you. And yeah, I said we. I had Bones take some blood and urine to run tests on me too. Didn't seem fair to ask you to do it without me doing the same. I always wear a condom, but can't be too careful."

"Maybe we should wait. We already tempted fate before," I said.

"I'm not going to force myself on you, baby girl. You don't want to do more than this right here, I won't try to push for more. But, baby, the second those results come back, you're mine. No more holding back. Unless you really and truly don't want me."

I cuddled closer. "Of course, I want you, Blake. That's the problem. I want you *too* much."

"No such thing. Let's get some rest, then we'll go

shopping in the morning. Ember needs a bed. You both need more clothes and other essentials."

"I found the playpen when I checked out the house," I said. "It's brand new."

"My brothers sent someone to pick it up. Figured Ember would need a place to sleep for a night or two until we could get a nursery set up."

"It was nice of them," I said. "Your President made sure we had the stuff we'd need immediately. I'm not used to all this, Blake. My only interactions with bikers were with Deuce and those who visited the Sadistic Saints. Your club was the first to show up who weren't evil like those men."

"Not all bikers are bad men, baby. There are completely legit clubs out there who don't get their hands dirty at all. The Hades Abyss have legal businesses, but we also have some which aren't so clean. What we aren't? Men like the Sadistic Saints. We don't hurt innocent people, or get off on being cruel, and we know a lot of other clubs like ours." He ran his hand up and down my back. "I want to introduce you to my club, and maybe bring in some friends from the other clubs. Ones with old ladies so you'll have someone to talk to, get a woman's perspective on this way of life."

"I think I'd like that." I breathed in his scent. "I'm not tired. Not even a little. Too wound up."

"You want to go to one of the twenty-four stores nearby? Go ahead and grab what we can? We can let Ember sleep, get someone to come sit with her."

I knew he trusted the people here, and if I was going to make a home with Kraken, then I needed to do the same. Even if I hadn't met many of them, they hadn't hurt me. Poison and Brick might not have been very talkative, but they'd gotten me here in one piece.

Titan had even been kind to make sure we had anything we might need until Kraken arrived.

"Do any of them know how to take care of a baby?" I asked.

"I could always get Bones to come sit with her. She seemed to like him, and as a doctor, I'm sure he knows how to change a diaper and keep our kid alive for an hour or two."

"All right. But I think I need to shower and change."

He swatted my ass. "Get to it, baby girl. I'll call Bones again and see if he's willing to come back for a little bit."

I hurried into the bathroom and started the shower. The hot water felt good as I scrubbed my body and hair. By the time I got out, the water had started to cool. I pulled on one of my only sets of clean clothes and went to find Kraken. Instead, I found Bones. He'd kicked back on the couch with Ember cradled against his chest.

"Your man went to get a club truck. Can't carry back a lot on a bike."

Made sense. "Um, about earlier."

Bones watched me, waiting.

"I'm sorry for the way I reacted. It just all came crashing down on me, and I guess it was too much. It wasn't your fault. I got scared and overwhelmed. I appreciate you coming to see us. Thank you for watching Ember tonight too."

"This little one reminds me of what I almost had," he said, a sad smile on his lips. "One day, maybe I'll get another chance. For now, you ever need a babysitter for this angel, give me a call."

A horn honked outside and I rushed out the door. Kraken got out and went around to open the passenger side. He gave me a boost into the truck, then shut the door. As he passed in front of the headlights, I admired him. The ink on his arms. The confident way he walked. Kraken was sexy as hell, and for whatever reason, he wanted me.

"Like what you see?" he asked as he slid behind the wheel.

"Just a little." I smiled.

Kraken winked and put the truck into gear. He turned on the radio as we left the compound, a classic rock station. His choice didn't surprise me. The fact he knew all the words *and* could actually sing did, however. Kraken had an amazing voice as he belted out the lyrics to "Cold as Ice." When the song changed to "To Be With You," and he cast glances my way as he sang, I got goose bumps, and some part of me fell for him even harder. Just when I'd thought he couldn't get more perfect.

He parked as close to the front of the store as he could and reached for my hand as we walked up to the doors. It felt… nice. Normal. We got a few looks as we entered the store, but I didn't care. I knew Kraken was older than me, and he looked like the kind of guy mommas warn their daughters to avoid. He leaned down and kissed my cheek.

"You're egging them on," I whispered.

"Good. They obviously need something to talk about."

I looked around, feeling as if people were staring at us. "Shouldn't they be home in bed? It's late. Like, really late."

Kraken's shoulders shook with silent laughter. "Baby, last I checked, we're here shopping late. Why wouldn't other people be here too?"

When he walked me to the jewelry counter, I

tried to back away. He pressed his hand to my lower back, holding me in place. The determination etched on his face told me this was a battle I wouldn't win. I didn't know what he was up to, but I didn't need shiny things.

"Kraken, I don't need anything from here."

"Yeah, baby. You do." He waved over a store associate. The older woman eyed him, then me, clearly disapproving of the fact we were together. If Kraken noticed, he didn't care. "Which one do you like?"

I looked into the case and realized they were wedding rings. I sagged against him, the fight draining from me. "You're buying me a wedding ring?"

"Look, I may not have gone about things the right way, but I want the world to know you're mine. You deserve something better than this store can offer, but I don't want to wait another second to put a ring on your finger so everyone knows I'm the lucky bastard who goes home to you."

"Kraken, that's…" Tears misted my eyes. It was the sweetest thing I'd heard in forever. I scanned the contents of the case. They were all so beautiful, and cost entirely too much. All I needed was a plain wedding band.

"Don't even think it," he said.

"What?"

"I see you checking out those bands. Nothing ordinary for my wife. Now which one do you like?" he asked.

The woman cleared her throat. "May I make a suggestion?"

Kraken arched an eyebrow at her. "Depends. Is it your suggestion she leave me for another man?"

The woman snorted. "No. But your wife has small hands, delicate bones. Anything overly large may be overwhelming for her. Unless you want people to see it from space."

"What rings would you suggest?" I asked.

The woman pulled out three different wedding sets. Each was beautiful, without being flashy. I pointed to the one in the center. "What about this one?"

Kraken took it from the box and slid it over my finger. It was a bit loose, but I loved it. The rings didn't feel heavy, and I liked the way they looked on my hand.

"We can send them out to be sized," the woman said. "Shouldn't take more than thirty days to get them back. Or you can take them to the jewelry shop on Clover. They might be able to do it within a few days."

"We'll take them," Kraken said.

"Do you need a ring as well?" the woman asked.

"Have anything indestructible?"

She put the rings away and locked the cabinet before opening another. The woman pulled out a black band with an inlaid green design and set it on the counter. "Tungsten steel. Popular with men who work with their hands."

Kraken slipped it on and flexed his hand. "Fits good."

"You'll have to pay for the rings here. If your wife wants to wear hers before you get it sized, I can help tighten it a little." She pulled out a package of what looked like clear rubber pieces. "Just put one of these on the bands."

Kraken paid for our purchases, then the woman helped me with the rings. I had to admit, it felt amazing wearing something showing I belonged to him. The fact he'd wanted a ring too surprised me. My father had worn a ring, but as a preacher, he'd been a pillar of the community. Appearances were everything to him. I'd noticed a lot of married men in the congregation didn't wear one. A biker seemed like the last person who'd ever want a wedding ring.

Kraken was right. He wasn't the same as the Sadistic Saints, not even a little. If my father, a man who preached from the Bible, had the respect of the community, and didn't abide liars, had sold his own daughter, why couldn't a man who looked as dangerous as Kraken be sweet and charming? I'd always thought when I met evil, I'd know it. With Deuce, it proved true. Everything else, though... My father looked like a sweet man. He clearly wasn't. Not even a little.

When we'd finished at the jewelry counter, we got a shopping cart before we started gathering the other things we needed. We went to the baby department to get another package of diapers, more wipes, and some clothes for Ember.

"What about this?" Kraken asked, holding up a pink shorts set with unicorns on the shirt. "Ember would be cute in it."

I couldn't help but smile. "She would. Although, I didn't think you'd pick something so... girly."

"We have a daughter not a son. *Yet*. Pink seemed appropriate."

I took the outfit from him, checked the size, then put it into the cart. He chose a few more outfits for Ember while I gathered baby shampoo, towels, and anything else she'd need. Kraken tossed in a rubber duck with a tiara, one of the more expensive thermometers, and anything else that caught his attention.

"Kraken, you're going to spoil her."

"Kind of the point."

He dragged me to the women's department. Once he learned my sizes, he started tossing stuff into the cart. I'd tried to stop him, or slow him down, but he was like a force of nature. There were far more clothes in the cart than I'd ever owned before, and I didn't know where he wanted me to put them all. I'd seen his closet and dresser. There wasn't much space available in either.

"Think we need another cart," he said.

"Exactly how much do you plan to buy tonight?"

He ran a hand down his beard. "Everything you need?"

I held up a lacy bra he'd tossed in. "And I *need* this?"

He smirked. "No. The pretty underthings are purely for my benefit because I have a sexy wife who will look hot as fuck in them."

"I can't even be mad at you. The things you say make me feel…" I shook my head. "I can't put it into words. Special? Yes, you make me feel special, Kraken."

He pulled me closer and gave me a quick kiss. "You are, baby girl."

By the time we checked out at the front, he'd filled another cart with a five-drawer chest for my new things, made sure I had no less than four pairs of shoes, and every possible bathroom or makeup item I could ever want. Although, I'd assured him I didn't care much for makeup, I did get a few things for times I wanted to dress up.

Kraken loaded the piece of furniture into the bed of the truck and all the bags went into the backseat. He stopped at a drive-thru on the way back and got milkshakes for us, a treat I hadn't had in years. The man beside me wasn't what I'd expected the first time I saw him. Deuce had done me a favor when he sent me off with Kraken.

I reached over and placed my hand on his thigh. "You're amazing."

He cast a glance my way before focusing on the road again. "I'm just me, baby girl. Only an idiot wouldn't treat you like the queen you are."

Yeah, he was pretty perfect, and I knew it wasn't a matter of *if* I completely fell for him, but *when*.

Chapter Six

Kraken

Four days passed. Quiet, uneventful days waiting on our test results, getting a nursery set up for Ember, drawing Phoebe out of her shell, and doing my best to show her I'd meant everything I'd said. Didn't stop the gnawing at my gut. There hadn't been a word from the Sadistic Saints since I'd carved up Deuce and left him on their bar top. No fucking way they'd let this go. I'd warned them, and I'd meant it. Smart men would heed my warning, but the Sadistic Saints were a bunch of dumb fucks.

Titan called in reinforcements from the Missouri chapter of our club, as well as three other clubs, under the guise of bringing old ladies here for Phoebe to meet. Those men really were bringing their families, but they were coming for another reason too. If the Sadistic Saints made a move, I wanted reinforcements here. We had a bunker where the women and kids would stay. It had been penetrated once, when Slider and his women were here. Since then, we'd made improvements.

The clubhouse was off-limits tonight for the club whores. Phoebe and Ember would meet everyone for the first time. I even had a special gift for her. I looked at the box on the bed, and the smaller gift bag next to it. I just needed my girls now. Ember giggled down the hall and I heard the splash of her playing in the tub. Smiling, I went to check on them. There was more water on the floor than in the tub as Ember smacked her hands, sending another wave over the side.

"Guess she loves bath time," I said.

Phoebe looked at me over her shoulder. "Well, she should. Do you see all this?"

Ember sat in a little bath seat I'd found online

and had overnighted, as her rubber duck bobbed beside her, along with the foam letters Titan had dropped off and a boat from Poison. Other things had started showing up on our doorstep too. A purple teddy bear from Wizard, a rag doll from Boomer, and a collection of baby-sized party dresses from Pretty Boy. I'd given him shit over it, but truth be told, Ember looked fucking adorable in them.

"Our girl about ready?" I asked.

"Think so." She pulled the stopper on the tub and lifted Ember out of the seat. I held open the soft baby towel and took my daughter from her. *My daughter*. The little cherub had me wrapped around her finger.

I carried Ember to her now-finished nursery and set her on the changing table. I'd become a pro at putting a diaper on my girl, and soon had one of the frilly little dresses on her. I cradled her against my chest and checked her diaper bag while Phoebe got ready. "Is Daddy's beautiful girl ready to meet some people?"

Ember babbled at me. I kissed her cheek and breathed in her sweet scent.

I heard the click of Phoebe's shoes and turned in time to nearly have a heart attack. The skirt of her dress swished around her knees. It was modest, but seeing her like this made something inside me shift. I'd admired her, cared about her, but it wasn't until this moment I started to fall in love with her. She'd put her hair up with little pieces curling around her face.

"Your mommy is beautiful, Ember."

"Bet you say that to all the women sleeping in your bed." She gave me a sassy smile.

"Only one woman in my bed. My wife." I pulled her to me, kissing the hell out of her. "And she's the prettiest woman I've ever known."

Her cheeks flushed and she bit her bottom lip. Cute.

"We'll be late if we don't hurry," she said.

"They can wait a minute."

She pushed at me. "Blake, be serious. You said they're here to meet me. It's rude to keep them waiting."

"And there's the proper preacher's daughter I married." Her lips tipped down at the corners. It seemed my words hadn't had the effect I'd hoped for. "Baby girl, what those bastards did to you doesn't define who you are. You were raised to be a proper young lady. Taught right from wrong. Your parents will get what's coming to them, and same for the Sadistic Saints."

"I'm not some naïve girl anymore," she said.

"No, you're not. You've seen the evil in the world. Survived it. You're stronger now than you were before. Instead of a scared young girl, you're a mom. A wife. An amazing woman." I kissed her again. "And I'm damn lucky to call you mine."

"You're going to make me cry," she said.

"It's all right, as long as they're happy tears."

The gifts I had could wait until later. I needed to get my girls to the clubhouse before Phoebe talked me into staying home. I led her from the house. Since I hadn't gotten a car for Phoebe yet, I still had one of the club trucks. Ember's seat was in the back, so I buckled her in. I helped Phoebe into the passenger seat, lingering a moment. She gave me a smile, and I couldn't help but think she was so damn beautiful. Didn't know what a pretty little thing like her wanted with a guy like me.

I shut her door, then went to the driver's side. It

didn't take long to reach the clubhouse, but it was far enough I hadn't wanted to walk. Especially with Phoebe all dressed up. I heard her indrawn breath when the line of bikes came into view, along with several trucks and SUVs. My particular chapter wasn't as large as some clubs I'd been around, but since we had guests, the place was packed.

I unbuckled Ember and carried her inside with Phoebe walking slightly behind me. I knew she was scared, or maybe just nervous, but everyone would love her. They'd never hold her past against her. Even if she'd chosen that life, the simple fact she was mine meant they'd welcome her with open arms. Just hadn't been able to convince her of it yet.

The sound of laughter and music spilled from inside as I pushed open the doors. It wasn't nearly as loud as party nights, and I didn't see a single club whore. I'd worried when the Pres had ordered them out of here at least one would cause problems. I saw Titan at the bar and moved farther into the room, reaching back to pull Phoebe up beside me.

"Come on, baby girl. Let's tell the Pres hi."

I held her hand as we moved through the crowd. Titan sipped his beer, leaning casually against the bar, but I saw the way he observed everything going on around him. These were our allies, but he knew as well as I did the Sadistic Saints could attack at any moment. In fact, so many clubs being here could very well lure them out. They couldn't just try to take down my chapter of Hades Abyss, but they could cripple a few other clubs as well.

"Good to see you, Phoebe," Titan said. "Although, you look about two seconds from bolting out of here."

"She thinks no one will like her," I said.

Titan snorted and motioned to someone across the room. Rocket came over with his woman and two girls. After the way he'd slaughtered the men who had hurt Violeta, I wasn't surprised Titan had asked him to come. Of course, he was also a great choice because of the age difference between him and his woman. Violeta was about four or five years older than Phoebe, and Rocket was a little older than me.

"Phoebe, let me introduce you to Rocket from our Missouri chapter," Titan said. "And his lovely wife, Violeta, and their two girls Zoe and Carlota."

Violeta gave her a little wave. "My sister would have come, but her husband doesn't let her leave the area without him."

Phoebe pressed closer to me. She gave the woman a polite smile, but I felt a tremor rake her. I released her hand and put my arm around her waist, drawing her tighter to my body. Violeta glanced at me, a flash of understanding in her eyes. She looked away, motioning for someone else, and soon we had more women gathered in front of us.

"I'm Mara," said a woman wearing a property cut for the Dixie Reapers. "I'm with Rocky. Our son, Owen, is with us but we left our daughter at home with Isabella and Torch."

"I'm Jacey and this is my daughter, Danica," said another woman. "I'm with Cowboy. Our boys, Jackson and Langston, are somewhere around here."

I saw Phoebe eyeing their property cuts and wished I'd given hers to her. "You have one of those too," I said. Her gaze lifted to mine. "I was going to give it to you earlier, but decided to wait. It's at home, along with a little something for Ember."

Titan snorted next to me and muttered something sounding like *dumbass*. He leaned over the bar and spoke to one of the Prospects and the guy took off nearly at a run. I had no doubt the Pres had just sent him after my woman's property cut so she wouldn't feel left out. Yeah, he was right. I was a dumbass.

"I'm Jordan," said another woman, elbowing her way closer. "Didn't bring my hellions with me, but Havoc is nursing a beer across the room. Don't worry. Those men come after you, we'll give them hell."

"We?" Phoebe asked, her eyes going wide.

Jordan smirked. "I'm not the kind to sit on the sidelines. Oh, I'm sure Havoc will tuck me somewhere safe, but don't worry. I'm always armed, so no one will get to you on my watch."

I glared at Titan, wondering why he'd invited the psychotic woman here. Havoc was one thing, but Jordan? I'd heard all about the way she'd gone after her man in South America, and how she'd located him. The woman was batshit fucking crazy. I didn't mind Phoebe coming out of her shell. Hell, I encouraged it. But the last thing I wanted was her trying to de-ball a man, and I had a feeling Jordan would talk her into it and so much more.

The Pres smirked at me and gave a nod of his head. I followed, hating to leave Phoebe behind. I didn't make it two feet before she rushed me, snatching Ember from my arms. I pressed a kiss to her cheek, then caught up with Titan as he claimed a seat at a table in the corner.

"Is there a reason we just fed my wife to the wolves?" I asked.

"The only rabid one over there is Jordan, and Havoc is here, so she'll at least moderately behave herself."

"Thanks for making sure some of the ladies

showed up, even if they did bring the kids."

Titan eyed someone across the room and I realized he was checking out Cowboy's eldest daughter, Danica. The more I studied her, the more I realized she was close to the same age as Phoebe, which meant if the Pres decided to make a move, at least it wouldn't be illegal. Cowboy might have something to say about it, though.

"You really think this is going to work?" I asked.

"Which part? The women giving Phoebe a sense of support and community? Or the Sadistic Saints making a move on your wife?" Titan turned to face me. "You left them a pretty powerful message, Kraken. They may give us a wide berth. To them, she was a piece of ass. Not sure they'll want to start a war."

"It's just odd. I killed their President, and we haven't heard a damn thing from them."

"Maybe they hated him as much as your wife does," he said. "There tends to not be much loyalty amongst men like those. No doubt someone was ready to step into Deuce's shoes."

It was possible, but my gut said trouble was coming. "Why did you send us there? I know it was to broker a deal, but no offense, Pres. I call bullshit. We've never dealt with men like those, so why now?"

Titan twisted his beer bottle on the table, rotating it several times. "A friend called in a favor. Wanted to know if the Sadistic Saints were as bad as he feared. Should have told you what was going on, or let the club know, but there are some secrets I can't share. They aren't mine *to* share. If I'd thought you'd be in any actual danger, something you couldn't handle, I'd have been more forthcoming with the information. Never counted on you finding Phoebe there, or killing their Pres."

A friend? I didn't like it when Titan got cryptic. There was more to the story, but I knew the Pres wouldn't share unless he was ready. The fact I'd been able to save Phoebe from the hell she'd been in made me grateful he'd sent us there, even if I didn't understand why he'd done it.

I cut my gaze to Titan and saw him watching Cowboy's girl again. "Pres, you keep watching Danica like you are, and Cowboy is going to take issue with it."

Titan ran a hand over his beard. "Yeah. She's just... different."

I eyed the young woman, trying to figure out what Titan saw in her. She had a girl-next-door kind of pretty, and a great smile. I could see the appeal, and I knew the Dixie Reapers were connected to several clubs through marriages or siblings, but I didn't see Cowboy taking it well if Titan made a move on his kid. Didn't matter if she was fully grown or not. I saw what he did, though. Innocence. We didn't see much of it in our world.

"Just tread carefully, Titan. When it comes to their women and kids, the Reapers will gladly bury anyone who fucks with their families. You break that girl's heart, and it won't just be Cowboy coming for you. It will be all of them."

"Which is why I'm sitting over here," he said, taking a sip of his beer. "She might have grown up in this world, but I don't think she has what it takes to be an old lady. Especially one to a President. I'll look, but I sure the fuck won't be touching."

The doors to the clubhouse opened and two women stumbled in. My body tensed as I scanned the room, wondering if anyone else had noticed. Titan had. He stood and started striding across the room, and I was fast on his heels. We'd declared the clubhouse a no-fly zone tonight for the club whores, but it seemed these two hadn't received the message. And once I found out who let them in here, I was going to kick their ass.

Titan grabbed Carla, but before I could get my hands on Dee, the woman flung herself at me. Her lips smashed against mine and her hand went straight for my dick. I wrenched her away from me and spat on the floor to get her taste out of my mouth. I shoved her, but she came right back, trying to wind herself around me.

"Enough!" I pushed her away again. "What the fuck are you doing here?"

"That's what I want to know," Titan said.

"Kraken." I froze at the soft voice and turned my head to see my wife and daughter coming toward me. "What's going on?"

"Someone forgot to not let the trash in tonight," I said.

Dee gasped and narrowed her eyes at me. "You didn't seem to mind my presence when I was sucking your dick."

I'd never condoned violence against women, but I smacked her. Not enough to do any damage, but it sure the hell got her attention. Her eyes went wide and her jaw dropped. "You will not *ever* speak to me with such disrespect again. In fact, you're banned from coming here. Next time I see you at the compound, the little love tap you just got won't compare to what happens to you. You disrespected me. My club. And my family."

Phoebe came to stand next to me, her presence soothing the beast inside me. Titan grabbed Dee and hauled her outside with Carla. I scrubbed at my mouth with the back of my hand, not wanting any part of that woman's germs on me. Yeah, she might have sucked my dick before, but the women at the clubhouse disgusted me now. All I wanted, or needed, was my wife.

"Baby, about Dee..."

She shook her head. "You weren't a saint, Kraken. I didn't exactly come to this relationship a virgin, and before you go off on how it wasn't my choice, I know that. Doesn't change the fact you weren't my first. We both have people in our past. As long as you haven't been with her since you brought me here, then I don't care what she has to say."

"Don't know what the fuck I ever did to deserve you, baby girl."

She leaned against me. "But just so you know, if I hadn't been holding our daughter, I'd have grabbed the bitch by her hair and dragged her out of here."

I tried to hold it in, but I couldn't. I burst out laughing. This woman. I never knew what to expect from her, and she amazed me every fucking day.

Titan came back in, dragging a Prospect by the collar. He tossed Sean onto the floor. "This one let them in, after given orders not to do so."

Phoebe stiffened next to me. She pulled away and moved closer to Sean with Ember still clutched in her arms. I watched as she knelt in front of him.

"I don't know why you let those women in, but I don't want them near my daughter. There are children here. Why would you do that?" Phoebe asked.

"You were supposed to get upset and leave the clubhouse," Sean said.

Wait. What? "Excuse me?"

Sean looked up at me, paling. "They have my cousin. If I didn't flush Phoebe out where they could grab her, they said MaryAnne would take her place. She's only sixteen, Kraken. She went missing two days ago. I have to get her back."

I didn't have to ask who he meant. The Sadistic Saints had made their move. It was sneakier than I'd expected. They'd seemed like the type to storm the gates. If what Sean said was true, we had to get MaryAnne back. There was no fucking way I'd let anyone suffer the way Phoebe had, and I knew my woman wouldn't want that either.

"Looks like we need a plan," I said.

Jordan elbowed her way through the crowd. "Then let's make one. I may not know who these men are, but it's clear the girl doesn't need to be with them. Let's get her back."

Havoc stepped up behind Jordan. "Whatever you need, let us know."

Titan looked around the room. "I need the bunker supplied. Enough to last a week for all the women and children present. I hadn't thought to move them down there tonight, but it looks like we're out of time. And, Jordan, don't even think of fucking arguing with me. You're going on lockdown with the others."

Jordan crossed her arms. "Fine. But I'm not going to be unarmed. Someone has to protect them if the rest of you fail."

Havoc snorted. "Do you really think they're getting past me? Or Kraken? He took down their President, by himself. But we can't have all of you running around here, out in the open. It would be a distraction, and you damn well know it, Jordan."

She sighed and nodded. "Fine. I get it. I don't like it, though."

Phoebe cuddled against me, and I wrapped my arm around her waist. My woman might not have the in-your-face strength Jordan did, but she was pretty damn perfect. With everything she'd suffered, it amazed me she'd even tried to talk to Sean, point out the error of his ways. Might not have been a fist to the face, which would have likely been Jordan's method, but she hadn't backed down.

Now I just needed to take care of the fuckers trying to take her from me, because no one was going to steal my wife and daughter.

Chapter Seven

Kraken

Instead of calling Church, once the women and kids were safe, Titan met with all of us in the main room of the clubhouse. Even the Prospects needed to hear his plan. He leaned against the bar, ankles and arms crossed, as he surveyed the room. I stood at his side with the VP. I got the feeling the Sadistic Saints would strike again, and it was coming soon.

"I appreciate all of you coming here," Titan said. "While we did want Kraken's woman to feel like she wasn't alone, you know there's more going on. The Sadistic Saints want her back."

"When you say back..." Cowboy trailed off. "We don't know the entire story. What are we getting involved in?"

I glanced at the Pres before taking a step forward. "Phoebe's family sold her to the Sadistic Saints. They raped and tortured her, treated her like a whore. I not only got her out of there, but I claimed her. And I left a little message for them by way of killing their Pres."

Titan snorted. "And he carved his message on the man's torso."

"Nice!" Havoc grinned.

"Only you'd get excited over something like that," Rocky said.

"The point is I won't back down. Phoebe is mine, and I'll be damned if I let those bastards get her back," I said. "She was scared, abused, and treated like garbage. I don't even want to think of what they'd do to Ember if they had the chance."

"Do you really think they'll come here and try to take her? It's one thing to attempt to lure her out of here, but to actually enter the compound and snatch her is another matter," Rocket said.

"They've let us know they want her back," Titan said. "Since we aren't dropping her on their doorstep, they'll show up sooner or later."

"You reinforced this place after Slider came here with his woman," Rocket said. "There's no way they'll get past your security. Or manage to get into the bunker. You'll need something to lure them into at least trying, or you'll have to leave a weak spot where they can breach the compound."

I scowled at Rocket. "We're not using my woman as bait."

He lifted his hands. "Didn't say you needed to. But with this place locked up like Fort Knox, there's no fucking way they'll get inside. Kind of hard to take them down if we're in here and they're out there."

"So we leave a weak spot," Titan said.

"What about the south corner?" Gravel asked. "It's far enough from the bunker. We could deactivate the cameras on that end, or at least make it look like they're not working, and make sure anyone patrolling the area does it at easily timed intervals. It would give them plenty of time to break in."

"I'm on it," Wizard said. "I'll have those cameras taken care of within the hour. I'll even head over that way, give them a good once-over to make it look like they're broken. I can be convincing."

"I'll make a patrol schedule," I said. "I want at least one Prospect to head down into the bunker until this is over. Everyone else, it's all hands on deck."

Brick snorted. "You're not in the Navy anymore, Kraken. We aren't on a fucking ship."

I flipped him off. It was no secret I'd been in the military, but only a select few knew I'd been a Naval aviator. When my brothers heard I'd been in the Navy, with my penchant for killing off our problems, they'd dubbed me Kraken. Except I hadn't struck from the depths of the sea, I'd taken out enemies by air.

"If there's anything you need to take care of, any last-minute tasks in case this shit goes south, I suggest you do it now," Titan said. "These sick fucks will fight dirty, and they won't be trying to just knock us out. They'll want to remove us from the equation permanently."

"How many chapters do those bastards have?" Rocket asked.

"Three that I know of," I said. "The one I snatched Phoebe from, another in California, and one up in New York."

"So, none close enough for them to call in reinforcements," Brick said. "Unless they already did and brought other chapters with them."

"Anyone had eyes on them?" I asked.

"Haven't seen them around here yet," Pretty Boy said.

"That's because you've been too busy keeping eyes on your sister," Gravel said. "How's that going?"

"The Wicked Mayhem are going to handle it. One of their officers is going to claim her." He ran a hand over his head. "Just hope Ophelia doesn't get all mouthy and fuck things up. They're her only hope."

I shook my head, not wanting to get involved in the family drama that circled Pretty Boy and his sister. I hoped he was right about Ophelia. I needed his head screwed on straight.

"Everyone get the fuck out, or stick around and have a beer. Whatever. I've got shit to do." Titan walked off down the hall.

I hoped his "shit" didn't involve a certain young woman down in the bunker. I wasn't about to tell the

Pres where he could and couldn't stick his dick, but I really hoped he wasn't about to fuck shit up with us and the Dixie Reapers. It was nice having allies, and I didn't think Cowboy would take it too well if his eldest ended up warming the Pres's bed.

Titan was right about one thing, though. There was always a chance we wouldn't all walk away from a fight with the Sadistic Saints. If this was my last day breathing, I wanted to make sure Phoebe knew what she meant to me. Until Wizard laid his trap, those bastards wouldn't be coming into the compound.

I motioned Patriot over. "I want you to organize some patrol rounds in the south corner using Riley, Sean, and Smoke. Make sure there's at least a thirty-minute break between their passes through that area. I want those fuckers to have a chance to break in. That being said, y'all try to give me at least forty minutes with my woman."

Patriot smirked, but I knew he'd do as I'd asked. I left the clubhouse and went back to the old barn, where we'd hidden the bunker. It had been improved since the last time we'd needed it. A hidden door still led downstairs to the bunker, but now there was a steel door that required not only a code, but another door with a retina scan before you could access the bunker. Every patched member could enter, but the Prospects hadn't earned the right just yet, which meant whatever Prospect came down here to watch the women would have to be let in by a brother.

I let myself in and scanned the area for Phoebe. Jordan held Ember as she chatted with Violeta. I made my way through the room and stopped outside the master bedroom. It was meant for the Pres, but I'd known he'd want Phoebe to use it. The sound of a woman crying had me turning the knob and stepping inside. Phoebe curled in the center of the bed, tears soaking her cheeks and the blanket.

"Baby girl, what's wrong?" I asked.

She gasped and jolted upright. "Kraken!"

I shut and locked the door. "Just us here, baby. You don't have to call me that right now."

"Blake, I thought you were trying to take down the Sadistic Saints."

"I am, just not right this very moment. Right now, I'm going to spend some time with a beautiful woman I happen to call my wife." I sank into the edge of the bed and reached out to run my fingers through her hair. "Why are you crying?"

"I don't know. It just felt like everything was pressing down on me. I don't know anyone here, and while they're nice, I feel out of place."

"Baby, you're not out of place. This compound is your home, which makes you the reigning queen of this Hades Abyss chapter, since you're the only old lady right now. Not to mention you're an officer's wife." I leaned down on my elbow and tugged her close to me. She cuddled up to me. "You know, we got the all clear from Bones and didn't even get to celebrate."

She bit her lip and looked like she was trying not to smile. "Blake, did you come down here to have sex before going off to war?"

"Can you think of a better way to spend the next half hour?"

Her shoulders shook with silent laughter. I didn't know if that meant she agreed, or found the situation amusing. Either way, my woman was a temptation I couldn't ignore another moment. I covered her body with mine, and kissed her long and deep. Phoebe wound her arms around my neck, opening to me.

"Not laughing now, are you?" I asked.

"Thirty minutes just doesn't seem all that long," she said between kisses.

"Guess we better make the most of it."

I peeled her clothes off before ditching my own. Her skin felt like warm silk as I pressed her into the mattress. My sweet Phoebe was every bit as eager as I was, her pussy already slick and swollen. As much as I wanted the moment to last forever, I knew we had limited time. I'd make it up to her later. I shifted my hips, sinking into her wet heat.

"Blake." She moaned and dug her nails into my shoulders. "So good. Don't stop."

"I thought you felt good before, but damn, baby. Nothing compares to taking you bare." I nipped her jaw. "Can't wait to put a baby in you."

"Less talk. More fucking."

I grinned and kissed the hell out of her. Her pussy rippled around my cock, making me want to slam into her. I gripped her hip and thrust deep. Her soft cries made my dick even harder. When all this was over, I was going to find a babysitter for Ember so I could keep my woman in bed for a solid twenty-four hours, only coming up for air long enough to rehydrate and eat.

"That's it, baby girl. Come for me." I stroked in and out of her. "Show me how much you love having my cock inside you."

She lifted her hips, taking me in deeper. I ground against her, pressing against her clit, and she came apart, crying out my name. Fuck! The gush of her release nearly sent me over the edge.

"So fucking perfect. Come for me again."

She clung to me. Her gaze held mine, all soft and trusting. I'd only had her in my life a short time, but I couldn't imagine having to go on without her. If anything happened to Phoebe, I'd want to die right alongside her. I took her hard and fast, not stopping until she'd come twice more, then I let go, filling her with my cum.

Sweat slicked our skin, and I'd have loved nothing more than to lie here with her for hours. I rolled to my side, holding her close. I'd never imagined having someone in my life that I'd love as much as I loved her. It was insane, since we were strangers.

"We need more time," she murmured, running her fingers through my beard. "That wasn't nearly enough."

"I know, baby. I know." My lips brushed hers. "When this is over, we'll take some time for ourselves. Just you, me, and Ember. But the nights will be just for you and me."

"Be safe, Blake. Please. I don't think I can do this without you."

I ran my fingers through her hair, then cupped her cheek. "I'm not going anywhere, baby. I'll put an end to those bastards, make sure you're safe, but I will do my best to still be standing when it's over."

"You better. I love you, Blake."

"Love you too, baby girl. So fucking much."

She curled her hands around my biceps and held on tight. "Can you stay just a little longer?"

"The sooner I put an end to this, the faster I can come get you. Be brave for me, Phoebe. Remember, you're the queen around here. Don't hide in this room crying. Get out there, make friends, and don't let anyone steamroll you."

"All right."

I kissed her again, wishing I didn't have to leave her. After I got dressed, I pulled her to me, holding her and just breathing her in. Before I could talk myself out of lingering, I let her go and went back upstairs. Morgan, one of the newer Prospects, gave me a nod. Looked like he'd been selected to watch the women and kids while we got things in order.

As I cleared the barn, I released the thoughts of Phoebe and Ember, focusing on the task at hand. If we were letting those fuckers into the compound, I wanted to be armed to the teeth. While I always kept a knife on me, it wouldn't be enough. I rode my bike to the house and raided the hidden compartment in my closet. With a little one in the house, I'd need to make my weapons more secure. Maybe a retinal scanner, or at least a lock that required a code.

I grabbed a 9mm, two extra full clips, and another knife. I didn't care that I smelled like Phoebe and sex. My brothers could give me shit over it if they wanted. When all this was over, I'd mark my body with her name, make sure she knew how damn serious I was about having a life with her. She had a property cut, but I'd have loved to get her inked. I just hated to ask it of her after all she'd been through with the Sadistic Saints.

After securing the house, I decided to do a sweep of the compound. If we avoided the south corner, except for the scheduled patrols, something would seem off. Assuming they were even watching us. There was a prickle along my skin telling me they were nearby. I didn't think the Sadistic Saints were necessarily smart, but they hadn't stayed alive this long by being stupid either. They were pathetic, but people with nothing to lose could be dangerous. I rode down the streets, leaning into the curves, and letting the wind in my hair calm my soul. It was only a matter of time before those fuckers made their move, but I needed to keep a cool head.

I circled the back of the property, not far from the barn where the bunker lay hidden underneath. The south corner had seemed undisturbed when I'd passed it. Just because we'd laid a trap didn't mean they would take the bait, but I sure the fuck hoped they did. Shadows moved along the fence line and I slowed my Harley. The shapes were low to the ground, but it was clear some men were already inside the property. I only saw four, and I doubted the Sadistic Saints had sent so few men. If Phoebe was right, when Deuce fell, his VP had probably stepped up. I remembered what that fucker had said when he'd walked into her room at their clubhouse. He wasn't going to give up easily.

Just one problem. They were too damn close to my woman. How the hell had they gotten into the compound and slunk this far into the property without anyone noticing? Hell, the stretch of fence we'd left unguarded hadn't even looked disturbed. Even if we'd left that area open, they'd still have needed to cut the fencing. They were either more talented than I'd given them credit for, or I'd missed something when I drove by.

They stopped, hunkered low. I eased my bike forward, taking the curve around the side of the barn. I pulled off farther down the road and cut the engine, then stuck to the shadows as I crept back to the barn. I gripped the handle of my knife, pulling it free of its sheath, and stuck close to the front of the structure. I didn't know if Morgan was still outside, or if someone had let him inside. With my back pressed to the wood, I listened for even so much as a rustle of leaves or the crunch of grass.

I heard the heavy tread of several men and braced myself. Their shadows moved along the ground. I knew the moment they saw my bike because they came to a halt. Dropping to my knees, I waited. If they rounded the corner, they wouldn't expect me to be low to the ground and would likely aim their weapons at chest level. I was counting on it. The first man crept along the wall of the barn. Idiot didn't even stop to see if someone was lying in wait. The moment he cleared the side of the barn, I attacked, driving the knife upward into his gut. As he staggered, I yanked the blade free and jabbed him in the ribs three times, then sliced his throat. The body fell to the ground and I lifted my gaze.

The other three wearing Sadistic Saints cuts seemed stupefied. What the fuck? These bastards had snuck in undetected? How? They didn't seem to be the brightest. Or seasoned for that matter. Had they never been in any sort of combat situation?

"Problem, boys?" I asked.

One of them blinked and his jaw dropped, then snapped shut. Jesus. These guys really were dumb. Had Leviathan sent the weakest of their club for this mission? If that was the case, how badly could he want Phoebe? He had to know these men would fail. Unless that was the point. Motherfucker. These bastards were a decoy, and I'd fallen for it.

I pulled my gun from the small of my back and sent a round into each of their chests. Too fucking easy. There was no damn way the Sadistic Saints had only sent these four men. They were a damn joke. As much as I wanted to check on Phoebe, I didn't dare. If anyone watched, they would see the barn held something of interest. I needed them to avoid this place.

Getting on my Harley, I started her up, then pulled out my phone. I dialed Titan, wondering if there had been a breach elsewhere. He picked up on the fourth ring.

"Where the hell are you?" the Pres asked by way of greeting.

"Back of the compound. Found four Sadistic Saints, but... Pres, there's something off. These guys were too easy to put down. Hell, they looked like scared kids. Something's off about all this. Not to mention, they were too stupid to pull off sneaking this far into the compound on their own."

"Agreed," Titan said. "Come to the clubhouse. I think we need to dig a little deeper."

"On my way."

I ended the call and got back on the road. The clubhouse wasn't much farther, less than a mile down the twisting path that ran through the compound when I heard the explosion. I revved the engine and pushed my bike, going fast as I dared. Smoke rose in the air and a feeling of dread filled me. I only hoped I wasn't too late.

Chapter Eight

Phoebe

The Prospect kept twitching, at first just his fingers, then I noticed him pacing and muttering to himself. I didn't claim to be an excerpt on behavior, but he seemed off. Not just anxious over the current circumstances. More like something else was going on. I glanced around, wondering if anyone else noticed. The others were watching TV or talking. Despite what Kraken had said, I still felt like an outsider.

What had they called this guy? Morgan?

I wondered how long he'd been with the club. It was obvious they trusted him, since he'd been left down here with us. I couldn't shake the feeling something bad was about to happen, and this guy was tied to it. Being around Deuce's club, I'd learned to watch for signs of impending doom -- usually mine. This guy's presence had everything inside me screaming I should run.

I couldn't. I'd seen how this place was accessed, and there was no getting out unless a club member came to release us. Which meant Morgan was stuck down here with us too. I didn't like that idea, at all. Speaking to the other ladies about it wouldn't be wise. Not if Morgan could hear us.

I edged closer to Mara, hoping I could speak to her without drawing attention to myself. She'd decided to make everyone food and stood at the counter, chopping vegetables. I turned my back to Morgan and lowered my voice.

"We may have trouble," I said.

The knife paused a moment before she resumed cutting. "What's that?"

"The Prospect. He seems twitchy. I think something's up."

"Your man wouldn't have put him down here with you if he'd thought the guy was trouble," she said. Nothing I hadn't considered myself. "Sure you aren't making more out of this than there is?"

"It's a feeling I have. I learned to trust my instincts when I lived with the Sadistic Saints. It kept me alive. Kept Ember alive, for that matter."

"If there is something wrong, we're all sitting ducks," she said. "We just need to have faith in our men. They'll protect us like they always do."

I wished I had her faith. It wasn't that I didn't trust Kraken, or the others. But I knew the men they were up against. Deuce's crew didn't play by the rules. They were underhanded, dirty, and got off on pain and suffering. I knew Kraken had killed Deuce, but could he take on the entire club? Leviathan was even worse. The VP would come for me. If anyone did, it would be him.

Somewhere above, there was a loud *boom* that made the very walls vibrate around us. My eyes went wide as I watched Morgan. His gaze flew to the steel door, and I knew he was anticipating something, but was it because of the noise upstairs, or something else?

Morgan's phone rang and he answered, talking low at first, then louder. "I can't! I don't have access. Only patched members can get in here. It takes a damn retina scan."

He muttered something else, then hung up the phone. My gut clenched and bile rose in my throat. He was working with the Sadistic Saints. I had no doubts to that, but I didn't understand why. What was in it for him? Kraken's men were so much better than Deuce's crew. Why would anyone want to be with those assholes? Unless they were holding something over his head. I wouldn't put it past them. We still needed to find MaryAnne, assuming they still had her.

The two teen boys were alert, casting glances toward Morgan and the door every few minutes. It seemed they'd overheard. Even though they were the size of full-grown men, I hoped they didn't try to do anything heroic. If someone did breach the bunker, I didn't want any of these people dying.

It felt like hours passed, but I knew it hadn't been very long. Booted steps sounded outside the metal door, and when it opened I knew my hell was just beginning. Two of the Sadistic Saints came in, tossing aside a set of eyes that I really didn't want to contemplate. I pressed back against the counter, wishing there was a way to run, to get Ember and just disappear.

I caught the gaze of the boys and shook my head, letting them know not to interfere. It was my hope they'd take me and leave everyone else. These women hadn't done anything to deserve this. Neither had I, but at least I'd survived it before. Kraken had called me the queen, and I was going to take that to heart. Sometimes a queen had to sacrifice herself to save her people.

Morgan pointed my way. My heart slammed against my ribs and I heard Ember crying. I didn't dare look her way. I knew Jordan had her and would protect her at all costs. If they had to take me, then at least my daughter would be safe. Kraken would take care of her.

The men advanced on me. I lashed out with my fists and kicked at them, but the bastards only laughed at me.

"Look, our favorite little toy grew a backbone," Pitch said with a grin. "It will be fun breaking you all over again. How many of us can you take at once? I've forgotten."

I closed my eyes and fought not to pass out. They meant to reenact my first night with them. I'd survived it once, but I didn't know if I could do it again.

Screwball grabbed his crotch. "We're gonna fuck you so good. Make you scream. Make you bleed."

I saw Jordan moving closer, and I held a hand out to her. I didn't need anyone else getting hurt. These bastards wanted me, and they wouldn't stop until they had me. I wasn't special. Not to them. They got off on the pain they caused. I'd been their favorite punching bag, their favorite little victim. Kraken had shown me what life should be like, that good men still existed. I only hoped he'd be able to move on when I was gone. There was no way they'd let me live this time.

I turned my head, holding Jordan's gaze. "Tell Kraken I'm sorry. Tell him…"

I shook my head and went with the Sadistic Saints. Fighting wouldn't get me anywhere. They dragged me up the stairs and outside the barn. Pitch tossed me over his shoulder and made a run for the tree line. They stuck to the shadows, moving swiftly through the compound. In the dark recesses of the compound, Screwball peeled back the fence. Pitch ducked through with me, and Screwball followed. A truck waited nearby. They tossed me into the backseat before getting in and taking off.

I'm so sorry, Kraken. I love you.

I pressed my hand to the window and watched the Hades Abyss compound get smaller and smaller. The truck hit the open highway and picked up speed, heading back to hell. It wasn't long before the sound of motorcycles filled the air and several Sadistic Saints zipped past us, with a few hanging back. The club Treasurer, Brimstone, winked at me as he flew by. I really hated these men.

"Running off like that was stupid," Pitch said. "Your ass is owned by our club."

"I'm not anyone's property," I said. "Not with the Sadistic Saints. I belong to Kraken."

Pitch turned to glare at me. "You'd be wise to never mention that fucker again. He killed Deuce. Carved him up. Left him on the bar for us to find."

"He was only protecting me," I said.

"Look how that turned out. Now we get to punish you. Not only for running off, but for your man killing our Pres. Shouldn't have done it, Phoebe. You're club pussy. You know your damn place. On your back with your legs spread."

I swallowed hard, fighting the urge to cry. I knew what was coming. It wouldn't be pretty. Would hurt a hell of a lot. They wouldn't go easy on me. Still, I loved the time I'd spent with Kraken, and I hoped he wouldn't come for me. It would be a suicide mission. I didn't know if Morgan had stayed behind. If he had, would he hurt the others? He wouldn't want to risk the women telling the Hades Abyss what happened.

The miles passed and eventually, we pulled up to the Sadistic Saints' clubhouse. Pitch got out and yanked me from the backseat. I stumbled as he dragged me into the clubhouse and threw me on the sticky floor. The few who'd remained behind crowded around. Looking in their eyes, I saw evil. If these men had souls, they'd been burned away long ago.

"Strip her," Brimstone said.

"What about Leviathan?" one of the men asked. "He'll want to have some fun with her."

Brimstone shook his head. "He'll get here when he can. This is all we've got right now. Everyone else is teaching those sorry bastards a lesson. Time to get the party going."

Pitch reached down and started cutting my clothes off with a sharp blade. The smile he gave me set a chill inside me, bone deep. He flipped the knife in his hand a few times, then grabbed a fistful of my hair. "I think you need a reminder of who you are. Every time you look in the mirror, you'll remember."

He sliced down my cheek, and I screamed out. The way he laughed, I knew it's what he'd wanted. My pain. Humiliation. He ran the blade down my other cheek, then went back to the first. I felt the blood drip down my face. Pitch shifted and looked at the others.

"Hold her."

Hands closed around my arms and legs, someone pressed their weight down on my shoulders. I couldn't see through my tears, didn't know who was surrounding me. The blade dug into my chest. Blackness rolled across my vision. Pitch took his time, carving me up like a piece of meat. My blood soaked the floor and gathered in my hair.

I felt the jab of a needle in my arm, then bliss. *No, no, no.*

"That's it. Good girl, Phoebe," Brimstone crooned. "Toss her in her room. We'll give the others a little time to get here. Then we'll teach the bitch a lesson she'll never forget."

Someone lifted me, carried me down the hall, then threw me onto a mattress. I floated, a haze settling over me where time had no meaning. I was vaguely aware of raised voices. I rolled to my side, knowing I needed to clean up. The last thing I wanted was infection to set in. Assuming I survived this, anyway. If I didn't, then it wouldn't matter. I managed to get to my feet and staggered my way into the bathroom.

The sight of my face horrified me, but it was the

word he'd etched into my chest that nearly broke me. *Whore.* The cuts were deep enough I knew they'd scar, especially since I couldn't properly treat them. Despite the burn from the soap, I cleaned my wounds best I could, even though I tumbled to the floor multiple times. The drugs coursing through my veins made me feel like I'd walked into one of those funhouse tunnels, with everything spinning around me.

I rubbed ointment into the wounds before collapsing on the floor. The darkness crept in, until I tumbled into nothingness, my last thoughts of Kraken and my sweet Ember.

Chapter Nine

Kraken

When I reached the clubhouse, chaos rained down on the Hades Abyss. The Sadistic Saints had blown the gate off the hinges and poured through. One of our Prospects, Robert, lay dead near the gate. Cowboy had taken a bullet through the shoulder and another to his side.

My brothers were scattered, bleeding from various wounds, and Leviathan stood in the center of all, a grin spreading across his face like it was fucking Christmas. I got off my bike and threw myself into the mix, stabbing and shooting anyone in a Sadistic Saints cut. I took down four of them before an arm came around my throat and someone lifted me off my feet.

"Who has the upper hand now?" the man demanded. I couldn't see him, didn't know which of them had gotten the drop on me.

"You'll never get Phoebe back," I said.

"You honestly think that has anything to do with that bitch? She's just a fucking whore. A place to put our dicks. There's plenty more where she came from. Only a select few liked holding onto that one. Stupid cunt wasn't all that special."

"Then why?" I asked, fighting for every breath. The way his gaze cut away, I didn't think he was being honest. Phoebe was a prize for them, even if I didn't understand why.

"You made a fool of us. Came to us wanting to make a deal, then not only stole the Pres's favorite whore, but killed him before slinking off like a damn coward. We can't let that stand."

I hung limp, giving him all my weight, and when he staggered, off-balance, I gripped my knife and slammed it back, driving the blade into him. He grunted and his grip weakened, dropping me back to my feet. I turned, recognizing their Sergeant-at-Arms. I didn't bother retrieving my knife. Instead, I pulled my gun and shot him right between the eyes. His body fell, collapsing on the ground, and I yanked my knife free, wiping his blood off on his clothes.

I turned in time to see Leviathan take aim at Titan. Without pausing, I pointed my gun at him, pulling the trigger. He staggered, but didn't fall, and got off two rounds. I saw the red bloom across Titan's shirt and unloaded the rest of my clip into Leviathan. Fucker still didn't go down. I reloaded, and kept shooting, not stopping until the blood bubbled from his mouth and he breathed his last.

When the fighting stopped, the bodies of the Sadistic Saints littered the ground. Their VP and Sergeant-at-Arms were the only officers among the deceased, and more than a dozen patched members, as well as a few Prospects. Which meant there were others elsewhere. Had they remained behind? Or was another wave coming?

I went to Titan, who'd sunk to his knees. He swayed, but remained upright. I ripped his shirt down the middle and assessed the damage.

"Pres, you took two to the chest, but it looks like they missed your heart. Need to get you flat and let Bones see what he can do."

Titan shook his head. "Take care of the others."

"Pres, if you fall, this club is fucked. I'll help with the others. Hell, I'll call in whoever I have to in order to get everyone patched up."

"How many?" he asked.

I knew what he meant. "Saw Robert when I pulled up. Gone. Ratchet didn't make it either. Fuckers gouged out his eyes. Everyone else is still breathing, but banged up."

Havoc lumbered over, blood running down his arm and a gash on his forehead. "Need help?"

"Yeah. His house is right over there," I said nodding to my right. "Let's get him in his bed. Have a feeling he won't be getting out of it for at least a few days, maybe longer."

Havoc helped me get the Pres to his home and stretched out on his bed. Bones entered with his bag, and Pretty Boy stayed to assist. I went to check on the others, and see who I could get to help patch everyone. We tried not to involve the citizens of the town, but this time we didn't have a choice. I got the attention of Brick and waved him over. He'd been beat to hell, but was at least upright.

"Need you to find some nurses or a doctor. We need more medically inclined people. Make it worth their while, and make sure they'll keep their mouths shut. Don't need the cops sniffing around."

Brick nodded. "On it."

I started grabbing bodies of the Sadistic Saints and tossed them into a pile. Getting rid of this many bodies wasn't going to be fun, but we'd handle it. Boomer limped over. He'd torn off his shirt and tied it off around his thigh, right above a bullet wound. Looked like he had a graze on his side and another hole in his shoulder.

"You okay, VP?" I asked.

"I'll live. The Pres?"

"Took two to the chest. Bones is in there with Pretty Boy, patching him up."

Boomer nodded before scanning the area. "Anyone checked on the women and kids?"

"I found a few men back there. Took care of them."

Boomer held my gaze. "Are you really that fucking stupid? You think a few men at the back and these here are their only effort to get in? Who's down there with the women?"

"Morgan."

Boomer pulled out his phone. His jaw tightened as he disconnected the call. "No answer. Get as many brothers as you can and go check on them. We promised to keep them safe. If we failed…"

I ran for my bike and started her up. Letting out a loud whistle, I caught the attention of Patriot, Gravel, and two Prospects. I motioned for them to follow. I heard the pipes of their bikes as we tore through the compound, heading to the old barn. My stomach knotted as I came to a stop. Morgan lay dead, his throat slit, and the bunker was wide open.

I rushed down the stairs, gun drawn. The women and kids were gathered in the center of the room, Ember clutched in Jordan's arms. Who I didn't see was Phoebe.

"Where is she?" I asked.

Mara came forward, tears misting her eyes. "They took her. She sacrificed herself for us. Went willingly."

I closed my eyes, the pain sharp like a knife in my chest. I should have stayed here with her. Protected her. I'd given her my promise she'd be safe.

"How?" How the hell had they gotten in here? Where had I gone wrong?

"She told me something was wrong with the Prospect. I brushed her off, but she said her gut told her bad things were about to happen. Those men came in, and…" Her gaze dropped to the left. I looked and saw the eyes. Rachet's, if I had to guess. "They took her and Morgan left with them. We thought if they'd made it down here, then the rest of you were fighting for your lives. None of us wanted to risk calling and distracting any of you."

"Morgan's dead," I said. And if they hadn't killed him, I damn sure would have.

Rocky pushed past me and gathered his woman in his arms. Havoc followed, embracing Jordan, my daughter smooshed between them. I felt the presence of Patriot and Gravel at my back. Patriot placed his hand on my shoulder.

"We'll get her back," he said.

Jordan brought Ember to me, placing her in my arms. "She said to tell you she was sorry."

"Not her fault. None of this was her fucking fault." I clutched Ember, breathing in her sweet baby scent. Whatever it took, I'd bring her mom home.

"Not many of us are in any condition to travel," Gravel said "But I'm with you, Kraken. We'll get some men and go after her."

I shook my head. "The Pres is shot. So's Boomer. I need to be here."

Wizard entered the bunker, his eyes haunted. "You're needed elsewhere, Kraken. I can hold things down. Boomer will be patched up in no time. The Pres will be on bed rest, for however long we can hold him down. You know he'll be up and doing shit even when he shouldn't."

Yeah, I knew it. I'd be the same way if it were me lying in the bed.

Wizard shoved my cut to the side and lifted my shirt. I looked down and saw the blood. Didn't feel a damn thing, except pure fucking rage over losing Phoebe. I'd slap a bandage on it and be on my way. If Wizard said he'd hold things down, then I wasn't staying. The more of a lead they had, the worse it would be for Phoebe.

"Rocket doesn't have so much as a scratch on him. Take him with you," Havoc said. "I'll put out some feelers, see who I know near the Sadistic Saints. You'll have backup by the time you get there."

"I can't take Ember with me," I said.

"I'll stay and watch her," Jordan offered. "And Havoc can go with you."

The man scowled down at his woman. I could tell he wasn't ready to leave her alone, and I couldn't blame him. We'd proven we couldn't keep anyone safe. First we'd failed Slider's woman, and now Phoebe was gone. I didn't think those assholes would come back, not now that they had who they wanted, but that didn't mean trouble wouldn't show up.

"Fine, I'll go," said Havoc.

"Go patch yourself up," Wizard said, slapping me on the back. "I'll get everyone here situated and keep an eye on things. We've got a few nurses coming in take care of those with severe wounds, like Titan."

It took longer than I'd have liked to make sure I didn't bleed all over the damn place and gather up a few men. By the time we got on the road, night was falling. The wind blew through my hair, but it didn't have the usual calming effect. My bike ate up the miles, and with every minute that passed, I worried what they were doing to my woman. It gnawed at me, nearly drove me insane, thinking of their hands on her. I knew what she'd been through before, and I didn't want her to live through it again.

My fault. I failed her.

It took too fucking long to reach the Sadistic Saints' territory. My body ached, and exhaustion pulled at me. A line of bikes was on the side of the road, along with two trucks. The men waiting had on cuts from various clubs. Reckless Kings. Savage Raptors. Wicked Mayhem. It seemed Havoc had been busy on the phone while I'd gotten my wounds patched. I glanced his way and he merely smirked.

"Told you there would be backup. These men want a piece of these assholes just as much as you do," Havoc said.

"Can't exactly go in guns blazing," I said. "I have no idea where Phoebe is and I won't risk her life."

"We scoped the place out already." I scanned the man's cut. *Socket. Wicked Mayhem MC.* "You won't like what you find inside."

"Phoebe..."

"It's bad, man." He held out his hand. "I'm Loch. Socket and I got here first. Did what little recon we could until the others got here."

"She's going to need a doctor. I'm Crow, by the way. With Reckless Kings."

"I appreciate all of you coming. I need to get her out of there, then I want to put an end to those bastards once and for all. Should have burned this damn place to the ground after I took out Deuce." If I'd done that, maybe Phoebe would be safe at home right now.

"They're all drunk as shit," said Socket. "Means they're dangerous, but they're also slow. I think we can take them."

Havoc folded his arms. "Not going to tell you what to do on your own damn mission, but if it were me, I'd get my woman the fuck out of there and run. Let the rest of us handle these assholes. We'll make sure there's nothing left."

"No. Not nothing. I need to handle this myself. Find out who hurt her the most, who started it. I want that man gift wrapped with a fucking bow, then I want to rip his insides out with my bare hands."

Havoc grinned. "Knew I liked you. Consider it done. Just focus on Phoebe."

Crow tipped his head to the trucks. "One of those is ours. There's a Prospect ready and willing to go wherever you need him to. Put your woman in the truck and follow on your bike. Get her to the nearest fucking hospital."

If she needed a hospital… what the hell had they done to her? I nodded and pulled both my gun and my knife. Crow and Havoc took point, clearing a path for me. Even though I'd said no to going in guns blazing, that's exactly what we did. A few men came in through the back. I scanned the area, not seeing any sign of Phoebe, but the blood on the floor drew my attention.

I gave myself a mental slap and hurried down the hall. A man in a Sadistic Saints cut tumbled out of the bathroom, still zipping his pants. I didn't hesitate, didn't even think. I just pointed and pulled the trigger. He fell to the floor and I knelt, dragging the blade of my knife across his throat. As he gurgled and choked on his own blood, I made my way to Phoebe's room, hoping I'd find her there.

I kicked in the door and saw her on the floor near the bathroom. I holstered my gun and put away my knife, dropping to my knees beside her. Tears burned my throat and eyes as I surveyed the damage they'd done.

"Oh, baby girl. I'm so fucking sorry." I moved her hair off her face and openly wept at the carnage. I pulled a blanket off the bed and wrapped her in it before lifting her into my arms. I carried her out the back and went back to the road. A Prospect leaned against one of the trucks and jerked to attention as I got closer. He opened the backdoor and I laid Phoebe on the seat. "Nearest hospital. I'll follow."

He nodded and got in, starting up the engine. I got on my bike and we took off down the road. I didn't have a fucking clue where anything was in this damn town, but the guy seemed to know where he was going. We pulled into the ER entrance of a hospital and I parked my bike on the sidewalk, not giving a fuck if it was permitted or not. I rushed to pull Phoebe from the truck.

"Keys," said the Prospect. "I'll move your bike so they don't tow it."

I tossed them to him and rushed inside with my woman, yelling out for a nurse.

"We need help! Right the fuck now!"

Someone pushed a gurney over and I eased Phoebe onto it. I answered their rapid-fire questions best I could.

"Name," a nurse asked.

"Her name is Phoebe Miller. She's my wife."

The woman nodded and tapped on her tablet. "What happened?"

"She was kidnapped. The men who took her did this. I... I don't know what else..." I bit my lip and stared after Phoebe as they wheeled her through the double doors.

The woman placed her hand on my arm. "She's in good hands, Mr. Miller. We'll need you to complete some forms, but as soon as we know more about your wife's condition, someone will come talk to you."

I nodded and followed her to the triage station. I didn't have insurance on Phoebe, but I gave them my credit card to put on file. It was something I'd need to handle after all this was over. She and Ember would both need a policy. Hell, I didn't have one for that matter. Now that I had a family, I needed to make sure I not only stayed upright and breathing, but I needed to get life insurance or some shit for my girls. Or at least start putting some cash aside.

I paced for a bit before sinking down onto one of the most uncomfortable chairs in the entire world. The men who'd had my back made their way inside and gathered around me. I noticed Havoc was missing, along with one of the others.

"It was Pitch," Crow said. "He'll be waiting for you whenever you're ready. Havoc is babysitting."

"Need to know how Phoebe is before I do anything."

Crow nodded. "Didn't expect anything less."

"Thanks for coming," I said. "Couldn't have done this on my own."

"Wiped those fuckers off the face of the earth," he said. "They won't be bothering anyone again. Won't be raping women, cutting them, or any other sick fucking thing they get off on."

"There's more of them. Elsewhere," I said.

"I know. I already talked to my Pres. He's going to make a few calls. We'll get it handled. No retaliation will come back on you for what happened tonight."

I watched the minutes tick by. Then the hours. When a doctor came out, and called for the family of Phoebe Miller, I stood. He made his way over, a mask around his neck and a cap on his head.

"Mr. Miller?" he asked.

"I'm Phoebe Miller's husband," I said. "But I go by Kraken."

He eyed my cut and nodded. "All right. Your wife is resting. We had to put a lot of stitches in her, but I couldn't give her any drugs. Tox screen shows she's got heroin in her system. Found a pinprick in her arm."

"Phoebe doesn't do drugs," I said. "She'd never

do that."

"Figured it was whoever cut her to pieces. It will ease your mind to know she wasn't raped that we can tell. No evidence of trauma. We'll need a DNA sample from you, but we didn't find much. I doubt her attackers left anything useful behind."

I briefly closed my eyes, thankful for that one small miracle. It had been my greatest fear.

"Is there any chance your wife is pregnant?" the doctor asked. "Once the heroin is out of her system, we'll need to put her on an antibiotic and a painkiller. I don't want to prescribe something that could be harmful to a fetus if there's even a chance she's expecting."

"We had sex right before she was taken. Decided we wanted to try for a baby. That was... not even twenty-four hours ago."

"Then I'll err on the side of caution. We'll keep her as comfortable as we can, but she needs to remain here at least overnight. I'll have a better idea tomorrow when she'll be able to go home." He folded his arms. "I saw your home address isn't exactly down the street. You might want to get a hotel for a few days, even once she's out of here. A long trip might be painful for her."

"Understood."

Gravel came to stand next to me. "Will she be out of it for a while? Long enough to secure lodgings and get some essentials?"

"Yes, by all means. She's in good hands, Kraken. If there's any change, someone will call you at the number on file."

Gravel steered me outside and I got on my bike. Pitch remained at the Sadistic Saints compound. I rode straight there, and pulled up with Gravel and Crow on either side of me. I walked inside, scanning the room. Havoc leaned against the bar, the asshole known as Pitch tied to a chair in the center of the main area.

I shrugged off my cut and removed my shirt, tossing both onto the bar. I yanked my knife free and approached the fucker who'd hurt my woman. "Shouldn't have touched her."

"Only made her prettier," Pitch said. "Didn't get to the fun part before you showed up."

My hand tightened on the handle and I willed myself to remain calm. The fucker was goading me, wanting me to end him quickly. I wouldn't give him that satisfaction. He'd carved up Phoebe, probably scarred her for life, given her a lasting reminder of this place. There was nothing I could do to him that would give her comfort, that would ease her pain, or satisfy the rage inside me.

"Where is MaryAnne? You took her, tried to turn Sean against us. What happened to her?"

Pitch grinned. "That bitch is long gone. You'll never find her."

I'd have Wizard look into it. Maybe he could check into their finances and see if money changed hands. If she was alive, we'd find her.

I got to work, taking my time, mimicking the marks he'd left on her face. Slicing into his cheeks, I made the exact cuts he'd given Phoebe. As I gazed into his eyes, I saw the nothingness. He didn't scream. Didn't beg. There was a void, the complete absence of a soul. I peeled the flesh from his arms, cutting off his tattoos. When I realized he wouldn't give in, wouldn't break, I decided I'd wasted enough time. I buried my knife in his chest, right where his black heart would be, if he had one.

Gravel placed his hand on my shoulder. "Go

clean up, brother. Get back to your woman. We'll take care of the trash."

I gave him a nod and went back to the room that had been Phoebe's. I washed off using her sink, checked my jeans and boots for blood, then went back for my shirt and cut. I shrugged them on and walked out, not so much as glancing back or hesitating. I'd done what I needed to do, and now my woman would be safe. No one would come for her.

I'd promised to protect her, and I damn well would. No matter the cost.

Chapter Ten
Phoebe

Three days. Three long, miserable days of being scared out of my mind. Kraken hadn't left my side since I woke up, but I could tell by the look in his eyes, what Pitch had done to me would haunt him. He wouldn't look at me the same as before. I'd bear scars that would never go away, both on my body and in my mind. I couldn't bring myself to look in the mirror at the hospital, but at the hotel it wasn't something I could avoid. They'd only kept me overnight, and only then because they'd wanted to run tests. A large mirror ran the length of the counter in the bathroom. I couldn't brush my teeth without seeing the stitches in my face, the lines on my chest that spelled out *whore*.

The worst part was having Kraken see me like this. Every time he looked at me, it would be a reminder of where I'd come from, what Pitch had done to me, and what the club had intended to do. His touch was gentle. He still whispered words of comfort and love, but in my heart, I worried he saw me different now than before. Damaged. Ugly. Someone to be pitied. Even though a plastic surgeon had tried to make the scarring minimal, no one could make it disappear completely. The stitches in my face and chest would dissolve within the next few days, or should according to the doctor. They'd said sometimes it took a little longer.

Standing long enough to wash or use the bathroom exhausted me. I'd heard the doctor tell Kraken I needed more time to heal before going home to Mississippi. I missed my daughter, and yet, I didn't want her to see me this way. She was so little. Would the cuts on my face scare her? I already knew people would stare if I ever left the hotel room. I'd felt their gazes on me when Kraken had brought me here from the hospital. We couldn't remain here forever, though, and my stitches could take over a week to dissolve.

The pills I had to take made me drowsy and unlike myself. The doctor had said what he'd given me wouldn't hurt the baby, if there was one. I hated them, but I didn't like the pain I felt without them either. Every day, I promised myself I'd stop taking them. Then I'd find myself reaching for the bottle. They didn't just numb the pain of my wounds, but they helped numb my mind and soul too. I knew it was a slippery slope, a path that would lead to addiction. My daughter deserved better. She needed me to be strong.

"Brought you something," Kraken said as he entered the hotel room. He set a bag on the bed next to me.

I reached for it, feeling the plastic crinkle under my fingers. I slid the bag closer and reached inside, pulling out two new books, but I'd felt other items. A puzzle book with pencils, scented lotion, and a card. I fingered the pink envelope and wondered what was inside. Get well soon? Thinking of you? Was there a card for someone telling you they didn't want you in their life anymore?

My hands trembled as I opened it, and tears gathered in my eyes as I read the words. The outside was simple with a bouquet of roses, but inside... Kraken had written his own special message to me. All the doubts and fears melted away as I read his words.

To the woman I adore --

You are the strongest, fiercest, bravest woman I've ever met, Phoebe. Life has given you a shit hand, but you keep brushing yourself off and getting back up for another round. I promised to protect you, keep you safe, and I failed. Not knowing if you lived or had died, and finding you battered and unconscious, nearly ripped me apart.

I've watched you the last few days. I see the way you try to hide. From others. Yourself. Even me. But I see you. The wounds you have don't define you, baby girl. They only enhance your beauty, remind me of how resilient you are, how determined to survive. I admire you, baby girl. More than you'll ever know.

Don't hide from me, Phoebe. Let me love you. Let me help you heal.

You're mine, and I'm yours.
Always.
Blake

He'd signed it Blake. Not Kraken. Not the name he used with everyone else, but the one that was only for me. I couldn't stop the tears from flowing as the card fell from my hand. I reached for him blindly and as his arms closed around me, I allowed myself to lean on him, to accept his strength and acceptance. His love.

"You're my everything," he murmured. "It kills me to see you like this. Nothing those fuckers did to you will ever diminish you in my eyes."

"I love you, too." I pulled up and looked up at him. "I'm sorry. I see my reflection and I hate the woman looking back me. I can't stand that I'll have scars the rest of my life, and knowing you can see them... it tears me up, Blake."

"Do you know what I see when I look at the cuts they gave you?" he asked.

I shook my head.

"I see a survivor. You've lived through brutality and abuse, their torture, not once but twice, baby girl. A lot of people would have given up, but not you. You kept fighting to stay alive. And I'm so fucking glad. If I'd lost you, I don't think I could have gone on."

I reached up and ran my fingers over his beard.

"You would have. For Ember."

He nodded. "Yeah, but I'd have been dead inside. You're the best part of me, Phoebe."

"I just don't know where to go from here. I feel ugly, and… it feels like they ruined me. I hate feeling like this, but I don't know how to turn it off."

He tunneled his fingers into my hair and kissed me hard and deep. "Not going to fuck you right now, even though I damn sure want to. You need time to heal, but, baby girl, you're far from ugly. Do I look like the kind of man who keeps an ugly woman around?"

I shook my head.

"All right, then. Guess that means you must be pretty fucking beautiful. Stunning. The most gorgeous woman in the entire world."

I bit my lip and giggled a little. His words gave me comfort, and eased the weight pulling me down. I glanced at the pills next to the bed and handed them to him. I knew if I kept them nearby, the next time I started to spiral, I'd reach for them. He was right. I was a survivor, and I wouldn't permit myself to get addicted to pain pills. Not when my daughter needed me, and *he* needed me. Even if it was the hardest thing I'd ever done, I'd refuse to take another one. I only hoped I was strong enough to not break and reach for the bottle again. I should throw them out, flush them so I wouldn't be tempted.

"How about we order room service, cuddle in bed, and watch movies all night?" he asked. "Sound good to you?"

"Perfect."

He ran his fingers through my hair. "Want me to fill the tub? You haven't tried the bubble bath I got you yesterday. Might help relax you before we eat. I'm sure the food will take at least a half hour, maybe longer."

I nodded and watched him walk off. I heard the water running in the bathroom and smelled a floral scent. It took me a minute to get out of bed and feel steady enough to walk. Kraken sat on the closed toilet, his fingers under the water spout. It must have seemed too hot because he turned the cold water knob some more. When he noticed my presence, he gave me a warm smile and stood, helping me out of my pajamas. He'd bought three sets for me, all soft cotton. They weren't sexy by any means, but I appreciated his thoughtfulness.

"Come on, beautiful. Let me help you into the tub, then I'll go place an order for us. Know what you want to eat?"

"Nothing too heavy, or greasy. Maybe some soup?"

His gaze narrowed. "You need more than just that. I'll get some for you, but I'll also see if they have some grilled chicken or something, just in case you're up to eating more."

I leaned back against the tub and closed my eyes. The water was perfect, and he'd been right. It was relaxing. I heard the murmur of his voice in the other room as he ordered our dinner. I didn't know if the others were sticking around too, or just Kraken. I'd seen two of his brothers at the hospital, but Kraken hadn't permitted anyone in our room. Was I keeping him from his duties with the club?

My fingers started to prune so I drained the water and got out. I hadn't thought to bring clean clothes in with me, so I wrapped the towel around my body and padded out into the room. Kraken sprawled in a chair at the little table, tapping on his phone screen. He glanced up as I pulled open the dresser drawer, taking out some clean panties and pajamas.

"We need to wash clothes," I said.

"I'll get the hotel staff to clean them. They have a laundry service."

I turned to him, pulling my pajamas on. "Blake, that's going to cost a fortune. I'm sure there's a laundromat nearby. Or maybe we can just go home."

"Baby girl, you're swaying on your feet. I don't think you're up for a road trip yet. When it's time, I'll make sure there's a club truck here to take you home, but for now, I want you to rest."

I crawled back into bed, pulling the covers up to my waist. He was right about one thing. Even something as simple as a bath really took it out of me. It felt like I'd run a marathon. I knew part of it was the drugs still in my system, but I'd been told I'd lost quite a bit of blood. I didn't know how long I'd been passed out in my room before Kraken found me.

Our food arrived and I managed to eat my soup and a few bites of the grilled chicken. I didn't have much of an appetite, but I ate because I knew I needed to. Not to mention, if I didn't eat regularly, Kraken would threaten to force-feed me. I knew he was worried, but I would be fine. Now, anyway. The words in the card he'd given me had changed things, made me realize how much he still loved me, wanted me. I might see a disfigured monster in the mirror, but he didn't. To Kraken, I was still Phoebe, the woman he loved. His wife.

He put the tray in the hall, then crawled into bed next to me. He drew me close to his side and I rested my head on his chest. Breathing him in, I let his scent wash over me. I'd held him at arm's length, worried about where I stood with him. I wouldn't do that anymore. If he wanted to comfort me, I'd let him. Maybe holding me helped him in some way too.

"Don't you need to be back home?" I asked. "You're an officer. I'd imagine they don't like you being gone so long."

"I'm right where I need to be. Titan took two bullets to the chest. He's on bed rest, which he fucking hates. Boomer is running things for the most part. They're patching up the compound and mostly lying low."

"Patching? What does that mean?" I asked.

"Sadistic Saints blew the gates off. We lost Ratchet and a Prospect. We got lucky it wasn't worse." He sighed. "And Morgan is gone too. But since he'd turned on us, we'd have gutted the fucker anyway. I don't know why he did it, but I'm sure Wizard is checking into it. Won't matter. There's nothing more sacred than our brotherhood, and he shit all over it."

"He seemed jittery, right before he turned me over to Pitch. I could tell something was off. I'd mentioned it to Mara, but we didn't have time to make a plan."

"If there's any sort of trail for Wizard to follow, he'll find out what was going on. But with Morgan dead, along with the Sadistic Saints, it doesn't much matter anymore. Knowing why he did it, won't change everything that happened."

"Maybe not," I said. "But it might give you closure."

"I'm more worried about MaryAnne. Pitch said she was long gone. I don't know if that means dead, or if they sold her. Hell, she could have been shoved into a brothel somewhere. We owe it to Sean to find her and bring her home."

I rubbed my hand across his chest, wanting to comfort him. "You will. The club will find her, if she's still alive. I have faith in you, Blake." The way he'd protected me, gotten me away from Deuce and the others, I knew he'd never stop searching for MaryAnne. My biker might be a bad boy, but he was a sweetheart when it came to women. A defender of the innocent. I just wasn't sure he'd appreciate me calling him that, even in my head.

Chapter Eleven

Kraken, Two Weeks Later

I kicked back at a table in the clubhouse, a cold beer in my hand. Phoebe's stitches had dissolved, and while she still had some scarring, it wasn't as bad as she made it out to be. I knew she felt self-conscious about them. Every time she left the house, her gaze darted around, like she worried people were staring at her. I wished we had more old ladies in our chapter. She needed some women around, but all our guests were long gone.

Wizard hadn't had any luck finding MaryAnne, but I knew he wouldn't give up. I'd thought about asking Titan if she could stay here for a bit. No doubt she'd be fucked up mentally if nothing else. I doubted someone like Pitch would have given her to a nice church-going family. Of course, Phoebe had learned all about those types and what they were capable of. I still hadn't given her father a visit, but I wanted to. If she hadn't needed me while we were in the Sadistic Saints territory, I'd have gone to have a chat with him.

Titan eased down into the chair next to me with a wince. I knew he didn't want to appear weak to the club, but he was still healing. The stubborn man hadn't even stayed on bed rest the required length of time. Couldn't blame him. I'd hate lying in bed every day all day too. He took a pull of his beer and set the bottle down.

"Something on your mind, Pres?" I asked.

"You were gone a while. There are a few things we need to discuss. I know you're still concerned about Phoebe, but I need your head back on club business. We have too much shit going on."

I nodded. "I'm back. I'm ready to work."

"We let Sean off with a warning. What he did

was dangerous and could have had dire consequences, but I understand why he did it. He knows in the future to tell us and we'll have his back," Titan said.

"Wizard ever find out why Morgan turned on us?" I asked.

"No. We can't find any connection to him and the Sadistic Saints. No huge deposits in his accounts, no missing family members. Nothing is out of the ordinary, so I have no damn clue what they had on him, or if we just fucked up and let the wrong guy prospect for us."

I pointed my beer toward some half-naked women dancing near the bar. "See we got some new talent while I was gone."

"Don't let your woman catch you eying them. She'll probably put you on your ass, or worse… leave."

He wasn't wrong about that. There were times my little Phoebe was timid as hell, but when it counted, she came out swinging. She'd only left with Pitch in order to save the others. If it had just been her, I knew she'd have gone down fighting. Now that she'd had a taste of passion, love, and acceptance, there was no way she'd ever go back to living the way she had before. Not willingly.

"I'm worried about her," I confessed. "You and I know her scars are barely noticeable unless you're looking for them, but to Phoebe, they might as well be huge craters. She feels ugly and like everyone is staring when she leaves the house. I don't know how to help her."

Titan tapped his thigh a few times, his brow furrowed. "I may know a way. Remember the nurses who were called in the day I got shot?"

"Yeah, what about them?"

"One them has some pretty bad scarring.

Beautiful smile, kind eyes." Titan's lips tipped up on one corner. "Doesn't take anyone's shit, including mine."

"Does this mean you're done giving Cowboy's daughter longing looks?"

Titan punched me in the shoulder, then grunted. I knew it had to hurt him more than me. "Told you I wasn't going there."

"Then call this nurse. See if she'll meet Phoebe here, or maybe out for coffee? I could drop her by the café."

Titan pulled out his phone and started typing. I didn't say a damn word about the fact he had the woman's number. Made me wonder if she was more than just his nurse. It would be nice if some of my brothers would settle down, find good women. Phoebe would probably like not being the only one here. The club whores didn't count. I didn't want them near my woman for any reason. Bunch of catty bitches.

"You up for dinner at the little Mexican place across town?" Titan asked.

"Did you just ask me and Phoebe on a double date with you and the nurse?"

He snorted. "What the fuck ever. You coming or not?"

"I'm always down for tacos. Just let me go get Phoebe."

I stood and stretched before walking out of the clubhouse. I got on my bike and headed home. First thing I'd done when we got back was buy Phoebe an SUV. It was big enough I didn't feel like I was crammed into the damn thing like a sardine, but not so large she couldn't handle it. When I got to the house, the living room light was on. I shut off the bike and went inside, smiling when I saw her stretched out on the couch, one of those romantic comedies on the large TV. She seemed to love those damn things, and I suffered through them because I loved *her*.

"Need to get ready, baby girl."

She jolted and glanced my way. "How did I not hear you?"

"Too busy mooning over the guy on TV? You cheating me on me with some actor?" I teased.

"Of course not." She stood and came toward me. "Where are we going?"

"Out for dinner. And before you get upset and decide you want to stay home, Titan invited us out. Can't exactly say no to the Pres, can we?"

"Guess not." She twisted her hands in front of her. "I need to shower and change. And Ember's asleep…"

"Get to it. I'll let Titan know we can head out in about a half hour, and I'll ask someone to come sit with Ember."

Her eyes went wide. "I only have a half hour?"

"Twenty-nine minutes now. Get moving, woman!"

She squeaked and took off to the bedroom. I smiled and shot Titan a quick text, then decided it wouldn't hurt for me to at least change my shirt. I smelled like cigarettes thanks to being at the clubhouse the last hour. As much as I wanted to spend every second of the day with Phoebe, I knew she needed some space, and I probably did too. I didn't give a shit about the whores at the clubhouse, but I liked having a beer with my brothers.

Pretty Boy volunteered to sit with Ember, since he had experience with kids. I knew the thought of taking care of Ember scared the shit out of some of my brothers. They'd never admit it, but I could smell their fear. It was almost funny.

By the time we rolled out, I noticed Titan's bike was already gone, which meant he'd left before us. I pulled into the lot of the little Mexican place, stopping next to Titan's Harley. I saw the Pres through the windows, a pretty blonde next to him. Phoebe tensed the moment she saw them.

"Blake, what's going on?" she asked.

"Easy, baby girl. I think the Pres likes this one. She's a nurse. Helped him when he got shot. Come on."

I got out and went around to her side. I opened her door and pulled her from the SUV, knowing if I didn't, she'd try to stay in the car. Leading her up to the front of the restaurant, I felt the tremor in her hand. I leaned down, my lips near her ear. "Remember, baby girl. You're fierce. Strong. A survivor. You've got this."

She gave a quick nod before we went inside.

I waved off the hostess and made my way through the restaurant. As we neared Titan's table, I realized why he'd wanted the nurse to meet with Phoebe. Her face was deeply scarred, the lines trailing down her neck and under her shirt. More scars marred her hands and what I could see of her arms, and yet she laughed at something the Pres said and looked happy. She also didn't seem to care if anyone in the restaurant stared.

I motioned for Phoebe to sit by the window and I slid into the booth next to her.

"Phoebe, Kraken, this is Aurelia. She's the nurse who patched me up," Titan said.

Aurelia gave an unladylike snort. "More like I threatened to tie your ass to the bed if you didn't lie still so you could heal."

Oh, I liked her. A lot. I grinned at Titan, but he

was too busy staring at the pretty nurse to care. And she was beautiful.

"What do you do, Phoebe?" Aurelia asked.

"Oh, um..." Phoebe chewed on her lip.

"Phoebe hasn't had a chance to think much about her future." I reached over and placed my hand over hers where they'd knotted in her lap. "I'm kind of hoping she might like to just be a stay-at-home mom. We have a daughter, Ember, and I'd love to have more kids with her."

Phoebe glanced my way, a smile curving her lips.

"Oh, where's the little one right now?" Aurelia asked.

"We left her at home since she was sleeping," I said.

"How did the two of you meet?" Aurelia asked.

Titan reached over, putting his arm around her and pulled her closer. "Why don't we check out the menus? The server will be by any minute, I'm sure."

Aurelia took the hint. I held Titan's gaze, letting him know I was grateful for the interference. I knew Phoebe wouldn't want to answer that question, or any other personal ones. Her life hadn't been easy since the Sadistic Saints had gotten their hands on her. While anyone in the club, or having lived this life, would understand, I didn't know if the nurse would. She'd probably seen her fair share of bad shit, and it was clear she'd suffered through something. I just didn't want her making Phoebe feeling inferior to her in any way, even if it wasn't intentional.

"Why did you become a nurse?" Phoebe asked. "I've always admired those in the medical profession."

Aurelia motioned to her face. "Got this, courtesy of an ex-boyfriend. Spent some time in the hospital and found an appreciation for those who could help people in my situation. Decided I wanted to do that too. Took some classes, knew I'd made the right choice, and studied to become an R.N."

"Your boyfriend did that?" Phoebe asked.

Aurelia nodded. "But seeing as how your man there can't keep his hands off you, and not in a violent way, I'm guessing he isn't the one who hurt you."

I ran my hand down Phoebe's hair. "Another club took her, cut her up. She's only recently healed."

Aurelia's eyes widened. "The day Titan was shot. They took you, didn't they?"

Phoebe nodded. "Yes. I went with him quietly so they wouldn't hurt the other women and children. It was better for one of us to suffer than all of us."

I pressed a kiss to her temple. "My fierce, protective baby girl. There's not another like her."

"So you and Titan are seeing one another?" Phoebe asked.

Aurelia's eyebrows went up and she looked at the Pres. "I don't know. Are we?"

Titan smirked. "Think you can handle me? The club? It's not exactly a cakewalk."

Aurelia leaned in closer. "Titan, I've worked in the ER during a full moon. Nothing scares me."

"Then I guess we'll see where this goes." He pressed his lips to hers in a hard kiss. "But be warned. I tend to take what I want."

"Looking forward to it, big guy." Aurelia smiled.

A server hurried over, a smile on her face. "Hi! Welcome to Maria's Cantina. Are you ready to order?"

We each placed an order for drinks and our meals, as well as getting a basket of chips and queso for the table. As we waited for our food, Aurelia and Phoebe got better acquainted. I didn't know if they'd ever be friends, but at least my woman now saw that scars didn't make someone ugly. If Titan did claim Aurelia, then she'd be around a lot. I wasn't sure if the Pres was ready for that, or just enjoyed the nurse's company.

Phoebe loosened up and seemed to enjoy herself.

When the food got to the table, she dug in, and seemed to actually enjoy her meal, something I hadn't witnessed since Pitch had snatched her. I liked seeing that spark again, even if it was over queso.

"Do you like to shop?" Aurelia asked.

"Oh, um. I haven't really done a lot of shopping, but I guess it's fun." Phoebe shoved a chip into her mouth, but if she'd hoped that would end the discussion, she was wrong.

"We'll have to go to the mall sometime." Aurelia leaned over the table and dropped her voice. "Without the men. We can get our nails done, have some lunch, and shop until we drop."

"You really want to go shopping with me?" Phoebe asked.

"Of course. I don't really have a lot of friends. I've found most women to be backstabbing bitches, but you don't seem like the type."

Phoebe gave her a cautious smile. "I think I'd like that."

"Maybe the four of us can go out again sometime," Titan said.

"I'm free on Tuesday night," said Aurelia. "But that could change. If anyone calls in sick, I might have to pick up an extra shift. It's kind of hard to make plans in advance because they could change at the last minute."

Titan shrugged. "I'm okay with that."

"What the Pres is trying to say is that if shit goes down with the club, he'd have to bail on you, so he's understanding that plans sometimes have to be broken." Titan narrowed his eyes at me, but he knew I was right.

"You ever been around a club like theirs?" Phoebe asked Aurelia.

"Not until I had to patch everyone up. I'd say I should steer clear, but with all the sexiness over there, I have a feeling you'll see me around." Her gaze slid to Titan. "Especially if this big beast wants to try dating."

"On that note, I think I'm going to get my wife home," I said, standing and throwing some money on the table. I helped Phoebe out of the booth. "Nice to meet you Aurelia. Phoebe can get your number from Titan so the two of you can set up a spa day or something."

I led Phoebe from the restaurant and helped her into the SUV. There was a slight smile on her lips as I got behind the wheel. I liked seeing her happy again. She'd needed to know that no one cared about her scars. They weren't as horrible as she thought and didn't detract from her beauty in the least. Not just to me, but to other people. I'd already told her how I felt, and she no longer tried to hide from me. But I'd worried I'd never get her out of the house and around other people.

"So your stitches are gone, and you seem to be healing nicely," I said as I pulled out onto the road.

"Is there a point to this?" she asked.

"Just wondering if that means you're cleared for... other stuff."

She turned toward me. "Is that your way of asking if we can have sex?"

"Maybe." I cut my gaze toward her. "Why? Do you want to?"

Her lips twitched. "Blake, I've been ready, even

before the stitches came out. There's no reason we can't be intimate."

"Then let's hope our girl is asleep when we get home because I have plans for you." I winked at her and her cheeks flushed. So damn adorable.

As I pulled up to the compound, the new automatic gate slid open. A Prospect patrolled just inside, and another sat in a guard booth, opening the gate only to those who were authorized to be here. I gave them a wave as I pulled down the road toward our home. Pretty Boy was on our front step, fiddling with his phone. Phoebe practically dove out of the car the moment it was parked.

"Is Ember okay?" she asked.

Pretty Boy smiled. "She's still sleeping. Just came out to take a call so I wouldn't bother her. She woke for about twenty minutes, but I changed her and tucked her back in. I think she's out for the count."

"Thanks for watching her," I said, shaking his hand.

"No problem. She's a little angel."

He stepped down onto the drive and walked over to his bike. I ushered Phoebe into the house, locked up, then lifted her into my arms and carried her to our room. I kicked the door shut before letting her slide down my body. I couldn't wait to get my hands on her. It had only been weeks, but it felt like months since I'd been inside her.

"Get naked, baby girl."

I reached back to twist the lock on the door, then shrugged out of my cut. I tossed it onto the dresser before taking off my boots and the rest of my clothes. Phoebe shifted from foot to foot, her eyes bright and her cheeks a rosy pink. I reached for her tracing the curve of her waist with my fingers.

"So damn sexy," I murmured. "Beautiful. And mine."

She melted against me. "Yes, I'm yours. Only yours."

I tipped her chin up and kissed her long and deep. My cock throbbed and I only hoped I could last long enough to please her. My hand hadn't been sufficient the last two weeks. I trailed my lips down her throat and nipped her shoulder.

"Blake, please… don't tease me. It's been too long."

On that we could agree. "Not fucking you until you come for me. You want my mouth or my fingers?"

She whined and squirmed against me. "Fingers."

I slipped my hand between her legs and stroked the lips of her pussy. "Damn, baby girl. You're already soaked."

"Need you, Blake. So much."

I worked her clit with my thumb and eased a finger inside her. I felt her quick inhalation and her nails bit into my back as she held on tight. Phoebe wrapped her leg around my hip, opening herself to me. She pressed her forehead to my shoulder and made the softest, sweetest sounds as I fucked her with my fingers. I added a second one, driving them into her faster. Harder.

"God, Blake. So close. Don't stop."

"Wasn't planning on it. Come for me, baby."

She held on tighter, her body trembling, as she came all over my hand. I kept thrusting my fingers, not stopping until she'd come a second time. I carried her to the bed and turned her to face it. With a gentle push against her back, she bent over the side, ass in the air.

"Gonna be quick this time, but I promise to make it last on the next round."

It was all the warning I gave her before sliding in balls-deep. I groaned at how fucking incredible she felt. Gripping her hips, I slammed into her again and again. I knew I was seconds from coming, and it was a dick move to not get her off again, but I couldn't hold back. A growl built in my chest and spilled from me as I came inside her. My heart hammered in my chest, and my cock twitched inside her. Pulling out, I rolled her onto her back and bent her legs, spreading them wide.

"Love seeing my cum all over your pussy." It leaked from her and appeased the possessive side of me.

She lifted her hands toward her breasts and I knew damn well what she was about to do. I released one of her legs and grabbed her wrist, stopping her. With a shake of my head, I tugged her hand away. No fucking way would she hide from me now. My dick was still hard, so I thrust deep, filling her up.

Phoebe's eyes went wide and her lips parted. I held her thighs, keeping her spread open, as I powered into her. I added a little twist when I was buried inside her, brushing against her clit. It wasn't long before her head was thrashing on the bed, and she'd fisted the bedding as if she needed something to anchor her.

I fucked her, driving into her with fervor, making the bed inch across the floor. Next time we'd do this over the foot so at least the wall would hold it in place. I reached down to grab the frame and haul it back in place. Phoebe giggled and I had to admit it was damn funny.

"Change locations?" I asked.

She nodded and I pulled out, then helped her up. She scrambled to the center of the bed and lay down with her head on the pillows. Looked like we were doing this the more traditional way. Didn't matter to me. Being with her was amazing, no matter the position.

I settled between her thighs and slid into her again, her pussy gripping me tight. "Missed this."

"Me too," she said softly.

"Reach up and hold the headboard."

Once she'd complied, I adjusted my hold on her, going deeper than before. Her eyes glazed and a flush worked its way up her chest and neck. Her pussy got hotter. Wetter. I reached for her nipple, pinching it tight and giving it a little twist. Phoebe cried out my name, her pussy clenching down as she came. I thrust into her, not stopping until I filled her with my cum.

"Note to self: Don't get injured again because I don't want to go this long without feeling you inside me ever again," she said.

"Same." I leaned down and kissed her. "But if I put a baby in you, we'll have to forgo sex for a bit. I might not have been a dad before, but I do know that much at least."

She sighed. "Well, in that instance, I think we'll both gladly suffer through it."

"Let's get cleaned up." I pulled out and rolled off her.

"Why? Aren't you just going to get me messy again? Or are you done for the night?"

"I see my sassy girl is back." I winked. "I like it."

She cuddled against me, tracing a pattern on my chest with her finger. "Let's just rest a bit, cuddle like this, and maybe you'll let me play some. I want your cock in other places tonight too."

Fuck if I was going to say no to that!

Chapter Twelve

Phoebe

I hadn't ventured out of the compound on my own, and I didn't like feeling as if I should look over my shoulder every few minutes. I knew Kraken had taken care of Pitch and the others, but what of the other chapters? Would they come for me in retaliation? Or did they not care? I couldn't help but feel this was far from over, no matter how many times the Hades Abyss assured me otherwise.

Kraken seemed to think they'd taught a lesson to the Sadistic Saints. Maybe he was right, but what if he wasn't? What if they were biding their time and would strike when Kraken and the others least expected it? I didn't think those other chapters cared about me in the least, but as the only female at the Hades Abyss compound, I knew it put a target on me. No one cared about a club whore, but an old lady? I'd be stupid to think someone wouldn't see me as Kraken's weakness.

I parked my SUV outside the mall and hurried inside. Aurelia had asked to meet for lunch and shopping, and Kraken had insisted I accept. I knew he worried about me and wanted me to make friends. It was sweet, and just another reason I loved him. But being out in the open like this, especially alone, made my stomach knot.

I spotted the blonde nurse as I neared the food court. She waved with a big smile on her face. I hastened over and tried not to think of the people who might be staring. If it didn't bother Aurelia, then I wouldn't let it bother me either. I sat next to her and wondered how it worked to shop in pairs. I'd never gone shopping with another woman, except my mother, and she hadn't been one to let me have any fun. I'd never been permitted to go anywhere without a parent or other adult with me, and even the times my sister had joined us, there had still been a reserved nature to our shopping trips.

"Never been shopping with a friend?" Aurelia asked.

"Is it that obvious?" I asked.

Aurelia held two fingers slightly apart. "Just a little. You look ready to bolt."

"My mother would take me shopping when I lived at home. My dad was a preacher, so it wasn't like I got to shop for the same sort of clothes all the other girls were wearing."

"What about after you left home?" she asked. "I'm assuming you're out of high school since you're married to Kraken."

"Something bad happened. Another club..." I shook my head. "I'd rather not talk about it, if that's okay. Kraken saved me. But to answer your question, no I've never been shopping with friends before."

"Then I'm honored to be the first." Aurelia smiled widely. "You hungry? We could eat first, or just get some coffee before we start shopping. Do you have anything special you need to get today?"

"I hadn't really thought about it. Kraken gave me his card and some cash, but I don't want to make him go broke either."

"How about some sexy stuff to tempt that hot husband of yours?" she asked.

"All right. But if I do, then you need to buy some to model for Titan." I nudged her with my elbow when she blushed. "I know you like him."

"Yeah, I do. I'm just not sure his world and mine will mesh very well. If something bad happens, like the day we met, I can't exactly just leave the hospital and go on lockdown because he's worried about me. And

Titan doesn't seem like the type to let me do my own thing. He'll want to be in charge."

I nodded. "Kraken is the same way, but I know he's trying to protect me. After the things I've been through, I appreciate that about him. In fact, it's one of the things I love."

"And for you, it's probably great. I'd feel suffocated, and angry. It wouldn't take long before I'd lash out at Titan, or any man who did that to me. I just don't see it working long-term, but I admit to being curious enough to at least attempt to date him. Maybe I'm wrong and it would work out fine."

She steered me into a boutique with lacy nightgowns and bras on display in the window. I'd never been permitted in this sort of store, and part of me was excited to go inside. There were so many textures and colors. I was nearly overwhelmed by it all. Aurelia talked me into nightgowns, scraps of lace and silk. They wouldn't cover much, but that seemed to be the point. I also grabbed a few bra and panty sets. The total astounded me, and my hand trembled a little as I handed over Kraken's card. I hoped he didn't get pissed I'd spent so much. We hadn't discussed a spending limit, but I wished we had.

I followed Aurelia into a few other stores before we had lunch in the food court. I couldn't seem to stop smiling and laughing, and couldn't remember the last time I'd enjoyed myself so much. I'd had friends in high school, but things were different then. My father was a preacher and I'd been expected to act a certain way. I'd followed the rules and they'd still tossed me away like I was nothing. Just trash they needed to get rid of. I hoped the roof of his church was worth it. No, actually, I hoped the entire building burned to the ground. It would serve him right.

"We should do this again," Aurelia said.

"Definitely." I smiled. "I had a great time today. I'd never realized shopping could be so much fun."

"You have my number. Call whenever you want to hang out. We'll just have to plan around my shifts at the hospital."

"What's it like being a nurse? I know you went to college, and you talked about your job a little at the diner. Was there ever a time you wanted to do something else with your life?"

She shrugged. "My father was a doctor. A heart surgeon. He died when I was little and my mother brought one loser home after another once he was gone. Becoming a nurse made me feel closer to him, but I really do enjoy my work. I like making a difference. I get yelled at by the hospital staff and the patients, but at the end of the day, I know I made a difference even if it was just a small one."

"I think I envy you." I twirled my cup on the table. "The bad thing I mentioned happened before I graduated high school. I know I could get my GED and maybe think about college, but I have everything I could ever want or need. Kraken loves me, and I love him."

"As long as you're happy, that's all that matters," Aurelia said. "There are plenty of women who enjoy being stay-at-home moms. I don't think I'd be one of them. I love the chaos at the hospital, even on the days I bitch about it or want to rip out my hair over the political crap that goes on. I don't think I could give it up. Not anytime soon."

She gave me a quick hug goodbye and I carried my bag out to the parking lot. The hair on my nape prickled and I stopped just outside the mall doors, keys clutched in my hand. I scanned the area, but I didn't notice anyone paying me undue attention. It was possible I was only feeling paranoid, but the churning in my stomach said it might be more.

I briskly walked to my car, popping the locks as I got close. Practically jumping inside, I threw my stuff onto the passenger seat and locked the doors. I started the car and backed out, then drove straight home. The entire way, I glanced in the rearview mirror a hundred times, worried someone might be following me. I couldn't shake the feeling, even as I pulled through the gates.

I saw Kraken's motorcycle parked in front of the clubhouse, along with several others and a few cars. I didn't know who was watching Ember, but I knew he'd never leave her alone. Instead of going to the house, I stopped to talk to Kraken. If there was someone watching me, he'd need to know. I didn't have proof but I hoped that didn't matter.

Getting out, I walked up the steps and pushed the doors open. My eyes took a moment to adjust to the dim lighting, and when they did, I wanted to fuck a bitch up. My teeth ground together as I made my way across the main floor and didn't stop until I stood directly in front of the whore shoving her ass in my husband's face. To make things worse, she only wore a thong.

I didn't say a word, just reached out and grabbed a handful of her hair, then yanked her until she fell to the floor. She shrieked and came up swinging, but I was prepared. I balled up my fist and let it fly, hitting her right across the cheek.

"Who gave you permission to shove your ass in my man's face?" I demanded.

"Kraken! Help me," she cried out pathetically.

"Help you?" I kicked her legs out from under

her, sending her ass back to the floor. "Help you? You honestly think my *husband* is going to help a whore over his wife?"

The woman launched herself at me, but Kraken wrapped his arm around her waist and hauled her back. "Enough!"

I narrowed my eyes at him. "If you're taking the side of that… that…"

He shoved the woman aside and took two steps toward me, the heat of his body pressing against mine. He reached out and tipped up my chin, forcing me to hold his gaze.

"Baby girl, I wasn't taking her side. There's a chance you're pregnant, and if she hurt you, I'd have to fucking kill her."

"There a reason you were letting her shove her ass in your face?" I asked.

His lips twitched. "I wasn't paying the slightest bit of attention to her. She doesn't do a damn thing for me. Most beautiful girl I've ever seen is in my bed every night. Why would I want anyone else?"

I sighed and pressed my forehead against his chest. I felt his silent laughter as his arms came around me. I didn't want to bring up my fear over being followed, not right this moment, but I didn't want to wait either. What if something happened before I got a chance to talk to him?

"We need to talk," I said. "It's why I came in here to find you."

He pressed a kiss to the top of my head. "What's wrong, baby?"

"I felt like someone was watching me when I was out with Aurelia. It might be nothing."

He sighed and pulled away, staring down at me. "But it could be something. You were right to tell me.

I'll tell the Prospects to keep an eye out, and I'll have a chat with Titan. Until then, I don't want you to leave the compound alone. If you meet with Aurelia somewhere, take a Prospect with you, or one of my brothers. I want you protected at all times."

I'd forgotten about the club whore until she pressed against Kraken's side. "You really preferred that scarred freak over me?"

I sucked in a breath and tried to keep my face impassive. I didn't want the bitch to know her words had hurt me. Before I could process what was happening, Kraken had spun and backhanded her across the face, sending her crashing against the table. I'd seen him smack a club whore once before, but not as hard as he did this time.

"You do not *ever* talk about my woman like that again." He advanced on her, fury rolling off him in waves. He fisted her hair, pulled her head back, then slammed her face onto the table. She screamed as blood spurted from her nose. "You're just a whore. You may be here voluntarily, but you're not an old lady. The only place you have here is as easy pussy. You're a wet hole and nothing more. That woman is my wife, my old lady, and you will show her the fucking respect she deserves or you can get your ass out of here and never come back."

Boomer pushed past me and placed a restraining hand on Kraken's shoulder. "Easy, brother. Know she insulted your woman, and you had a right to deal with it, but I think she's learned her lesson. Let her up."

Kraken backed off, but growled at her like some sort of feral beast. I went to him, trembling at his show of temper. I didn't think for a moment he'd ever hurt me or Ember, but it still left me rattled that he'd make a woman bleed.

"Phoebe felt like someone was watching her while she was out shopping," he said, drawing Boomer's attention. "This may not be over yet."

Boomer nodded. "We'll discuss it. I'll get Wizard on it and call Church whenever he's dug up some shit."

I tugged on Kraken and he let me lead him from the clubhouse. He helped me into my SUV, pressed his lips to mine, then shut my door. He gave me that sexy wink I loved so much as he walked to his bike and started it up. He followed me to the house and I saw Pretty Boy's bike out front again. Somehow, the club's Treasurer had become our babysitter. It didn't bother me, and I knew Ember loved him, but I found it slightly strange. Didn't the man have better things to do?

I stepped through the front door and heard singing. My feet stuck to the floor as I listened to Pretty Boy sing to my daughter. His voice was deep and rich, and surprisingly, he could carry a tune. Kraken came in behind me, giving me a nudge, and I went into the kitchen where Pretty Boy walked the floor with Ember.

"Quit flirting with my daughter," Kraken said, taking Ember from him. "She's too young for you."

Pretty Boy smirked. "In eighteen years she won't be."

"Don't even think about it," Kraken warned.

"Thanks for watching her," I said. "I feel like we're taking advantage of you."

Pretty Boy shook his head. "I love sitting with her. Makes me miss my nephew a little less. He and my sister are in good hands, though."

I didn't press for more. Since his sister didn't live here, she'd obviously not paired off with one of the club members. Wouldn't he have wanted her close? Or did he feel like his brothers weren't good enough for his sister?

Pretty Boy made his farewells and put Ember down on the living room floor with her toys. Kraken had his phone to his ear, but he murmured so low I didn't hear what he said. I figured that meant it was club business. Even though I'd had lunch with Aurelia, I needed to figure out a plan for dinner. If Kraken got called away, I wanted to make sure he'd eaten. I wasn't the greatest cook, but I liked taking care of my little family.

I dug through the fridge and cabinets, then decided to make pork chops with mashed potatoes and green beans for dinner. I'd looked up some recipes on the phone he'd given me, but I wasn't brave enough to try something as adventurous as making rolls from scratch. Instead, I bought some from the bakery at the store and just warmed them in the oven while I put the finishing touches on everything else.

Kraken ended his call and came closer, pulling me back against his chest. He kissed my cheek, then my neck. "Love you, baby."

"I love you too. Pork chops okay for dinner?"

He nodded. "Sounds good. I'm going to go play with our girl while you do your thing in here. Just give a shout if you need anything."

I waved him off and got to work mixing the ingredients for the homemade marinade I'd found online. It was the first time I'd tried it, and I hoped it turned out okay. With some luck, the pork chops would be flavorful. I heard Ember giggle in the living room and smiled. Kraken was so good with her. For such a tough-looking guy, he was an amazing dad, and so sweet to the both of us. I'd be forever grateful he'd walked into the Sadistic Saints clubhouse that night.

Chapter Thirteen

Kraken

The news wasn't good. It wasn't the Sadistic Saints with their eye on Phoebe. It was worse. Her parents had hired someone to bring her home. I didn't know why, but I'd damn sure never let them have her. They didn't deserve Phoebe, or Ember. I wasn't entirely sure they wouldn't sell them both the first chance they had. Wizard's words still rattled around my brain. The phone call hadn't gone the way I'd hoped. Another club would be easier to take on. But a preacher and his wife? What the fuck was I supposed to do with that?

Ember chewed on the ear of her bear, babbling at me. I wasn't sure when she would start talking in a way I could understand, but I had to admit she was just too fucking cute for words. I hoped one day we had a house full of kids. Although we'd need more rooms. Right now, I only had two bedrooms other than the one I shared with Phoebe. I'd always sworn if I had kids, they wouldn't have to share a room. Sharing a closet-sized bedroom with two other siblings had been hell.

I heard Phoebe humming softly in the kitchen as she cooked our dinner. If anyone had ever told me I'd be playing on the floor with my daughter while my wife made dinner, I'd have laughed in their faces. I'd never thought of myself as the settling down type, but Phoebe had needed me, and just maybe I'd needed her too.

My phone rang and I pulled it from my pocket, answering it while keeping an eye on my daughter. "Kraken."

I heard a snort and glanced at the screen. *Wizard*. "No shit. Listen, I've been trying to follow the paper trail from the parents. Looks like they used part of the money from the Sadistic Saints to hire a P.I. He either lost her trail, or learned what the parents had done and refused to help. So where did they turn but to another club. One we're a little familiar with."

"Who'd they call?" I asked.

"Reckless Kings. I can promise you Beast doesn't know a damn thing about how Phoebe came to be here. I'm betting the parents spun some sob story about you snatching the girl. Need to call him and nip this shit before it gets out of hand."

"I'm on it," I said, then disconnected the call. *Son of a bitch.*

I shot off a quick text to Titan to give him a heads up, then dialed the Sergeant-at-Arms for the Reckless Kings. Forge answered on the fifth ring, right before I was about to give up.

"What the fuck do you want?" Forge asked.

"Nice greeting, asshole. Heard your club is watching my woman."

I heard him shift and something rustle on the other end of the line. "Phoebe Whitlow?"

"Not Whitlow anymore. She's not just my old lady but my wife. Don't believe me, check the marriage records."

"Well, fuck. Why the hell are the parents paying us to find their kid if you have her? They're claiming she got snatched or some shit. When my guys said they'd seen her drive into your compound earlier, I didn't believe them."

"They sold her to the Sadistic Saints. No clue why they're suddenly so concerned, but I'll be damned if they'll get their hands on her or my daughter. I don't fucking trust them."

"I'll call my guys off, but, Kraken, you need to

handle this shit. Those people aren't going to back down. If we won't do the job, they'll hire someone else. I can put the word out their money isn't good, but you know some stupid fuck somewhere will take the job just the same."

Yeah, I knew it. Didn't like it one damn bit either. "Thanks, Forge. Next time, instead of lurking around our fucking town, come knock on the damn door. You'll be lucky if Titan doesn't bust some heads."

"Shit," he muttered. "On it. I'll call your Pres and my guys. We'll sort it all out."

I shook my head and hung up the phone. At least I knew they wouldn't be taking Phoebe, but he made a good point. Her parents wanted her back for some reason, and I doubted they'd stop just because the Reckless Kings decided to back out. No, they'd find someone else. Someone as unscrupulous as the Sadistic Saints had been, and there'd be no reasoning with them. My woman and kid were in danger every second those sorry sons-of-bitches were breathing. Preacher, my ass. The man was no better than... *Damn.*

I pulled up Wizard's name on my phone and shot off a message. *Find me proof the parents sold her to the Sadistic Saints.*

They'd either see reason, so they didn't see the inside of a prison for trafficking their own underage kid, or I'd fucking kill them. As much as I didn't want Phoebe to know I'd gotten her parents' blood on my hands, I'd do whatever was necessary to keep her safe. I had to wonder just how rotten the preacher was if he could sell his own kid. What would stop him from doing the same to some other girl, or Phoebe's sister?

My phone rang again and I saw the Pres's name light up the screen. "Did the Reckless Kings call you?" I asked.

"Yeah. Spoke with Wizard too. He can't find any sort of communication between the parents and the Sadistic Saints, and the money deposited was cash. He's going to keep digging, but there's a chance they were smart enough not to leave a trail."

"I can't let this lie, Titan. She's not safe."

"I know," he said. "Spend some time with your family, Kraken, but later tonight I want you to ride out. Go visit her family. They have another daughter. Younger than Phoebe."

Right. So if money got tight, they'd find a way to earn some easy cash again. I didn't know what the hell to do with Phoebe's sister. I really didn't want her in my house underfoot, but I wouldn't abandon her either. If they had other family, it would make sense to send the girl to live with them. Unless the others were as bad as the preacher.

"I'll have Grizzly meet you there," Titan said.

"The Pres for the Devil's Fury? Why the hell would he do that?"

"Because he takes in strays. Has a thing for giving teen girls a second chance. He'll raise her right, and he'll make sure Phoebe can see her whenever she wants."

"All right. I'll head out once my girls are in bed."

I disconnected the call and picked up Ember, carrying her into the kitchen. Phoebe already had our plates on the table and was in the process of getting drinks from the fridge. She froze mid-reach and stared at me.

"What?" I asked.

"You have that look."

"Need to make a run later tonight. I'll be gone until sometime tomorrow. Possibly longer. But I'm not going anywhere until bedtime. I'm going to spend as much time with my girls tonight as I can."

Phoebe gave me a tight smile, but I knew she wouldn't ask questions. She was the perfect old lady. I put Ember in her high chair, then claimed a seat next to her. When Phoebe sat down, I noticed her hand trembled. It was her number one tell when something made her anxious. I reached out and placed my hand on top of hers, giving it a slight squeeze.

"It's going to be fine, baby girl. I'll come home to you. It's not something that will detain me for long, but I need to make sure you're safe, and your sister too."

Her gaze held mine. "My sister?"

I nodded. "I don't want to risk your family doing the same thing to her. Do you?"

"Of course not."

"I'm going to make sure she's safe, baby. And I'll ensure your parents can't harm anyone ever again. I just need you to trust me."

"I do. But if anything happened to you…" Tears filled her eyes.

"Hey, hey. What's wrong, Phoebe?"

"I don't know. I'm overly emotional, I guess."

Emotional? Now that she'd mentioned it, she did seem rather sensitive lately. I'd assumed it was due to her scars, but maybe it was something else. I squeezed her hand once more, then pulled out my phone, shooting off a message to Bones. *Need you to come see Phoebe. Bring your kit.*

Once the task was finished, I devoured my food. I'd lived off diner food before, but Phoebe was going to fatten me up in no time. For someone who hadn't had a lot of opportunities to cook, she caught on quick. Dinner was amazing. "Baby girl, you are one wonderful cook. I've never eaten so good."

Her cheeks flushed. "I'm not that great at it, but I

want to learn. I've been looking up recipes to try. I want to be a good wife and mom."

"Baby, you're the best. Never doubt it."

"Love you, Blake."

I winked, knowing she liked it when I did that. Her cheeks always flushed and she'd get this little half-smile on her face. "Love you too."

While she bathed Ember, I packed a small duffle in case I was gone overnight. By the time our daughter was ready for bed, I was able to tuck her in. I placed a kiss on her brow and ran my fingers over her cheek.

"Sleep well, little princess."

Phoebe lurked in the hall. The worry in her eyes ate at me. I took her hands in mine and pulled her in close for a kiss. My lips lingered, and I wished I didn't have to leave her tonight. I backed her to the wall, my lips devouring hers until she was breathless. The doorbell rang, making me draw back.

"Be right back, baby."

I opened the front door and found Bones on the doorstep. He held up his bag. "I came prepared. Now what's wrong with your woman?"

I let him in and Phoebe wandered into the room. I probably should have warned her I'd asked him to stop by. "She's overly emotional. I know she's been through a lot lately, but I wanted to make sure nothing more was going on."

Bones nodded and started asking questions. "When was your last period?"

Phoebe's gaze clashed with mine and skittered away. "Before I met Kraken."

"That means it's been a month or longer," Bones said. "I'm going to take some blood and test for pregnancy."

"There isn't a faster way to find out?" I asked,

knowing at this time of night, there was no way we'd get an answer right away.

"If you want to find out before the lab can run it, get one of those home pregnancy kits. I'll take enough blood to check a few other things as well. No harm in double checking, but if she's missed her period, there's a good chance she's pregnant. I seriously doubt the two of you have been abstaining."

"Only when she was too hurt," I admitted. I pulled my phone out and texted a Prospect to pick up a home pregnancy test.

I'm on gate duty and Titan assigned Sean to the clubhouse. Fucking great. I'd forgotten for a moment we were still down to two Prospects after the shit went down the day Phoebe had been grabbed from the compound. Last thing I wanted to do was run to get a damn pregnancy test when I was leaving tonight.

Bones narrowed his gaze at me. "Something wrong?"

I showed him the text from Riley and he grunted. Perfect. No fucking help. Bones motioned Phoebe over to sit, then he withdrew the items he needed to get a blood sample. While he did that, I paced the room, and sent off a text to Stone, hoping he'd run to the store for us.

Did you seriously just ask me to get a pregnancy test?

I grinned at Stone's response. *Yeah, asshole. I did. Phoebe might be pregnant and I want to know before I leave tonight.*

I could imagine the cussing he was doing right now. But I knew he wouldn't let me down.

Fine.

"Stone is dropping a test off in a bit," I said.

Phoebe seemed paler than usual since the mention of a possible pregnancy. We'd talked about starting a family. I'd thought this was what she'd wanted. Had I been wrong? I wanted to be excited over the chance to have a baby with her, but if she didn't want this...

"I'm done. I'll get this to the lab and get back with you. Until then, take the home pregnancy test. If it's positive, get some over-the-counter prenatal vitamins for now. I can call in the stronger stuff later," Bones said.

He packed up and left. I sat next to Phoebe, reaching for her hand. She leaned against me, placing her head on my shoulder. I wrapped my arm around her shoulders and tugged her closer.

"I know we talked about having another baby," she said, "but with everything going on, I'm a little scared."

"The people following you have backed off," I said. "And my trip tonight will ensure no one comes after you again."

"Until the club faces another threat. I knew what I was signing up for, Blake, but the thought of our kids being in danger scares the hell out of me. What if I'm out somewhere and someone takes me or our kids? Or all of us? I don't want them to suffer the way I did."

I ran my hand up and down her arm. "Baby girl, we can't live our lives worrying about the monsters lurking in the shadows. If we did, we'd never enjoy a single second of our time together. Yes, there's a chance you and Ember, or any other kids we have, could be in danger at some point. Just know not only will I protect you, but so will this club. We will always come for you, Phoebe."

"I know." She sighed. "My mind is racing with a million worries."

"You going to be okay with me gone tonight? Do

you want me to ask someone to stay here overnight?"

She shook her head. "I don't want to put anyone out, Blake. I'm just being silly and overly sensitive. Maybe Bones is right and I'm pregnant."

I pressed a kiss to her temple. "If you are, I will be the happiest of men. And before you ask, it's not going to make me love Ember any less. She's mine, end of story. I'm the only dad she's going to know. Doesn't matter if she has my DNA or not."

"How long before you have to leave?" she asked.

"Soon, baby. Just waiting on Stone to get here because I want to know before I leave if you're pregnant or not."

She nodded and cuddled closer. She didn't fill the silence with idle chatter, and didn't ask me to put on the TV. I breathed in her scent and found comfort in her presence. I knew she worried I wouldn't come back, but there was no fucking way a preacher would put me in the ground.

There was a soft knock at the door and I knew it would be Stone. I got up to let him in, but he remained outside, merely handing me the plastic sack.

"There's a shit ton of different ones. Didn't know what she'd want so I got three one of the ladies at the store recommended." Stone shrugged. "Never exactly shopped for one of those before."

I clapped him on the shoulder in thanks, then shut the door. Phoebe had been silent as she'd stood and came closer. When I turned, she was right in front of me, her gaze fastened on the bag. I gave it to her, then steered her down the hall to our bedroom and bathroom. Leaning back against the counter, I folded my arms, intent on waiting.

She blinked at me like a little owl. "You're not staying in here while I take these."

"Yeah, baby girl. I am."

"But... Blake..." Her cheeks went scarlet. "I have to... *pee* on them."

I rolled my bottom lip into my mouth and bit down, not wanting to laugh. She stared me down, and when she realized I wasn't leaving, she heaved a sigh and dropped the sack on the counter. Phoebe removed the three tests inside, read the instructions for each, then, with her gaze cast away from me, she dropped her pants and hovered over the toilet, taking all three tests.

"I've had my mouth on your pussy, share a bathroom with you, and you seriously thought you peeing on a stick would be revolting?" I asked.

"It's embarrassing," she muttered.

When she'd finished, she capped the little sticks and set them on the counter. While she righted her clothes and washed her hands, I stared at the little innocuous-looking plastic sticks. It was hard to believe something so small, so breakable, could tell me if I was about to be a dad again. I hadn't lied to her. Far as I was concerned, Ember was mine, but this time, I'd get to be there for all of her pregnancy and see our kid when they were born.

"It said three minutes," she said.

I set a timer on my phone, then led her into the bedroom. I made sure I had everything I needed for my impromptu trip while we waited. Phoebe sat on the edge of the bed, eying my duffle like it was a poisonous viper. She'd have to get used to me being gone overnight. It didn't happen all the damn time, but often enough. Being a husband and father wouldn't change my duties with the club.

The timer went off, and I took Phoebe's hand, as we went to check the results.

A smile spread across my lips as I stared at each little stick. "Looks like we're having another baby."

She wrapped her arms around me and held on tight. "That means you have to be extra careful and make sure you come home to us. I can't do this alone, Blake."

I tipped up her chin and kissed her. "You can, but you won't have to. I'll be back sometime tomorrow."

"You're leaving now, aren't you?"

I nodded. "Gotta go, baby girl. You call Titan if you need anything, understood?"

"I will."

I kissed her one last time, grabbed my bag, and walked out before she could tempt me to stay.

Chapter Fourteen

Phoebe

My stomach knotted as I heard the front door shut, but I tried to take a calming breath. Then another. I knew this wasn't the first time he'd gone out on club business, and it wouldn't be the last. I'd been around bikers long enough to know they did what they wanted when they wanted, and followed their own code. Even though the Hades Abyss weren't monsters like the Sadistic Saints, I figured some things would remain the same. Like the club whores. Except the ones here weren't forced into that way of life and came of their own free will.

Didn't mean I wouldn't try to kick their asses if they touched Kraken. He was mine, and hands off. I knew Blake wouldn't encourage them, but he hadn't exactly seemed inclined to shove them away either. I'd have to learn to trust he wouldn't do anything to hurt me.

Just like I had to believe he'd come home in one piece tomorrow.

In such a short time, he'd become everything to me. I'd thought my parents loved me. I knew better now. There was no way they'd cared even a little if they'd been willing to give me away for a large chunk of cash. Which meant other than Ember, the only person who had ever loved me was Blake. I'd gladly given him my heart, and it would be his until I drew my last breath.

My phone rang, and I hurried to answer before it could wake up Ember. *Titan*. My stomach clenched. Had something happened to Blake?

"Hello," I said, my voice not as steady as I'd have liked.

"I've knocked twice. You going to open the

door?" he asked.

I scrambled to the front of the house and pulled open the door. Sure enough, the club Pres was on the doorstep. I hung up the call and stared, not quite sure why he was here. Kraken hadn't been gone that long. I knew accidents happened anywhere, but Titan had a smile on his face, which eased my worries.

"Kraken insisted you didn't want company tonight, but I had a feeling you were here pacing the floor."

"Not quite pacing, but... I don't like the idea of him going after my parents. Not because I care what happens to those monsters, but because I don't want *him* to get hurt."

Titan nodded. "Figured as much. Just so you know, that man of yours can handle himself. Now let me in. We have some movies to binge-watch. I even brought popcorn."

I glanced down and saw the sack in his hand with the box peeking out of the top, along with what looked like a few different types of candy. I backed up and let him into the house, then shut and locked the door. Titan made himself comfortable in the living room while I grabbed two sodas from the fridge. When I returned to the living room, he'd already found an action movie.

"Come sit," he said, patting the couch next to him.

I plopped down next to him. "You know, this is probably the strangest thing I've experienced in the last year or so."

"Strange?" he asked, opening a package of Twizzlers and handing me one.

"The President of the Hades Abyss is in my living room, offering to watch TV with me, and is feeding me candy. Aren't you supposed to be throwing back beers with the rest of your club and chasing women right now?"

His eyebrows rose. "And forgo the pleasure of your company? Never."

I snorted and opened my soda, taking a gulp before setting it aside. At the Sadistic Saints, I'd feared their President. Deuce had made my life hell. He'd abused me. Hurt me the worst way a man could harm a woman. Done everything in his power to knock me down. Titan felt more like the older brother I'd never had, but I didn't for a second think he was a fluffy cute bunny. I had no doubt he'd gladly make his enemies bleed, but I also felt safe with him.

"Thank you," I said.

He just smiled and kicked his feet up on the table. I eyed his boots and he slowly dropped his feet back to the floor. I wondered if I should tell Aurelia he was trainable. Maybe it would make her more accepting of his lifestyle. If he put the seat down and had good aim, there would be a line of women waiting to be claimed by him. Titan and the others were far from ugly. Of course, Pretty Boy looked like he'd stepped off the cover of a magazine, but the others could hold their own.

"Did Kraken tell you the news?" I asked.

"News?" He shifted to face me.

"I'm pregnant."

He yanked the candy from my hand and pulled my soda out of my reach. "No, he didn't. If he had, I'd have brought you a salad and bottled water."

"Did you seriously just take candy from a pregnant woman?"

"Not my first rodeo. I know you aren't supposed to have a lot of sugar or caffeine." He stood, gathering the goodies and carrying them to the kitchen.

I followed, wondering what he was doing. When he handed me a banana and pulled out the gallon of milk, my jaw dropped. He didn't really mean to... He took down a glass and filled it, then slid it over to me. Yep, he really did.

"You took away my candy and soda and gave me a banana and milk," I said, staring at the items in my hands. "I feel like a kid being punished."

"Eating for two now," he said. "Need to keep a nutritious diet for the little one growing inside you."

"Ember turned out fine," I pointed out, and I'd been damn lucky to get much of anything to eat or drink when I'd been pregnant with her. It was a miracle I hadn't lost her with Deuce's treatment of me.

He leaned against the counter and stared me down. "Kraken is my Sergeant-at-Arms. You're his woman, which makes you part of my club. Know what my job is as President?"

"To be a big bossy pants who takes candy from women?"

"It's to ensure the well-being of those in this club. I make sure we prosper. Help keep everyone safe. And right now, that means making sure the only old lady this club has eats something healthy for the first Hades Abyss baby born in my chapter. We adopted Ember when Kraken did, but this little one will be here from the very beginning."

I peeled the banana, then savagely bit into it. He winced and shifted, which made me smirk. Served him right. I finished it off before I drained the milk. I had to admit, he was probably right about it being better for the baby. I hadn't had a clue what I was doing with Ember, and I still didn't know much about the right and wrong things to do during a pregnancy.

"Bones came earlier to check on me," I said. "But I think I need a special doctor. Think he could recommend an OB-GYN to me?"

"Do I look like I know anything about lady doctors?" he asked.

I waved to the now empty glass. "You know something about pregnant women. So, yeah. I'm going to assume that means you know about lady doctors, as you put it."

"Ask Aurelia who she recommends. I'll see about getting some insurance for you, but the club will cover any medical costs. That baby is going to have lots of uncles."

"I feel sorry for Ember," I said. "I can see it now. Her date will show up at the gates and be met with a line of armed bikers."

Titan nodded. "Exactly right. And if they hurt our girl, we'll bury them six feet under."

"Well, this conversation got dark fast."

"Come on." Titan came closer, then hooked his arm around my shoulders, dragging me along with him. "We'll finish the movie, then you can pick the next one. But if it's one of those sappy things, you better not breathe a word to the club about me watching it. Have to maintain my image as a badass."

"You're still a badass," I assured him. "You just have a mushy center you don't let too many people see."

"Don't tell anyone."

I pretended to zip my lips. "Your secret is safe with me."

"You're such a dork."

"Takes one to know one."

He froze and looked down at me. "You didn't just say that. Are you twelve?"

"For Kraken's sake, you better hope not."

He groaned and reclaimed his seat on the couch. I wished Aurelia could see him like this. I didn't know what the two of them were like when they were alone, but if she saw this sweet, funny side of Titan, I knew she'd fall for him. Any lady would be lucky to have him.

"What are we watching anyway?" I asked as I sat down again. "And what made you think I wanted to see anything that seems to involve car racing?"

"You're no fun." He tossed me the remote. "Go ahead. Put on that romantic shit women like. Just don't start yelling at me if my snoring bothers you."

I smacked his shoulder before flipping through the movies. Just because he'd taunted me, I did indeed put on a romantic comedy. Titan gave me the side-eye, but didn't so much as grumble. Even more surprising, he didn't fall asleep either. Although, I decided not to torture him with a second one when the first movie went off. Instead, I compromised on an old favorite -- *Top Gun*.

"Thought you liked the romantic movies," he said.

"It has romance," I pointed out. "Not to mention shirtless military men. What's not to like?"

He pretended to gag, but grinned at me. "Don't let Kraken catch you gawking at halfway naked men on TV or in person. I bet he'd spank your ass."

He was most likely right. But Kraken wasn't here right now, and I needed a distraction. I leaned against Titan and put my head on his shoulder. He tensed for the briefest of moments before putting his arm around me.

"Thanks for coming. If I'd been here alone, I probably would have worried myself to death. I know he'll be gone like this again, but it's the first time and…" I shrugged, not really knowing how to explain everything I felt.

"Kraken can handle himself, but I called in reinforcements. They'll let him run the show and only step in if needed," Titan said. "And your sister is going to live with the Devil's Fury. Their President tends to take in stray girls. He's got two living with him right now."

"Stray girls?" I asked, not sure I liked the sound of that.

"Grizzly lost his wife a while back. They never had kids, so he tends to take in teen girls who have nowhere else to go. He gives them a stable home, a chance to improve their lives, and spoils the hell out of them. Two of his adopted daughters married men in his club. One is off running wild right now, and the latest two are still in high school so they're still at home."

"He sounds nice," I said.

Titan shook with silent laughter. "Don't say that to his face, but yeah. When it comes to women and kids, he's a big softie. Wouldn't know it to look at him."

"I don't know. You and Kraken look pretty badass and intimidating, but you're both really sweet to me. My father is a preacher, an upstanding member of the community, and someone people look up to. He looks like a kind man, never has a harsh word for anyone, and look what he did to me. The way someone looks doesn't mean anything. I will never again judge someone based off their appearance."

"You're pretty smart for someone so young," Titan said.

"I learned the hard way."

He nodded. "That you did. You also discovered you're tough as hell and a survivor, which means the next time Kraken leaves and says he has to be gone for a day or a night, you're not going to freak out. I know this time it's different. He's going after your family."

"No. Not my family. Not anymore."

"The point I'm trying to make is this time it's personal for you. When I send him out on a run that has nothing to do with you or your children, it won't bother you as much. Yes, he could still get hurt, but nothing has taken that man out yet and I don't see it happening anytime soon. He was in the military and they trained him well. Kraken knows what he can and can't handle on his own."

"It's not that I don't trust him, or you. I know you and this club would protect me with your lives. Some of you already have. I'm sure part of it is just me being overly emotional right now. The other part... my relationship with Kraken is still new. I guess we're in the honeymoon phase, as they call it, and I really don't like being separated from him for very long. It makes me anxious."

Titan gave me a slight squeeze. "You'll be fine, Phoebe. You'll settle in more over the upcoming months, get to know everyone here better. You already know how a club works, somewhat. I know the Sadistic Saints were rotten to the core, but the politics are basically the same. Far as Kraken is concerned, you're the perfect old lady for him, and I have to agree. You need to find your groove, your place here at the compound."

I knew he was right.

He pointed to the screen as Tom Cruise took off in a jet from the deck of a ship. "That right there is what your man used to do. He was a Naval aviator."

Looked like I'd married my very own superhero. I'd watched this movie once at a friend's house my freshman year of high school. My parents never would have let me see anything like this, and I'd only been allowed over that day because my parents wanted to go to some retreat a few towns over. My sister had spent the day with one of her friends too. It was the only taste of freedom I'd had while living at home.

"I don't think I can picture him in the military," I said. "Kraken without a beard?"

Titan laughed. "Yeah, guess that is hard for you to picture. If you ever ask him to shave it, make sure you film that shit. His reaction will be priceless."

I tipped my head to look at him. "Are you on drugs? Why the hell would I want him to shave it?"

He shook his head and we went back to watching the movie. Having Titan here eased my worry a little, and he helped keep my mind off things. I had to wonder if this was what friendship actually felt like. If it was, then I'd never truly experienced it before. And that was even sadder than my father selling me to Deuce.

Chapter Fifteen

Kraken

I'd ridden straight through to Phoebe's hometown, only stopping once for gas. When I'd checked my phone, the Pres had sent a selfie of him and my woman sitting on my damn couch. I'd shaken my head, but I'd been damn grateful he'd gone to my house. At least I knew my woman was taken care of while I handled this shit.

I eyed the house where she'd grown up. Looked like a nice enough neighborhood. All the yards were neatly mowed. Homes were freshly painted. Not so much as a broken window or patched roof in sight. I'd always thought kids in these types of places had it easy. Maybe Phoebe hadn't faced many hardships growing up, but what her family had done to her was beyond horrific. Who the fuck sold their own damn kid?

I parked my bike in the shadows and pulled out the items I needed from my saddlebags. Grizzly stood beside me, ready to extract Phoebe's sister and get her to safety. He'd also brought along his son-in-law, Dragon, as backup. I didn't think a preacher and his wife would give me too many problems, but I wouldn't argue over having another set of hands. Titan had also put in a request with our Missouri chapter and their newly patched Prospect, Iron, had come as well.

I knew the kid had been with the Hades Abyss a long time. He'd more than proven himself, and I was grateful to have him here, even if I only asked for help with the clean-up or made him a lookout. I wanted these people to suffer, but I didn't want to be away from Phoebe longer than necessary. I could have easily asked someone else to handle this, but she was my wife and my responsibility. Which meant getting vengeance for all she'd suffered was also mine.

"You ready?" I asked the men standing with me.

They all nodded and we fanned out. Grizzly went with me through the front while Dragon and Iron took the back. It was early morning but not quite light outside. Getting through the front door was almost too easy, and it didn't make a sound as it swung open. With my gun in one hand and my knife in the other, I entered the house and scanned each room. Silence. Utter and complete silence.

Grizzly jerked his head toward the stairs, then motioned something to Dragon. I went up to the second floor and nudged open the first door. The room was empty, but I could tell immediately it had been Phoebe's. Even after all this time, her scent still faintly lingered in the air. A picture set on the dresser of her and what I assumed to be her family.

The second room belonged to the sister. Wizard hadn't said much about her. Grizzly entered the room and I stood guard, waiting to see if the parents made an appearance. He covered the girl's mouth to stifle any screams as he woke her. Poor kid. Her eyes were wide, and I could practically hear her heart racing she was so damn scared.

"I'm married to your sister," I whispered. "We're going to take you somewhere safe."

She seemed to calm a little and tugged at Grizzly's hand. He released her, but I could tell he was braced to grab her and run if she screamed.

"Phoebe's okay?" she asked.

"She's fine. We have a daughter and another baby on the way." I smiled. "Go with Grizzly. I'll make sure you see your sister soon."

The girl got out of bed. "I'm Meredith. Are you

really married to Phoebe?"

I nodded. I'd show her the pictures on my phone, but I wasn't about to relinquish my weapons. Not until her parents were at least restrained.

Her lip quivered. "They did something bad, didn't they? I knew she'd never leave like that. She told me she was sneaking out for a party, but she never came back."

"Your family isn't all that nice," I said. "We'll talk later. Right now, you need to go."

"Pack a few things," Grizzly told her, "but be quick about it."

She hurried to her closet, opened the door, and took out a small suitcase. While she threw things inside, I listened intently for any sounds in the house. I heard the soft tread of steps coming from behind and clocked Dragon coming up the stairs. He must have left Iron downstairs as a lookout. When Meredith finished packing, Grizzly took her suitcase and he ushered her downstairs.

"I'm with you until you say otherwise," Dragon said. "Brought my bike so I have my own way home. Griz will take the girl in the club truck."

We checked the next room, finding an office, then the jackpot with the fourth door. The preacher and his wife lay sleeping, each in their own twin-size bed. Made me wonder how they'd managed to have two daughters if they didn't even sleep together. I jerked my chin toward the wife and Dragon crept to her side. I tossed him a length of rope and while he secured her, I pressed my gun to the preacher's head. His eyes snapped open.

"We need to have a talk," I said. "About Phoebe."

He audibly swallowed but didn't so much as

blink. I yanked the covers to the foot of the bed and made him stand, then forced him to his knees.

"Whatever she's done --" Before he could finish the sentence, I slammed my fist into his jaw.

"What *she's* done? That girl is an angel, and you threw her away. Sold her to the Sadistic Saints. They raped her. Repeatedly. Made her their little whore. Was the money worth it?" I asked.

"You don't understand," the preacher said. "She was a willful child. The blood of monsters ran through her veins."

"Well, at least you admit what you are," I said.

He shook his head. "She wasn't ours. Not really. Her daddy was some biker filth who blew through town, got a local girl pregnant. We took her in, decided to raise her as our own. But I could see the evil in her."

"Evil? Evil!" I rammed my fist into his face twice. "My wife is not fucking evil. You are! Do you honestly think a seventeen-year-old girl deserved to be raped by an entire club of bikers? You're supposed to be a man of God. What happened to forgiveness and all that other bullshit you spout on Sunday mornings? Isn't that kind of the mantra of a man like you? Turn the other cheek and all that shit? But you didn't protect an innocent girl. Tossed her to the wolves and didn't even look back."

Dragon shifted his eyes on the preacher. "What club?"

My gaze jerked to him, then back to the man at my feet. He was right. We needed to know where Phoebe's real father had come from. The bastard probably didn't even know he had a kid, much less what had happened to her.

I pointed to my cut. "I'm with Hades Abyss. The men you sold Phoebe to were the Sadistic Saints. What club was Phoebe's father from?"

The man pissed himself and started shaking.

"What. Fucking. Club?" I yelled, shoving my gun against his temple.

"Yours," he said in a near whisper. "Her dad was from your club. The woman told us the man's name, but it wasn't a real name."

"His road name," Dragon muttered. "What was it?"

"Titan," the preacher said.

The world tipped under my feet and the breath in my lungs stalled. *Holy shit*. Titan? My Pres was going to flip the fuck out, and so was Phoebe. He wasn't much older than me. Only two years for that matter. If he'd knocked up some girl around these parts, it must have been right after he patched in. With Phoebe being nineteen -- and I didn't want to think about the fact I'd forgotten her birthday -- it meant the Pres had only been her age when she'd been conceived. Our chapter was relatively new, but most of us had come from other Hades Abyss chapters, and Titan had been one of them.

"I need to make a call," I said. "What was her mother's name?"

The preacher held my gaze. "Mary Chambers. She was only eighteen and scared. I'm sure that filth took advantage of her. She came to the church for help."

I snorted. Yeah, right. The Pres only had to crook a finger for a woman to drop her panties. I had no doubt even back then he'd had the girls falling at his feet.

"I'll watch them," Dragon said. "He needs to know."

I agreed. I stepped into the hall and pulled the

door shut, then dialed Titan. I could hear Phoebe laughing in the background when he answered.

"You done yet?" he asked.

"No. I hit a… snag."

"What the fuck kind of snag?" he asked.

"Do you remember ever being in these parts before? Maybe shortly after you'd patched into the club?"

"Vaguely. The Sadistic Saints weren't there back then. Another club was, but they disbanded about a decade ago. Why?"

"Preacher says Phoebe isn't his kid, that he took her in when a girl named Mary Chambers dropped off her infant daughter. A daughter conceived by her and a biker."

I waited a moment, then Titan started cursing a blue streak. I heard him moving through the house and a door slammed.

"Are you fucking with me right now? Are you telling me Phoebe might be my daughter?" he asked.

"Not fucking with you. He's claiming you're Phoebe's dad. Is it possible? The name Mary Chambers doesn't seem even a little familiar?"

"I… I don't…" He sighed. "I hooked up with some girl in that town back then. I honestly don't remember her name. Met her at a party."

"Look at my wife. Really look at her. Anything familiar at all?" I asked.

I heard him go back inside, then heard Phoebe saying something.

"Titan, put me on speaker. She needs to hear this."

I heard a click. "All right. She can hear you."

"Baby girl, I need you to listen. The preacher says he's not your real dad. Looking at him and his wife, I honestly don't see any resemblance to you. He claims your mom was a teen mother who didn't want her baby."

"Tell her the rest," Titan said.

"And the preacher claims the father of that baby, of *you*, was a man called Titan wearing colors like mine."

I heard a crash, then more cussing.

"What the hell is going on?" I demanded.

"She fainted. I'll handle it. Go deal with that sick fuck, and, Kraken, you better make him suffer. If she's my daughter and I've lost all this time with her, I want his blood. Every last fucking drop."

"On it."

I hung up and went back into the bedroom. The wife was crying and pleading with Dragon, claiming she'd had no part in what happened to Phoebe, but I could tell the bitch was lying. She'd known. Might not have planned it, but the preacher here hadn't kept her in the dark.

"Titan wants this one to pay," I said, pointing at the preacher. "Can you handle the bitch?"

"You got it. Any requests?" Dragon asked.

"Don't care as long as she's not breathing."

Dragon grabbed the now hysterical woman, gripped her head in both hands, and snapped her neck. She slumped to the floor, her lifeless eyes staring at the wall. The preacher pissed himself again and bawled like a fucking baby. Not even over his wife. No, the bastard only thought about himself.

"I'll give you anything you want. Don't kill me. You can have all the money in our accounts. My daughter! You can have Meredith."

"Didn't learn the first time, I see. Don't worry. Meredith is safe and will soon be far from you." I used a length of rope to tie his hands behind his back, knocked him flat and tied his ankles too. "How's your tolerance for pain, preacher? Because you're in for a world of it. Better start talking. Why did you try to get Phoebe back?"

He babbled and cried as I cut his shirt from his body.

"I just wanted..." He gaze darted around the room.

"What? More money?"

He nodded. "One club paid for her. I thought maybe another one would too."

Sick fucking bastard! I used the material to gag him, shoving a wad into his mouth, then tying a strip around his head to hold it in place I slid my blade along his tender skin. Shallow cuts along his back. I didn't stop until every inch was covered in blood. Slicing his pants off, I carved *Traitor* down the length of one leg. I nicked a vein and the blood started to pool under him, which meant I was running out of time.

Rolling him over, I removed the gag from his mouth. "There's one thing you're going to do before you die. If you don't, I'll make you suffer more."

"Anything."

I saw his phone on the bedside table and brought it over. Damn fool didn't even have it locked. I pulled up the number for the church and showed it to him.

"Anyone there right now?" He frantically shook his head. "Then you're going to leave a voicemail and admit to what you've done. You'll tell them you sold Phoebe to men who raped and abused her. Tell them where the money for the roof came from. And only then will I think of ending your pathetic life."

"I'll do it," he said.

I pressed the button to call and put it on speaker.

The church voicemail picked up and when it beeped, he started rambling about what he'd done. When I was satisfied, I ended the call and tossed the phone aside.

I heard Dragon murmuring on his phone, and the words *clean up*. While he made sure we wouldn't get caught or leave any evidence behind, I made good on my promise to Titan. I carved up the preacher like he was a damn Christmas goose, and watched as he bled out. When I was finished, Dragon clapped his hand on my shoulder.

"Come on. There's a crew coming by to make sure there's no trace we were here. They'll handle the bodies too. Make it look like the preacher and his wife skipped town."

I eyed the blood covering the floor. "Don't think you can hide that so easily."

"They'll do whatever is necessary. Even burn this bitch to the ground." Dragon looked me over. "Better wash some of that off before you hit the road. Thankfully, you're wearing dark colors, but you still might want to clean up and change."

I nodded and followed him from the house. Outside, Iron was waiting, but I noticed Grizzly was already gone. I was glad. They needed to be far the fuck away from this place. I hoped like hell the girl could handle what she'd learn about those parents of hers, assuming they even *were* her parents. If they hadn't given birth to Phoebe, there was a good chance the sister wasn't related either.

I texted Titan one word. *Done*.

He sent another selfie of him and Phoebe cuddled on my couch. My woman looked pale but happy. Maybe finding out she hadn't been related to these fucks had lifted some of the weight from her shoulders.

I had a feeling Thanksgiving and Christmas at the club were about to get interesting. Not only would this be our first holiday season with an old lady on the premises, but Phoebe wasn't just my woman. She was Hades Abyss by blood and the President's daughter. Never saw that fucking coming, and I knew Titan hadn't either.

As tired as I was, there was no fucking way I'd stay anywhere overnight. I needed to get home. But first, I pulled out my overnight bag and went back into the house. I washed up in the kitchen sink and changed my clothes, rolling up the dirty ones and shoving them into the bag. I'd either clean them or burn them later. When I got on my bike, I started her up and eased down the road. I opened up my bike on the highway and let the tires eat up the miles. The sun beat down on me as it rose to its peak just as I passed the town limits sign. Every part of me ached and fatigue pulled at me. I stopped at the gates to the compound and Riley let me through. Heading straight for the house, I saw Titan's bike was still outside. When I entered the house, I heard the TV going and stepped into the living room, smiling at the scene before me.

Ember sat on Titan's lap as he stared at her in wonder. Phoebe was next to them and looked at the Pres with a bit of awe.

"So... does this mean I have to call you Dad?" I asked.

Titan flipped me off. "Fucker."

Phoebe bolted from the couch, but I held up my hands and she threw herself into my arms. "You're home. You're safe!"

"Told you, baby girl. Nothing was going to keep me from coming back to you. You doing okay?"

She nodded against my chest. "It's so strange and yet... I feel relieved."

"How's it feel to be a dad and grandpa, Titan?" I asked.

"Pisses me off I missed so much of her life. If you hadn't already taken care of Deuce and the others, I'd have ended them. The way they hurt my girl." He shook his head. "They died too easy."

"Where's Meredith? Where did you send her?" Phoebe asked.

"Remember I told you she'd be in good hands. She's with the Devil's Fury. Their Pres is going to take her in, give her a home. You can talk to her later." I ran my hand down her hair. "She may not be your sister by blood, but you were raised with her. Makes her family."

"What if she's like me?" she asked.

"You mean not really the daughter of those sick bastards who raised the two of you?" I asked.

She nodded.

"If there's a way to find out, I'm sure the club hackers can do it. Between Wizard, Surge, and Outlaw, they'll dig up whatever they can."

"Already had Outlaw working to change Phoebe's birth certificate. I know he feels hampered because of his hands, but figured he could easily handle something like that. She might be married to you and have your last name, but I want to make it damn clear she's my daughter," Titan said.

"What happened after you hung up?" I asked.

Phoebe's cheeks pinked. "I fainted. Then we talked. The shock wore off after a few hours. He pointed out I was already family because I'm with you. Being his daughter just makes it even more official. And now Ember will have a grandfather she can look up to."

"It's going to take a little time to adjust," Titan said. "We'll find our way. She's not going anywhere and neither am I. We have all the time in the world to catch up."

"As much as I want to sit here and enjoy all this, I'm dead fucking tired. Going to shower and crash for a few hours."

Phoebe put her arms around my waist and kissed me. "I'll make something special for dinner. You gave me peace, not only knowing I'm not related to those hateful people but making sure they'd never hurt anyone else. And you gave me a family."

"No, baby girl. You're the one who's given me everything I could ever want or need. Love you."

I kissed her again, then waved to the Pres as I walked out of the room. Shower. Sleep. Then I'd sort out our new family dynamics with a clearer head. Life just kept throwing curveballs, but this one was pretty damn amazing.

Epilogue

Kraken, Five Months Later

I sprawled in a chair on Titan's back deck, watching my woman eat ice cream straight from the container. She glowed with health and happiness, and the slight roundness to her belly was a constant marvel for me. My kid was in there. We still didn't know what we were having, but we'd find out soon enough. Or so I hoped. Phoebe kept saying she might want to be surprised.

Titan handed me a beer. "Grizzly called earlier."

"How's Meredith?" I asked.

"Adjusting. Kind of wishing we'd talked to that preacher a little more. How the fuck did he end up taking in two girls who were both related to clubs? Seems too orchestrated if you ask me. No way it's a coincidence."

"Except in Meredith's case, her daddy isn't part of the club anymore. Hell, I don't even think the bastard is still breathing in all honesty. Heard Twister went after Grizzly's daughter over a decade ago. You really think Griz or Badger left that man alive?" I asked.

"Probably not," Titan said. "I wouldn't have."

"Any word on MaryAnne?" I asked.

"Yeah, but it's not good. Wire and Lavender tracked her down. Found her in a brothel. They sent some men after her. She was drugged out of her mind. Right now, she's under medical care."

"Sean know?" I asked.

"He knows we found her, but I haven't told him where she is. He doesn't need to see her like that," Titan said.

Ember toddled over and yanked on Titan's jeans. "Paw, paw, paw, paw…"

My lips twisted. "I'm still pissed at you, Pres. My own kid didn't even say my name first. Nope, she calls for her grandpa."

Titan chuckled and lifted Ember into his arms. "You have another chance with the next one."

Phoebe yanked the spoon from her mouth. "Uh-uh. I'm the one carrying these babies. They need to say Momma first."

I froze and looked at her. "Babies? What the... Baby girl, what the hell have you been keeping from me?"

Her cheeks turned crimson. "I may have asked the doctor not to tell you. The day you thought you heard two heartbeats? You were right. We're having twins."

I narrowed my eyes at my wife. "You'll pay for that."

Titan grunted. "I do *not* want to hear that shit about my daughter. What you do in your own home is one thing. But this is my house."

Phoebe smiled at Titan, then gave me a calculating look. "If you're mean to me, my daddy will just let me move in with him."

Titan stood up with Ember in his arms. "On that note, I'm going inside and I think the two of you need to go home. Phoebe, don't even try to pull that shit. I love you, but Kraken is my Sergeant-at-Arms. I need his head screwed on straight, so stop fucking with him."

"Fu, fu, fu... " Ember babbled.

I pointed to the Pres. "I'm not the mean one. Your *daddy* just taught our daughter to cuss."

Titan laughed as he went inside. Even though he'd taken to Phoebe and Ember, claimed them as his family, I knew the fact Aurelia had stopped returning his calls bothered him. Phoebe had confided in me, saying the pretty nurse found it too strange that her new best friend was the daughter of the man she'd been dating. I hoped she'd come around, but if not, it just meant she wasn't the right one for Titan.

Phoebe worried about him, as only a daughter could. She'd flourished the last five months and I was so damn proud of her. I stood up and swung Phoebe into my arms, her ice cream tumbling to the ground. "You know, there are plenty of ways I can punish you."

"Oh yeah?" she asked, her fingers curling around the back of my neck.

"Um-hm."

"Like what?"

I stopped at the side of Titan's house and shifted her so that her legs went around my waist and her back was to the wall. I worked my hand under her shirt and pulled down the cup of her bra. Her eyes dilated and her lips parted. I stroked her nipple with my thumb, back and forth, until it was nice and hard, then pinched down.

"Oh, God! Kraken..."

"You like that, baby?" I asked, tugging and twisting the hard peak.

"Yes! Don't stop."

I could tell she was already close to coming. Her nipples had been so damn sensitive lately I'd gotten her off just by playing with them. When she was right at the edge, and I could tell she was about to fall, I backed off. She gasped and arched her back, trying to entice me.

"Nope. You don't get to come."

"B-but..." She licked her lips. "I need it, Kraken."

"What you need is to take that shit home," Titan

yelled from the other side of the wall.

Phoebe shrieked and buried her face in my neck. I laughed as I carried her to the little SUV she drove and placed her in the passenger seat. Caging her in, I held her gaze and reached under her shirt again. I dragged my knuckles across her exposed nipple.

"You wet for me?" I asked.

She nodded.

"You want my cock?"

"You know I do."

"Then come for me. Right the fuck now." I pinched down and she cried out, her hips bucking. I released her breast and shoved my hand inside the leggings she'd worn. My finger slid along her wet slit and I drove two inside her.

"Oh, God. Oh, God." She whimpered and thrust against my hand. I got her off, then licked my fingers clean before getting in the car.

"If you weren't already pregnant, I'd say I'd put a baby in you."

She grinned at me. "Too late. You knocked me up pretty much immediately."

"Guess that means we'll just have to practice so I don't forget how it's done." I slid my gaze over her, lingering on the swells of her breasts. "We may need a bigger house."

I pulled to a stop in the driveway and Phoebe bolted from the car, racing inside. I followed and found a trail of clothes leading to our room. When I stepped through the bedroom door, I found my wife bent over the bed, ass in the air.

"Don't make me wait," she said, looking at me over her shoulder.

"I don't get a little foreplay too?" I asked, teasing her.

She eyed my crotch. Yeah, I was hard. Had been since I'd started playing with her at Titan's house. I chuckled as I undressed, then placed my hands on her hips.

"How do you want it? Soft and slow?"

She shook her head.

"Hard and fast?" I asked.

"Yes. Yes!"

I gripped my cock and dragged the head up and down her wet slit before pressing inside. She felt like fucking heaven. I pulled back and slammed into her. Phoebe cried out, pushing back against me. I took her, claimed her, fucked her so deep she'd feel me for hours. If the doctor hadn't assured us I wouldn't hurt the baby, I'd be treating her with kid gloves. Of course, now I knew there were two…

I paused. "Um, baby. Maybe we should…"

"Don't. You. Dare. Stop." She waggled her ass. "Fuck me, Blake."

I slapped her ass and drove into her again. This time I didn't stop until she'd come on my cock twice and I'd filled her with my cum. We cuddled in bed, and I marveled at how much my life had changed since meeting her.

I cupped the mound of her belly. "You're my everything, Phoebe. You and our kids. I love you. More than my next breath."

"I love you too, Blake. *We* love you." She rolled to face me. "I may have gone through something horrible and scary, but if it meant I had to survive all that in order to be here with you, I'd do it again."

"I never want you to hurt like that again, baby girl. Only wish I could turn back time. Let the Pres find out about you sooner, bring you here. We'd have still ended up together."

"You sound so certain."

I smiled and kissed her softly. "I am. You're mine, Phoebe. My one and only. We were destined to be together. Nothing will ever change that. Wouldn't have mattered when or how we met."

She ran her fingers over my beard. "You're rather romantic for a badass biker."

"Only with you."

She smiled and cuddled closer. To the world, I was Kraken, Sergeant-at-Arms for the Hades Abyss, and a man not to be trifled with. But here, with her, I was just a man completely in love with a woman. *My* woman. My love. My wife. My everything.

Demon (Devil's Fury MC 6)

Harley Wylde

Farrah -- I've spent my entire life at the Dixie Reapers MC compound -- one of the perks of being the VP's daughter. Except it's suffocating. Leaving to start a life of my own was the only solution. I knew what it would mean if I went to the Devil's Fury MC compound, even more so to flirt with their Sergeant-at-Arms. Getting involved would ruin the little bit of freedom I've found. Then I ended up in the man's bed. Leave it to me to find trouble around every corner. My daddy is going to be so pissed, especially when I run from Demon, get snatched off the streets, and shoved into a trunk. I'm not winning at the adulting thing.

Demon -- She was a one-night stand. Until the condom broke. Then I found out she'd lied to me. The hot little number in my bed wasn't just any woman, she was the daughter of a Dixie Reaper. Maybe I shouldn't have barked orders at her, or spanked her ass. Feisty little Farrah ran, pissing me off even more. When she disappeared and I realized trouble had found her, I knew I'd do whatever it took to make sure she was safe. Only after I had her back did I realize she was fucking perfect for me. Watching her handle the club whores was hot as hell, and she didn't take shit off anyone.

I'll make her mine -- permanently.

Prologue

Farrah

"I'm not a child!"

My dad stared me down. "Really? Because you're acting like one."

"Why is it so hard for you to admit I'm all grown up? I'm not a kid anymore, Daddy. I want to go on dates, do things other girls my age are doing."

"Like drugs and getting knocked up?" he asked.

"You're wrong for that and you know it. I've been around drugs my entire life and know better than to touch the stuff. As to the other, I can't very well get pregnant if you won't let me date."

He waved a finger at me. "Now you're getting it."

"It's not fair. I want a boyfriend. A life! You're suffocating me."

My mom placed her hand on my dad's shoulder. "Venom, you can't keep her locked up forever."

"Damn it, woman. What the fuck is it going to take for you to call me by my name? Been together eighteen years and you still use my road name." He cast her a glare.

"Don't take your anger out on me unless you want a case of blue balls," my mom retorted.

I winced, not wanting to think about their sex life for even one second. I wasn't stupid. I knew why the doors were locked sometimes and we couldn't get in the house, not to mention they weren't exactly quiet. It was romantic, sort of, and gross at the same time.

"I'm leaving, Daddy. You can't stop me."

He folded his arms over his chest. "Fine. You want to leave? Pack your shit and get out, but whatever money you have is all you're getting. You can take your truck, your clothes, and that's it. When your phone plan expires, I'm not renewing it. We'll see how long you last out there on your own. It's a hard, cruel world, Farrah."

My mom blinked back tears and I hated doing this to her, but I couldn't live in this cage another moment. I hoped she'd forgive me someday, and my daddy too. I loved him, more than anything, but I needed to spread my wings and fly. He had Mariah and Dawson if he wanted to smother someone.

I stomped down the hall, grabbed two bags from my closet, and started filling them. Clothes into one, other essentials into the second one. I slid my laptop into my backpack, along with some photos and other things I didn't want to leave behind. I shoved my shoes into another one. I couldn't bring myself to look my parents in the eye as I carried my stuff to the truck. I went back inside long enough to get my purse. Mom handed it to me, heartbreak written all over her face. I felt like shit hurting her this way, but it needed to be done. My heart felt heavy as I took out my keyring and removed the house key. I set it on the table inside the front door and walked out, hoping I hadn't made a huge mistake.

At eighteen, I knew I had a lot left to learn, but I'd never get to experience anything if I stayed. The Dixie Reapers were my family, and my daddy was their VP. I'd led a life most would envy, but I couldn't sit back and watch the world pass me by another moment. The only kisses I'd had were with boys at school.

My dad had never permitted me to go on dates, or do much of anything outside the compound unless he knew exactly where I was, and I knew he had a tracker on my phone and my truck. If I'd lied to him, he'd have known about it.

My eyes misted with tears as I stared at my childhood home. I saw my mom peeking through the curtains and gave her a little wave. I hoped she understood and could talk my daddy into letting me come home again soon. Not to stay, because I was ready to stand on my own two feet. But I wasn't ready to walk out for good. The thought of never coming back here nearly gutted me.

I pulled out of the driveway and headed for the gates. It was bittersweet pulling through them. Once I hit the highway, I didn't look back. I had no idea where I was going or what I'd do to put food on the table and keep a roof over my head, but I'd figure it out. I passed through the Florida panhandle, then drove into Georgia. I could have stopped by the Devil's Boneyard and bought myself some time, but I knew Scratch would call my dad the second I showed up there. No, it was better to keep moving.

My neck and back started to ache as I crossed into Blackwood Falls. I knew the Devil's Fury lived in the area, so if I got into trouble, they might help me. Stopping for a bit seemed like a good idea. I found a motel, got a room for a few nights, and decided to make a plan.

I'd need money before too long, which meant finding a job. I dug around in my purse and pulled out a white envelope with my mom's handwriting on the front. *For an emergency.*

Peeking inside, I saw a few hundreds. If daddy found out, he'd be pissed as hell, but I was grateful she'd looked out for me one last time. I got back in my truck and drove around town. There wasn't a lot open this time of night so I pulled off in front of the diner.

Some hot food would help. I was tired and starving, which made it more likely I'd make a rash decision I'd later regret.

A waitress waved at me. "Sit anywhere you want. I'll be right there."

I slid into a booth by the window and picked up a menu tucked behind the napkin dispenser. Once I'd decided on food, I set it aside and studied the town through the window. It was small, much like home had been, but at least it was a change of scenery.

"What can I get you?" the woman asked as she hurried over.

"The special, a sweet tea, and a job." I smiled.

"New in town?" she asked.

I nodded. "Just got here tonight. I'm staying at the motel for the moment, but I thought I'd see if I could find some work around here."

"You come back tomorrow before lunch. The manager will be here and he'll be able to help. We're short-staffed so it may be your lucky day."

I smiled and thanked her, thinking maybe I'd made the right decision after all.

I had to hope the Devil's Fury didn't ask me to leave. If my dad tracked me here, and I knew damn well he had the ability to do so, he could very well place a call and have me run out of town. I hoped he wouldn't, but if he thought it would teach me a lesson, I wouldn't put it past him.

I pulled my phone from my purse and sent a message to my little sister, Mariah. *I'm safe and have a place to stay for the night. Love you.*

I saw the dots blinking across the screen and waited, but they stopped and a message never came through. It seemed my dad wasn't the only one angry with me. She'd get over it, and once she got older, she'd understand. I had no doubt my dad would eventually suffocate her too with all his rules.

I was free. I breathed in the scents of the diner and felt the tension in my body ease. For the first time in my life, I was on my own, in charge of my own destiny. I hoped I didn't fuck it all up.

Chapter One

Demon

The music blasting from the speakers in the ceiling pounded against my skull like a sledgehammer. Maybe I was getting too old for this shit. Forty-three didn't sound ancient until I got around the younger generation at the clubhouse. Partying had lost its appeal over the last few years. Watching my brothers settle down had caused a strange twinge in my chest, an ache I absently rubbed. I hadn't been serious about a woman in a while. I'd thought one of the little señoritas staying at the compound could be something special, but it hadn't worked out. She'd since moved on, along with the others. Except the younger ones.

Glancing around the room, it seemed far emptier than before. Even the Pres wasn't here tonight. Now he had three little chicks under his roof and had turned into a ferocious papa bear. I hadn't seen him walk off with any of the club whores, ever, but at least he'd come to drink and hang with the brothers. Since those girls came to stay here, we'd seen less and less of him on nights like this. Couldn't blame him.

Starla, one of the newer club whores, sashayed over. Her red lips were slicked to a high shine and her eyes had been rimmed in black. There'd been a time I might have been tempted by the sway of her hips, the come-hither look on her face. Now she just came across as desperate. She moved closer, her perfume nearly suffocating me, as she trailed her nails up my arm and across my shoulder.

"Looks like you could use some company," she said, settling on my lap.

Part of me wanted to shove her off, but all she'd done was make my headache worse. No harm in letting her sit for a minute. Her hand grazed my chest and headed for my zipper. I closed my fingers around her wrist, halting her progress.

"Not tonight," I said. Or any night.

Her lip stuck out in what she probably thought was a sexy pout. It didn't do a damn thing for me. When I released her, I gave her a nudge off my lap until she stood next to me. As the Sergeant-at-Arms, and single, the club whores tended to flock my way, in hopes I'd claim them as my old lady. Never would happen, but it didn't stop them from trying.

The doors to the clubhouse swung open and a curvy blonde stepped through. No, not stepped. She sauntered into the room, head high, shoulders back, and gazed at her surroundings as if she owned the place. Her tongue flicked out to wet her lower lip and my cock hardened behind my zipper. A quick sweep of the room told me I wasn't the only one checking her out, but I'd damn sure be the one balls-deep in her later.

I stood and made my way across the room, my prey in my sights. Stopping close enough I could feel the heat of her body, I waited for her to acknowledge me. When she ignored me, it only made me want her more. Reaching out, I tipped her chin up, forcing her to meet my gaze.

"You lost, little girl?" I asked, realizing she was far younger than I'd thought. No way she'd gotten past the Prospect at the gate if she wasn't at least eighteen, but she was still young enough to be my daughter. No fucking way she was a day over twenty-five, if that.

"No, I'm not lost. You're in my way."

Oh, I liked the sass on this one. I smiled and placed my hand at her waist, tugging her closer. "Your way? Did you get a good look when you came in? Pretty little things like you only have one place in this clubhouse. On your knees or bent over a table."

A flush worked its way up her neck and settled in her cheeks. Her eyes darkened and her pulse fluttered. Seemed she liked the idea. The way her dress hugged her body, it left little to the imagination, but I still would prefer to have her naked and spread out so I could feast on her. Only one problem. I didn't have a room at the clubhouse anymore and I didn't take random women back to my house.

"Maybe this isn't my first time seeing this sort of thing," she said. "You may not have seen me here before, but it doesn't mean I'm stupid when it comes to bikers. I know more than you think."

I stepped back and scanned her. "No property cut. No ink claiming you as an old lady. You making the rounds? Whatever club you came from, I promise to treat you better."

"Full of yourself, aren't you?" she asked, but I noticed she leaned a little closer.

"Oh, sweetheart. You're the one who's gonna be full of me."

I didn't give her a chance to pull away or run. I swept her into my arms and carried her down the hall. The bathroom wasn't the cleanest place, and this one seemed special somehow. She deserved more than a quick fuck against the wall. The Pres would have my ass if he ever found out about it, but I nudged open the doors of Church and stepped into the darkened room.

"You're not going to get in trouble, are you?" she asked, looking around. "Pretty sure I'm not supposed to be in here."

"Let me worry about that. Right now, all I need you to do is undress." I let her slide down my body until her feet touched the floor. She gave me a coy smile as she reached for the hem of her dress and slowly eased it up her thighs, over her hips, and pulled it all the way off, tossing it onto the table.

Black lace hugged her breasts and barely covered her pussy. Fuck but she was the sexiest thing I'd ever seen. I prowled closer, backing her against the table. Bracing my arms on either side of her, caging her in, I claimed her mouth. Her lips were soft and pliant under mine, and she opened eagerly as I thrust my tongue inside. Tasted sweet as candy.

I reached down to unbuckle my belt and unfasten my jeans, pausing to pull a condom from my pocket. I set it aside and shoved my pants down enough to free my cock, and ripped open the foil packet, my lips never leaving hers as I kissed her breathless.

I leaned back and rolled the latex down my shaft, then gripped her hips and put her ass on the edge of the table. Shoving her panties aside, I stroked her pussy, groaning at how fucking wet she was. My cock jerked in anticipation. I wrapped my fingers around her hip, holding her still as I pushed inside.

"So damn tight." I groaned and closed my eyes a moment, my heart hammering in my chest. She felt like fucking heaven. My gaze found hers as I slammed into her. The way her eyes widened and her cheeks paled made me pause. "You all right?"

She seemed to struggle to draw breath and I pulled back, only to freeze at the smear of blood on the condom. What the fuck? I tried to take a step back, but she reached out and grabbed hold with both hands. "Don't. Please. I want this."

I slid inside her again, filling her. "You have some explaining to do."

"Later. Just… just fuck me."

The damage had been done. If I'd known she

was an innocent, I'd have given her a wide berth. I'd popped her cherry. Might as well finish the job. I reached down to stroke her clit as I thrust in and out, using a slow, steady rhythm. For whatever reason, she'd chosen me, or rather accepted my caveman act and let me take her innocence. I'd be damned if I made it a bad experience for her.

My balls drew up and I knew I was close. Too damn close. I worked her clit faster until her pussy clenched tight and she cried out, her nails digging into my arms as she held on. I slammed into her, taking her harder and deeper. I'd always pulled out, even when I wrapped my dick, but with her, I wanted to feel everything. Or as much as I could with the latex covering my cock. I grunted, my hips jerking, as I came, my gaze holding hers.

She looked so fucking pretty. Her lips parted, eyes bright, and a flush riding her cheeks. Made me wish I had all night to take her over and over. Then again, maybe I did. I hadn't taken any of the club whores home, but it didn't mean I couldn't take this sweet thing back to the house. The fact I'd taken her virginity made her different.

I kissed her again and eased out of her. I went to dispose of the condom but reconsidered leaving it anywhere in the clubhouse. I tied it off, shoved it inside the wrapper, and decided I'd toss it in the trash at home. I pushed it down into my pocket and made a mental reminder to wash these jeans later.

"Come on, pretty girl. You're coming with me."

"I am?" She sat up and adjusted her panties before pulling her dress over her head. "You take my V-card and decide you're the boss of me?"

I leaned into her space, noticing her quick inhalation. "More like I'm not done with you yet. What

I have in mind requires a bed and more condoms. You going to lie and say you aren't interested?"

She rolled her bottom lip into her mouth, shaking her head. I righted my clothes and helped her off the table. With her hand in mine, I led her back through the clubhouse and out into the night. A blue truck I'd never seen before drew my attention. I scanned it as we walked past and I stopped beside my bike. She eyed the Harley, then her dress and I had to fight not to smile.

She swung a leg over the seat, smoothing her skirt under her ass. She surprised the hell out of me by tucking the top of it under her thighs. Looked like it wouldn't be her first time on the back of a bike, which was something we'd discuss later. Like what the fuck she'd been doing at the clubhouse if she wasn't there to party.

I got on and started her up and backed out of the parking spot. I eased the bike down the road, winding through the compound. My house wasn't far and I quickly pulled into the driveway and up under the carport. The woman pressed to my back got off as I shut off the engine.

I took her hand and led her inside. The carport door opened into the kitchen and I tossed my keys onto the table. I yanked the used condom from my pocket and threw it into the trash. I didn't give her a chance to see much of the house before I dragged her to my bedroom.

"Someone seems eager," she said, humor lacing her words.

"Damn right." I came to a sudden stop and pulled her into my arms. "Not every day I'm gifted with a virgin. Figure I better make the most of it."

She looped her arms around my neck. "I'm not

exactly a prize. If you don't believe me, ask my daddy. Pretty sure I'm the reason his hair is going gray."

"I'll just have to disagree with him." I backed her toward the bed and kissed her hard. Best damn night I'd had in a long time. "What's your name, beautiful?"

"Farrah." Her gaze searched mine, as if looking for something. Was her name supposed to mean something to me? A little warning bell went off in my head, but I shoved it aside. Sweet thing like her couldn't be as much trouble as she claimed.

"I'm Demon."

Her lips twitched in a near smile. "I know. I read your cut."

Another piece of the puzzle, but damn if I wanted to put it together right now. She knew what a cut was, had ridden on a bike before. Who the hell was this little goddess?

I removed her dress and this time stripped her all the way bare, including the fuck-me shoes she'd been wearing. Faint blonde hair covered her mound, trimmed super short. I removed my cut and tossed it aside before toeing off my boots and taking off the rest of my clothes. She reached out, tracing her fingers over the ink on my chest.

"So we're clear, I don't bring women here."

"What do you call me? Because I'm here," she said. "Last I checked, I'm a woman."

"Special. Different." I skimmed my fingers over her cheek. "Fucking beautiful."

Her face flushed pink. "I'm too jiggly to be beautiful. Too much around the middle, and my thighs are too big."

I reached behind her and smacked her ass hard. She gasped and pressed closer to me. I ran my palm over the cheek I'd struck, then spanked her again. Her nipples hardened against me.

"You don't talk bad about yourself. Not around me."

"Or what?" she taunted.

"Or your ass will be red and you won't be able to sit for a week."

"You'll have to do better than that."

Little spitfire. "Maybe I should fuck the sass out of you."

Her eyes darkened and she pressed tighter against me. Yeah, she liked that idea as much as I did. I spun her to face the bed and gathered her wrists in my hand at the small of her back. I kicked her feet apart so I could see her pretty pussy before I spanked her ass until I could feel the heat coming off it. I leaned down putting my lips near her ear. "Maybe when I'm done spanking this fine ass I should fuck it."

She jolted like she'd been electrocuted, but I noticed she didn't say no. I reached for the bedside table drawer and pulled out an unopened box of condoms. After ripping into the package, I pulled one out and tore it open. I released her long enough to roll one down my cock. When I'd finished, I gathered her wrists in my hand again.

I didn't give her a chance to break free. Holding her still, I surged forward, entering her hard and fast. Farrah cried out, her body tensing a moment. I trailed kisses along her shoulders and upper back until she relaxed. Flexing my hips, I fucked her, driving into her with every stroke. Changing my angle, I brushed the secret spot inside her, making her orgasm almost immediately. She soaked us both and the bed as she screamed out my name.

When I came, it damn near felt like my soul left my body. I couldn't remember a time I'd ever felt like this. The chemistry between us was intense as fuck, and not something I wanted to necessarily walk away from. At least, not until I'd had my fill. I pulled out and everything in me froze as I stared at the bare head of my cock.

"Motherfucker," I muttered.

She tried to twist and turn. "What? What's wrong?"

I glanced at her pussy and saw my cum running down the inside of her thigh. It should have scared the shit out of me, but instead, I had the insane urge to shove it back inside her and fill her up with more. *What the fuck is wrong with you?*

"Demon. You're scaring me," she said.

I released her, letting her turn around and sit up. I ripped the condom off. "It broke. Fucking condom broke."

Her hand shook as she shoved her hair behind her ear. "O-okay. Well, I'm clean. Are you?"

I nodded. "Got tested recently and haven't been with anyone since. Not the only problem we have here, sweetheart. You on birth control?"

Her face went deathly pale and she would have surely hit the floor if she weren't sitting on the bed. As it was, she swayed a little. Yeah, that's what I thought. Pretty little virgin wasn't on anything, and I'd filled her up. I already knew the odds weren't in my favor.

"Never had this happen before," I said. "I don't go around fucking virgins, or coming inside anyone bare. Not once has a condom broken, nor have I had any pregnancy scares."

She licked her lips. "Looks like I'm not the only one experiencing some firsts for tonight."

I couldn't hold back my smile, my lips tilting up on one corner. "Stay the night."

She shook her head. "I should go. And I definitely need to get the morning after pill."

I stared at her stomach, slightly rounded and soft, and imagined her big with my baby growing in her. No. Just fuck no. She wasn't taking the damn morning after pill, even if it meant I had to handcuff her ass to my bed.

"Sorry, sweetheart. Not happening."

"What's that supposed to mean? You don't get a say in this! It's my body."

I nodded. "Yep, it is, but if there's a baby, it's not only yours. Not going to let you kill my kid. If it makes me an asshole, so be it."

"Oh, I…" She placed a hand over her belly. "I hadn't thought of it that way."

"Let's rinse off in the shower, get some rest, and we'll discuss this in the morning. Think we both need some sleep to clear our minds."

"All right."

She followed me into the bathroom and I started the shower. When steam billowed out, she stepped inside and I followed. Couldn't remember a time I'd enjoyed washing a woman, but I liked having my hands on her. She felt like silk, and fit against me perfectly, her head tucked under my chin. As much as I wanted to take her again, I knew now wasn't the time. We cleaned up and I tugged her down onto my bed, wrapped my arms around her, and slept with her naked body curled against mine.

Best damn night's sleep I'd had in forever.

Chapter Two

Farrah

A sound pulled me from sleep. It took a minute for the cobwebs to clear and I realized it was a phone ringing. Damn it. I'd left mine, along with everything else, in my truck. I hadn't spoken much to my dad since I'd left two weeks ago, but Mom still called every few days. I felt the arm across my waist tighten before Demon rolled away from me.

Shit. I'd slept with the Sergeant-at-Arms. Not only would my dad be pissed if he found out, but I knew Grizzly would be too. I'd let him know I was in his territory the day after I'd gotten a job at the diner. It had seemed like the right thing to do. He'd extended an invitation to drop by anytime I wished, and last night I'd needed to cut loose a bit. No way in hell he'd be happy about this, though. Letting me stop by was one thing. Setting my sights on one of his officers? Probably wasn't going to go over well. I needed to get dressed, get to my truck, and get the hell out of here.

I heard the low murmur of Demon's voice as I got out of bed and scrambled for my clothes, pulling them on. I'd only managed to pull on my panties and fasten my bra when the silence struck me. I looked over at Demon, who stared me down, arms folded over his rather impressive chest. The look on his face wasn't lost on me. I'd seen it plenty of times on my dad. He was pissed, which meant I was no longer just Farrah-the-one-night-stand. He'd discovered who I was.

"You're in a world of trouble, little girl," he said, his voice a deep growl.

"I'm on my way out. If you don't want to drop me back by my truck, I can walk."

He tossed his phone aside and advanced on me. It didn't escape my notice he was still completely naked. I nearly sighed at the perfection of his body. Maybe he wasn't movie star amazing, but Demon was in shape, had massive amounts of ink, and I'd always been a sucker for a nice, thick... beard. The fact he was older than me didn't bother me in the slightest. Hell, my dad was about twenty years older than my mom, and they'd been happy together all this time. If anything, it had taught me age was nothing more than a number.

"Something you maybe forgot to tell me last night?" he asked.

I cocked my head to the side. "No, not really. I mean, you fucked me before you asked for my name. I thought it didn't matter who I was. You wanted to get off and I was tired of being a virgin."

He advanced on me and I stumbled back until I collided with the wall. I'd seen my dad angry plenty of times, but I'd known he wouldn't hurt me. Demon? He wasn't like my dad. I'd heard about the things he'd done, even if no one realized I'd eavesdropped on those conversations. He was brutal when he felt someone should be punished and didn't shy away from hurting a woman who had done the club wrong.

My heart slammed against my ribs as my gaze skirted the room looking for an escape. He pressed closer to me, his arms caging me in. I locked my knees and forced myself to look up. The fury rolling off him was tangible, and for the first time in my life, I was scared. I'd never admit it, but this man wasn't like any other I'd ever met.

"You fucking knew it would change things if you told me you were Venom's kid, so you kept it from me." He reached up and fisted my hair, tugging the strands and holding me immobile. "You *lied*, Farrah. I don't like lying little bitches. What did you hope to get from this?"

He tugged harder and tears pricked my eyes, but I refused to give him the satisfaction of seeing how scared I was. "I wanted a night of fun. I'm tired of being *Venom's kid*. He never let me go on dates. Never let me go anywhere unless he tracked my every step. Do you know what it's like to be put on a leash? So I left. I don't live with the Dixie Reapers anymore. If I'd known you'd be such an asshole about it, I'd have picked someone else last night."

"Someone else?" he asked, his voice deceptively low and calm. "Someone. Else."

I nodded. "I was just another hole to you. Did it ever occur to you you're not more than a dick for someone to ride? You aren't using those women. They're getting what they want from you and moving on to the next man."

"Is that right?" he asked. "And you intend to do that too? Hop from my bed to the next? Maybe you want to make your way through the Devil's Fury? Your daddy would be so proud. His precious little girl, nothing more than a club whore."

I gasped as the barb found its mark. Without a single thought other than inflicting pain, I lashed out, my hand cracking against his cheek. The sting of my palm was enough to tell me I'd done a very stupid thing. Demon hauled me from the wall, dragging me by my hair. He sat on the edge of the bed and tossed me across his lap. He ripped the fabric of my bra and panties, tearing them from me.

"Want to act like a spoiled little bitch? Fine." He brought his hand down on my ass so hard I screamed out and kicked my feet. "You'll be punished like one."

Smack. Smack. Smack.

"Think you can do whatever the fuck you want?"

he asked. "This is what happens when you sass me, Farrah."

Smack. Smack. Smack. Smack. Smack. Smack.

Tears streaked my cheeks and my ass felt like it was on fire. He lifted me, standing and turning, before he tossed me facedown on the bed.

"Just a dick to ride? Plan on sampling my brothers? We'll fucking see about that."

I squealed as he shoved his fingers inside me, but it quickly turned to a moan. No matter how upset I was, I couldn't deny something about the big brute turned me on. *You're fucked up, Farrah.*

"Anyone else ever made you this wet?" he asked.

I held still, refusing to answer.

"Fine. Have it your way." His hands gripped my hips. Demon thrust hard and deep, filling me up. He slammed into me over and over, taking what he wanted. An ache started to build inside me, and my clit throbbed. Demon took me like a man possessed, not stopping until he'd come inside me. He leaned down, his chest pressed to my back. "This tight little pussy belongs to me, Farrah. You gave up your virginity to me on a silver fucking platter. And now you think you'll run along and spread your legs for someone else?"

He tugged on my hair again.

"Answer me," he demanded.

"I-I-I…"

He pulled out and his hand came down on my poor, abused ass cheeks again. *Smack. Smack. Smack.*

I cried and twisted under his grip. "Stop. Please, Demon."

He paused, his breath sawing in and out of his lungs, the harsh sound filling the air. He flipped me over and pinned me down, my wrists held captive over my head. The fact he was still hard made me squirm.

"I told you last night you weren't a piece of ass. You should have told me the truth, Farrah."

"I wanted to be myself," I said, sniffling. "I'm tired of being known as my dad's daughter. I don't have my own identity. How is that fair?"

He smoothed my hair back from my face, his gaze softening. "Did I hurt you?"

"My ass hurts."

"It's supposed to, but the spanking wasn't what I meant," he said.

"It didn't hurt. I didn't come, but…"

He kissed me, the stroke of his lips almost tender. "I'm sorry, sweetheart. Lying is one thing I can't condone. Not ever. You hear me? Don't ever lie to me again."

"All right. So… you plan to see me again?"

"Again?" He arched an eyebrow. "Little girl, you're not leaving this house anytime soon. Not until I know for damn sure you don't want any dick but mine."

My eyes went wide. What the hell?

He kissed my lips. My jaw. Nipped my ear. "In case you forgot, you might already be carrying my kid. I plan to make damn sure you are."

"You can't do that!"

He chuckled and drew back enough to look down at me. "Oh yeah, I can. I can do whatever the fuck I please. You're in my territory. Lied to me. You think you've been punished enough already? No, sweetheart. I'm only getting started. When I'm done with you, you'll damn well know not to sass me again, or fucking lie to me."

"I have a job. I can't just… stay here."

"Should have thought of that before you didn't

tell me who you were. Now I've got my Pres calling thinking something happened to you. He saw your truck and no one knew a damn thing about you being here last night, except the fucking Prospect who let you through. Not a damn person who saw you recognized you last night."

"I didn't mean to make him worry," I said.

"Oh, he's more than worried. He's called your daddy."

My heart took off at a gallop. No. No, no, no. I shook my head and fought to break free, but Demon shifted his hips, using the bulk of his body and his cock to pin me to the bed. My nipples hardened as he thrust into me, brushing against my clit as he filled me up.

"If Venom is going to come here and start shit, I'd damn well better get something out of it," he said.

"Like what?" I asked.

"Already told you. You. Pregnant. Mine." He slammed into me. "Mine. My woman."

His caveman act should have turned me off, but secretly I loved it. I liked having his big, strong body holding me down. Wanted more of his bossiness and demands. He angled his hips and I saw stars. On the next stroke, I came so hard I couldn't draw a breath. I felt the heat of his release as he pounded into me. He released my wrists and I immediately reached up to cling to his shoulders, needing to touch him.

I ran my fingers over his beard and his lips. He kissed my fingertips before I explored more of him.

"Doesn't bother you I'm old enough to be your dad?" he asked.

"You realize my dad is fifty-seven, right? There's no way you're that old."

"Maybe not, but I'm forty-three. Still old enough to have a kid your age."

I wiggled my hips, feeling his still semi-hard cock inside me. "Don't feel old to me. In fact, you're around the age my dad was when he claimed my mom. Does it bother you? Our age difference?"

He shook his head before kissing me soft and slow. Demon drew back and pulled out. I felt his release as it slipped from my body and my cheeks burned. I knew I had to be making a mess of his bed.

"You're not really claiming me, are you?" I asked, sitting up.

"Hadn't planned on it, until the condom broke. Spent a good bit of the night thinking it over. I've been wanting something more. A family."

I stood and faced him. "Wait. So if you'd fucked one of the club whores last night and the condom had broken, you'd be claiming her right now?"

He shrugged. "Can't say. Don't know since it didn't happen that way."

My hands fisted at my sides. Right. I wasn't special. Wasn't anything other than convenient. Property. I was property and nothing more. I'd forgotten for a moment, but I wouldn't do it again. I'd lived the club life for so long, I knew exactly how this played out. My dad adored my mom, but Demon didn't give a shit about me. The moment he had what he wanted, he'd be back to fucking club whores and expecting me to be here waiting for him. I'd been around enough clubs to know they weren't all like the Dixie Reapers and Devil's Boneyard. There were plenty of bikers who had a woman at home and still fucked the club whores. I didn't know enough about the Devil's Fury to discount Demon doing such a thing. No way would that happen to me.

"I'm taking a shower. When I'm done, I'll run a bath for you. Sit your ass down, Farrah." He pointed to the bed and I sat like a good little puppy.

The moment I heard the shower running I grabbed my dress and pulled it over my head. I snatched my shoes from the floor and tiptoed out of the room. Every muscle in my body clenched tight as I approached the front door, worried he'd discover I wasn't where he'd left me. If Demon didn't want me to leave, there wouldn't be much I could do to stop him. He was so much larger than me. I made it outside, put on my shoes, and practically ran for my truck. I huffed and puffed by the time I reached the clubhouse and jumped into the cab of my pickup. I jammed the key into the ignition and started it up, then my tires spit gravel as I backed out and barreled toward the gate.

The poor Prospect didn't have a choice but to let me out. It was either open the gate, or I'd have gone straight through it. Tears trickled down my cheeks as I headed for the motel. I'd been so stupid. Letting him take my virginity was one thing. I should have left it there and walked out, but no, I'd let him tempt me into more.

Stupid. Stupid. Stupid.

"Way to go, Farrah. First taste of freedom and you possibly get knocked up by a Neanderthal biker," I griped to myself. I'd been around the type my entire life and knew better. Why I'd thought Demon would be different wasn't something I'd figure out anytime soon.

At the motel, I parked outside my door and hurried inside. I locked the door stripped out of my dress and shoes and hurried to the shower. It wasn't too late, I didn't think. Maybe I could still take the morning after pill. The last thing I needed was a reason for Demon to hold onto me. What he'd done today was just a taste of what I'd likely get if he caught up to me.

This town was only so big, but I couldn't run. Not yet. I needed more money, and the job at the diner was a sure thing.

I washed away all traces of Demon, except for the purplish marks on my hips where he'd held me tight. The way my ass stung when the hot water hit it told me I'd likely bruised there too. When I got out, I twisted and turned to inspect myself in the mirror and winced when I saw the damage. I'd been in such a hurry to escape the pain hadn't registered, but now was a different story.

I dressed quickly, wishing I had leggings or something soft but put on jeans and a tee along with my tennis shoes. I pulled my hair up in a bun before I grabbed my keys and purse. Pharmacy. I needed something for the pain, and the morning after pill. If the thought of taking it made me a little sad, it was for me to know and no one else. There was plenty of time for me to start a family, preferably with the right man. One who would love me the way my dad loved my mom. I wanted what they had, so damn much.

I'd no sooner stepped out the door than a hand wrapped around my arm and yanked me off my feet. I cried out, losing my grip on my stuff. My keys fell to the ground along with my purse, the contents spilling across the pavement. At first, I'd thought it was Demon, but this was so much worse. The stench assailing my nose told me the man hadn't bathed in weeks, if not longer. His hair hung in greasy strands around his face, and his teeth were rotted.

"Been waiting on you, girly."

"What do you want with me?" I asked, almost afraid of the answer. I remembered him. He'd come to the diner four nights in a row now. Always sat in my section and eyed me like a slab of meat. No one had tossed him out, despite his unkempt state. I'd thought maybe he was harmless, but it seemed my instincts had been right.

"Pretty thing like you is just what I need. Come along." He dragged me behind him. I couldn't keep my feet under me long enough to lash out at him. My dad had prepared me for this. I knew what to do, in theory, but I needed the right moment.

We neared an old rusted heap, the bald tires looking seconds from blowing out. He opened the trunk and shoved me inside. I immediately skimmed my hands over the surface, hoping for a tire iron, or something I could use as a weapon. All I found were empty beer cans. Before I could launch one at the asshole trying to kidnap me, he slammed the trunk shut.

Panic welled inside me, but I pushed it down. I wasn't some weak woman. My daddy had taught me to defend myself. Maybe I'd bungled it right now, but I'd get my chance. As long as I remained calm, I should have plenty of air, and time to make a plan. Suddenly, facing Demon didn't seem so bad. If I'd waited for him like he'd said, I wouldn't be locked in a stupid trunk.

Way to go, Farrah. One stupid mistake after another.

No wonder my dad hadn't wanted me to go anywhere alone. I sucked at adulting, and now I'd been kidnapped and faced who knew what. One way or another, I'd get out of this stupid trunk, get free of the bastard who snatched me, and I'd prove once and for all I wasn't a kid who needed rescuing.

The alternative wasn't something I wanted to contemplate.

Chapter Three

Demon

"You have to be fucking kidding me," I said, staring at the empty bedroom. The little bitch ran. I should have known. With a shake of my head, I finished drying off and got dressed. She'd probably made her way back to her truck and headed to her motel room. I'd have to haul her ass right back.

I'd slipped my cut over my shoulders and grabbed my wallet when someone pounded on my front door. I hurried to open it only to find the Pres and VP waiting for me. Grizzly looked pissed, but Slash... he looked worried. A worried VP scared the fuck out of me. Not much ever bothered Slash.

"What's going on?" I asked.

"Nox was assigned to the gate this morning," Grizzly said. "He saw Farrah tear out of here like her ass was on fire, so he contacted me. I had to deal with something so I asked Slash to call her, see how bad you'd fucked up. Her phone's ringing, but she won't pick up."

"She's a little brat with her tail feathers in a knot," I said. "I was on my way to go get her and drag her back here."

Slash and Griz shared a look before the VP focused on me. "What exactly were you going to do when you got her here?"

"Handcuff her to the bed until she saw reason."

Griz opened and shut his mouth. Before I could process what was happening, his fist flew at my face and clocked me right across the jaw. I staggered back a step and tried to shake the stars from my eyes.

"What the fuck, Pres?" I asked.

"She's Venom's daughter, not a fucking club whore. You'll treat her with respect," Grizzly said.

"Yeah well, she's possibly carrying my kid, so I'll do whatever I damn well deem necessary to keep her safe and talk some sense into her."

Slash held up his hands and stepped back. "Nope, not going there. Of all the times for you to not wrap your dick. Jesus, Demon. Are you fucking stupid? Do you have any idea what Venom will do to you?"

"Not my concern right now," I said. "I have a wayward brat to bring back."

"She left the Reapers because her dad kept treating her like a kid," Grizzly said. "You do the same and she's not going to stay."

"Then she shouldn't have fucking run like a kid," I said. "Not to mention she lied to me. Didn't say a fucking word about who she was before she let me take her virginity, or after. It wasn't until you called asking if I'd seen her I put two and two together. I hate fucking liars."

"What did you do?" Slash asked.

"Spanked her ass and reminded her where she belonged."

Grizzly cursed under his breath and looked up at the sky, as if needing divine intervention. "You're a Goddamn moron, Demon. She's probably well on her way to leaving the state by now."

"We'll see about that." I gripped my keys and went out to my bike. The Pres and VP stuck close as we approached the gates and followed me out onto the streets. It seemed I was going to have an audience when I confronted Farrah.

I was beyond pissed by the time I reached the motel, until I saw her truck and noticed the room in front of it stood open. A purse and keys lay on the ground, and a feeling of dread filled me. I cut the engine to my bike and went to check it out. When I picked up the keys, I accidently hit the alarm button. Farrah's truck beeped and the lights flashed until I shut it off.

"We're so fucked," Slash said, holding a small wallet in his hands, Farrah's license on display in the little window.

"We have to call the Dixie Reapers," Grizzly said. "Venom is no doubt on his way here already. I want Outlaw to pull any video feed from this area. We need to find out who took her and which way they were going. Maybe we'll get lucky and find them if he can hack into the traffic cameras."

I tightened my hold on her keys and scanned the area. Not a single fucking person was out, which wasn't too strange for this time of day in this place. It was nighttime when everything came to life. The drug dealers, prostitutes, and other people making a buck however they could would fill this parking lot by the time night fell. But which one of them had taken Farrah, and why? And why the hell had she been staying here? Fuck! If I'd known I'd be tempted to keep her... It was too late to play the *what if* game. Letting some random pussy stay at this Godforsaken place was one thing, but not the woman I intended to claim.

Grizzly shoved me until I slammed against Farrah's truck. "This is your fault! Damn it, Demon! You had to put your dick in her, didn't you? Then you lost your fucking cool and let her have it. If anything happens to that girl, I'm going to gut you my own damn self."

I swallowed hard, not wanting to admit he was right but... he was. It was my fault she'd run off. She could be safe right now, in my house, if I'd calmed the fuck down and talked to her. Listened to what she had to say.

"You won't have to," I said. No, if she'd been hurt, or God forbid, killed, because of my fucking temper, I'd make damn sure I couldn't hurt anyone ever again. Whatever it took.

I heard the Pres talking to Outlaw and I took the time to scan the area again, looking for anything that might lead me to Farrah. I heard a phone ringing and Slash pulled one from Farrah's purse. He showed me the screen. *Rick.* I took the phone and answered it.

"Who is this?" I demanded. "Why the fuck are you calling Farrah's phone?"

"Because I need her to cover a shift tonight. I'm her boss." There was a pause. "And you are?"

"Demon."

The man muttered something I couldn't quite catch. "She told me she was giving the Devil's Fury a wide berth. Should have known the pull would be too strong. Is she coming back to work, or do you plan to keep her locked up at your compound?"

"Farrah is missing," I said.

The line was silent a moment. I glanced at the screen to make sure the call was still connected.

"What happened?" Rick asked.

"I don't know yet. Has she had any trouble at work? Any customers causing problems?"

"Not exactly, but there was a man making her uncomfortable. Said it felt like he was watching her," Rick said. "It's why I gave her last night off and let her work the lunch shift instead. Thought she needed a break. The man has been in lots of times with no issue, but I didn't want her to not feel safe."

She'd been worried, and this asshole's solution was changing her shift for a day? What the hell? He should have asked the fucker to never come back. Still, if he'd followed her to the motel and knew where she was staying, it wouldn't have mattered. He'd probably still have her right now.

"What can you tell me about the guy?" I asked.

"Never saw him, so I don't know. The waitresses have dealt with him before. I'll see if they remember anything useful. Listen, whatever I can do to help, let me know. Farrah's a sweet kid. Always on time. Works hard. I hate to think of someone hurting her."

He wasn't the only one. I ended the call and paced the sidewalk. Slash and Grizzly ended their calls.

"It was her boss calling her phone. Said a customer was making her nervous. He didn't know anything else, but he's hoping the waitresses might remember something about the guy." I ran a hand through my hair. "How long will it take Outlaw to find something?"

"Outlaw said since Farrah is technically Reapers' property, he's asking Wire to handle it. He didn't want to step on any toes, and he's right. I'm sure he'll help if he's needed, but Wire and Lavender can work faster," Grizzly said.

"I called a friend at the local police department," Slash said. "She'll keep her eyes and ears open for any sign of Farrah, but I told her this was a club matter and we'd handle it."

She? I eyed Slash. He'd never gone for the ballsy sort, so I didn't think the woman was a love interest. Still, I found it interesting he had a connection to the police and hadn't said a damn thing before now. Either it was a new thing or he was keeping shit to himself.

Griz's phone rang and he winced, which told me it was most likely Venom. I didn't have a single doubt the man would try to put me on my ass, and I'd have to let him. I'd fucked up. Not only had I possibly knocked up his kid, but I'd chased her off and now she was in danger. Being fourteen years younger, I had no doubt I could take him, but it was his right to put me in my place. Once, anyway.

Instead of listening to the conversation, I walked the area again. I didn't see signs of any cameras in or around the parking lot. There was one over the motel office door, but the way it was angled meant it only tracked who was coming and going from the lobby. Wouldn't be of much use to me right now.

I saw a curtain flicker and glanced over. A woman quickly yanked the material back over the window, but now I had to wonder if she'd seen or heard something. I went over to knock on the door and waited for her to open it. The chain remained across the top, only allowing her to open it a crack.

"What do you want?" she asked.

"My woman got snatched from this parking lot earlier. You hear or see anything?"

She frantically shook her head and started to slam the door, but I put my boot up, halting it. I reached for my wallet and pulled out a twenty. She eyed the money, a hungry gleam in her eyes. She reached through and ripped it from my hand.

"Heard something a little while ago. I ain't no snitch, though." Her gaze darted around the parking lot. I understood her concern. People in this part of town, especially this motel, didn't take kindly to those who ran their mouths. "Man took your girl. Name's Earl and I ain't sayin' nothing else."

I let her slam the door and went to tell Grizzly and Slash what I'd discovered. Earl wasn't a lot to go on, but it would give Wire and Lavender at least a crumb to work with. Something was better than nothing.

"What did the whore say?" Slash asked.

"Man named Earl took Farrah. She wouldn't say anything else. Too scared."

Slash nodded. Grizzly shot off a text to someone and I figured he was imparting the name to Wire or Outlaw. Maybe both. Hell, I'd take whatever help I could get at this point. The more people searching for Farrah, the better the chances we'd find her before something bad happened. Being kidnapped was horrible enough, but if the man put his hands on her, or worse, I'd fucking kill him. Assuming Venom didn't beat me to it.

I got on my bike, ready to get back to the compound. No sense in sitting around the motel lot. It wasn't like the man would bring Farrah back. She might be a pain in the ass, but with the wrong sort of man, it would only get her killed. I heard the Pres and VP follow me out of the lot. I didn't know how long it would take Venom to arrive, or who he'd bring with him. As much as I didn't look forward to seeing him, we needed more men to help find Farrah. I'd call in every favor I had if I thought it would make a difference.

Was she scared? Hurt?

My gut clenched when I thought of all the things the bastard, Earl, could do to her. I'd seen enough shit my imagination ran wild. Wouldn't be the first time one of our women got hurt in the worst way possible, but I fucking hated it. And yeah, Farrah was mine. She might not admit it, and her daddy damn sure wouldn't, but it didn't change a thing. I'd claimed her virginity, filled her with my cum, and I'd be damned if I let her walk away.

The moment I'd seen her, I'd known there was

something different about her. I might not have thought about keeping her at the time, but the moment I'd felt her tight pussy wrapped around my dick, I'd known once would never be enough. Hell, all night wasn't enough. I'd planned to keep her in bed all day, until the Pres called and I'd realized who she was. Pissed hadn't begun to describe how I'd felt. I could have handled it better. Should have.

I stopped at the clubhouse and went inside for a cold beer. I'd have preferred something stronger about now, but I knew I needed to keep a clear head. Farrah needed me. I'd failed her once. I sure the fuck wouldn't do it again.

Grizzly hadn't called Church, which meant he wasn't telling everyone about Farrah. Not yet at any rate. I didn't know if he wanted to wait for Venom, or if he hoped she'd magically appear all on her own. He'd said he'd been busy earlier. I hadn't asked with what and I honestly didn't give a shit. If it had been club business, he'd have told me. Assuming I needed to know.

"You're quieter than usual," Dingo said, sliding onto the stool next to me. "Shouldn't you be busting heads or something?"

"Only head needs busting right now is mine. Fucked up. Bad."

He shrugged. "Can't be all bad. Grizzly hasn't ripped you apart."

"Think he's waiting to let Venom do it." I glanced at him. "Slept with Farrah but didn't realize she was a Reaper's kid."

He nodded as if it made all the sense in the world, which meant he'd already heard something. Did the club already know what I'd done? Were they aware she was missing? I glanced around the room and noticed nearly everyone was present. It wasn't a common sight, especially in the morning.

"Grizzly sent out a mass text to everyone," Dingo said. "He left out the part of you fucking up, in case you wondered. We know Venom is coming and his daughter is missing."

"Chased her off by being the bastard I am. Should have done better."

"So she was a notch on your bedpost and nothing more?" he asked. I glowered at him and he grinned. "Didn't think so. You acted like a caveman, didn't you? Barked orders at her and expected her to obey."

"Maybe."

He snorted. Yeah, there was no maybe about it. I'd done exactly what he'd said and look how it turned out. Had I been too damn hard on her? I didn't understand why she'd run. She had to see I was trying to do the right thing. There was no fucking way I'd let her leave if she had my kid in her belly. She'd been around a club her entire life. We might not be the Dixie Reapers, but Griz ran things close enough to the way Torch handled shit for her to have an idea of how this all worked. Had she been so sheltered she didn't realize what I'd been trying to do?

"The Reapers should be here soon. You up for facing her daddy?" Dingo asked.

"Not like I have a choice."

"We should probably have the med kit handy. I have a feeling he's going to tear you apart. Not only did you deflower his precious daughter, but you scared her off. Now she's gone and he's mostly likely losing his damn mind."

"I know the feeling," I muttered. When I got Farrah back, we needed to have a talk. Obviously, I'd terrified her, or pissed her off. Whatever I'd said to make her run, it seemed like I needed to clarify a few things. We weren't on the same page, and we needed to be. She'd stayed in my bed all night. No woman had ever stayed the night. Hell, I didn't take them back to my house, but she'd been different. I needed her to understand I wasn't letting her go. Not now, not ever. She was mine, plain and simple.

I'll find you, Farrah, and I'll bring you home where you belong.

Chapter Four

Farrah

The trunk felt like it was a million degrees and sweat soaked my clothes. I felt every bump in the road and wondered where the hell we were going. Too much time had passed. Were we even still in Georgia?

The car finally came to a halt and I tried to gather my strength so I could break free. My mouth was dry as cotton and I ached from head to toe. Not a good combination, and it meant I was probably dehydrated. I heard the murmur of voices before the trunk opened. I struggled to get out, but only succeeded in collapsing on the ground.

"What the fuck is this?" a man demanded.

I squinted up, my vision blurry. I blinked a few times before denim-covered legs and the bottom of a black leather cut came into view. My gaze went higher and I couldn't help the rusty laugh I let loose. This idiot. The moron who'd decided to kidnap me had brought me to the Devil's Boneyard. Fucking priceless.

I gave Havoc a little wave.

"Motherfucker," he muttered.

My eyes slid shut as the world around me tilted and spun. I heard the sound of flesh hitting flesh and had no doubt Havoc was pounding on the man who'd snatched me from the motel. Served him right. What the hell had he thought would happen? The Devil's Boneyard didn't deal in human trafficking. Hell, they saved women from assholes like this one.

A strong hand gripped me and the next thing I knew Havoc had cradled me against his chest.

"What the fuck were you doing in that idiot's trunk?" he asked, striding through the gates and up to the clubhouse.

"He kidnapped me," I said. "Duh. Did you think

I volunteered?"

"Smart ass." His lips twitched as he fought not to smile. "Your daddy know where you are?"

"What do you think?"

"Right. Think I'll let the VP handle this one. No way I'm telling Venom some junkie just tried to trade his kid for drugs."

"Thought y'all didn't deal in the hard stuff anymore," I said.

"For the most part, we don't." He shrugged as he carried me into the cool air and eased me down onto a chair at a nearby table. "Can't help it if everyone knows you come to us for the good shit. He could have easily gone to Devil's Fury for a fix."

I rolled my eyes before letting my head rest on the table. Whatever energy I'd had seemed to have disappeared. Being locked in a trunk was no joke. A chill skated over me as the air conditioning cooled my wet clothes.

"Why exactly were you in their territory?" Havoc asked.

"Know that asshole a little too well if you know where he's from," I mumbled.

"He's come around before. Several times. Had him checked out. Now answer my fucking question, Farrah."

I sighed and looked up at him. "I left home. I've been working at the diner in Blackwood Falls and staying at the motel until I save enough for an apartment or something. If I hadn't been so pissed, he never would have gotten the drop on me."

"Why were you pissed?" he asked.

"Demon." I figured the name alone would make him understand.

"Venom know you hooked up with the Devil's

Fury Sergeant-at-Arms?"

"Nope. Or rather, he didn't. If someone's noticed I'm missing, he probably knows by now."

Havoc sighed and pulled out his phone. I heard him talking to Scratch. A cold bottle of water pressed against my cheek and I smiled at Jin. He popped the top for me and I tried to sip it so I wouldn't get sick. I wanted to drain the damn bottle and ask for another, but I also didn't want to puke all over the floor.

"Scratch is calling your dad, and he's going to send Janessa over with a change of clothes for you. She's probably the closest to your size."

Yeah right. Last time I'd seen her, even post-baby weight, she was skinnier than me. I hoped like hell she brought something stretchy or it would never make it over my fat ass. My cheeks warmed when I remembered Demon's reaction to me calling myself fat. He seemed to like me the way I was, until he'd discovered I was a Dixie Reaper's kid. Maybe I should have told him up front, but I'd known he'd never touch me.

"So much for getting to use those skills my dad taught me," I said. "I wanted to take the guy out myself. Prove I'm not helpless."

Havoc folded his massive arms. "Uh-huh. He might have been strung out and jonesing for a hit, but I don't think you'd have been able to take him down. Not without a weapon. Start carrying a fucking knife, Farrah. Mace. Anything! Jesus, girl. You know better. Hell, you want a gun? We got plenty. Take your pick."

"Won't happen again."

"Damn straight it won't," a new voice said. I turned to look over my shoulder. Jackal. Fucking awesome. "I can't believe your dad let you leave without making sure you could handle yourself. I know for a fact Tank has worked with you, your sister, and Torch's daughter to make sure you could take down any handsy boys. Did you even try to fight him off?"

"He caught me by surprise." I was starting to feel like a broken record, but it was the best I could do. I'd fucked up. I could admit it.

Jackal narrowed his eyes. "You need to have your ass beat."

I winced. "Please don't. It still hurts from…"

I clamped my lips shut and felt my cheeks burn. Oh hell. I'd done it now. The last thing I needed was anyone hearing what had happened between me and Demon. Admitting I'd slept with him was one thing, but how rough he'd gotten? Probably best I kept it to myself. I didn't know what sort of reaction I'd get from this crew, but it wouldn't go in my favor either way.

"From what?" Jackal asked.

Havoc snickered. "My best guess? Demon. Is that it, Farrah? Demon spank your ass when you didn't shut your sassy mouth?"

I shrugged and refused to give them an answer. Wasn't any of their business anyway.

"This is fucking priceless," Havoc said. "Does Bull know you and Demon have a thing?"

"Why would Bull care? And I never said I had a *thing* with Demon. It was the one time. Won't be happening again."

"Uh-huh." Havoc didn't look convinced. "You know, I heard Bull gave your daddy hell when he claimed your mom. Then your mom gave him shit for claiming Darian. Can't wait to see how this one plays out."

I flipped him off, then finished off the bottle of water. The more I thought about the man who'd grabbed me, the more I realized things weren't adding up. He'd come all this way with me for what? Drugs? Why me? There were plenty of single women in Blackwood Falls, and I knew for damn sure a lot were prettier than me.

"Hey, Havoc. Where's the man who kidnapped me?" I asked.

"Being detained," he said. "Why?"

"You don't find it strange out of all the women he brought here, he picked me?"

Havoc shared a look with Jackal, then stomped out of the room. I might not have protected myself, but it seemed I'd figured out something before the Devil's Boneyard, so I'd call it a win. I drank three bottles of water, and managed to keep them down, by the time Irish arrived with a change of clothes for me. Janessa must have known her stuff wouldn't fit because everything in the sack was brand new.

"Thanks," I said, taking it from him.

"You can shower in my room," Jin offered. "It's clean. I don't take women in there, but I keep the place picked up."

I stood, bracing myself on the table until I knew my legs would hold me. The heat from the trunk must have sapped all my energy. I followed Jin to his room and went into the bathroom, shutting the door. The space was tiny, but it would do for a quick shower.

I left the water on cold while I scrubbed my hair and body, then pulled on the brand-new panties, sports bra, tee, and leggings. It wasn't stylish, but at least the clothes were dry and clean. There was even a pair of flip-flops in the bottom and I quickly slipped them on. I shoved my dirty stuff into the sack and contemplated throwing it all out. I wasn't sure I'd get the smell out. Not just from my sweat, but the trunk as well. It hadn't exactly smelled like roses.

When I went back to the main room of the clubhouse, I saw more Devil's Boneyard members. Scratch made his way over to me, pulling me in for a hard hug.

"Girl, you know how to get into trouble, don't you?"

"At least I didn't cause it this time," I said.

He chuckled and released me. "True enough. Don't guess your daddy will care either way. He's already heading into Devil's Fury territory so he's not about to turn around and come get you. Looks like one of us will have to take you home."

"My dad went to Blackwood Falls?" I asked.

Scratch nodded. "Devil's Fury called him. Said you were missing. I've let him know you're okay, but he's not going to rest easy until he sees you."

"I'll just end up in another trunk. His."

Scratch smiled and shook his head. "No doubt. He'll do his damnedest to get you back home to Alabama, but you're a grown woman now, Farrah. Think he's learned by now you're too stubborn to hold in one spot if you don't want to be there. You just need to convince him you're really okay."

I licked my lips and looked around before dropping my voice a little. "The man who took me. Did he say why he picked me?"

All traces of humor were wiped from Scratch's face. "Not for me to say, Farrah. Club business."

I had to bite my tongue. I wanted to call him out on his bullshit. It wasn't just club business. The asshole had snatched me, stuffed me in a trunk, and brought me here. It was pretty fucking personal. I didn't know why he couldn't see it. Being carted across state lines and being traded for drugs gave me a vested interest in what the man had to say, or what would happen to him.

I'd never been one to keep quiet, but I wasn't with the Dixie Reapers right now. Scratch was the VP here and he deserved respect. Didn't make it easy. I sat at a nearby table and waited to see who was taking me back to Blackwood Falls. I already knew it wouldn't matter what I wanted. Bikers were more caveman than anything else. They'd do what they wanted and in this instance it would be whatever they felt was the safest thing for me.

Magnus came over, nudging my chair with his boot. "Come on, girl. Time to go home."

"You drew the short straw?" I asked.

He smirked. "Something like that. Your dad is fit to be tied. Let's get you back to him so he can see you aren't hurt."

"Just my pride."

I'd always said I'd never been one of those women. The ones who go without a fight. What had I done? Not paid the fuck attention to where I was going. It was the number one rule when I became a teenager. Always pay attention to my surroundings. I'd known the motel wasn't the best place to be, had seen the criminal element lurking there. Should have checked before opening the door. I knew better, I'd screwed up just the same. I had no doubt Demon was pissed as hell right now. I only hoped he kept his mouth shut around my dad.

I got up and followed Magnus out of the clubhouse, my dirty clothes left behind. I didn't want to see them again. Even if I didn't have much money, and couldn't afford to replace them, I didn't think I'd ever be able to wear them again. The club could wash and donate them, or toss them into the trash for all I cared.

Magnus helped me up into a large SUV parked outside, then cranked the AC when he started up the engine. He didn't fill the silence with idle chitchat, and I didn't feel the need to either. I rested my head against the window and eventually closed my eyes. The day caught up with me and I managed to fall asleep, only to jolt awake when I realized the car was no longer moving.

I looked for Magnus, but the driver's seat was empty despite the fact the SUV was still running. Rubbing at my eyes, I stretched and got out of the car. My feet no sooner hit the ground than I found myself pressed back against the vehicle. I stared up at Demon and my heart skipped a beat. Beyond the fury I could see how worried he'd been.

"You're in trouble, little girl," he said, his voice nearly a growl.

"Demon, can we not do this? I've had one hell of a day and I just… I need to get something to eat and sleep for a while."

He backed up a step right about the time my knees gave out. Demon caught me easily and swung me up into his arms. He carried me over to a truck and eased me down onto the passenger seat. When he got behind the wheel, I wanted to bail out of the truck. Last thing I wanted to deal with right now was an angry Demon. My ass still hurt from the last time. Was it really this morning? Seemed like longer.

He drove straight to his house. It seemed there would be no avoiding him, or the confrontation I could feel brewing. I waited for him to open my door, then he lifted me once more and took me into the house. Instead of going to his room like I'd expected, he sank onto the couch and held me in his lap.

"Do you have any fucking idea how I felt when I realized you were missing?" he asked.

"It's not like I asked to be kidnapped."

He framed my face with his hands, forcing me to hold his gaze. "If you'd stayed put like I'd told you to, then you wouldn't have been at the damn motel to get snatched. I can't protect you if you aren't here, Farrah. Not knowing where you were, who had you, or why you'd been taken… it about tore me up inside."

"We barely know each other, Demon."

"For starters, we're past the point of you calling me Demon when it's only us. Call me Cody. Second, we're going to get to know one another real damn well, Farrah. I cleaned out your motel room and moved your shit here."

I took a moment to process everything. "Does my daddy know?"

He shook his head. "Not yet. I wanted to wait until I knew you were safe before I said anything. I know he's going to kick my ass, and I'm going to let him. To a point. Man has a right to defend his daughter. But, Farrah, you're mine. Don't even think of fucking walking out the door again. I'll tie your ass to the bed next time."

"I need to see him."

Demon nodded. "I know. I'll ask him to bring you some food. You can eat while he takes his frustrations out on me."

I cocked my head to the side and stared at him. "You're really not going to fight back?"

He shook his head. "I'll let him get some hits in, then deflect whatever he sends my way. But no, baby, I'm not going to hit your daddy."

I leaned against him, resting my head against his shoulder. I didn't have a clue how this would even work between us. He was so controlling, and I liked being able to do what I wanted when I wanted. After being on lockdown my entire life, I wasn't ready to jump right back into the club life. I'd come here to spread my wings and experience life. Not shackle myself to the first biker who came along.

Even if he was a big, bearded, tatted sex god.

"This isn't what I wanted," I said softly.

"You shouldn't have gone to the clubhouse looking for a hook-up if you didn't want to risk getting claimed, Farrah. You've been around clubs your entire life. You know how this shit works."

"I know. I only wanted to have a good time. My dad hasn't let me have any fun. I came here to have a fresh start, experience new things. Now I'm on lockdown again."

He rubbed his hand up and down my arm. "I'm not your jailer, Farrah, but I also won't let you risk getting yourself hurt. Until we know why you were taken, I don't want you leaving my sight. I'm sorry if you don't like it, but I won't budge on this one. You could have died, or worse. What if he hadn't taken you to the Devil's Boneyard? Another club might have turned you into a whore or sold you. What then?"

I knew he was right, but I didn't have to like it.

Looked like I was back on a leash for the foreseeable future. At least this one came with lots of orgasms.

Chapter Five

Demon

As much as I wanted to spank her ass for walking out earlier, I couldn't help but feel relieved she was okay. I had no idea why Earl wanted her. The fact he'd dropped her with the Devil's Boneyard was a damn miracle. The thought of her ending up in a brothel or as some pervert's sex slave made my stomach turn. Having her in my arms calmed my inner beast for the moment.

I breathed her in, holding her close. How the fuck someone I'd only known for a day could be so important to me I couldn't explain. I'd known *of* Farrah, and probably saw her a few times as a kid, but until last night, our paths hadn't crossed since she'd grown up. I'd told myself I only wanted her to stay because she could be carrying my kid, but I knew damn well I was lying to myself and everyone else.

For whatever reason, she'd become important to me. She'd crawled under my skin and there was no digging her out. She was there, holding on like a damn tick. The fist pounding on the front door had me setting her aside. I'd barely pulled the fucking thing open before Venom's fist met my jaw. My head snapped back and I staggered a step or two, but remained upright. I worked my jaw back and forth as he advanced into the room. For a man his age, he still fucking hit hard.

"That was for fucking my daughter," he said as he set the food down. He landed two more blows, one to my ribs and one to my temple. "And that's for Goddamn losing her!"

"Daddy!" Farrah tried to work herself between us, but I didn't need her fighting my battles. I shoved her behind me so she wouldn't get hurt, and Venom drew up short. He eyed me before glancing over my shoulder at his daughter.

"Couldn't keep your hands to yourself?" he asked and I knew it was directed at me, even if he was attempting to stare his daughter down despite the fact she hid behind me.

"I didn't know who she was. Not until the next morning, then I spanked her ass for lying to me."

Venom snorted. "Good luck. Spankings never worked on Farrah. Too damn stubborn like her mom."

"Mom says I'm stubborn like you," Farrah said, her words muffled where she'd pressed her face to my back.

"We good?" I asked the VP of the Dixie Reapers MC.

Venom nodded. "We're good. For now. You hurt her, lose her, or fuck up in any other way and I will end you. Don't give a shit who you are. No one hurts my baby and lives to tell the tale."

"If she'd stayed where I put her, she wouldn't have been kidnapped," I said. "She got pissed at me and ran."

Venom took a step to the side and looked at his daughter, folding his arms over his chest. "That true, Farrah?"

"Maybe," she said, drawing the word out. "In my defense, he was being all high-handed and barking orders at me."

"Jesus Christ," Venom muttered. "Sit your ass down. You need to eat."

I felt Farrah move away from me and I turned to see her heading for the kitchen through the archway off to the left. I followed with Venom at my heels. He placed a sack of food in the middle of the table and unloaded what had to be at least fifty tacos and two containers of sauce. Farrah reached for a taco, unwrapped it, and ate the damn thing in three bites. I'd never seen a woman do that, but I had to admit I was impressed.

I reached for one and Farrah growled at me. Venom snickered and pulled out a chair, sitting across from his daughter. He pointed to the spot between the two of them and I sat. Farrah inhaled eight tacos before she sighed and leaned back.

"Is my grocery bill about to go up?" I asked.

She flipped me off.

"When it comes to tacos or pizza, I've seen Farrah outeat the men at the clubhouse," Venom said. "If she's going to be here with you, you should be prepared. Her favorite ice cream is Neapolitan because she can never pick just one flavor. And keep kettle corn stocked. It's one of her favorite snacks."

I braced my arms on the table and leaned forward a bit. "You seem awfully accepting of this. Figured you'd beat the shit out of me and drag her out of here."

Venom shook his head. "I tried to lock her down. Didn't work. If she wants her freedom, I'm going to give it to her. But if you're claiming her, you better make damn sure she stays safe. If I get another call about her missing, they'll never find your body."

Even though he was in Devil's Fury territory, I let the threat slide. For one, he outranked me. For another, he was my woman's daddy. Had to respect the fact he wanted to keep her safe, even if he wasn't able to do it in person.

"Anyone ever find out why he took me?" Farrah asked.

No, or at least I hadn't heard anything. The look Venom cast my way said he hadn't either. If the

Boneyard crew had pulled any info from the guy, they hadn't shared it. So either he wasn't talking, or they were keeping it to themselves. Either way, I wanted to know what the fuck was going on. Why had Earl taken Farrah?

"You can't claim it's club business when it directly involves me," she said. "I have a right to know why he picked me."

"You'll know what I let you know," I said. When she tried to stand and storm off, I grabbed her arm and forced her ass back down onto the chair. "Farrah, you've proven you're not as badass as you seem to think. A junkie stuffed you in a trunk and took you across state lines. Last thing I need is you trying to handle shit on your own."

"He's not wrong," Venom said. "You know I love your mom, and she can hold her own against most people, but do you honestly think I'd take the sass you're throwing at Demon right now if she were sitting in your place? Fuck no. If she'd gotten kidnapped, her ass would already be red and she'd damn well better think twice about disobeying again."

"Should I call and ask Mom what she thinks about you saying she needs to obey you?" Farrah asked.

"Go right ahead. Do you know what she'd tell you?" Venom asked. "She'd say I'd never do anything to hurt her and would protect her with my life. And she'd be right. Even if it means I can't share everything with her. I tell her what I'm able, and when I say she needs to keep her ass at home, she does it. Or at least stays inside the compound."

I leaned back in my chair, eyeing her. "What exactly do you think it means to be mine?"

* * *

Farrah

I shrugged. "You'll boss me around and expect me to do as you say, like I'm a stupid dog or something. I'll be locked behind these gates, unable to go where I want when I want. You'll want to know my every move and I'll lose what little freedom I've found since leaving home."

Disappointment and sadness crossed my dad's face. He stood and walked to the kitchen door, pausing with his back to me. "Farrah, I'm sorry you think being part of a club is so horrible. It means I fucked up raising you. I'll send your grandpa over to say hi, but I think I'm heading home. It's clear you don't need me here or want to be here yourself. I love you, and I always will, but... I can't be around you right now."

He walked out and it felt like I'd just lost the most important person in my entire world. My dad had been angry with me plenty of times. Not once had he ever walked off like this. It felt... final. I heard the front door open and shut. Demon didn't say a word. Didn't so much as move. He stared at the table, as if the woodgrain had all the answers he sought.

"You were wrong for that," he finally said. "You want to get pissed at me? Fine. Let me have it, but you just threw your entire life in your dad's face. He came here to make sure you were safe and you told him how much you'd hated living with the Dixie Reapers. Those people are his family. *Your* family, and you shit all over everything they stand for."

I opened and shut my mouth because he was right. I couldn't deny I'd done exactly what he'd said. It hadn't been my intention, but it happened just the same. I owed my dad an apology, and Demon too.

"I'm sorry," I said. "I don't hate the club life. For

the men, I'm sure it's amazing. Not so much if you're the daughter of the VP. He wouldn't let me date. If he caught me talking on the phone with a boy, he'd threaten them. I couldn't leave without him knowing where I was going, who I'd be with, and even then he had a tracker on my truck and phone."

"He was protecting you, Farrah. If you weren't being such a spoiled little bitch, you'd see it. The trackers, the constant worry over where you were? Did you ever stop to ask why?"

Well, no. I hadn't.

"I haven't been real close with your dad's club, but I do know some shit you may not. Like the fact your mom showed up on the run. Her mother and stepdad were going to sell her to someone who wanted to destroy her, use her up and make a whore out of her. And Rin… Do you think she hates the safety of those gates? After all she's been through, would she see your dad's protective measures as being too much?"

The more he said the lower I felt. He was right. My dad had done his best to keep the evils of the world at bay. He'd done the only thing he knew how, protected me the best way he could, and I'd made it sound like I'd lived in a prison. I knew there were girls out there who had it worse than me. I'd never gone without food, clothes, or shelter. He'd bought me a truck, made sure I knew how to drive, taught me self-defense, even showed me how to shoot a gun.

"I need to talk to him," I said.

"Not sure he wants to hear it, little girl. What you said was downright hateful to a man like him. Venom needs some space."

Tears misted my eyes and I nodded. I hated knowing I'd hurt my dad. The tacos I'd eaten suddenly felt like lead sitting in my stomach. I bolted out of the chair and down the hall to the bathroom, barely hitting my knees before I threw up. I'd been horrible. My dad had called me a brat often enough, but he'd always said it with a smile. This was different. I'd gone too far, and I knew it. What if he never spoke to me again?

I sniffled as tears streaked my cheeks. Booted steps came closer, then I felt the heat of a large body behind me. The scent of my grandpa surrounded me as he wrapped his arms around me. His blond hair was liberally streaked with silver now, but he still was one of the strongest men I knew, and he gave the best hugs.

"I messed up," I said.

"Yeah, you did. I convinced Venom to have a beer and cool off. He hasn't left yet. We've talked about this before, Farrah. You have to think about your words before you speak. You hurt him bad."

"I know. I'm sorry." I hiccupped and turned, burying my face in his chest as he hugged me.

He ran his hand down my hair, like he'd done all my life. I'd missed him while I'd been gone. If I stayed here, moved in with Demon, how would often would I see my family? I'd enjoyed my independence, but I'd known I could always go home to visit whenever I'd wanted. Even if my dad had been intent on teaching me a lesson, my grandpa would let me stay with him. He'd kept a room at his house for me and my sister, even after he met Darian and had more kids. My brother usually slept in the same room as their son, since the two weren't just related but were best friends too.

"I'll convince your dad to stay another day or two," he said. "But you owe him an apology, Farrah, and I don't mean a half-assed one."

"I know. I will."

He kissed my forehead and stood. "Now brush your damn teeth and stop giving Demon such a hard time. He's not going to take your shit."

"That's all you have to say about it?" I asked.

He snorted. "Fuck, no. I'm going to give your daddy hell. He claimed your mom when she wasn't much older than you. I didn't like it. I didn't sit back and take it quietly either. Now it's Venom's turn to see how it feels."

Before I could say anything else, he left. I went to find my things. Demon had said he'd brought everything here, and I found my toothbrush in the master bathroom. I scrubbed with toothpaste, wanting to get the vile taste out of my mouth. I spat in the sink and rinsed my mouth, only to look up and catch Demon's reflection as he waited in the bedroom. I patted my lips with a hand towel and went to face the music.

"Bull give you something to think about?" he asked.

I nodded. "I've always listened to my grandpa. Didn't always do what he said, though."

"I have a feeling you've always fought against anyone trying to boss you, as you put it. You finished being a brat? That shit you pulled was juvenile, hurtful, and wrong."

"I know. I'll tell Dad I'm sorry. My grandpa convinced him to stay a little longer."

"Why don't you shower and get ready for bed? It's been a long-ass day and you need to rest. I'm going to make some calls in the other room, then I'll come join you."

I knew he wasn't asking but telling me. "Where are my clothes?"

He pointed to the dresser. "Bottom two drawers.

The rest is in the closet."

I went over and pulled out a clean pair of panties and a nightgown, then went back to the bathroom and started the shower. He'd already put my hair stuff and body soap inside, along with my razor. I got the water so hot my skin turned red when I stepped under the spray. I scrubbed myself and shaved. After I put conditioner in my hair, I let it set for a few minutes and closed my eyes, enjoying the water beating against my back and shoulders.

I hadn't realized until now how much everything hurt. Rattling around in the trunk of the car had left some bruises on my body, to go along with the ones Demon had gifted me. I'd preferred his. At least I'd had fun getting them.

I cooled the water down to rinse my hair, working out the tangles with my fingers. I shut off the water and dried off before I pulled on my clothes. The shower had helped a little, but I still ached everywhere. After I shut off the light, I crawled under the covers and shut my eyes. Maybe Demon was right. Even though it wasn't very late, I was definitely tired.

He'd been right about other things too.

I didn't know why I was acting like this, but I'd hurt the people I loved. I hoped tomorrow I'd feel more like myself.

Chapter Six

Demon

I couldn't deal with the family drama bullshit with Farrah, Venom, and Bull. Not right now. What she'd said at the table left me with too many questions. Not only about our future, but about her kidnapping as well. A quick call to Havoc hadn't provided the answers I'd wanted. One thing I did know, he hadn't told me everything. Something was going on and I wanted to know what the fuck it was.

As much as I hated to disturb Grizzly when he was home with the girls, I needed to give him a heads-up about the shit going on. His phone rang six times, and I damn near hung up, when he finally answered.

"Is the clubhouse on fire?" Grizzly asked instead of giving me a somewhat normal greeting.

"Not that I'm aware. Have you talked to the Devil's Boneyard?"

"Not since earlier. Why?" he asked.

"Just spoke to Havoc. Get the feeling he's hiding something. This whole thing with Farrah seems off, doesn't it? Why her? And if the Boneyard crew knows something, why the fuck aren't they telling us? Farrah isn't theirs. We have a right to know why she got snatched."

"I'll see what I can do. Right now, Meredith is having a meltdown of some sort. Bawling her eyes out and fuck if I know why. Girl won't talk to me, or anyone."

I knew someone she'd talk to, but Griz might not like it. "Get Doolittle over there. Seen her talking to him several times."

"Fuck me," he muttered. "I guess if she's going after a brother, might as well be Doolittle. She's too fucking young, but I know he won't hurt her."

No, he certainly wouldn't. Although, the girl had a few years before she wouldn't be jailbait. I hoped he had the sense to wait. Meredith was still new to our compound, but Griz already doted on her, just like the others. Didn't matter none of those girls were his biological kids. He'd taken every one of them under his wing, adopted them, and raised them like they were his own. I knew damn well he'd do anything for them. Only one was out in the wind. Shella.

"If you get anything from the Devil's Boneyard, would you let me know? I don't know if I need to keep a close eye on Farrah or if this was more a crime of opportunity. I'm thinking it's not. The entire thing feels off," I said. "I'll rest easier knowing exactly what we're facing."

"Let me get Meredith calmed down and I'll see what I find out. You better hope you have boys. These girls may drive me to drink," the Pres said.

I snorted. "You already drink."

I heard his laughter as he hung up and shook my head.

I shot off a quick text to Doolittle. *Hope you know what you're getting into.*

If he hurt Meredith, Griz would rip him a new one. I scrolled through the messages on my phone, making sure I was up to speed on everything. One in particular caught my attention. I clicked it and my stomach twisted. A young girl, bound to a chair, begged for her life. As much as I wanted to close the damn thing, I made myself watch as some sick bastard tortured her.

They'd left her bleeding and more than likely permanently scarred. A man wearing a ski mask over his face got right up in the camera. "Bitch is gonna be the best little whore when we're through with her. I'll be taking bids on who gets her first."

I didn't know why I'd received the clip until I saw who it had come from. Kraken. I typed out a quick response. *That your missing MaryAnne??*

It only took a moment for him to answer. *Yes. Might need backup.*

Well, fuck me. There was no damn way I was leaving town while things were unresolved with my own club, but if he needed more hands I'd send a few men his way. I knew Griz wouldn't mind, but I'd run it past him first. It could wait until tomorrow.

I locked up the house, something I'd never bothered with before, and shut out the lights. When I got to the bedroom, Farrah was already asleep, curled in a tight ball on her side of the bed. I stood in the doorway and studied her. In sleep, she looked angelic. Sweet. Innocent. Hell, she'd been innocent until I popped her cherry. I didn't know what the hell to do with her. No fucking way I'd let her walk out of here if there was even a chance she was carrying my kid, but at the same time I didn't want her to feel trapped like she had with the Dixie Reapers. Maybe she wasn't cut out for club life, even though she'd been born into it.

Last thing I wanted was a miserable woman giving me hell at every turn. If I thought she could be happy, I'd hold on with both hands. I'd never brought a woman home. Never thought much about them past me getting off. Then Farrah came into my life. It only took the one night for her to turn everything upside down. Her bratty attitude tonight had earned her a spanking, but the way she'd gotten sick when she'd realized what she'd done had been punishment enough.

I removed my boots, tossed my cut onto the dresser, and stripped down to my underwear. Even though it was dark, moonlight filtered through the blinds letting me find my way to the bed without tripping over anything. I slid under the covers and folded my arms under my head. The ceiling didn't hold any answers for me. No matter how much I wanted to pull Farrah into my arms, I knew she needed some space tonight. Hell, the fact she practically hugged the edge of the bed told me plenty.

I'd never taken shit from anyone. Had gone after what I wanted. Same way I'd done with Farrah the night she'd come to the clubhouse. Now things were different. She wasn't some nameless, throwaway one-night stand. She meant something to me, even if I didn't want to analyze exactly *what*.

Did it make me an asshole for wanting to keep her here when she clearly didn't want this life? Probably. No. More like definitely. Hadn't given a shit before. Shouldn't give one now.

She whimpered in her sleep and rolled toward me. Her brow furrowed and even in sleep she looked troubled. It took me less than a minute to cave in to my desires and I pulled her against my side, hooking my arm around her. She snuggled in closer and every muscle in her body seemed to relax.

"Demon," she murmured.

A quick glance told me she still slept. If she was dreaming about me, I sure the fuck hoped it was a good one. I'd thought Farrah would be a good fit for me, once I got un-pissed about her lying to me, but it was clear we had some issues to work through. I didn't remember the others having trouble keeping their women by their sides. I reached for my phone and pulled up a text to Steel.

Did Rachel give you trouble? Don't think Farrah wants to stay.

I hit send before I could second-guess myself. I didn't want to sound like a damn pussy, unable to hang onto my woman. Maybe it was karma trying to fuck me over for all the shit I'd done. Could be the fates didn't want a guy like me having a woman and family. Someone hurt the club, in any way, and I didn't care if they were a man or woman. I'd been known to torture them equally. Wouldn't hesitate to slit a traitor's throat and didn't matter to me who the fuck they were.

My phone chimed with a response. *Did you order her to stay or tell her why you want to keep her?*

What the hell did he mean? *What the fuck?*

Christ! It's like talking to a toddler. You have to give her a reason to stay, dumbass. You telling her she's not leaving is only going to make her want to run. Glad my second kid will be a boy.

Well, fucking hell. I'd already figured out she was a runner. How the hell did I convince her to stay? It was doubtful she'd want to. Not after everything she'd said earlier. I'd given her something to think about, and I knew Bull had too, but would it be enough?

"Who are you texting?" Farrah mumbled. "All the clicking is loud."

I hadn't thought about the sound my phone made when I typed out a number or message. When I was at the compound, noise didn't matter. I put the device on silent whenever I dealt with club shit. Should have realized I was too fucking noisy.

"Steel. Had a question for him," I said.

She stretched and hummed, then cuddled closer. "I'm sorry I'm such a bitch. I don't mean to be. There are times I open my mouth and can't seem to stop what comes out. I didn't mean to hurt my dad, or you."

I hugged her tighter. "I think we all have those moments. You're under a lot of stress too after being kidnapped. You must have been scared."

"More like pissed," she said. "Asshole left bruises from rattling me around in his trunk. I hope Havoc hurt him."

"I have no idea what Havoc did because the Boneyard crew is keeping silent on this one, which I hate. If I don't know why you were taken, how the fuck can I keep you safe? Pisses me off. They have women and wouldn't stand for this shit, but I'm supposed to?"

She rubbed her hand across my chest. "Havoc knew the guy, or of him. Said he'd been there before to buy drugs. Still don't know how I fit into everything. He'd been at the diner a few times. Always gave me the creeps."

"Don't think we're getting any answers tonight, baby."

"You hurt me too, you know?"

I shifted so I could look down at her. "What do you mean?"

"You only want me here because you think I could be pregnant. If I'd told you I was on birth control, you'd have let me walk out of here. It's not me you want."

Fuck. Steel was right. I flipped on the lamp so I could see her better.

"Farrah, it's not just because of the baby, or possible baby. I told you before you're different. I don't bring women to my house. Sure the fuck don't move them in. I'm not so good with words. Never know what to say to a woman." I snorted. "Never had to. Women have been dropping their panties for as long as

I can remember, but I want more from you."

She twisted until she lay on her stomach and propped her chin on my chest. "You know, women don't like hearing about past conquests when they're lying in bed with you. Kind of a turnoff."

"Wasn't what I meant. I only wanted you to know you're special. The others weren't. They were convenient and nothing more."

"You plan on fucking them still? If you claim me?" she asked.

"What the hell kind of question is that?" I demanded.

"One I want answered. My dad and his brothers are different from others who have visited in the past. Some don't care if they're married or have an old lady at home. They still fuck around and see nothing wrong with it. I need to know which category you fall into. I think I deserve to know."

Fucking women. Always wanting to talk about shit, wanting to know about your *feelings*. Relationship were too damn complicated, which is why I'd mostly avoided them. I'd had some fun with one of the little señoritas we'd taken in a while back, until she'd decided to strip for a living. Now she was out there on her own, and I'd walked away. No fucking way I'd ever be cool with my woman showing off her body to a bunch of men for money. I didn't think poorly of those women, but I knew damn well I was too jealous to ever handle dating one of them.

"In the past, I haven't been committed to anyone enough to stop fucking other women. Doesn't mean it's going to play out that way with you. Also never wanted to keep those women. Maybe it would have headed down that path eventually, but when we parted ways, I didn't give a shit. Just moved on."

"You're not painting a pretty picture," she said.

"Not supposed to be pretty. But it's the truth. That's what you wanted, right? Honesty? Well, there it is. I'm an asshole who likes women, but I'm offering to be exclusive with you, Farrah. I won't fuck around behind your back, and I expect the same of you. I ever catch you with another man and I'll fucking rip his dick off, gut him, and make you watch."

She winced. "Thanks for the visual."

"Like your dad and grandpa haven't done worse," I said.

"They may have, but I certainly didn't witness it, and I have a feeling it happened before my time. Dad's too… Dad. And Grandpa? He's a big teddy bear."

I'd love to see Venom's face, and Bull's, if they heard Farrah say that shit. Teddy bear? Too Dad? As the VP, I knew damn well Venom could still tear a man apart, and probably had far more recently than Farrah realized. Bull had gotten his name for a reason. Age might have mellowed him a little, or having a family, but deep down, he was still the same guy he'd been twenty or thirty years ago. People changed, but not as much as Farrah thought.

"You go on believing that, baby. I guess you can keep your delusions."

She blinked, opened and shut her mouth, and ended up not saying anything, but I could practically hear the gears turning.

"You think your daddy is VP and remains in his position by what? Asking people nicely to do shit? Not likely. His hands are dirty, but like a good dad, he keeps it from you."

"Guess I never thought about it like that," she murmured.

I ran my hand up and down her back. "Need you

to think about something. I want you here, Farrah. Doesn't matter if there's a baby or not. You're mine, but I don't want a constant fight on my hands. I have too much shit to worry about around here. Last thing I need is an old lady who can't follow orders."

She traced patterns on my chest and after a moment, I realized she was drawing hearts. "You really want me here? For me and not because I could be pregnant?"

"Said it, didn't I?"

She nodded.

"Then it must be true because I don't fucking lie."

She leaned closer and put her lips to mine. I buried my fingers in her hair, holding her to me as I ravaged her mouth. Her little nipples hardened and pressed into me. I slid a hand down her back, over her ass, and cupped her pussy through her panties. Wet. So fucking wet.

"Thought you were pissed at me," I said and tapped her pussy. "This tells another story."

She squirmed. "Maybe I want angry make-up sex?"

I tried not to laugh. "Baby, we've already had angry sex. Then you walked out. Although I do owe you a spanking."

I reversed our positions, putting her under me, her stomach to the mattress. I backed off, lifting her hips and ripped her panties off. Rubbing her ass cheeks, I noticed she had several bruises. I hoped like hell they weren't all from me. It was one thing to leave my fingerprints on her hips, which I noted were there, but I didn't like hurting her. Not this kind of pain anyway.

"Why didn't you tell me?" I asked.

"Didn't think you'd care. Wasn't the entire point to punish me?" she asked.

"Yeah, but I didn't know I left bruises."

"They're not all from you. I wasn't kidding when I said I got bruised bouncing around in that asshole's trunk." She eyed me over her shoulder. "From what I've heard, you aren't the type to give a shit about leaving bruises behind."

She was right. Somewhat. With anyone else, I hadn't cared. But Farrah wasn't just anyone. She was… mine. Didn't mean I wouldn't punish her when she deserved it, but I didn't like the idea of hurting her enough to leave bruises. I might be an asshole, but I wasn't an abusive asshole.

"With other women. Not with you," I said.

"Are you getting soft on me?" she asked.

I rubbed my hard cock against her ass. "Do I feel soft to you?"

She snickered. "No, so maybe you should put your cock to good use and fuck me."

"You aren't too sore?" I asked, trailed my fingers over her pussy.

"A little bit," she admitted. "I still want you."

I leaned over her, kissing along her spine until I reached her neck. I gently sucked the skin, leaving a mark. My woman was so damn wet I knew she'd take me easily. I lined my cock up and sank into her, not bothering with a condom this time. The damage had been done, and if she was mine, there wouldn't be any barriers between us. She moaned and clutched at the bedding.

I braced my weight on one hand and placed the other against her belly as I started to thrust. I'd always been more into self-gratification before. Hard, fast fucking with no emotions involved. Wasn't really sure

I *had* emotions -- not the romantic type anyway. Still, it seemed important I take my time with Farrah, prove to her I wasn't some rutting beast.

She clasped me so tight, her pussy nearly squeezing my dick to the point of pain. The soft sounds she made urged me on. I slid my hand from her belly up to her breasts, cupping one and rubbing my thumb across her nipple. I hadn't thought it possible, but she got even hotter and wetter.

"That's it, baby," I murmured. "Come for me. Show me how much you love my cock."

"Cody! Don't stop. Please…"

"Not stoppin'. Nothing could pull me away right now." I stroked in and out of her. When she cried out, her pussy clamping down tighter, I damn near came. I drove into her faster and harder. Her climax seemed to roll into another, and soon I was filling her up with my cum. I grunted on the last few thrusts, emptying my balls. "Fuck, baby. So damn good."

I kissed her neck. Her shoulder. I didn't know how she could think I'd want anyone else. Now that I'd had a taste of Farrah, no other woman would ever compare. She'd ruined me for anyone else. It wasn't only because she'd been a virgin, although knowing I was her first -- and last -- was a big fucking turn-on. No, it was more. She fit me, both physically and in every way it counted. She might have a temper and a mouth on her, but her softer side would calm the fury usually running through my veins. Maybe with her I could be a better man. One who deserved her.

I pulled out and leaned back, watching my cum slide down her thighs. "Now that's a beautiful fucking sight."

Her cheeks flushed and she buried her face in the pillow. Too damn cute. I stretched out on my side and tugged her against me. She sighed softly and cuddled close. Within minutes, she was asleep, and I followed soon after.

Chapter Seven

Farrah

I didn't know if I had a shift at the diner or not. Would Demon even let me keep my job? He seemed like the type who would prefer I stay home. Even though he'd said he'd give me some freedom, I wasn't sure what his version of freedom was, but I had a feeling it didn't mesh with mine. As much as I'd loved being my own person, doing what I wanted when I wanted, I had to admit there were upsides to being here with him. Besides the orgasms.

Demon made me feel safe. I hadn't realized until last night what exactly it meant to be behind the gates of an MC compound. Sure, I'd lived with the Dixie Reapers my entire life, and I'd known my dad protected me and the others. Having Demon break it down made it more... real. I loved my dad, and all my family, but I'd always felt suffocated. Being thrown into a trunk made me realize something. They had a reason for the gate and fence. My dad hadn't put me on lockdown to be mean or show how much power he held. He'd wanted to keep me safe.

Now Demon had taken over the task.

Meiling, Dingo's woman, had stopped by to keep me company. Although, it was more likely she was keeping an eye on me while Demon handled club business, in the event I decided to run away again. But she'd convinced Demon to load his credit card to the shopping app on my phone. I only hoped he didn't get pissed as hell once he saw the bill.

"Is this a retail therapy thing?" Meiling asked. "Or is this a get even with Demon thing? Either way, I think you definitely need the tablecloth and kitchen curtains."

I flipped through the different color schemes of

the set on my screen. Too many choices. "To be honest, maybe it's a bit of both."

She pointed to the blue-checkered curtains with daisies along the hem. "I dare you to buy those. If you do, you need to record his reaction when he sees them."

Uh, no. I wasn't about to buy those. "I'm not into… what is that anyway? Country chic or just country?"

"Does it matter?" Meiling asked.

"Nope. I'm not buying them. I kind of suck at this. I've never decorated a house before."

Meiling's phone chimed and she checked it. Her adorable little girl's face filled the screen, along with the word *Home*. "I better get this. Wen is probably driving Dingo crazy."

I tried not to laugh. I really did. But hearing Dingo and crazy in the same sentence was too much for me. As I wiped the tears from my eyes, I tried to suck in a breath and calm myself. "Sorry, but aren't dingoes considered crazy dogs or something?"

Her nose wrinkled, but I saw a slight smile curve her lips as she answered the call. Deciding to give her a little privacy, I took my phone into the living room and looked around the space. Everything in Demon's house was dark. I had to wonder if the man was allergic to colors.

The sofa was brown leather, along with the loveseat. The floors were hardwood and seemed to be a dark walnut, if I had to guess. No curtains hung in the windows, only blinds. A massive flat screen TV hung on the wall over a fireplace. Every piece of wood furniture was dark as well. The closest color I could associate with the walls was taupe. The quality of the furniture was nice, but all the drabness was going to get to me.

I scrolled through the app and picked out an area rug with some reds, blues, and greens. A few more clicks and I added throw pillows. I scanned the room again and realized there wasn't a single picture. Not of him, friends, not even something scenic for the walls. I found a contemporary oil panting with lots of color and added it to my cart. I also tossed in some scented candles, picture frames for photos I planned to put out eventually, and some cutesy things I thought would add some personality to the room.

When I saw the total, I winced. Demon might very well kill me later, but we seriously needed these things. Or at least I did. I couldn't live in this drab house. If he wanted me to stay, to make a life with him, he needed to give me a few things too. Like letting me make this house my own.

Meiling stopped in the doorway. "I hate to run, but Dingo said Wen is running a fever. He's called her pediatrician, but needs to run to the pharmacy, so I need to get home and watch her."

"It's fine. I'm not going anywhere. Besides, it's kind of fun spending Demon's money."

She waved and headed out the door. I hadn't had a chance to meet any of the other old ladies yet, but Meiling seemed sweet. Being part of a club, I knew she also had to be pretty tough. Even though we hadn't discussed much in the way of personal stuff, there was something in her eyes telling me she'd had a hard life before coming here. It was a story I was all too familiar with, seeing as how several of the Dixie Reapers ladies had been in trouble when they'd found their men. Until now, I hadn't known my mother was one of them. She'd kept the ugliness from me, and I could understand her reasoning. It made me feel like an ungrateful bitch for all the times I'd given her grief over the years.

I heard a motorcycle pull up and peeked out the window. My dad swung his leg over the seat of his bike and headed for the front door. He looked a little less pissed today. I dashed to the entryway and let him in. Before he even crossed the threshold, I threw my arms around him and hugged him tight.

"I'm sorry, Daddy. I'm a mean, hateful, ungrateful bitch and you didn't deserve anything I said last night."

He pressed a kiss to the top of my head like he'd done all my life. "I should have sat you down long ago and explained things better. Demon told me about the talk he had with you. It was never my intention for you to feel like you lived in a prison. There's so much ugliness in the world. I didn't want any of it to touch you."

"I know, Daddy. I understand. Now, anyway."

"Maybe we haven't done you any favors by not letting you see the darkness that lurks around the club. We wanted you to enjoy your childhood, be as normal as possible. It seems like we need to make a few changes when I get home."

"You leaving already?" I asked.

"No. Your grandpa convinced me to stick around a little longer. Besides, I can't very well take off until I know you're safe. Your man and the other Devil's Fury officers are trying to get info from the Devil's Boneyard. If all else fails, I'll have Bull call Scratch."

My family tree was a bit screwed up but having my dad and my grandpa in the same club was pretty awesome, and my grandpa's wife was the daughter to the VP of the Devil's Boneyard. Even though my grandpa's woman Darian was no blood relation to me,

Scratch had always been like another grandpa for us. The fact he hadn't told my dad or Bull anything yet worried me.

I had a feeling there was more to the story than any of us knew, and I didn't like it. Not only did I worry someone would come for me again, but it made me wonder if this hadn't been about me and something much bigger. Like club level big. But the question was whether or not they'd come for me because I'd spent time with the Devil's Fury or because I was the daughter and granddaughter of a Dixie Reaper.

I'd thought the man was just a junkie. Had I been wrong?

My dad led me to the kitchen and pulled out a chair. "Sit. Your grandpa will be here in a minute with some food. He ran to the diner where you work and said he'd bring something back for the three of us."

Work. Shit. "I don't know if I still work there or not. We haven't discussed whether or not Demon will let me work."

I tried really damn hard not to snarl at the thought of needing permission to have a job, but the smirk on my dad's face told me I hadn't succeeded. He reached over and patted my shoulder before sitting in the seat next to mine.

"You picked the Sergeant-at-Arms, Farrah. How much freedom does Tank give his woman and kids? He knows their every move, sends men out with them to keep them safe. Know why?" he asked.

"Because he's controlling like the rest of you?"

"No. Because he's the one who takes out the trash when the club has an issue. He sees the worst of it all and knows there's a big fucking target on him out of all of us. Demon is the same. He can't be relaxed about letting you run off to do whatever you want whenever you want because you will always be in danger. Anyone who wants to hurt him will do so through you." He leaned back in his seat. "If you wanted a safe, normal life, you should have hooked up with a tax accountant. Worst trouble they'll get into is either with the IRS or getting a papercut. No bad guys tossing you into trunks."

He had a point, but I'd always been attracted to what my mom called the bad boys. A few years ago, my dad had lost his shit when he'd discovered I was talking to one of the Prospects. Threatened to toss the guy out of the club. I liked the way men like Demon made me feel. And yeah, maybe the danger surrounding them was a turn-on too. Until it took me across state lines in a trunk with no air conditioning.

It didn't matter. I'd made my decision and I'd stick with it. If Demon wanted me, I was staying. I had no doubt we'd argue, but the hot makeup sex would be worth it. I put a hand over my belly and wondered if even now there was a tiny life growing inside me. I didn't feel the least bit prepared to be a mom, but it seemed my big, bad biker didn't want to use condoms anymore. I hadn't said a word last night when he'd taken me bare. Honestly, I'd enjoyed it.

"I love you, Daddy," I said. "I'm sorry I was such a pain growing up. I know I gave you and Mom a hard time."

"You're strong, Farrah. If you hadn't been so sassy and troublesome, I'd have worried this life would gobble you up and spit you out. Instead, I know you can handle being the old lady of the Devil's Fury Sergeant-at-Arms. Although, he'd better make it fucking official by the end of the week or your grandpa and I will stomp his ass into the ground."

I wasn't about to tell him Demon could probably

take on both of them and come out the victor. I loved my family, but my daddy and the Pres were starting to get up there in years. I'd honestly been waiting for the day Torch and my dad both stepped down. My grandpa was older than them, but he wasn't an officer for the club. With the exception of the Road Captain, Gears, all of them were in their fifties and sixties now. At the same time, I couldn't really picture anyone else as Pres or VP.

The front door opened and shut, and I heard the heavy tread of my grandpa's steps as he neared the kitchen. The smell of food made my stomach growl as he set down two bags from the diner. I eyed the smothered pork roast sandwich he set in front of my dad and knew Mom had no idea he was eating something so greasy. Grandpa had a chicken-fried steak, which wasn't any better, and he set meatloaf and mashed potatoes in front of me. Which still left another bag of food, and I knew damn well it had dessert in it.

"So, do Mom and Grandma Darian know the two of you are eating like this?" I asked.

"Nope," my grandpa said. "And if you tell them, you don't get the slice of cherry pie I got for you."

I dug into my lunch, knowing better than to argue. There was no doubt in my mind he'd follow through on his threat, and cherry pie was one of my weaknesses. Really, just about any dessert made my mouth water.

"How are Mariah and Dawson?" I asked.

"Your sister has decided since you aren't there to flirt with the Prospects, she's going to step up and fill your shoes," my dad said. "And Dawson learned how to change the oil on your mom's SUV last week."

I blinked and tried to process what he'd said. "Um, Dad. Dawson is like eight. Why is he changing the oil?"

"Because if we didn't show him how, he'd take apart any vehicle he found to see how they worked," my grandpa said. "It was self-preservation. He took the seat off my bike right after you left. We don't need anything else like that happening."

Someone banged on the front door, but my dad stood up, put his hand on my shoulder to keep me in my place and went to answer it. I wasn't sure who he thought would come to Demon's house unless they were permitted. I highly doubted I'd get snatched again, especially if I stayed inside the compound. I heard the sound of women's voices, then two ladies strolled into the room, each carrying a large shopping bag from the local grocery.

"I'm Grizzly's daughter, Lilian, and this is Elena. She's with Outlaw. Oh, and I'm with Dragon."

I eyed them both and gave a little wave. "I'm Farrah. My dad is the one who let you in, and this is my grandpa, Bull."

"We thought you could probably use some groceries," said Elena. "I doubt Demon has anything edible in the house. Unless you're into beer and pretzels."

"That was nice of the two of you," my dad said, retaking his seat.

I stood and took the bags from them before unloading everything onto the kitchen counter. Fresh vegetables and fruits, pasta, herbs and seasonings, fresh meat. The more items I pulled out, the more concerned I became because I'd never had much of a chance to cook and had no idea what to do with any of it.

"Thanks, I appreciate it," I said, giving them a smile

My grandpa laughed, but tried to cover it with a cough. I glared, but he only winked at me. He knew damn well I had no clue how to make anything from scratch or cook healthy crap. My dad looked rather amused as well.

"Laugh it up, you two," I said pointing at them.

"Something wrong?" asked Lilian.

"Um, no. It's just… I don't really know how to cook other than the basics. I'm sure I can find some recipes or something. It can't be too hard to follow the instructions, right?"

Elena hugged me. "We'll help. In fact, I bet we could have a cooking day once a week. Zoe, Rachel, and Adalia would join us. Even China!"

"China?" I asked, thinking it sounded more like a road name than someone's actual name. Although, it was rather cool.

"Meiling's mother. Blades always calls her China and it kind of stuck. Her real name is Xi-wang. You'll like her, but she's a little reserved around new people. Once she opens up to you, she's really sweet," Lilian said.

"We'll help you get everything put away before we leave. You should enjoy the time with your family while they're here," Elena said. "There will be plenty of opportunities for us to get to know one another better. You're not alone here, even if it might seem like it."

We put the groceries away while my dad and grandpa stuffed their faces. I hadn't expected help from them anyway. If it had been the three of us, they would have gotten up, but with two other ladies here they would give me a chance to make new friends. They'd always been like that.

Elena and Lilian each hugged me before seeing

themselves out, with a promise to stop by again soon. Once they were gone, I sat down to finish my food. After my dad and grandpa had stared at me in silence for at least ten minutes, I set my fork down and waited for whatever they felt they needed to say.

"You'll be fine here," my dad said. "But I'm not leaving until I know what the fuck is going on with your situation and see either a property patch on you or some ink. I'm sure things will be wrapped up within a few days."

My grandpa nodded. "I already called Darian this morning. She knows I'll be gone for a bit and wanted me to give you a hug from her."

"How's Mom?" I asked.

"Pissed as hell she's not here in the middle of everything, but I reminded her she needs to be there with Mariah and Dawson. I'm sure Rocky and Mara would let them stay over for a few days, but I'm not sure the Devil's Fury are ready for your mom to be here in mama-bear mode."

He wasn't wrong. I didn't know the guys here very well yet, but I wasn't sure how they'd handle my mom when she got all protective of her little chicks. I could easily see her pissing someone off. Possibly even Demon.

"The Devil's Fury may be your family by association," my grandpa said, "but we're blood. You're a Dixie Reapers legacy. If you weren't a girl, you'd have already been patched in. Toughest kid I know."

"You do realize that's sexist, right?" I asked. "I can't patch in just because I'm a girl? The Stone Age called, Grandpa. They asked when you're returning."

He swatted my arm. "Smart ass."

"Don't go giving your mom any ideas," my dad

said. "She'd have an all- women's MC up and running before any of us know what happened."

He made it sound like a horrible idea, but I rather liked it. I'd never ridden a motorcycle by myself. Not because I hadn't wanted to, but more because all the ones my dad and his brothers owned were too heavy for someone my size. I knew there were smaller Harleys, though, and I suddenly wanted one. I wondered how much of a fit Demon would have if I bought one.

One thing was for certain. I wouldn't be buying anything too pricey without his permission if I didn't have my own money. As much as I didn't care for working at the diner, I needed to do something to earn money. It made me wonder if there was anything I could do at home. Did the other old ladies work? Or did their men have them firmly under their thumbs too? I knew Lavender helped Wire whenever the club needed some hacking done, but I didn't know of any Reapers who let their women work.

It might be time to shake things up a little at the Devil's Fury.

Chapter Eight

Demon

I was getting tired of the Devil's Boneyard and the bullshit they were throwing our way. They fucking knew something. I didn't understand why they were hiding the information about Farrah's abduction. It was clear they knew the guy who'd taken her. What the fuck were they keeping from us and why?

"No offense, Scratch, but my woman is in danger and y'all are jerking us around. It's pissing me the fuck off," I said, earning a glare from Griz and Slash. Fuck them too.

"Your woman?" Scratch asked. "Since when is Farrah yours?"

"Since now."

Slash rubbed his beard. "Well, if you want to be technical and shit, you haven't said a damn thing about claiming her. You want a property patch for her, you need to do it the right way."

"Fuck you," I said. "Y'all practically forced Dingo to keep Meiling. While Griz wasn't too thrilled about Dragon knocking up Lilian, he didn't stand in the way of him claiming her. Everyone did their best to shove Adalia and Badger together. Why do I have to jump through hoops like a damn circus monkey?"

"Because she's the daughter of the Dixie Reapers VP," Slash said.

"Not to mention my daughter is her grandmother," Scratch said. "Far as I'm concerned, that kid is my family. What if I don't think Demon is what she needs?"

What. The. Fuck. "You do realize you aren't part of this club, or the Dixie Reapers, and therefore get no say in the matter, right?"

Grizzly pushed back from the table, as if putting

space between him and the phone would change anything. Even Slash threw up his hands. Hot Shot and Savage both looked away. I heard a growl through the phone and realized I'd pissed off the Devil's Boneyard VP, and everyone at the table had known it the moment the words had left my mouth.

"I'm not trying to step on toes, but Farrah is mine. If her dad is okay with it, I don't see what fucking business it is of yours or anyone else." At least, Venom had accepted the decision. I wasn't too sure he actually liked the thought of his daughter with me. Couldn't blame him. I'd done a lot of fucked-up shit in my life. "So yeah, I need a property patch for her. She's already moved into my house."

"Earl brought Farrah here for a reason," Scratch said. "He didn't realize the girl was related to me. All he knew was I have a man here who likes her. Thought he'd trade her for some drugs and get in our good graces."

Wait. What? "Who the fuck wants my woman?"

"Rooster. He won't be happy to hear Farrah is off-limits, but he's not going to tear shit up either. They've met a few times and he liked her spirit," Scratch said. "I'd hoped I could get Farrah here and everything would work itself out. It never occurred to me she'd be delivered by a junkie, or kidnapped."

"But you knew we were looking for her, knew I'd said she was mine," I said.

"Yeah well, what the fuck I hear and what actually happens are often two different things. What do you say, Griz? You accepting Demon's claim on Farrah?"

Grizzly paced the room a moment. "What I say is I'm getting too old for all this shit. If he wants her, and she's agreeable, I don't have a problem with it. But… I think I may seriously think of stepping down as President of the Devil's Fury. I want to spend time with my girls, give them a good life, and make sure they get the attention they need. I'm tired of getting bogged down in all this crap."

We stared at the Pres, not quite sure what to say. He'd said often enough he was getting old, but I knew Scratch, Cinder, and Torch were all around his age. While Cinder had decided to spend more time with his family and hand the reins over to Charming, I hadn't realized Grizzly was serious about doing the same.

"Who are you naming as your successor?" Scratch asked.

"Badger. He knows it's coming," Grizzly said. "We've talked a few times, but he always brushes me off. Time to step aside and let a younger generation take over."

Scratch sighed. "You're making me feel old, damn it. We're close to the same age, but I damn sure don't feel like I need to step down yet."

"Didn't say you have to," Grizzly said. "Honestly, if May were still here, I'd have handed everything over to Badger a few years ago. I knew Shella and Lilian were getting old enough to move out and sitting at home alone doesn't hold much appeal. Now I have two more adopted daughters to look after, and Meredith. There's plenty to keep me occupied."

"This is getting depressing as shit. Scratch, do I have anything to worry about with Farrah? If Earl only grabbed her…" No, something was still off. "How the fuck did Earl know to grab her? You said Rooster has a thing for her, but why would Earl know that?"

"Motherfucker," Scratch said. "Maybe I am getting too old for this shit. We have a rat. There's no other way anyone who wasn't part of this club would know about Rooster and Farrah."

"Where's Earl now?" I asked.

"Havoc worked him over, got what he thought we needed, then cut him loose."

"So he could be back up this way?" I asked.

"Possibly. You think he's going to come for Farrah again?" Scratch asked.

"I'm not sure. But I'm not letting her leave the compound without at least three brothers with her." I leaned back in my chair. "And I damn sure want to know how Earl knew to grab Farrah. He had to have watched her. Learned her routine. He's not stupid."

"In other words, not just a junkie looking for a fix," Slash said. "Faking it?"

I shrugged a shoulder. Without speaking to Earl, it was anyone's guess. If he was in the area, I wanted him picked up and brought here. It seemed we needed to have a discussion. If my fists accidentally connected with his face a few dozen times, I didn't think anyone would care.

"Anyone have a picture of this fucker?" I asked.

"I'll have Shade contact Outlaw," Scratch said. "I'm sure Wire will want in on this too. He's watched Farrah grow up."

"Get me something and I'll have eyes all over this fucking county watching for Earl. His ass is mine. No one hurts my woman and gets away with it."

"Oh, how the mighty have fallen," Slash said.

"Fuck you."

He grinned and flipped me off.

"Grizzly, you want to stay in the loop on this or do you want me to contact Badger when I call back?" Scratch asked. "How imminent is your retirement?"

"Call Badger. I won't officially hand everything over just yet, but I want him to take point on anything for the next few weeks. Get used to shouldering the responsibility of the club," the Pres said.

"Fair enough. I'll check back when I know something," said Scratch.

The line went dead and I eyed my brothers. I wasn't sure how I felt about Grizzly stepping down. I'd known it would happen eventually, but I'd thought he'd stick it out a while longer. What he said made sense, though. He loved those girls, and I knew he hated shit with the club pulling him away from them. He may not have his wife anymore, but he kept her memory alive by taking in stray teens, just like she'd done with Adalia.

"Need a property cut. Soon." I stood and walked out, not giving them a chance to argue. I stopped in the main part of the clubhouse and grabbed a cold beer. Venom and Bull were at my house visiting with Farrah. I wanted to give her as much time as I could with her family before I intruded.

I felt a hand slid up over my shoulder and down my chest. The sparkly purple nail polish told me enough. I gripped her hand, twisted slightly, and pulled her away from me.

"Not now, Ray."

The pretty blonde stuck her lip out in a pout and batted her eyelashes. Might work on some, but not me. She could play all the games she wanted. With someone else. Now that I had Farrah at home, I didn't want the likes of her or any other club whore.

"We always have fun," she said.

"I'm off the market. Besides, you know better than to touch me without permission, and I don't recall you asking."

"Off the…" Her lips pressed together and fury flashed in her eyes. "Who the fuck are you claiming? I didn't do all that shit with you only for you to toss me aside."

Fucking bitch. "Really? Because you didn't seem to mind any of it at the time."

"Who's the bitch who thinks she can come in here and take our men?" Ray demanded.

I towered over her, getting in her space. "One, none of us are *your* men. You're here for a purpose. Either do as you're told or get the fuck out. I don't have time for your shit and neither does anyone else here."

I could tell by the way she tossed her hair and sashayed off she wasn't nearly done. Sooner or later, she'd pull some stunt and I'd have to boot her from the club. Or worse, make an example of her. I thought I'd already handled this shit, made sure the damn club whores knew their place, but it seemed they needed another lesson.

Gator slid onto the stool next to mine. "Why is it when a guy finds himself a woman, suddenly everyone wants a piece of him? Maybe I should get fake engaged."

I snorted. "Yeah, because you never get laid."

Gator smiled and leaned his forearms on the bar top. A Prospect brought him a cold beer and replaced mine with a fresh one. I popped the top and took a swallow, studying the room around me. A few club whores were already here, despite the early hour, but it was mostly the younger patched members at the clubhouse tonight. Gator being the exception, but then the man was always up for a party if it involved women.

The clubhouse doors opened and Badger entered, not stopping to talk to anyone. He walked straight through to the back and into Church, where

Grizzly had remained behind. I wondered if the club would feel broadsided by Grizzly's decision. It also made me wonder how I'd feel when the time came for me to step down. Wasn't going to happen anytime soon, but it was sobering to realize I was no longer twenty with my entire life ahead of me. I didn't have one foot in the grave, unless I got shot or stabbed in a fatal spot, but I had to face the fact I was getting older.

"So you're claiming Venom's daughter?" Gator asked. "Wasn't even aware the two of you were seeing each other."

"More like it was supposed to be a one-night stand and ended up something else." I took a swallow of my beer. "Took her home with me before I knew who she was."

Gator's eyebrows lifted. "You don't take women home."

"Exactly."

He whistled. "Well, damn. I hope you plan on marking her as yours. I don't think her daddy will take it kindly if you plan to keep her without patching or inking her."

He wasn't wrong. The moment Venom showed up, I'd known I'd have to make things official between me and Farrah. Just hadn't been sure how it would go until she'd talked to me last night. I had no fucking clue how long it would take to have a property cut made. Seemed like the others had gotten theirs pretty quick. While several clubs did ink their women, I didn't think Farrah would agree to being branded in a more permanent way. Not after everything she'd said.

"Why are you still here?" Gator asked. "Shouldn't you be home with your woman?"

"Giving her time with her family. They'll leave before too long. Not sure when she'll see them again."

Gator nodded. He opened his mouth to say something, then shut it and pushed his stool back a bit. My nape prickled and I whirled to see what or who was behind me. Ray practically wrapped herself around me, planted a wet kiss on my cheek and neck before I could pry her off, and raked her nails down my upper back. The burn told me she'd left a mark. Fucking bitch!

I shoved her off, not caring if she fell.

"What the fuck, Ray? You were Goddamned warned about this shit!"

"You don't belong with some bitch from another club," she said. "I've been here, given you anything you've asked for."

"What makes you think I'd ever make a whore my old lady?" I asked. "Know what you are? A place for someone to put their dick. Lots of someones. Anyone in this fucking club wearing a patch, and any visitors we may get. That's what you are and nothing more."

Her face flushed, her eyes flashed, and she fisted her hands. "So I give the club what they want and it makes me a whore?"

"You knew what you signed up for. No one ever gave you fucking hope you'd be something else," I said.

The doors to the clubhouse opened again. Farrah stepped inside with Venom and Bull on her heels. Fuck my life.

Her gaze went to where Ray had kissed me, and I knew then and there the bitch had left a lip print. She looked from me to the club whore, her gaze narrowed. Her dad and grandpa hung back, both alert and ready for anything. There was no doubt they had Farrah's back.

"Farrah, meet Ray. She's a club whore," I said.

My woman looked Ray over from head to toe. "Wouldn't have thought she was anything else, not dressed like that and reeking of desperation."

Ray gasped and swung at Farrah. I tensed, ready to handle the situation, but Farrah ducked the blow and came back with an upper cut to Ray's chin. The whore's eyes went wide as she fell to the floor, but Farrah wasn't finished. She kicked the bitch in the ribs, dropped to one knee and punched her in the tits before going for the woman's face again.

Ray screeched and flailed, trying to get away. Venom and Bull snickered, letting Farrah handle things herself. As the Sergeant-at-Arms, I should step in, but it was a big fucking turn-on to see my woman beat the shit out of a club whore. I grinned as Farrah whaled on Ray.

"What the fuck is going on out here?" Badger demanded as he came up beside me.

"My woman took exception to Ray trying to make a claim on me," I said.

"And you're just going to let her beat on the woman?" Badger asked.

I shrugged. "Figure she's earned it. What do you think will make a bigger impression? Me dragging Ray out of here and branding her, or letting Farrah handle her shit?"

"Good point," Badger said and winced as Farrah knocked out one of Ray's teeth. "But if she kills the bitch, I'm not helping you dig a hole."

I flipped him off because the fucker knew damn well I wouldn't bury the bitch in a six-foot hole. Not just one hole anyway. No fucking way I'd ever make it that easy to find or identify a body. Only amateurs did something that damn stupid.

Farrah stood up, her chest heaving as she shook out her hand. She looked over at me. A soft growl slipped past her lips as she marched by me and grabbed a handful of napkins. She scrubbed at my cheek and neck.

"Want me to drag the bitch out of here?" I asked.

"No. Make her crawl her way out of here," Farrah said. "But she better not come the fuck back here again. I won't be so nice next time."

I glanced down at Ray. Both eyes were blackened and swelling shut, her lip was split and bleeding, she'd lost at least one tooth, her nose was bleeding, and she was favoring her ribs. If this was Farrah's version of nice, I didn't want to see what sort of damage she'd do if she got well and truly pissed.

"Did you just issue an order?" Badger asked, his tone soft and deceptively calm.

Farrah folded her arms around herself. "No. Just stating a fact. If I see her again, I'll finish what I started. Unless Demon wanted her attention?"

I shook my head. "I'd already shoved her off once before she pulled this shit."

"Then if she touches him again, all bets are off," Farrah said. "Or do you take the side of club whores here over old ladies? Say so now, because if that's the case, I'm out of here."

Badger looked from her to me. "Old lady?"

"Griz didn't fill you in?" I asked.

"Didn't mention you claiming anyone," Badger said. "I'll get a property cut ordered. Welcome to the family, Farrah."

She moved in closer and leaned against me. I wrapped my arms around her, holding her against my chest. The slight tremor told me she was either still high on adrenaline and about to crash, or she'd been more upset than I'd realized. Deciding not to wait and see if she fell apart, I led her outside.

I spotted her truck near the steps and helped her into the driver's seat. Venom's bike, and Bull's, were both parked next to her. Since they hadn't come outside with us, I figured they were staying for a drink, or to speak with the Pres. I hoped they were done visiting with Farrah for the day. As much as I knew she'd miss them, I was ready to have her to myself for the night.

I pressed a hard kiss to her lips, then shut her door before walking down to my bike. My phone jingled with a text and I checked it quickly. Damn. I'd forgotten what I'd promised Kraken.

Any news for me about MaryAnne? Can't wait any longer.

I felt like an ass for leaving him hanging, especially while that poor girl suffered. *I'm tied up. My woman got kidnapped.*

Didn't take Kraken long to answer with a thumbs-up emoji. I hated fucking emojis. What were we? Twelve? Why the fuck couldn't grown-ass men just use words?

I glanced down the road, but Farrah was too far ahead for me to see her. I backed out and pulled on the road that wound through the compound. I revved the engine to catch up to her, coasting into the driveway alongside her truck before she'd had a chance to shut off the engine. Had to admit she looked pretty damn cute in the big-ass truck.

She hopped down as I turned off the bike and got off. It seemed the energy had drained from her and she looked damn tired. She'd only taken two steps before I swept her up into my arms and carried her inside. I kicked the door shut and went to the living room, sinking down onto the sofa with her on my lap.

"It was hot as fuck watching you handle the bitch at the clubhouse," I said. "You okay? Hurt your hand?"

"I'm fine, Demon. Just tired."

I tapped her nose. "We're alone at home."

She smiled slightly. "Cody. I'm sorry. I think I'm a little overwhelmed. I met more of the old ladies today. They brought some groceries over."

"You'll like them once you get to know everyone." I ran my hand up and down her arm. "Did your dad say how long he's staying?"

"Until he knows why I was taken. And he wanted to make sure you weren't planning to keep me without making it official. Since you've cleared that up now, he'll just hang out until he knows more about the man who grabbed me."

I knew a bit more than I had this morning, but still felt like something was off. It was possible I was overthinking shit. Since it was Farrah involved, I could admit I might not be seeing things as clearly as I normally would.

Same could be said for Venom and Bull. Still, my gut said Earl wasn't just a junkie who bought from the Devil's Boneyard. He'd been in this area for a reason, nowhere near the Devil's Boneyard.

Why go to them when he could just come here for some drugs?

Farrah rested her head on my shoulder and I decided to let it go for now. Sooner or later, the truth would come out. I only hoped she wasn't in danger still.

Chapter Nine

Farrah

I'd never been the overly emotional type. Angry, perhaps. But not the type of woman who wanted to cry when she became stressed or tired. I felt out of sorts. It had been two weeks since I'd been kidnapped, and no one seemed to know anything. Seemed like a good enough reason to not feel like myself, but I needed someone to talk to. I didn't know what my dad had told my mom, so I didn't dare call and talk to her. The last thing I wanted was to cause trouble between them, and if I said something to contradict whatever Daddy had been saying, all hell would break loose.

My sister was also out. She had a big mouth and couldn't keep anything to herself. I had a few friends. I wouldn't consider them the sort I'd share secrets with, which meant I had no one. Unless I opened up to the Devil's Fury old ladies. I didn't know them. Even though a few had introduced themselves, I had no idea if I could trust them not to run blabbing to Demon.

I scrubbed the kitchen counter for probably the twentieth time and threw the sponge into the sink. There wasn't a single spot in the house I hadn't cleaned. Demon was off on club business. My dad and grandpa were still hanging around, but they were apparently too busy to be here today. With them, and Demon, MIA I had to wonder if something had come up pertaining to my kidnapping. Had they found out something new?

I'd peeked out the front window earlier and noticed a Prospect lurking outside. Every time Demon left the house, he made sure someone was nearby in case I needed anything. At least, he'd said that was the reason. Now I had to wonder if maybe he was concerned for my safety instead? Surely he didn't think

I was in danger in his house? I knew things had gone badly not too long ago with the Hades Abyss MC and the gates to their compound had been blown off, from what I'd overheard, but it didn't seem to be the norm. I couldn't remember too much trouble when I was growing up. Then again, my dad was good at hiding stuff from the kids, so it was possible trouble had come knocking plenty of times and I'd just never been aware of it.

A knock sounded at the front door and I hurried to answer. I knew the Prospect out front wouldn't let anyone past who wasn't permitted in Demon's house. I threw open the door and blinked at the man on the steps. We hadn't met before, but he had on a Devil's Fury cut. *Stitches* was on the front.

"Demon asked me to stop by and make sure you were okay," the man said.

"Why wouldn't I be?" I asked.

"He said you were a little, um…" The man rocked back on his heels. "Snippy?"

In other words, he'd said I was being a bitch. I should have been offended, except he was right. I *was* being bitchy and I didn't even know why. I stepped back, letting Stitches into the house. It was only then I noticed a bag clutched in his hand.

"What's that?" I asked.

"A few medical supplies. I was a medic in the Army and I'm a licensed EMT." He set the bag down. "I only brought it as a precaution. Demon said you'd seemed off and it concerned him."

"I'm fine. I think it's been a stressful few weeks and maybe it's getting to me."

"Mind answering a few questions?" Stitches asked.

"I guess that's okay," I said.

"Have you been running a fever?"

"No, I don't think so."

"Any aches anywhere?" he asked.

"No. I feel a little off, but not like I'm sick."

He cleared his throat and glanced away for a moment. "My next question might embarrass you a little."

"Do you honestly think I've been in Demon's house for weeks and we haven't had sex?" I asked.

He nearly choked trying to hold back his laughter. "Wasn't my question but it does lead up to it nicely. When did you last have your period?"

My brow furrowed as I thought about it and realized I had no idea. I did try to keep track using the calendar on my phone. I pulled it from my pocket and opened the app, then scrolled back a month.

"About five weeks ago." Five. Weeks. More than a month. Three weeks before I'd slept with Demon the first time. Shit. I looked at Stitches and realized he was pulling something from his bag. When he handed me two pregnancy tests, I bit my lip and contemplated what this meant for me.

"Go take both," he said. "We'll figure things out after you get the results. Only takes a few minutes."

I gripped the two boxes and carried them to the hall bathroom. When I shut the door, I twisted the lock. I didn't think Stitches would come barging in, but the idea of me being pregnant had me rattled. I read the instructions and took both tests, setting the little sticks on the bathroom counter while I washed my hands. I noticed they were shaking and it felt like my heart was racing.

Secretly, I hoped they were negative. I didn't know a damn thing about being a mother. Honestly, I didn't know if I wanted to be one. Not right this moment. Someday I'd wanted to be a wife and mother, have children under foot. I'd thought I had my entire life ahead of me. Time to have fun, see the world a bit. Things were changing too fast. I watched in horror as one of them flashed a plus sign and the other showed two lines. Both were positive. I staggered back and hit the wall, sliding down it to the floor.

The doorknob rattled and Stitches yelled at me through it, but I couldn't make out what he said over the buzzing in my ears. Pregnant. Me. I was going to have a baby. Maybe it shouldn't be so surprising, but… I gasped, trying to draw in air. It felt like my lungs were starving and spots swirled across my vision. A loud crack sounded right before Stitches came tumbling into the room, the door broken.

"Farrah! What's wrong?" He knelt next to me, taking my pulse.

"P-pregnant." I sucked in more air. "Can't breathe."

"Come on. Let's get you up and out of this room." He lifted me to my feet, put his arm around my shoulders, and led me back to the living room. He eased me down onto the couch and walked off only to return with a bottle of water. "Sip this."

"I can't be pregnant. I can't." I shook my head feeling like my world was unraveling. "I don't know how to do this."

He reached out and squeezed my shoulder. "Want me to call Demon? Or your dad?"

Oh, shit. My dad. My chest started to hurt and I rubbed it absently. "Not Daddy. Not Demon."

"Then I'm calling Bull." He moved away and pulled out his phone. I heard the low murmur of his voice, but I couldn't focus on what he was saying. "Your grandpa will be here in a minute. Just stay calm,

Farrah."

Calm. Right. A little human was growing inside me, someone I'd be responsible for the next eighteen years, and he wanted me to be... calm. Sure. Piece of cake. It wasn't like my entire life hadn't been turned upside down. I was still adjusting to being Demon's old lady. Now I had to figure out how to be a mom.

I heard the tread of my grandpa's boots, then his arms were around me. As his scent surrounded me, I felt myself relaxing a little at a time. Finally, I felt like I could breathe. The panic had abated a tiny bit.

"So, it wasn't enough I became a dad for a second time after becoming a grandpa, now you're making me a great-grandpa?" he asked.

"Could be worse. Darian could be pregnant too," I mumbled.

"Don't even go there. Owen and Isadora are more than enough. Besides, the last time Darian was sick, I got snipped. She was so out of it, she never noticed," my grandpa said.

I started laughing. I couldn't help it. "You're in your sixties now and you got snipped?"

Stitches coughed and fought back a smile. "Men have been known to father babies into their eighties. As long as his woman hasn't gone through the change, there's no reason she couldn't get pregnant still."

It was a sobering thought. If Demon knocked me up this easily, and I wasn't even twenty, how many kids would we have over the next two or more decades if he didn't get fixed? I knew birth control wasn't a guarantee. I didn't know if I could handle one kid, much less several. I had a hard time picturing Demon as a father. Did he even like kids? We hadn't discussed having children together. I knew it was bound to happen sooner or later, since the man didn't seem to like condoms, but I hadn't thought I'd get pregnant right away either.

"Try not to stress too much," Stitches said. "You'll also need some prenatal vitamins. They have some you can get over the counter, but whenever you see an OB-GYN, it's possible they'll put you on prescription ones. They're stronger and work better."

"I don't know how to be a mother," I said.

"Sure you do," my grandpa said. "You've had a lot of good examples back home. Your mom, Darian, Isabella, and all the other Dixie Reaper old ladies. I know you feel overwhelmed, but you've got this, Farrah. You're not a quitter, or weak. You helped make that baby and you're damn sure going to do your best by him or her."

I knew it wasn't a suggestion but a decree. My family wouldn't let me do anything less. It wasn't like I could undo the pregnancy. My grandpa was right. Demon and I had made a baby together, and I had a responsibility to the child. Once I calmed and had a chance to adjust to the idea, I knew I'd love the little one growing inside me. I'd been excited both times my mom had been pregnant. I remembered the way she'd smile and rub a hand over her belly.

"I have to tell Demon," Stitches said. "He wanted to know what was going on with you. It's not something I can hide from him."

Part of me wanted to be the one to tell him, but another part thought he might take the news better from someone else. After everything we'd been through, I wasn't sure if he really wanted a kid with me or not. Yes, the condom had broken and he'd said he was going to get me pregnant on purpose, but… what if he'd changed his mind? Condoms broke all the time. What if his desire to get me pregnant had only been in the heat of the moment and he'd now be angry over my current condition?

My grandpa gave my hand a squeeze. "It's going to be fine, Farrah. Demon's not a bad sort. He officially claimed you. Surely you realized kids would eventually be part of the equation."

"I guess I didn't think about it being this soon. We haven't really talked about it. He brought it up once, but it wasn't the type of conversation where we decided when we wanted them or how many. More of a…" I clamped my lips shut. The last thing I wanted to tell my grandpa was Demon demanded I'd had to stay put in case I'd gotten pregnant after our one-night stand. Not to mention, he hadn't used a condom since the first night.

"More of a what?" my grandpa asked, his body going tight.

"Nothing."

He tipped up my chin and stared me down. "Farrah, did he do something he shouldn't have?"

"I didn't exactly say no, Grandpa. Things just escalated and he said there was a chance I could be pregnant. He wasn't going to let me leave until he knew for sure."

My grandpa growled and stormed off, the front door slamming into the wall as he left the house. My heart pounded and I took a step, then another. Soon I was running to my truck. I threw myself into the driver's seat and peeled out of the driveway. I saw my grandpa's bike ahead and pressed the accelerator a little harder, wanting to catch him before he could say anything, or worse, do something he shouldn't.

He beat me to the clubhouse and was already inside before I could even park my truck. I ran inside, scanning the interior, but I didn't see Demon or my family. Raised voices from the back caught my attention and I headed toward them. One of the Devil's Fury men stepped in my path, arms spread so I wouldn't get past him.

"Easy, Farrah. You know you aren't permitted in Church."

My gaze landed on his cut. *Colorado.* "I said something I shouldn't have. You don't understand. I need to get in there and defuse the bomb."

His eyebrows lifted. "Bomb?"

"My grandpa. He's going to destroy Demon if I don't get in there."

Colorado laughed. "Sweetheart, I'm more concerned Demon won't hold back enough not to hurt Bull and Venom."

If he'd meant to reassure me, he'd said the wrong thing. I nailed him in the nuts with my knee and darted around him, then ran full tilt toward the doors at the end of the hall. I heard him groan and knew I'd pay for it later, but I needed to make sure my family was safe. I slammed the doors open and stood panting inside Church. The men all stopped to stare at me, Demon's eyebrows both lifting nearly to his hairline.

"What the fuck, Farrah?" my dad demanded. "Since when do you *ever*, and I mean fucking-ever enter Church?"

"I need to…" I panted for breath. "Grandpa, it wasn't as it sounded."

"What the hell is going on?" Demon asked.

"I was talking to my grandpa and I think he misunderstood something I said. He got mad and came here. I didn't want anyone getting hurt." I pressed a hand to my chest, then covered my mouth. My stomach rolled and flipped. With a squeak, I frantically searched the room. My grandpa handed me a trashcan

-- thankfully empty -- and I threw up.

"Fucking hell," Demon muttered. "Stitches was supposed to come check on you. Do you have the flu?"

I shook my head and closed my eyes, hoping I wasn't about to embarrass myself further. When I didn't think I'd be sick again, I held Demon's gaze. "No flu."

"You knocked her up," my grandpa said.

Demon rocked back on his heels. "You're pissed because I got her pregnant?"

"I'm pissed because you had a one-night stand with my granddaughter, then told her she couldn't leave until you knew she wasn't pregnant. Which makes me think you either weren't too damn careful, or the condom broke. Either way, you had no damn right to tell her she couldn't leave."

My dad ran a hand over his hair and took a step back. The quick flash of a smile told me more than I'd ever wanted to know. It seemed Demon was more like my dad than I'd realized.

Demon came closer, his steps slow and steady. When he reached me, he slid his hand around my side to the middle of my back and tugged me against his chest. He held me, then lowered his head, his lips near my ear. "Pregnant?"

I nodded. My stomach started to knot, worry eating at me. Would he be angry about it? Or did he want to be a dad right now? Being strangers had been great for a one-night stand, but not so much when I would now be spending the rest of my life with him. We really needed to talk more and fuck less. It didn't help I couldn't keep my hands off him, or vice versa. And since neither of us seemed to think about protection whenever we were in the bedroom...

"I'm sorry for barging in," I said.

"We'll talk about it later."

The doors opened behind me and I heard a growl. I clenched my eyes shut and pressed closer to Demon. I had no doubt Colorado had caught up to me, and I knew he'd be pissed as hell. I nearly winced. I'd known exactly how and where to hit to cause the most damage. Tank had made sure I knew how to escape any unwanted attention, and so had my dad. Moment of truth. What would Demon do when he found out what I'd done to his brother?

"That little bitch kneed me in the nuts," Colorado said.

"What were you doing at the time?" Grizzly asked.

"Tried to keep her out of here. Women aren't allowed in Church. Told her so."

"You let my tiny-ass woman not only get past you, but she took you out in the process?" Demon asked. "And you want us to what? Punish her?"

"Yes." I heard him shuffle closer. "Not even sure my dick still works."

I felt the presence of my dad and grandpa, and the heat of their bodies as they came closer. My grandpa ran his hand down my hair, and the scent of my dad's cologne teased my nose. I had no doubt if Demon said he was going to punish me, both of them would have something to say about it.

Demon tightened his hold on me. "She's pregnant, asshole."

"You branded a damn club whore, not to mention the other shit you've done in the past. Because she's pregnant she gets away with hurting one of your brothers? I'm a patched member of this damn club," Colorado said.

I lifted my head and looked over at him. "I'm

sorry I hurt you. I was scared and when you said Demon was going to hurt my grandpa and dad, it didn't make things any better. I needed to see they were okay."

Demon set me aside and advanced on Colorado. "You told my woman I was going to beat on her family? What the fuck is wrong with you?"

"Why don't we just consider this all a big mix-up?" another man asked.

I read his cut. *Badger*. I'd met him before, but it had been so long ago I hadn't placed him right away. I knew he'd claimed Grizzly's oldest daughter.

"A mix-up?" Colorado muttered.

Badger nodded. "Yep. A mix-up. Otherwise, I have to assume you're too weak to not let a woman get the drop on you. Not sure how the club would feel about it."

Colorado audibly swallowed and took a step back. "Right. Yeah, it was a mix-up."

"I really am sorry," I said. "I never meant to hurt you."

He gave a jerky nod and left. A quick glance at Demon didn't reassure me in the least. His gaze was dark as he stared me down, and I worried what he'd say or do when he got home. I'd known better than to come in here, and to knee Colorado in the nuts, but I'd done both anyway. Looked like I'd have to pay the price, despite what he'd told Colorado.

"Go home, Farrah. We'll talk when I get there," he said.

I bit my lip and gave a quick nod. Without looking at anyone, I hurried from the room and went back to my truck. I drove slower going home and parked in the driveway. When I got inside, I paced a moment, trying to figure out something I could do to sweeten Demon a little when he got home. Besides getting naked. While I knew it would work, I wasn't the least bit interested in sex right now.

I rummaged through the kitchen cabinets and pulled out a cake mix and can of frosting. It wouldn't be gourmet, but men liked dessert, right? I preheated the oven and took some eggs from the fridge and got the vegetable oil out of the pantry. I mixed the cake batter and set it aside so I could pull out a baking pan. After I greased it so the cake wouldn't stick, I poured in the batter and placed it in the oven, setting the timer.

I took my time cleaning the kitchen. When the timer beeped, I removed the cake and set it aside to cool. I didn't know when Demon would come home, but I hoped I had time to take a shower and change my clothes. I'd run out the door earlier in my holey jeans and a ratty T-shirt. With my luck, I'd embarrassed him not only by barging into Church, but because of how I'd looked.

I let the water get nice and hot while I stripped off my clothes. I shoved them into the hamper and climbed under the spray, closing the glass door behind me. The heat beat down on me, easing muscles I hadn't even realized were tense. I shampooed and conditioned my hair, then scrubbed my body. I made sure to shave and used my shower oil to moisturize afterward. Even though I knew I should get out, I wasn't quite ready yet. I pressed my forehead to the tiled wall and let the water hit my shoulders and back.

"Cake on the counter and naked woman in my shower," Demon said.

I slowly turned to face him, not having heard him come home. His gaze traveled over me as he shrugged off his cut, then toed off his boots. He reached behind him and gripped the collar of his shirt, yanking it over his head. I didn't know why men looked so damn sexy doing that, but they did. I'd end up getting stuck if I tried it. He finished undressing and got into the shower, crowding me against the wall.

"I could get used to coming home to this." He skimmed his hands down my sides and settled them on my hips. "So fucking beautiful."

"I'm sorry about earlier."

He quieted me with a kiss. Slow. Soft. Completely unlike Demon. It almost worried me. Then he pressed his hand to my belly and I understood, or thought I did. The tenderness wasn't for me, necessarily, but because I carried his child.

"Stitches stopped by the clubhouse. Said you'd be overly emotional and I needed to make sure you didn't get too upset. You knew better than to come into Church, and if Colorado had pressed things, I wouldn't have had much choice but to discipline you for hurting him. Thankfully, Badger turned the tables on him."

"My grandpa got so mad. I didn't know if he'd attack you. I tried to explain to Colorado, but he laughed and said you'd be more likely to hurt my grandpa and dad. I can't explain what I was thinking or feeling, but I had to get in there and make sure none of you were hurting each other."

He tucked my hair behind my ear. "Everything's fine, Farrah. I'd have understood if Bull felt the need to take a swing, same way I let your dad hit me."

"I know I need to trust you, and I do. I guess I feel like despite everything, we really don't know one another. We're still strangers for the most part. Everything with us is happening so fast. I feel like I'm spinning and I..." I pressed my forehead to his chest. "No one has ever made me feel the way you do. The chemistry between us is insane, and so damn intense. I want to know you better, Cody. The real you, not the version you show everyone else, but I'm worried you'll never let me get that close."

He was quiet, just stroking his hand up and down my side. I worried I'd said too much, but when he finally spoke, some of the tension eased from me.

"You're right about us being strangers, and about me not letting too many people get close. The club knows more about me than anyone else, but there are some things I keep to myself. I'll try to let you in, Farrah. I'm not letting you go, and I damn sure don't want you to be miserable. We'll figure it out, even if it means we both make mistakes along the way."

"Why were you gone so long? Or is it club business and you can't say?" I asked.

"Partly club business. Some of it was trying to figure out the shit swirling around you, except I'm not sure if it's you or me who's the real target in all this. Were you taken for being tied to the Reapers and Boneyard crews? Or because of me? Scratch seems to think Earl snatched you as a way to appease someone in his club."

I lifted my head and looked up at him. "What? Who?"

"It seems Rooster mentioned he liked you. How the fuck Earl would know about it, or who the hell you are for that matter, is something I'm trying to figure out. I don't like any of this, and until I know more, I want you to stay behind the gates."

I didn't like it, but I understood. The last thing I wanted was to be tossed into another trunk or have something even worse happen to me. Especially since I now had a baby growing inside me. The panic I'd felt when I saw the positive tests had abated a little.

Knowing Demon wasn't upset had helped. I'd always wanted children, even if I hadn't thought they'd come until I was older. I just hadn't wanted them this soon in my life. I'd thought I'd have more time to explore, learn new things, and maybe see the world a little.

"As much as I want to fuck you right now, I think it might complicate things at the moment," he said. "The reason we don't know much about each other is because I'm balls-deep inside you every chance I get. So, let's finish showering, go get a slice of that cake you made, and have a conversation."

I opened and shut my mouth, staring up at him. Was he serious?

He kissed me, a quick hard brush of his lips against mine, then he backed away. Yeah, it seemed he'd meant every word. I wasn't sure what to make of this version of Demon. How many different sides did he have?

Chapter Ten

Demon

I'd given up sex for cake and talking. Jesus. If my brothers had heard that shit come out of my mouth, they'd ask what size panties I needed. With any other woman, I wouldn't have given a fuck. But Farrah wasn't anyone -- she was *my* woman. If she needed to talk, I'd make the sacrifice. I fucking hated talking about myself, even if she'd been right. We didn't know a damn thing about one another other than the basics.

It wasn't just me anymore. I'd have to make changes and be willing to compromise on occasion. I'd let her win some battles along the way. When it counted, I'd hold my ground. Being an asshole to the club whores was one thing. I didn't want Farrah to hate being here, or regret being mine. There were two clubs who would take her in if she decided to leave. Hell, probably more than two.

She'd had to frost the cake when we got to the kitchen. I'd taken a seat at the table, watching her. I couldn't remember the last time I'd had a woman in my home, before Farrah anyway. There'd been one or two women I dated seriously when I'd been younger, but no one in a while. She'd been here several weeks and I liked having her around. One night had always been enough in the past. I should have known the moment I wanted to bring her here, keep her overnight, she'd be different from all the others.

Seeing Badger, Dingo, Outlaw, Dragon, Dagger, Guardian, and Steel all settle down had made me realize my life was pretty fucking lonely. Yeah, I had my club, but when I came home at night, it was only me here. Or had been until now. It hadn't escaped my notice she'd added a few touches to the house. I now had some sort of decorative pillows on my couch, a colorful rug on the floor, pictures on the wall.

I hadn't told her, but I liked what she'd done with the place. Even in here she'd made changes. Lace curtains hung at the window. A bit too girly for me, but it made the place feel like a home and not a bachelor pad. She'd even bought new bedding for our room, steering clear of flowers and shit. The blues and greens weren't bad, and I had adjusted to the bold contemporary design on the comforter.

She cut two slices of the cake and pulled a bottle of water from the fridge as well as a soda. Farrah gave me the larger piece and the soda before sitting in the chair next to mine. She cast me a shy smile before taking a bite.

"You feeling more like this place is home with all the changes you made?" I asked.

She froze. "I'm sorry I didn't ask first."

I waved off her concern. "Not what I meant, baby. I don't mind you adding your own touch to the place. Everything looks nice. And don't think I didn't notice you used my bank account to pay for it. Every penny you spend, I get a notification from my bank. I didn't add it to keep tabs on you, but so I'd know if anyone fucked with my accounts. But it means you can't spend money in secret. I'll always know."

Her cheeks flushed, but she didn't deny it. She took another bite of cake, licking the frosting off her lips. "I would have covered it, but since I couldn't work I didn't have any money to spare."

"With a baby coming, I don't think you'll have much time to work. The other ladies here have enough to do without watching our kid too. You're a mom now, Farrah. Your life is changing, and I know it wasn't what you'd planned, but you've got to go with the flow."

"You mean go along with *your* flow."

I smirked but didn't answer. I didn't have to. She already knew what I'd say. Same thing her dad and grandpa would likely have said to their women if they'd made such a remark.

"We need a nursery," she said.

"You pick a room and a color. I'll get it painted. Can't leave to go buy shit until I know you're not in danger, but we can look at some things online. You either get something local a Prospect can pick up, or we can have it delivered. When all this is over, you can go to as many baby stores as you want."

"I'm starting to wonder if we'll ever figure out what's going on."

I'd had the same thought more than once. I had Outlaw, Wire, and the other hackers Outlaw knew checking into things, and I hoped to have an answer any day. It was shitty to go behind Scratch's back when all this seemed to involve the Devil's Boneyard too, but if he had Farrah's safety as a priority, it wasn't showing. I couldn't risk anything else happening to her, and not only because she carried my child. I'd grown rather fond of her. My house finally felt like more than four walls and I knew it was all due to her.

"You wanted to talk. Said we don't know enough about one another. So ask your questions. I'll answer what I can," I said.

She nodded and seemed to think it over a moment. "Do you have any family outside the club? Anyone who's still alive?"

"Not that I know of. My parents are long gone. Good riddance when it comes to my father. The man was no prize. Never knew my grandparents. I don't remember any siblings growing up, unless either of my parents had affairs that resulted in kids who didn't live with us. As much as they hated one another, anything is possible." I shrugged a shoulder. "Only have the club. And now you and our kid."

"You already know my family," she said. "Or at least on my dad's side. All he has is the club. If I have any family on Mom's side, other than my grandpa, I don't know anything about them. She said her mom was dead."

I wondered why they'd kept her in the dark. I remembered the rumors circulating through the various clubs when Venom took out Ridley's mom and stepdad. I also knew Ridley had a half-brother, even if I didn't know what ever happened to him. It was curious no one had kept up with the kid. Shouldn't he have met his nieces and nephew at some point?

"What else do you want to know?" I asked.

"Well, I'm pretty sure your favorite drink is beer and your favorite food is hamburgers, because you consume a lot of both. Any other favorite things I should know about?" she asked.

I snorted. "While I am partial to beer, hamburgers aren't my favorite food. It's steak. I like listening to classic rock, don't care much for wearing bright colors, and I like to watch *Die Hard* at Christmas."

Saying I didn't like wearing colors was an understatement. Nearly every shirt in my closet was black, gray, or navy. I did have a dark green and a maroon in there, but they'd been gifts from the old ladies. Apparently, the somber colors made me less approachable, which worked in my favor as the Sergeant-at-Arms.

"What about you?" I asked, feeling like I should want to know the same things about her. As long as she was honest, faithful, and we got along, I didn't really need to know anything else. But women were different from men, and the last thing I needed was her going off about me being an insensitive asshole. I'd heard it often enough over the years. The difference was this time the woman lived under my roof and I couldn't kick her ass to the curb.

"My favorite drink is sweet tea. I'm partial to cherry pie. I love blues and greens the most, and I don't really have a favorite movie but Lavender did get me hooked on *Dark Crystal* and *Labyrinth*. I'll listen to just about any music except modern rap." She finished her cake and pushed her plate away. "I also know how to change the oil in my truck, maintain my tire pressure, can change a tire, and while I haven't had to personally do it yet, I do know how to change the brakes on my truck too."

"Impressive. I'm not sure the other old ladies around here have the first clue what to do with a car other than put gas in it and drive."

"Doesn't sound very fair of you. Maybe they know more than you think," she said.

It was possible, but doubtful. My brothers had a type. Damsel in distress with an inner strength that usually surprised everyone. But their strength was subtle, not at all like my woman. For me, I liked the fact Farrah was a fighter. If she'd been a complete pushover, or too docile, I'd have been bored. Instead, I never knew what she'd say or do next. Might cause a few issues with the club here and there, like her kneeing Colorado in the nuts, but all in all, I'd rather have feisty over demure any day.

Knowing she wouldn't be helpless if she broke down on the side of the road was a bit of a relief. Didn't mean I wouldn't put extra precautions in place. Farrah had quickly become high on my list of priorities, as well as the kid growing inside her. My club still did and always would come first, but I also knew she'd understand, having grown up in this world.

"That it? Talk's over?" I asked as quiet descended over us.

"Guess I'm not too good at all the girly shit," she said. "I'm more tomboy according to my family."

"Nothing wrong with being a tomboy." I much preferred Farrah in her T-shirts and jeans than the skintight outfit she'd worn the night we met. She'd been sexy as fuck, but the more I got to know her, the more I liked her in a more natural state.

"If you'd seen me as a kid, you wouldn't utter those words. I climbed trees, even dive-bombed Tank one time. I've had broken bones, knocked out a tooth more than once, gotten black eyes. I think my mother despaired of me ever acting like a girl. Then I discovered I liked boys and I'm almost certain she and my dad were wishing I'd go back to climbing trees instead of wanting to climb the Prospects."

I rubbed the back of my neck, not liking the idea of her *climbing* anyone but me. Stupid, since I knew she'd been a virgin when I took her, so I was the only man she'd ever been with. Didn't mean I liked the thought of her checking out anyone else. I knew damn well if I voiced my opinion she'd call me a caveman, or worse. Heard it plenty of times before.

"I expect faithfulness from you, Farrah, not just in our relationship but to this club as well. You're my old lady, and I know you understand what it means. I won't treat you like a kid who needs to be led around. You handled yourself just fine with the club whore. Should probably not knee any other brothers in the nuts like you did to poor Colorado. That being said, I don't want you letting anyone push you around. You're mine and not some club whore they can fuck with. Understand me?"

She nodded. "Right. Tough, but hold back with the brothers in your club. Club whores are fair game."

I couldn't help but smile. "Yeah, you can put them in their place all you want. It was hot as fuck. Long as you realize you're getting bent over the second we get home."

"Until I can't bend."

The thought of her belly swollen with my child made my dick hard. Yeah, I was a sick fucking bastard, but at least I owned up to it. I reached across the table and took her hand, lacing our fingers together. There was more to Farrah than most probably realized. She had the hard-as-nails exterior down, but I'd seen the sweetness in her, the insecurity at times, and the need to be accepted. She wouldn't take shit from anyone, even me, but she got hurt the same as everyone else.

"I don't know what this relationship will look like, but I can promise you're the only woman I'll be fucking. I'll come home to you every night, unless I'm out on club business, and I will protect you with my last breath. You'll never want for anything, you or the baby. If there comes a time I'm not here, the club will watch over the two of you."

Her fingers tightened on mine. "Let's not off you this soon. At least wait until you've pissed me off good and proper, then I may decide to lend a hand."

"Don't ever change, Farrah," I said, smiling. I'd give her shit because it was fun, and I'd spank her ass whenever she disobeyed, but it would be entertaining, never knowing what tomorrow would bring. I knew for damn certain she'd never stay where I put her, unless *she* decided it was a good idea.

"I'm afraid you're stuck with me as I am," she said. "Smart mouth and all."

I tugged her closer and leaned over the corner of the table to kiss her.

As much as I'd love to fuck her, she'd made a good point. We didn't seem to do much of anything else. If I just wanted sex, I could have gotten it at the clubhouse. Farrah was mine, and the mother of my child. She deserved more than for me to treat her like a club whore. I didn't have a fucking clue how to be in a relationship. Hadn't been in one in forever, and even back then, I'd screwed it all up. Hell, I'd only ever dated two women, and I hadn't exactly been faithful to them. I'd made them promise not to fuck around, but I hadn't given them the same courtesy. If I'd had a sister and some asshole had treated her the way I'd treated my somewhat girlfriends, I'd have kicked his ass. The closest I'd come to a relationship in the last decade was a little Mexican señorita who'd been dropped on the club's doorstep, but it hadn't lasted long or gotten overly serious. Since I'd claimed Farrah, I needed to make sure I did shit the right way this time.

It was different. Not like before. This time, if I fucked shit up, I'd have hell to pay. Not only because of who she was related to, but she lived in my home, had been officially claimed in front of my club, which meant she was here to stay. I couldn't just toss her out and wash my hands of her. The thought of keeping a woman should have scared the piss out of me. I'd never really wanted to in the past. Even the women I'd dated somewhat seriously I'd known I'd never hang onto indefinitely.

"So, a nursery... any ideas what you want in there?" I asked.

"Where should we put it?"

I stood and motioned for her to follow me. The first bedroom was empty so I pushed open the door and let her check out the space. At the moment, I had a few things stored in here, like my gun safe. With the help of my brothers, I could move it elsewhere. Might be the prime time to add a room to the back of the house like I'd thought about for a while now. The second room held some gym equipment and a desk I used on occasion.

"I'll be adding a room to the back of the house off the kitchen. I can move the gun safe out there, along with the shit in the second bedroom. Shouldn't take too long to get it framed out and finished. Long before the baby gets here, as long as the weather holds. Still, I can shift it from the wall and get the painting done in here, go ahead and put together any furniture you pick out." I glanced around the space and back at her. "Think it will work?"

"Sure, but… if you have another spare room, why not just move the gun safe in there?" she asked.

"Well, I could, but as fast as I knocked you up this time, something tells me we'll need the bedrooms for our kids." Her cheeks flushed. "So, do you want this to be the nursery? We can work on getting the other room set up for any future children further down the road."

She nodded, then rubbed her toe across the carpet. "Can we put new carpet down? This one is a little…"

"Ugly?" I asked and laughed. She wasn't wrong. "Yeah, we can put in new carpet. This was part of a leftover roll I got cheap when my house was put up. I didn't much care at the time."

She worried at her lower lip before lifting her gaze to mine. "Is this going to work?"

"For a nursery?" I glanced at the room again. "I don't see why not. We can get it fixed up quick enough."

"Not the room," she said. "Us. You. Me. This baby."

I'd thought we'd already settled this in the kitchen. She'd wanted to talk, to get to know me better. But she still doubted what exactly?

"Farrah, what do you want?"

She opened and shut her mouth, not seeming to have any idea what to say.

"You wanted to know more about me, so I sat down and talked with you. I know it's not enough, but you can't learn everything about a person in the span of a few days or even weeks. Hell, people married twenty years probably still learn new shit about their spouses. Do you think I'd do this for anyone else? The talking, moving my damn guns to another location… any of it? Because I wouldn't." I folded my arms over my chest. "I have never, not once, given a rat's ass about a woman's feelings. Until you. I don't know what the fuck else you want from me, but it seems like you've got one foot out the damn door."

Her cheeks flushed a deep pink. "I'm sorry, Cody. My emotions are all over the place. It's not an excuse, and maybe I've always been a brat. I'll try to do better, but it won't happen overnight."

"You're young, Farrah. Really damn young. I don't expect you to act like a forty-year-old woman, but you're not a kid either. You walked into the clubhouse that night, begging to get fucked. Now you're mine, and so is the kid in your belly. I'm trying to give you what you want, to some extent, but I'm not a fucking lap dog, or someone you can run roughshod over. I'll see to your needs, make sure you're safe, but I will also spank your ass when you deserve it."

She gave a short jerky nod before eyeing the room again. I had no doubt I was about to face an uphill battle with her, but hopefully we'd come out the other side without killing one another. I liked feisty women, but she was right. Farrah was a brat, and I was more than happy to spank it out of her if need be.

Chapter Eleven

Farrah

Demon had been right, about a lot of things. I'd never admit it to him. His ego was big enough already. But I wasn't a kid anymore and had one of my own on the way. It was time to grow up. I'd left the Dixie Reapers for a chance to spread my wings and stand on my own two feet. I'd yelled at my daddy about treating me like a child, and yet, I still acted childish at times. I missed him now that he and grandpa had gone back home. Since it didn't seem this mess with Earl would be fixed anytime soon, they'd returned to their club with a promise from me to check in every day.

I didn't think for one moment at eighteen I had everything figured out. I'd wanted the chance to try, though, and had hoped moving away would give me more opportunities to learn who I was and what I was capable of doing. So far, it seemed I was capable of finding trouble and getting knocked up. Although, to be fair, I'd found trouble since I'd been old enough to walk.

Which was why I now found myself driving to the clubhouse in the late afternoon with two pans of lasagna on the seat beside me. My cooking skills had slightly improved, mostly thanks to the help of Lilian and Rachel. Making a cake from a box was one thing. The lasagna was a new skill level I'd recently achieved, at least somewhat, and I was nearly certain I wouldn't poison the club, so I'd decided to do something nice for the single men and feed them. As much as I wanted to take credit for the idea, I was merely doing my part. Steel's woman, Rachel, had stopped by to introduce herself two days ago, a little black pug dancing at her feet and her daughter by her side, and mentioned all the old ladies chipped in and chose an afternoon or night to feed the single men in the club, although the frequency was up to them. Some only cooked once a month, while others made something once a week. I doubted anyone wanted my cooking very often, so I'd most likely take a meal once a month.

I pulled to a stop in front of the clubhouse and parked as close to the steps as I could. Already a line of bikes filled the parking area. The Prospect at the gate gave me a slight wave but I knew better than to pull him from his post in order to have help carrying the dishes inside. Instead, I held my head high and marched inside, hoping to snag the first guy I came across. If I even attempted to carry both inside, I'd likely drop them. They'd nearly ended up on the ground just getting them to my truck.

Smoke hung in the air and stung my eyes and nose. I waved a hand in front of my face, but it didn't help much. Considering it was still daylight outside, I was a bit surprised at the number of both bikers and club whores lingering in the main room. Then again, the Devil's Fury had far more single men than the Dixie Reapers. It made me wonder if my dad's club had been like this back before I'd been born.

I scanned the room, but the cigarettes and whatever else they were smoking made my vision blur. I knew it couldn't be good for my unborn child either, so I stumbled back outside. How did the other ladies deliver the meals? I highly doubted the Devil's Fury men liked their women wandering into the clubhouse when it had mostly, if not fully, naked women running around. I hadn't seen Demon in there, but I knew his bike was parked in the lot. My gaze narrowed. If he hadn't been in the main area, exactly *where* had he been?

I pulled my shirt up over my nose and went back

inside. I shoved my way through the crowd looking for him, then eyed the darkened hallway. I'd only made it two steps down the corridor before a door opened and he came out, zipping his pants. Everything inside me went tight, hoping like hell he'd just used the bathroom and there wasn't a woman in there. My heart fell to my feet and shattered as the door opened again and a naked woman strolled out, wiping her lips. She smirked at Demon before pushing past me, which was the exact moment he realized they weren't alone.

"Farrah."

I shook my head, turned, and bolted.

"Goddamnit, Farrah!"

I heard him chasing after me, but I didn't dare stop. I fought my way through the clubhouse and dashed out the door. Rushing down the steps, I blindly reached for the handle on my truck door. Tears blurred my vision as I yanked on the damn thing, finally flinging the door open. I scrambled onto the seat and jammed my key in the ignition. My tires spun as I backed up and shot toward the gate, the poor Prospect diving out of the way as I barreled through.

I heard the pipes on several bikes and saw them in my rearview mirror, but they damn sure weren't Devil's Fury. My heart pounded and my palms grew slick as I took a corner a little too fast. I didn't know where I was going, except away from Demon. On the next turn, the lasagna slid into the floor but somehow managed not to splatter all over the place. Still, I wasn't sure anyone would want to eat them now. A quick glance told me they were a hot mess after the tumble to the floorboard. When the diner came into view, I pulled over and stopped. Pressing my head to the steering wheel, I tried to take calming breaths.

How could he do that to me? He'd sworn not to

touch anyone else. Maybe I should have been more specific and told him I didn't want him to trip and his dick accidently fall into anyone's mouth either. Anger and hurt flickered through me, and my eyes stung from unshed tears. I wouldn't give him the satisfaction of making me cry!

Someone opened the door of my truck and pulled me out. I should have fought, but I didn't have it in me right then. I'd survived being kidnapped once, which meant I could do it again if it came to it. Since they didn't seem to have a vehicle with a trunk, I didn't feel threatened just yet. I eyed the patches on the guy's cut. *Savage Raptors MC. Lynx.*

"And just where the hell are you going like that?" he demanded. "You could have gotten yourself killed."

I sniffled and wiped at my tears, the ones I'd sworn not to shed, looking up to focus on his face. I didn't recognize him, but the way he spoke to me made it seem as if we knew one another.

"Lynx, we need to get her out of here before they come looking. Whatever happened, it's clear she wanted to leave the Devil's Fury," another man said.

Lynx nodded and helped me back into the truck. "You okay to drive?"

"Drive where?" I asked.

"We'll take care of the truck. Just take her on your bike," the other man said again.

Lynx assisted me back out of the truck and over to the most badass Harley I'd ever seen. All sleek black paint and chrome, the bike was slung low to the ground. He swung his leg over the seat and held out a hand.

"Why should I go with you? I don't know who you are or why you're here," I said. "I wasn't born yesterday."

His lips twitched as if he wanted to smile. "Get on the bike, Farrah."

I jolted at his use of my name. "How do you know who I am?"

"Because I'm your uncle. Now get on the damn bike," he said.

Numb. In shock. And having no idea what he meant by being my uncle, I found myself reaching for his hand. He helped me onto the back of his bike and pulled out of the parking lot. We hit the streets of town and soon the highway. As the wind whipped through my hair, I realized we were leaving Blackwood Falls. I gripped him tight, not wanting to fall off as the bike picked up speed. By the time he pulled over, my bladder was screaming for a pitstop.

Lynx stopped in front of a motel that seemed decent enough and patted my thigh. I got off the bike, thankful for all the rides I'd been on with my family because my legs held me up and didn't feel like jelly. One of the other men from Savage Raptors went inside and came out a few minutes later with several room keys. He handed one to Lynx.

The biker stood and reached for my hand, leading me over to the nearest room. He unlocked the door and motioned for me to go inside. If he was kidnapping me, this was the strangest way to go about it. I gave him a cautious glance as I scurried past and went straight to the bathroom, where I shut and locked the door. Once I no longer felt like I'd pee in my pants, I unlocked the door and went to wash my hands at the sink.

Lynx sat in a chair by the window, or perhaps sprawled was a better word since it looked like he'd melted.

"Why did you say you're my uncle?" I asked. "And where are we? Why did you take me away from Blackwood Falls?"

He held up a hand. "One question at a time, dear niece. First, I said I'm your uncle because I am. Your mother, Ridley, is my half-sister. I go by Lynx these days, but the name on my birth certificate is Wilson Benton. Ridley and I share the same mom, but her stepdad was my father. Unfortunately."

If my mother had a brother, why hadn't we ever met before now? Why hadn't she said anything about Wilson, or Lynx as he called himself now? Were the Savage Raptors a rival club? Had that been why he'd been kept a secret from me all these years? He didn't look too much older than me, for that matter.

"As to where we are, I'm taking you back home. To my home."

I opened my mouth to protest, but he held up a hand, silencing me.

"I'll tell you what you need to know, when you need to know it. At the moment, I'm trying to keep you safe. The man who kidnapped you isn't who you think he is."

"The junkie? Earl?" I asked. "How did you know about that?"

"It's a long story. Right now, you need to rest. Write down your sizes and I'll have someone get some clothes for you. I'm sure you'd like to eat as well."

I pressed a hand to my belly. Oh hell! I'd ridden on the back of his bike, who knows for how many miles, while I was pregnant. Demon was going to kill me. For that matter, he might kill me anyway for getting onto Lynx's bike to begin with.

I sank onto the edge of the bed. I'd ridden off with a stranger, all because Demon had hurt me. I didn't want to stop and analyze why it felt like my heart had broken. I didn't love him, barely knew him. Right? I wasn't certain who I was trying to convince. It seemed I'd done something incredibly stupid and fallen for a biker, like I'd always said I *wouldn't* do.

I felt Lynx's gaze on me. For whatever reason, the man didn't unsettle me. It was almost comforting being in his presence. I wasn't sure what to make of it, but perhaps he'd spoken the truth and we really were related. It didn't explain why my mother had never mentioned having a brother, or why we'd never met before.

"What do you need right now, Farrah?" he asked, his voice soft and coaxing.

"I-I don't know."

"Why did you come tearing out of the Devil's Fury compound? I was on my way there to speak with you, but the moment I saw your truck fly through the gates, I knew I had to follow you."

"How did you know what I drive? Or anything about me?" I asked.

"You think Wire is the only hacker who's part of a club?" He smirked. "I've kept tabs on my sister over the years, and her family. Which is why I knew you were in danger."

"Danger?" My eyebrows went up. "From Earl? The man is a junkie. If he hadn't caught me by surprise, he'd have never managed to shove me into the trunk."

He rubbed his chin and I noticed he had the dark shadow of stubble but not a full-out beard. "Earl isn't a junkie. Or rather, he sometimes pretends to be one, if he thinks it will get him what he wants."

"I don't understand."

"Earl isn't really Earl at all." He leaned forward,

bracing his elbows on his knees. "The man is a shadow. The face you saw probably isn't even his real one. He takes on whatever persona will help him blend in."

I shook my head, starting to get a headache. "That makes no sense at all. He took me to the Devil's Boneyard to trade me for drugs."

"Did he?" Lynx asked. "Or did he want it to appear that way? Maybe he used you as a way to gain entrance into their compound and thought it would also hurt the Dixie Reapers and the Devil's Fury at the same time."

"I have no idea what you're talking about."

He leaned back in the chair again, looking so relaxed, except for his eyes. They were nearly the same shade as my mother's, but Lynx's looked troubled. What was going on? He'd said I was in danger, but why? I wasn't anyone special. Yeah, my daddy was the VP of the Dixie Reapers, and I'd now been claimed by the Sergeant-at-Arms for the Devil's Fury, but why would anyone care?

"You want to eat here or go somewhere?" he asked. "We need to talk, and not just about this mess. Something else is going on and you're going to tell me what it is."

Damn it. He wanted me to tell him about catching Demon with the club whore. My stomach knotted and a sharp pain spread across my chest. I absently rubbed at the ache, hoping it would go away.

"You may not know me, Farrah, but I've kept an eye on you. Same for your sister and brother. You're my family, and there's nothing I won't do to keep you safe. Understood?"

"Yeah. I get it."

"So talk to me, niece. What had you running out of there like your ass was on fire? And why the fuck were you crying?" he asked.

"Demon," I said, as if it would explain everything.

His gaze scanned me. "I don't see any property ink, or a cut."

"I only recently got my property cut and I didn't think to put it on. Wouldn't have made a difference anyway." My eyes burned again as I thought about Demon walking out into the hall as he zipped his pants, and that bitch coming out after him. We hadn't been having sex much the last few days, but it wasn't because of me. He'd pulled away and I didn't know why. Had he gotten tired of me already?

"Talk to me, Farrah. What did Demon do?"

I bit my lip so hard I tasted blood. "I caught him with a club whore. He said he would be faithful. I should have known better. A guy like him can have anyone, and probably has. Why would he give that up?"

"Damn." Lynx stood and came to sit beside me, reaching for my hand. "I don't know why he'd want anyone else, Farrah. You're beautiful, bold, and if you're anything like your mom, I'm sure you're not the quiet sort to take things lying down. He's lucky to have you."

If only Demon felt that way.

"I hadn't even realized how attached I'd gotten until then. It felt like my heart broke. How is that possible? We've only been together a short while. I can't love him already, can I?"

"Sure you can." Lynx stood and tugged on my hand. "Come on. We're going to get some food, some clothes for you, and we're going to have a little chat. Maybe realizing you're gone will give him the wake-up call he needs."

Or freedom to do whatever he wanted. The thought made me miserable. I shouldn't have run. It was cowardly, but it had hurt so damn bad seeing him with that woman. I'd always fought for what I wanted. Until now.

Chapter Twelve
Demon

I'd fucked up. Badly. Even I could admit it. I knew what she'd thought. The fact Sasha, a damn club whore who kept trying to get in my pants, had followed me to the fucking bathroom pissed me off. And she'd be dealt with. Harshly. If she cost me Farrah, I'd do far worse than brand her. The catty bitches at the clubhouse needed another lesson.

"Where the fuck is she?" I demanded as I paced. I'd called Church the moment I realized Farrah was nowhere to be found. I hadn't realized the idiot guarding the gate had just let her through, or that no one had thought to follow her. I'd already reamed them out and wanted someone's blood. They'd known she was in danger. Bunch of drunken and high idiots had been too deep in alcohol and pussy to keep her from driving off. If anyone in Blackwood Falls knew where she was, they weren't talking.

Outlaw clicked away on his laptop, stopping now and then to flex and stretch his fingers. It was shitty of me to make him do this, knowing it caused him pain, but I needed to find Farrah. I had Outlaw hacking into any security cameras around town, hoping we'd be able to at least get a direction. If I knew whether or not she'd headed back toward Alabama, at least I'd be able to hit the road.

I glanced at Outlaw and saw him pale. His gaze lifted and met mine, and I didn't like what I saw. Not even a little. He turned his laptop around and I watched as a Savage Raptor hauled her out of her truck. The way he held her spoke of a familiarity I didn't much like. When he led her to his bike and she climbed on without complaint, fury ignited inside me. Who the fuck was that guy and how did he know

Farrah?

"Who is he?" I asked.

"I don't recognize him," Outlaw said. "And I can't read his cut. I can make a call. I have friends there."

"Do it. I need to know why he came for Farrah. You make it real fucking clear she's mine. Anyone touches her and I will end them. I don't give a shit if you're friends with the club or not."

Outlaw nodded and picked up his cell phone. As he talked to his contact, I started pacing again. I couldn't remember a time I'd felt so enraged, and I only had myself to blame. I'd been too lax with the club whores. Farrah had put one on her ass, and I'd hoped it would be enough. I knew my brutality tended to bother my brothers at times, and it damn sure didn't endear me to the old ladies. They thought I took things too far, but it was clear I hadn't gone far enough. If these bitches didn't fear me, fear what would happen if they fucked us over, then I hadn't done my job.

I clenched my fists, the need to spill blood nearly overpowering. When would we fucking learn? We kept letting these whores in, not putting an end to their foolishness right off. Look where it got us every fucking time. One thing was for damn sure. Once I got Farrah back home, my time at the clubhouse was at an end, unless we had some family nights like a few other clubs, including the Dixie Reapers. I knew I couldn't entirely avoid the place. Even Badger and Dingo made appearances to have drinks with our brothers, but I'd try to spend more time at home with my woman. The Reapers had gone so far as to add a pavilion and play area for the kids, an area where the old ladies could get together and let their children play while they socialized. I kind of liked the idea of a safe place for all the club kids to play.

It was time for some changes around here, but I'd have to get Badger to agree. I didn't think it would be too difficult. The man loved his woman more than anything in the world. If he thought Adalia would be pleased with the changes, he'd probably get out there and swing the hammer himself to get shit built.

Outlaw hung up the phone and closed his laptop. The soft *snick* sounded too damn loud. And final. Why wasn't he still searching for Farrah? And why the fuck wasn't he talking? I moved closer, folding my arms over my chest as I stared him down.

"Farrah is with Lynx. He'll keep her safe. It's why he was in town," Outlaw said.

"What the fuck?" I glanced at Badger and Slash, seeing it was news to them too. "They came here uninvited, didn't give anyone a heads-up, then took off with my woman?"

"I didn't get the entire story," Outlaw said. "But we need to go to Oklahoma. Or at least you do, and a few others. That's where Lynx is taking Farrah, back to the Savage Raptors."

"Why does he have Farrah? What is he to her?" I asked, nearly dreading the answer. She'd been a virgin when I'd taken her, but it didn't mean the other man hadn't met her somewhere and fallen for her. Hell, even I had to admit she made me feel things I'd never felt before.

"He's her uncle," Outlaw said. His gaze flicked over to Badger, then back to me. "Lynx is Ridley's half-brother. And according to Spade, the Savage Raptors VP, no one knows about the connection. Not even Ridley."

What the... I shared a look with Badger and Slash, wondering just what the hell we were about to get into.

"So, Pres. Who's going with me?" I asked.

Badger cracked his neck and scanned the room. Grizzly hadn't made an official announcement so much as he'd just removed his patch and handed it to Badger. It hadn't caused as much of a stir as I'd thought it would. Everyone understood Griz's reasoning, and he'd always be a respected member of the club. Not a damn one of us wanted the job and we'd all been happy to have Badger step into the role.

"I'm going with you," Badger said. "I'll get Griz and Lilian to keep an eye on Adalia for me. Slash, you stay behind and keep things running smoothly here. Outlaw, since you have contacts with the Savage Raptors, I want you to go. I know you can't ride a bike that long so take one of the club trucks. Might need it anyway. Savage and Colorado, you'll go with us."

I growled, thinking of how Farrah might react to seeing Colorado. Badger silenced me with a look. I didn't like it, but if the Pres wanted Colorado to go, then that's exactly what would happen. He also asked for Beau to go along. I knew it was getting close to time to patch the kid in. He'd fucked up before and had paid the price. Since then, he'd toed a fine line and done everything we asked.

"As much as I know you want to leave right the fuck now," Badger said, looking my way, "we'll head out in a few hours. It gives anyone with old ladies time to get their families settled."

"I'll keep them safe," Steel said. "I'm sure Rachel would love to have them over tomorrow. If they're all in one spot, it will make it easier. I don't know why the Savage Raptors thought Farrah needed their protection, but it can't be good."

Badger nodded. "Appreciate it, Steel. No damn

club whores here while we're gone. I want them cleared the fuck out immediately, and if any slip through the gates to come back, I'll be having a little chat with whoever let them in. The kind that leaves a lasting impression."

I winced remembering a time he'd used a blow torch to remove someone's eye. Badger wasn't someone to fuck with. I'd done some bad shit in my time and wouldn't hesitate to gut those club whores if I thought they deserved it, but he was another type of monster altogether. When it came to women and kids, he'd do anything to keep them safe. Even go to jail, like he'd done for killing Adalia's attacker when she'd been a kid.

"Demon, pack your stuff, but gather some of your woman's things, including her property cut if she's not wearing it." Badger stood. "Two hours. I want everyone ready to ride. If I have to track down any of you fuckers, it won't end well."

"I'll call Tank and let him know about Farrah," Slash said. "Venom and Bull will want to know, and I have a feeling Ridley may have something to say about a long-lost brother absconding with her daughter."

Fucking hell. This was about to become a damn circus. Badger dismissed Church and I went straight to my house. When I reached the bedroom, I stopped and stared at the bed. The sheets were still rumpled. Pain shot through me when I realized what I'd lost. Since Farrah had told me about the pregnancy, I'd tried to be gentler and not reach for her as often. Had it been a mistake? Did she think I didn't want her anymore?

I hadn't even realized I'd gotten closer to the bed until my knees bumped the mattress. I reached down and ran my fingers over Farrah's pillow. I knew I was a bastard and an asshole. The moment I'd known who she was, I should have released her. I'd been selfish, wanting to hold onto her, loving her feistiness. With my past, I wasn't sure she'd believe anything I said about Sasha.

I hadn't touched her, even though she'd shoved her tits in my face all damn night. No one could ever compare to Farrah. It wasn't just her outward appearance, even though I thought her to be the sexiest woman I'd ever met. Her inner strength, her fire, had drawn me to her like a moth to a flame.

I didn't know a damn thing about being in a relationship with a woman. I'd told her as much, but maybe I should have tried harder. Given her flowers. Taken her out on dates. I'd wanted to keep her safe behind the gates, and instead I'd driven her from the compound, given her a reason to doubt me.

You're an idiot. You love her and you damn well know it. Should have told her.

I got my duffle out and threw in a few changes of clothes, then got another bag for Farrah's things. I lifted her nightgown to my nose, breathing in her scent. If this went sideways, if she refused to come home with me, it would fucking gut me. I could demand she leave with me. Wouldn't stop her from hating me. In fact, she'd hate me more than she probably did right now.

I pulled my phone from my pocket and pulled up her name. I hesitated, wondering if she'd even read a text from me. Only one way to find out.

It wasn't what it looked like. I didn't touch her.

I hit send and waited. It showed the message was delivered. After another moment, it said she'd read it. I waited, hoping she'd respond. Even if she told me to go fuck myself. Anything was better than silence. Another minute passed, then another.

I'm sorry I hurt you. I hit send again. *I don't want anyone else.* Hit send again. Then I sent several more messages, each showing as read, but none getting a response.

Scared the shit out of me not knowing where you were.

I need you, Farrah.

Tell me how to fix this. Fix us.

Little dots appeared and I stared, waiting. When I saw her reply, I dropped the phone on the bed, knowing I'd fucked up worse than I'd thought.

You can't fix us. It's obvious there isn't an us to fix.

Shit. Goddamnit. I had to do something. A glance at the time told me I had a little over an hour before Badger wanted to leave. Just enough time. I threw the rest of the stuff into the duffle bags, then managed to carry them to the clubhouse on my bike. I tossed them onto the clubhouse steps at the feet of one of the Prospects.

"Put those into whatever truck Outlaw is taking. I'll be back before we leave but I need to do something first."

I pulled away from the clubhouse and left the compound, heading into Blackwood Falls. My first stop was the jewelry store. I hadn't asked Farrah to marry me. Just claimed her and given her a property cut. Needed to fix that before anything else. I selected an engagement ring I thought she'd like and purchased it, then went to my next stop.

Doolittle was on his way out of the clinic when I pulled up. Even though he'd been taking a more active role in the club, and now kept a house at the compound, he still didn't attend every Church meeting. With his day job, it wasn't always possible for him to drop everything and come running. But he knew about Farrah missing, and I knew he'd do whatever I asked to help get her back. Except what I wanted wasn't just another brother riding along.

"Can we talk inside?" I asked, shutting off my bike.

"Yeah, but we've closed up for the night."

We entered the lobby and I heard the dogs barking in the back, and cats going crazy. They always had some overnight patients. Even better, they also took in puppies and kittens to adopt out. That's what I counted on right now.

"I need a dog, or a puppy. Something for Farrah. I want a guard dog," I said, thinking of how little Victoria had done her best to keep Steel's family safe. The tiny pug hadn't been much of a deterrent even though she'd tried. All healed up, she got spoiled daily by Coral, Rachel and Steel's daughter.

"Is she back?" he asked. "I heard what happened. Steel keeps me up to date on things when I'm bogged down at the clinic, but I haven't gotten any messages from him since she took off."

"No, and that brings me to another point. Can you leave here for a few days?"

He nodded. "I don't have any surgeries scheduled the next few days. Someone else can handle the routine exams. Why?"

"Need you to come with me. Farrah is with the Savage Raptors. We're riding out in…" I pulled out my phone to check the time. "Thirty minutes."

Doolittle whistled. "Not giving me much time to pack."

"Need a dog first. You got anything I can adopt for Farrah? Something to keep her safe?" I asked.

"I do. He's not exactly a puppy, though. Flunked out of training so the police don't want him."

"Flunked?" I asked.

"Trigger is a German Shepherd. He was in training to be a K-9 officer, but he gets distracted too easily. I don't see why he wouldn't make a good guard dog for the house. He can't be a service dog because of his attention span, but he's a good boy."

"Can I see him?" I asked.

Doolittle motioned for me to follow him. I'd expected something smaller. I knew he'd said Trigger wasn't a puppy. Still, the mountain of dog I saw wasn't what I'd anticipated. Trigger had jet black fur, intelligent eyes, and stood taller than most German Shepherds I'd seen.

Doolittle gave him a silent hand command and Trigger sat, his tongue lolling. My brother opened the cage and Trigger's tail started wagging, sweeping across the concrete floor. I knelt in front of him and held out a hand. He sniffed me, then gave a tentative lick.

"How old is he?" I asked.

"Not quite a year."

"Jesus! He's a fucking horse already!"

Doolittle nodded. "German bloodlines. He has impeccable breeding. If you want him, he's yours. I was told to place him with the right owner. I think you and Farrah just might be it. I don't know that I'd put him with someone who had small kids, and before you say anything, I know Farrah is pregnant, but Trigger would grow up with your kids and it makes a difference."

"I'll take him."

"Let me get a leash. Good thing I didn't ride my bike to work." Doolittle smiled. "Guess I'm taking him with me in the SUV to the Savage Raptors? Is that why you asked if I could take some days off?"

"Yeah. I want to take him to meet Farrah. I fucked up, Doolittle. So damn bad. Not sure Trigger here can fix the mess I made. Hoping he'll help smooth the way at least. Maybe she'll talk to me."

Doolittle rocked back on his heels. "Don't remember ever hearing you give a shit about what a woman thought or wanted."

"Never loved one before."

"That would do it." He slapped me on the back. "I'll bring him with me and grab some stuff he'll need. We can use a set of the clinic's bowls for now, but you'll need to buy him some when we get back home. I have a small bag of food I give out to adopting families so it will hold him over until we reach Oklahoma."

"Thanks. I owe you one."

He got a strange look in his eyes. It was gone so fast I'd thought I imagined it.

"Just toss a good woman my way if you run across one."

I didn't know what to say. I'd known a woman from his past had fucked him over. She'd been at the compound a short while, living in the house with him, until he'd had enough and kicked her ass out. Since then, I hadn't seen him pay much attention to any of the women who came around. Except little Meredith, but I knew they only had friendship between them. Hell, the kid was sixteen and even though Doolittle wasn't all that old I knew he'd never go there. He'd given the club whores a wide berth, but then again, he'd never much cared for them to begin with. They'd popped his cherry, and he'd had a little fun here and there, but not like the rest of us.

I gave Trigger one last pat on the head, then went back to my bike and drove straight to the compound. Whatever items the dog needed would have to wait until we stopped riding for the night. I pulled through the gates and Outlaw waved me over. He leaned against the club's truck, his woman pressed against him and his daughter on his hip. I rolled closer and cut the engine on my bike.

"I know where Farrah is right now," Outlaw said. "Spade is going to have his man remain where they are until we can reach them. They stopped at a motel so Farrah could rest and get a bite to eat. She was distraught when she left earlier. Guess Lynx was concerned about her."

"Badger know where we're going?" I asked.

"I gave him the name and location of the motel. It's not too far from here. A few hours. We might be able to get a little rest before we drive the rest of the way to the Savage Raptors."

My brow furrowed. "If we get Farrah back, why would we go all the way to Oklahoma?"

"Because they know about Earl, who he really is, and what the fuck is going on. It would be wise to hear them out, and it sounds like they've been preparing for Farrah's arrival. Not just hers, actually. Venom is bringing Mariah and Dawson too, along with Ridley."

None of it made any sense to me, but I'd go along with it if it meant Farrah would be safe. I still didn't know what to think about her uncle. I'd wait and see how things played out. The moment I thought she was in danger I'd get her the hell out of there, assuming the trouble came from the Raptors and not outside forces. If they could help in some way, I'd be grateful for the assistance.

"Let's ride," Badger yelled out as he walked over to his bike.

Doolittle shot past us in his SUV, heading for his house. I waved Badger over, hoping to buy the vet a little time.

"Doolittle is coming too. My present to Farrah is riding with him. He needs a minute to pack."

"What the fuck kind of present did you get her?" Badger asked.

"A dog." I smiled. "A guard dog. You know Doolittle won't take long. Give him ten minutes, Pres. If he's not here by then, I won't say a word about rolling out of here without him."

Badger ran a hand through his hair and glowered at me. "You picked a fucking fine time to get a Goddamn dog."

He wasn't wrong, but it was something I'd felt I needed to do. Not only would Farrah have company when I wasn't at the house, she'd also have protection. I needed her to see how important she was to me. My texts hadn't made a dent in the wall she'd put up between us. I could only hope Trigger would soften her a little, at least get her to let me explain about Sasha. When we came home, I'd deal with the club whore. All of them. It was time they learned their damn place.

"I know that look," Badger said. "What are you planning?"

"Think the club whores need a refresher on how to behave. Sasha started this shit. Farrah would still be here, or at least wouldn't have run. She saw me come out of the bathroom zipping up my pants. Only went in to take a piss, but Sasha followed, trying to get me to fuck her. When it didn't work and she saw Farrah in the hallway, she wiped her mouth like she'd just sucked me off. I hate these fucking cunts!"

Outlaw winced and cast an apologetic look at his wife. I normally wouldn't use that particular word to describe a woman, especially not with one of the old ladies around, but this latest batch of club whores fit the word. Every last one of them was close to being out on their asses if I had any say in the matter. Caused too much fucking trouble.

"Sorry, Elena," I said. "Didn't mean to use such a crude word in front of you or little Valeria."

She waved me off. "Sometimes it's justified. Sounds like it was the perfect label considering the trouble she caused."

Doolittle's SUV came barreling down the road and I started my bike up again. It wasn't long before all of us were on the road. I didn't care how late we got there, I needed to see Farrah. The fact I'd hurt her, even unintentionally, made me want to kick my own ass. I should have known Sasha was up to something. Could have locked the fucking door. Lesson learned.

Chapter Thirteen

Farrah

The way Lynx kept looking out the curtain made me nervous. What was he waiting for? Or worse, *who*? Did he think Earl, or whatever the man's actual name was, would attack us here?

"Aren't you going to sleep?" I asked. He'd insisted I lie down after we ate, and I'd taken the bed closest to the bathroom, leaving the one near the door for him.

"No." He glanced at me, then away. "Sleep while you can. You'll need your rest for what's coming."

If he thought those words would inspire me to relax and close my eyes, he was fucked in the head. My body tightened even more and I fisted the covers. I hated the ominous shit men tended to say, thinking it somehow made women feel more at ease if we didn't know the details. It was obvious he didn't have a woman in his life, or if he did, I had to wonder if she wasn't some doe-eyed innocent who skittered away from the Boogeyman like a frightened rabbit. If something bad was heading my way, I wanted to know as much as I could.

"When are we leaving?" I asked.

"In the morning. Farrah, shut your eyes. And your mouth. Sleep while you can."

I narrowed my eyes at him and flipped him off. Even though he faced the window, it was clear he'd known what I'd done. Slowly, he turned to face me, his jaw tight and his eyes flashing with anger.

"Little girl, don't try me. You may be eighteen, and my niece, but don't think for a second you're too old for a spanking."

I gasped and my cheeks burned at his words, knowing it's exactly what Demon would do if he got his hands on me. Spank me until I couldn't sit for a week. The way Lynx smirked said plenty. He knew exactly where my thoughts had gone, and apparently thought Demon needed to discipline me. Men! There were times I didn't know why we put up with them.

I heard the pipes on quite a few bikes and tensed even more. Were those the men he'd been waiting for? More Savage Raptors, or someone else? Lynx moved away from the window about the time someone banged on our motel room door. He opened it and stepped back. Demon entered the room, his gaze landing on me, burning with something I couldn't quite discern. He let out a whistle and a large black dog trotted in, sitting at his feet.

Bolting upright in bed, I stared at the beast before focusing on the man again. "I left and you went to get a dog?"

I was trying not to be offended. Then again, being replaced by a dog was better than him getting another woman. Of course, he'd already *had* another one, which was why I'd left in the first place. It reminded me I was angry with him, even if he did look sexy and rumpled from the ride here. I curled my fingers tighter, my nails biting into my palms, to keep myself from doing something stupid like going to him and throwing my arms around him.

Lynx stepped out and shut the door, leaving me alone with Demon. The black German Shepherd came closer, his nose twitching as he took in the scents from the room. He slowly approached me and placed his chin on the bed. I reached for him, not daring to move too quickly for fear he might snap my fingers off, and gently petted the top of his head before scratching behind his ear.

"His name is Trigger, and I didn't get him to

replace you. I got him *for* you. Doolittle says he'd be an excellent guard dog for you and our kids."

I stared at the dog before looking over at Demon, only to realize he'd moved closer and now stood merely a foot away. My heart gave a hard kick, reminding me of what he'd done.

Demon sat on the side of Lynx's bed, his hands dangling between his knees. "We need to talk, Farrah. What you saw... it wasn't what you think. I didn't touch Sasha. She'd been trying to get in my pants all night and I'd sent her packing each and every time. I went to take a piss and she followed me in there. Since I was mid-stream, I couldn't exactly walk the fuck out or boot her ass out the door. She didn't suck me off. I didn't fuck her. Nothing happened."

I wanted to believe him, more than anything, but what he said and what I'd seen didn't seem to mesh very well. She'd seemed very satisfied, and his pants had still been undone. But if he'd truly been using the bathroom, it was possible he'd just stepped out before he'd zipped his pants all the way.

"I tried to stop you so I could tell you right then, but you ran. When I realized you'd disappeared, I about had a fucking heart attack. I didn't know if you'd left on your own or been abducted again. When Outlaw showed me security camera footage of someone pulling you from your truck and you getting on the back of the man's bike, I about lost it. No." He shook his head. "I *did* lose it. I wanted to beat on someone, tear something apart."

"Demon, it hurt so much when I saw you walk out with her. You'd promised to be faithful and I'd trusted you but..."

"Sasha put on a convincing performance. When we get home, I'll be teaching her a lesson, one all the club whores better learn from or they're all out on their asses. I'm sick of their shit."

I rubbed the head of Trigger again and he closed his eyes, groaning in doggy contentment. "You really got me a dog?"

He slid off the bed onto his knees and pulled something from his pocket. "Actually, I got you more than that."

It took a moment for me to realize what he held in his hand. A small, black velvet box. When he opened the lid, the engagement ring inside sparkled. I'd never seen anything so beautiful, or unique. It wasn't a plain diamond, but a pale yellow stone.

"It's a canary diamond," he said. "I knew you needed something unique. No ordinary diamonds for my beautiful Farrah. I'm sorry I fucked up. I can't promise I never will again because it could happen, but you need to know I'd never willingly hurt you. I…"

He clamped his lips shut and seemed to fight some sort of inner struggle. I wasn't sure he'd say anything else when he finally spoke again.

"I love you. I should have told you sooner, but I didn't even want to admit it to myself. I don't know when it happened, or how, but you burrowed under my skin and into my heart. I'm not so great with words. Or actions it seems. I already claimed you, made you my old lady and mine in every way as far as the club is concerned, but I want the world to know it too. Marry me, Farrah. Take my name. You already stole my heart."

My vision blurred with tears and I bit back a sob. I struggled to get free of the covers and dropped to my knees on the floor in front of him. Holding out my hand, I noticed it shook as he slid the ring onto my finger.

"I love you, Cody. It's why it hurt so much when I thought you'd been with that other woman. I didn't mean to fall for you. Didn't really want to, but it happened anyway. Leaving you was the only thing I could do because it felt like I'd been ripped in two."

He cupped my cheek and gently pressed his lips to mine. "I'm so fucking sorry, Farrah."

I clung to him, holding him tight as I could. I knew there wasn't a guarantee some other club slut wouldn't try to get her hands on him. He was an officer, sexy, and had a dangerous vibe I knew women loved. As long as he promised to be mine and only mine, I'd have to trust him to keep his word. The next time one of those women tried to come between us, I wouldn't let her.

I drew back and ran my fingers over his beard before kissing him. As much as I wanted more, I knew now wasn't the time. Lynx could return at any moment. I had no doubt he'd give us a little space, time to work things out, but he wouldn't stay gone forever.

"Are we going home?" I asked.

He shook his head. "Outlaw said the Savage Raptors have information we need, and they've already made preparations to keep you safe. Your dad and mom are on their way there, along with Mariah and Dawson. For whatever reason, your entire family seems to have been targeted. Badger wants to hear what they have to say. He came with me, as well as Doolittle, Outlaw, and a few others. We'll stay here overnight and head out first thing tomorrow."

I sagged against him, suddenly more tired than before. Now that Demon was here, and things were okay between us again, it no longer felt like my world was crumbling around me. Knowing he was here was enough for me to sleep for a bit. I stood and got back into bed, then patted the space next to me.

Trigger took it as an invitation and leapt onto the bed, making me laugh. I caught Demon's smile before he gave the dog a stern look and pointed to the foot of the bed. Trigger gave a doggy grumble of complaint but ended up lying across my legs. I tugged them free and he pressed close to me, even though he no longer pinned me down.

Demon removed his boots, folded his cut and placed it on the dresser, pulled out more weapons than I'd realized he had on him, then he slid into bed next to me, tugging me into his arms. I rested my head on his shoulder and breathed him in.

"I'm glad you're here," I said softly, then closed my eyes.

He stroked his hand up and down my arm, the steady thrum of his heartbeat a comfort to me. I heard the motel door open and shut. Since Demon didn't react, I knew it was either Lynx or one of the Devil's Fury. I cracked my eyes open and smiled when I realized it was Doolittle.

"No one else wanted to sleep in here with the dog," he said. "Hope you don't snore."

Demon flipped him off and I giggled before shutting my eyes again. Even though I was exhausted, I still didn't quite fall asleep. Instead, I drifted, feeling weightless yet still conscious of everything around me. I heard him speaking with Doolittle and Trigger's deep breathing. Even the sounds from the parking lot reached my ears.

"They have Farrah's truck here. You going to let her drive it to Oklahoma?" Doolittle asked.

"She'll be safer there than on the back of my bike. Have to wonder if Lynx would have let her ride with him if he'd known about the baby. Doesn't seem like the type to put a kid at risk," Demon said.

Great. He'd known I rode with Lynx. He'd mentioned seeing me get on Lynx's bike, but I hadn't thought much of it until just now. I had no doubt a spanking was in my future, unless he gave me a free pass since he'd been the reason I was so upset to begin with. I could hope. The thought of my last spanking was enough to make me wince.

"Everything okay between you two now?" Doolittle asked.

"Yeah."

"Badger got a call from Hades Abyss. About MaryAnne," Doolittle said. "They lost her again. All the hackers are banding together to try and locate her. Seems she got sold, but they don't know who bought her."

I heard a mumbled *Fuck*. "I dropped the ball. Kraken asked for my help, then Farrah got kidnapped and keeping her safe has consumed my every thought. If anything happens to MaryAnne, worse than she's been through already, it will be my burden to carry. I could have done something, even if it was just sending Kraken help from another club, or telling him I couldn't make it."

I could feel his pain over the situation and hated I'd been part of it. I didn't know who MaryAnne was, or what was going on with her, but I hoped they found her safe. It wasn't Demon's fault, even if he felt it was. Earl, or whatever his name really was, should be blamed. If he hadn't snatched me from the motel, or had other devious things in mind, none of us would even be here right now.

"I hope they find her. Poor girl was beat to hell and back. I can only imagine what they've done to her since," Demon said.

"Guess we'd better get some sleep. Morning will be here soon," Doolittle said.

He shut off the light and I felt Demon exhale, but his body didn't relax. I cracked my eyes a little to observe him. It was clear he was troubled, and I wasn't sure if it was because of me or MaryAnne. Maybe both. He placed his hand over my belly, either not realizing I was awake, or pretending he didn't know.

"I will keep you safe, little one. I claimed your momma. You're both mine."

He nuzzled my hair and pressed a kiss there.

"I fucked up so many times, especially with Meiling."

I heard a snort across the room. "Heard about that. And yes, I'm eavesdropping. You should apologize to Meiling and Dingo. Putting Beau to the test and using Meiling to do it was all sorts of wrong. But they'll forgive you. It's what brothers do."

Demon sighed. "Have to end this shit with Earl first and get my woman back home. I'm sure she'll want some time with Lynx, him being her long-lost uncle and all, but I doubt we're going to resolve this issue overnight. Just hope the fucker is trustworthy. If I have to gut the fucker and start offing Farrah's family, I don't think she'll take it well."

No, he was right about that. I certainly wouldn't.

Slowly, the tension eased from his body and after another few minutes his breathing evened out. Now that my big, bad biker was asleep, I was able to relax and do the same.

Chapter Fourteen

Farrah

I'd never been to Oklahoma before. I wasn't quite sure what to think of the place. The Savage Raptors had a nice compound and clubhouse. From what little Lynx had told me, they'd made a lot of upgrades over the last six months. I could hear the pride in his voice as he showed me around. They had a set of guest quarters not far from the clubhouse. All one level, but small like apartments. Each had one bedroom, a mini-kitchen, bathroom, and small living area. But they seemed like they were comfortable enough. Since I'd be sharing one with Demon, I'd soon find out.

My mom, dad, and siblings were in another, and my grandpa had come with Darian and their kids, Foster and Tara. The other two were taken by Scratch and Rooster. Knowing the Devil's Boneyard member had feelings for me made things a little awkward. When he'd shaken Demon's hand, I'd noticed the wince and had no doubt Demon was trying to break every bone in the man's hand. He couldn't have made things clearer if he'd stopped to pee on me.

Women weren't allowed in Church, which seemed to be true of every club, so instead, their President, Atilla, had suggested we meet outside. All of my family, as well as everyone who'd come to help, gathered behind the clubhouse with every member of the Savage Raptors present. Trigger sat at my feet, panting and scanning the area as if he were searching for threats. Since Demon had confessed the dog had been a police K-9 dropout, it was quite possible he was doing that very thing. I did feel a little safer with the large beast next to me.

"Sorry for the unconventional meeting," Lynx said. "Doubt all of you would have fit into Church anyway."

A few people chuckled and Lynx flashed a quick smile.

"As some of you know, my niece, Farrah, is in danger. I've kept quiet about where I came from, or who I'm related to. It's time to confess everything. My father was Richard Benton III and Ridley is my half-sister."

I heard my mother suck in a breath and I looked over to see tears misting her eyes. She mouthed the name *Wilson* and looked up at my dad. He gave her a reassuring squeeze and I focused my attention back on Lynx.

"Earl is actually something of a ghost. He doesn't technically exist, and most people prefer it that way. My father wasn't a good man, as Ridley can attest to, and he had shady dealings with a lot of people. I devoted my teen years and adult life to finding out everything I could about him, the men he worked with, and how I could make them all fall." Lynx met my father's gaze and held it a moment. "My father isn't an issue as he's been dead a long time, but the others are another story."

I stroked Trigger's head, hoping it would calm me. I felt like I was shaking so hard I'd cause an earthquake and noticed my hand visibly trembled. I didn't know where this was going, but I knew it couldn't be good.

"While I'm skilled at what I do, I'm not the best. That title is reserved for Wire and his woman. It seems my poking around was finally noticed and it put my family at risk. Poor Farrah is getting the brunt of it because of her tie to Demon with the Devil's Fury," Lynx said. I didn't understand why it would matter if I were Demon's or not. None of this made any sense to me yet. For that matter, I'd only spent the one night with him. How had Earl even known? Did that mean he'd not only been spying on me, but had someone found a way to watch me with Demon? My skin crawled at the implication.

"Earl's real name, before someone tried to erase his existence, was Darius Somers."

I felt Demon stiffen next to me and wondered if the name meant something to him. I knew they shared the last name. Were they family?

"Darius Somers is just one of many bastard sons of Terrell Somers. Demon's father. It seems Darius knows about his half-brother. I think the idea of Demon being happy, and Farrah being the cause, put more of a target on my niece," Lynx said.

"Why the fuck would some asshole I've never met care about me? And why kidnap Farrah only to deliver her to the Devil's Boneyard?" Demon asked.

"Darius is, for lack of a better word, crazy. He's worked as an assassin for men like my father. At one time, he was greatly feared, and labeled Diabolus. The last few years, he's gotten sloppy and his trail was easy to find. I noticed female family members of those who opposed him or his employers started to vanish. Unfortunately, he's now after me, which means Farrah, Ridley, and Mariah are in danger. I wouldn't put it past him to even snatch my nephew, Dawson. But Farrah has especially captured his attention."

"Earl has been getting drugs from us for a while now," Scratch said. "He wanted to exchange Farrah for his next hit because Rooster liked her."

Lynx folded his arms. "And how did he know Rooster liked her? What made him think you'd ever accept such a trade?"

Scratch didn't seem to have an answer.

"Because he's been studying Rooster. He used a drug habit as a reason to get close to your club. Rooster has something in common with Darius, and Demon." Lynx held my gaze a moment before looking out over the small crowd. "He shares DNA with them."

"Bullshit," Rooster yelled. "My father was from Ireland."

"Your mother was married to a man from Ireland," Lynx said. "But that man wasn't your father. Your mother had an affair. Several in fact, from what I've been able to find. One of those men was Terrell Somers. I believe, and I think Darius does as well, that you're actually the son of Terrell Somers."

Rooster glanced over at Demon. I could tell he didn't know what to make of the news, and my sexy biker seemed to be a little in shock as well. To everyone else, he probably appeared calm and unmoved, but I knew different. The corners of his eyes were a little tighter, his lips flattened a little more. Despite his loose posture, I felt the steel of his muscles and the tension running through him.

"You're giving me a headache, Lynx. What's it all mean?" I asked. I worried if he didn't hurry this along, Demon might erupt.

"You were on Darius' radar after he heard about you from Rooster, indirectly. Found some messages on the dark web where Darius was searching for you, wanted to deliver you to his brother in hopes of gaining favor with him. He's had people watching you, Farrah, across several states. Any glimpse and he was notified. Which is how he found you working at the diner. He'd only thought to use you to get closer to his brother, until he found out about your connection with the Devil's Fury." Lynx looked like he didn't want to share whatever else was on his mind. "He has a lot of high-tech equipment. I found, um… he has pictures. Of you and Demon. I'm not sure how he managed to get so many when you were clearly inside the compound and nowhere near the fence line, but they're rather detailed. And something I never wanted to see. Demon, you might want to make sure you don't have any cut fencing around the compound. Or a rat."

My stomach knotted and I felt sick.

"Demon is the only son Terrell Somers even attempted to raise, and I think it's twisted something inside Darius, knowing he wasn't wanted. He wants to destroy Demon and was going to use Farrah to do it. I think he'd hoped Rooster would accept Farrah as a gift and cause trouble between the clubs."

"Well, he didn't," Demon said. "And I got Farrah back, so what the hell does he want now?"

"Darius has a rather lucrative business. He owns multiple brothels across the globe, ones that specialize in… brutality. For the right price, you can do anything, including kill the whore you purchase for the evening. Since the Devil's Boneyard didn't give Farrah to Rooster, and it didn't have the result he'd hoped for, I think his mind has warped and twisted even more. He wants revenge. Against you. Me. And he'll use Farrah to get it, most likely by putting her in one of those wretched places," Lynx said. "There's no other explanation. He's tried to abduct women before, and once they were out of his reach, he moved on. Don't get me wrong. His success rate is high, unfortunately. Only a few have slipped through his fingers. Since he always uses a different name, the police haven't connected the kidnappings, especially since they cross various states. If he didn't have shit documented so well, I'd have never known about them. But he didn't back down this time, which tells me it's personal."

"So what exactly is the plan? Why are we all here if you think he only wants Farrah?" my grandpa asked.

"Because if he can't get to Farrah, he may decide to use her siblings or other family to lure her out. I needed to make sure everyone stayed safe. As for the plan... You won't like it," Lynx said. "We need to use Farrah as bait. I have no doubts he's kept an eye on her and knows she's here. If it doesn't work, then maybe he's moved on, but I think he's too focused on her to walk away at this point."

"Are you fucking kidding me?" Demon demanded. "You want to use my pregnant fiancée as *bait*?"

Lynx blinked a moment, his gaze swerving to me. "Pregnant?"

I gave him a slight nod and reached over to take Demon's hand, hoping it would keep him from doing something reckless, like beheading my uncle. He squeezed my fingers once, then released me.

"I don't want to risk her, or your kid, Demon, but I don't think anything else will work. Mariah is too damn young to even attempt something like this. There's no one else. Darius will want Farrah if for no other reason than to hurt the two of us. She's our best bet at getting him to come out of hiding," Lynx said.

"He's right," I said, putting my hand on his arm. Demon yanked free of me, fury rolling off him as he glared down at me. "This is our best shot at getting Darius to come out of hiding. Do you want to look over our shoulders the rest of our lives?"

"You're not doing this," he said, his teeth clenched as he snarled at me. "I will tie you to the fucking bed if you even attempt it. Don't push me, Farrah. I won't let you risk yourself or our child."

"It's not your call," I said. The moment the words

left my lips, I knew I'd made a grave mistake. My eyes went wide as Demon tossed me over his shoulder and walked off. Too stunned to do much but hang limply, I tried to process the words shouted from my family and the others.

Trigger trotted after us, but I didn't know how he'd react when Demon finally exploded, letting out all the anger I felt inside him. I motioned to the dog and yelled for him to stay. The German Shepherd halted and sat, even if he didn't seem pleased to be left behind.

Demon didn't stop until we entered the small quarters we'd been given for our stay, then he slammed the door and bolted it. Demon went straight back to the bedroom, sat on the edge of the mattress, and pulled me across his lap.

"Not. My. Call. That's what you said." He yanked my clothes, tearing them until I lay bare and at his mercy. His hand came down hard on my ass cheek and I yelped in both surprise and pain. He spanked me without mercy, each blow harder than the first. I heard the breath sawing in and out of his lungs as if he'd run a marathon. My ass felt like it was on fire as he ran his palm over the abused cheeks.

Demon stood, lifting me, then pressing me belly down over the side of the bed. I heard the clink of his belt and the slide of it through his belt loops. He yanked my arms behind my back, binding my wrists with the leather. The heat of his body pressed against me as he leaned down over my back, his lips near my ear.

"Your safety and that of our child is *not my call*. Is that what you said?" he asked, his voice deep and low, sending a shiver down my spine.

"I need to do something, Cody. I can't live in

fear."

He pushed his hips against me tighter, the hard ridge of his cock unmistakable. "And now? Are you afraid right now, little girl? Worried the big bad wolf might gobble you up?"

"I'm not afraid of you, Cody," I said softly.

He worked his hand between our bodies, his fingers prying my thighs apart. The cool air hit the lips of my pussy. "Still not afraid? Or maybe you like it when I get rough with you, punish you and spank that pretty little ass."

"It hurt," I said, but even I could hear my words lacked heat. Yes, he'd probably bruised my skin, but I couldn't deny my nipples were hard and my clit throbbed. He was right. I did like it when he got a little rough. I *liked* having him punish me. Maybe it was why I always pushed him so hard.

"It hurt," he said in a mocking tone. "If I were to shove my cock inside you right now, I bet you'd be wet, wouldn't you? I remember the last time I spanked you. You liked getting fucked hard afterward, got off on it."

"Cody, I..." I stopped, not knowing what I wanted to say.

He unfastened his pants, the rasp of his zipper loud in the otherwise quiet room. I felt his cock rub against my pussy right before he plunged hard and deep, filling me up. I cried out, my body going tight. He pounded into me, unrelenting as he took what he wanted.

"Mine, Farrah. You're mine. I won't let you risk yourself." He thrust harder. Faster. I squirmed under him, wanting more, needing him to touch me. My nipples rubbed against the bed as he hammered into me, the friction nearly enough to make me come. "If I have to fuck you into obedience, I will."

He slammed into me again and I screamed out as an orgasm ripped through me, leaving me breathless. Demon grunted as he filled me with his cum, his cock twitching inside me. I shifted and realized he was still hard. He pulled out and removed the belt from my wrists, only to lift me onto the bed and stretch my hands up to the headboard. Using the same belt, he secured me to the bed.

"Not done with you. When I am, you won't be thinking about putting yourself in danger. You'll be too fucking tired. Too sore." He leaned down gently biting my nipple. "Going to make you come until you can't anymore. Fill you up. Your thighs and pussy will be covered in my cum. Maybe your ass too."

His words had me gasping and arching toward him. We hadn't done that yet, but I'd wanted to. The books I'd snuck when I was younger had always made me curious. Not to mention the things I'd heard when no one realized I was lurking near the clubhouse.

Demon gripped my hair, tipping my head back and forcing me to hold his gaze. The anguish and anger I saw were enough to make my heart nearly stop. "Do you have any idea what would happen if Darius got his hands on you and we couldn't save you in time? Do you? Despite the world you've lived in, Farrah, you're still rather sheltered. The places Lynx mentioned, the type of brothels my half-brother owns, would destroy you. You'd be beaten. Raped. Eventually killed, all for the pleasure of depraved men who like to cause pain. I won't... *can't*... let you risk yourself."

I studied his face as his words sank in. Not just the words themselves, but what he didn't say as well. It wasn't just me he worried about, or our child. If

Darius were to succeed in taking me again, and this time not handing me over to Rooster, it would destroy Demon.

"I love you, Farrah. I won't let you do this. I can't." He kissed me hard and deep. "I would die without you."

"If I don't, they'll try to use Mariah," I said softly. "My little sister. She's not even out of high school, Cody. What do you think would happen if you couldn't rescue her? You think I'm sheltered? She's never thought to question anything in her life. She just does as she's told. Even though she ran a bit wild with me when we were younger, it's not the case now. Being kidnapped would have broken her. I came out fighting, but her? She'd have fallen apart."

"I know you're strong, baby. It's part of what I love about you, but don't ask this of me. Anything else, but I can't stand the thought of him getting his hands on you again. And now that Lynx has brought you here, he'll know he's no longer just Earl the junkie to us."

"Do what you must, Cody. But so will I."

His jaw set in determination and I knew I was in for a long day and night.

Regardless, I'd find a way to sneak out and go to Lynx. If he needed me to be bait, it's exactly what I'd do. Anything to protect my family.

Chapter Fifteen

Demon

"What the fuck did you do?" I demanded as I shoved Lynx. I'd woken to Farrah missing and nearly had a heart attack.

"She needed to do this," he said. "But I admit, shit went sideways. I took her to the local café and left her alone outside for a few minutes, hoping it would lure Darius out of hiding. Except he turned the tables on me, made sure I was distracted, and snatched Farrah."

I snarled and hauled back my fist, then let it fly, cracking Lynx across the jaw. I didn't give a fuck if he was Farrah's uncle or not. He'd used her as bait, after I'd expressly forbid it, and then he'd fucking lost her! Darius had my woman, my pregnant fiancée, and no one knew where they were.

"How." *Crack.* "Did." *Crack.* "You lose her?" The last of my words were a near roar as I let the blows land on the fucking moron. I couldn't remember ever being so damn furious in my life.

Lynx yanked himself from my grasp and wiped the blood from his mouth and nose. "I didn't lose her on purpose! She's my family!"

"You should have never used her as bait. You knew I didn't want her out there, vulnerable and at the mercy of a man like Darius Somers. He's going to kill her. And it will be a blessing to her when he does because I have no doubt she'll suffer greatly before then. I will fucking kill you if we don't get her back safe."

Lynx gave a quick nod. "And I'll let you."

Doolittle came up, placing a hand on my shoulder. "Trigger is missing, Demon. I don't think Farrah is alone. He must have followed her and Lynx this morning."

"What the fuck good does that do? It's obvious the dog let her get taken, or worse, Darius killed him if he tried to protect her." I pulled at my hair, wanting to yank it out.

"Trigger is microchipped, more specifically, he's got a tracker in him. If he's with Farrah, which I suspect he is, then we'll know exactly where they are," Doolittle said. "I've got the app on my phone."

He pulled the device from his pocket and with a few swipes, he had the app open and a map came up on the screen with a little red blinking dot. I didn't know this area, but Lynx did and cursed.

"He's taken her to the warehouses outside town. They're ours but are currently empty," he said. "I'll get everyone together. Now that we know where she is, we can make a plan."

It took a half hour before the Savage Raptors, as well as the Dixie Reapers, Devil's Boneyard, and my brothers were in the same room. We'd decided to take things to the interior of the clubhouse and leave the women and kids out of it. Prospects were guarding them in one of the guest quarters.

Atilla scanned the room and leaned back against the bar top, arms folded and ankles crossed. As silence fell, he took a breath and seemed to contemplate what he wanted to say.

"We offered protection to Farrah if she came here, and we've failed. Not just her, but her old man, her family, and one of our own -- Lynx. Diabolus is more cunning than any of us were prepared for and he's gotten the upper hand. The good news is thanks to Doolittle, we know where he's keeping Farrah and it seems her dog is sticking close to her. So we need a plan. We can't go in guns blazing or she could end up dead," Atilla said.

Before anyone else uttered a word, my phone went off, as well as several others in the room. I pulled up the message and saw it was from Wire. Another video. An ache tore through my chest as I opened it and saw my feisty Farrah tied to a chair. Her shirt had been sliced so her breasts spilled out, her bra apparently cut away if she'd worn one to begin with. He'd put duct tape over her mouth, but her eyes flashed with fury and fire.

"I have a special treat in store for you today. This lovely little spitfire is the daughter of a Dixie Reaper, the old lady of a Devil's Fury member, and is desired by someone in the Devil's Boneyard. Even better, she's got spirit and won't break easily." The man came into view, and it was the same hooded figure who'd had MaryAnne. He knelt and leaned in closer. "The first round of bidding will remove her clothes. I've already given you a taste by letting you see her tits. You want more, you'll pay. Then you get to decide her fate, my friends. Tick, tick, tick. This offer won't last long."

I threw my phone so hard it shattered against the wall. My gaze met Venom's and I saw every bit of fury I felt blazing inside him as well. Same for Bull and several others who'd come to help Farrah. Rooster, the half-brother I'd never known about, came to stand beside me.

"We're going to get her back," he said. "If I'd had any idea about all this, I'd have kept her when he brought her to my club, or at least made it appear as if I were keeping her."

"I didn't see Trigger," Doolittle said.

He was right. The dog hadn't been in the video. Did that mean the warehouse was a dead end? Had he killed or injured the dog and left it there, somehow knowing we could track it? Or was Trigger biding his time to rescue Farrah?

"We can't take the bikes," Lynx said. "He'd hear us coming before we even got close. Every truck and SUV available will need to be used for this mission."

The doors opened and Ridley came in, her head high and shoulders back. She knew she shouldn't be here, but there was a small bundle clutched in her hands. She didn't stop until she reached me and handed it over. I glanced down, seeing a change of clothes for Farrah.

"She may need those," Ridley said. "When you find her."

I nodded. "When." Not if.

"Ridley, you can't be here," Venom said.

"That's my little girl. I'll not stand by and do nothing." Ridley lifted her chin, but I saw the sheen of tears in her eyes and I knew Venom did too. He yanked her into his arms and held her as she cried.

"She may need her mom," Bull said. "We don't know how fast we can find her, or what that asshole will do before then. Might be a good idea to take a woman with us, just in case. Besides. I know Ridley. She won't stay put if we try to leave her behind. Not this time."

It seemed my woman got her stubbornness from her mom. I almost pitied Venom. On the other hand, he'd survived living with her for nearly twenty years. It meant there was hope for me and Farrah.

It didn't take long before we loaded up into the trucks and SUVs. The drive to the warehouse wasn't far but we parked a ways off so Darius wouldn't see us pull up. We crept through the trees and underbrush to reach the buildings. The app on Doolittle's phone guided us to the last warehouse. Trigger prowled the exterior of the building and didn't stop to even take notice of us. Although, the dog was too smart to not realize we were there. The fact he didn't glance our way told me he was focused on Farrah.

"Looks like the dog didn't die after all," I said.

I edged closer to the building and found a crack in the wall. I could barely make out the interior but Farrah drew my gaze. The bidding must have started. She'd been stripped completely bare and had blood running down her arms. My hands clenched into fists, realizing he'd cut her.

"What will Trigger do if we let him inside?" I asked, my gaze going to Doolittle.

"Attack. If the man doesn't have a gun, then the chances of Trigger being harmed or killed are relatively low. He's been trained for this."

I heard Farrah scream and I fought the urge to rush to her rescue.

"I'm going after her," I said. "Hold the dog back. I need to take care of Darius on my own, or at least make him suffer a little."

The next time I couldn't hold back. I ran for the front of the warehouse, barreling inside. Darius spun to face me, a demented smile on his face. The coldness in his eyes chilled me as he shoved his arm back, burying a knife in Farrah's arm. After she screamed this time, she passed out.

I circled Darius, pulling two knives out. I could end it quickly and shoot him, but I wanted him to hurt. To bleed. I needed him to suffer the way he'd made Farrah suffer.

"Don't you want to know what's on the menu for your woman?" he asked, trying to goad me.

"Won't matter. You'll be too dead to do anything else to her."

Darius snarled at me. "Maybe so, but I think I'll give you a gift anyway. They want me to slice her up, make her bleed. My bloodthirsty audience wants to watch as she's raped by multiple men, then finally sold off to the highest bidder. I'd planned to gift you a copy of the video so you could see what your precious Farrah suffered."

The maniacal laugh he let loose had the hair raising on my arms. Bile rose in my throat just thinking about what he'd planned for her. I lunged, slicing my knife across his abdomen. It didn't seem to slow him even a little. Darius came for me, slashing at me like a madman. His blade found its mark several times. Not enough to stop me. I went after him, not stopping until I had him on the ground, blood pooling around his body.

He coughed and still grinned as if he'd somehow won.

I heard Trigger barking, then the large beast knocked me out of the way as he latched onto Darius. I didn't know why he'd come to me and not Farrah, but now that Darius was handled, I could take care of my woman. I stood and moved toward Farrah, only to freeze. Two men flanked her, also wearing black masks. He hadn't been working alone. How had we missed it? My heart slammed against my ribs as I watched in horror. They fondled her, laughing at the anger they must have seen in my face.

The first slash of a blade across her chest had me growling as loud as Trigger, except the dog beat me to it. He launched himself at the man who'd just hurt Farrah, latching on with his teeth and not letting go. I rushed the other one, taking him to the ground. Soon, I heard my brothers surrounding me and realized more masked men had moved in from the shadows. It seemed it wasn't just Darius, or even Darius and a few men, but an entire operation.

I heard someone scream and grinned as I saw Trigger tearing into one of them. He ripped the flesh from the bone and went back for more. A hard kick from another assailant sent the dog flying, but the German Shepherd got up and leapt into the fray again.

While the masked men were distracted, I rushed to Farrah. Her head slumped and her eyes were closed, which was a blessing. I hoped it meant she wasn't in pain for the moment. The pulse in her throat was steady. I worked the ropes loose and freed her arms and legs before I gently eased the tape from her mouth.

"I've got you, baby," I murmured, cradling her in my arms.

Pain seared into me and I turned, nearly dropping Farrah. Somehow, Darius had managed to get up. I'd thought for sure he'd breathed his last already. The knife in his hand dripped blood and as the room spun I realized the fucker had stabbed me. It wasn't just Farrah's blood on that knife, but mine as well.

"Nothing personal. Brother." He sneered and lunged again. I couldn't deflect the blow without dropping Farrah. I turned, trying to keep her safe as his knife sank into me again.

I heard shouts and Farrah was taken from my arms right before my knees hit the concrete floor. I glanced over in time to see Doolittle slice Darius' throat, ending his miserable life. Someone helped me stand and I staggered my way out to one of the trucks. Nothing made sense for a while, everything going in and out. Voices blurred, the light was too bright, and I felt like I was slipping away.

"Don't you dare die on me," someone

whispered.

I fought to open my eyes again and saw Farrah, her brow creased as she clung to my hand. A glance around the area showed we were no longer in the truck. I didn't remember it stopping, or the ride back to the compound for that matter. I lay stretched out in a bed, with Farrah next to me.

Doolittle leaned over, catching my attention. "Keep in mind I'm a vet and not a human doctor, but I think you'll both live. I had to put stitches in Farrah's arms. She had three gaping wounds and some shallower cuts that just required bandages. You, on the other hand, we nearly lost."

"What's wrong?" I asked, my voice croaking a bit. Jesus. How long was I out of it?

"The stab wounds were deep, Demon. You lost a lot of blood and it was hard to keep you conscious. Even when you weren't completely out, you weren't quite with us either. Delirious is a good way to put it. I patched you up best I could. The rest is up to you, but you won't be leaving the Savage Raptors for at least a few days. Even then, you may not be healed enough to ride your bike."

"I'm sorry." I glanced at Farrah and saw tears in her eyes. "If I hadn't left, you wouldn't be hurt right now. It's my fault."

"Later," I said, not having the strength to argue with her. She'd defied me, but I didn't have it in me to punish her when she'd been injured.

I struggled to sit up, but Farrah pressed me back to the bed. "Not right now. Please. Rest a little more."

"How long?" I asked.

"It's been two days," Doolittle said, knowing what I meant. "And Farrah hasn't left your side. We placed her in the bed next to you, patched you both up at the same time, and she's stayed here ever since. You have quite a woman there, brother."

I smiled, knowing he was right. She was something else, even if she didn't obey for shit. By the time I'd eaten some soup, and managed to get to the bathroom on my own, I knew I was ready to find out exactly what the fuck had happened, and if Darius was responsible for MaryAnne as well.

Farrah was a stubborn woman and didn't want me leaving the guest quarters, so Atilla came to me. The Pres sat on the sofa and studied the two of us.

"If ever there was a perfect match, I do believe it's you and Farrah. I think I'm envious." He smiled.

"The men with Darius… who were they?" I asked.

"His lackeys. Henchmen. Whatever you want to call them." Atilla shifted. "Lynx worked with Wire and two other hackers. Darius has been doing this a long time. There are countless videos of the women he's abused and killed, as well as those he's sold. Hades Abyss was particularly interested in one. Pretty little thing named MaryAnne. They're tracking her down now. I heard the Pres himself is looking into it."

"Good. Any others?" I asked.

"Who can be saved?" Atilla asked. "Probably not. We're going to track down any we can and try to help them, but it may be too late for most. Some are long dead, or so used up they may as well be. Right now, you focus on healing and taking care of that amazing woman by your side."

"Need to get home."

"Soon. I've been assured your club has things in hand in Blackwood Falls. They left Beau here in case you need him to ride your bike. Doolittle thought it would be a good idea for you and Farrah to take her truck home, along with Trigger. That dog is something else! I've already asked Doolittle to send one my way if he finds another like him." Atilla stood and shook my hand. "Let us know if you need anything."

He let himself out and I made my way back to the bedroom with Farrah's assistance. The next several days were spent mostly sleeping and trying to regain my strength. By the time we left, I was more than ready to be home.

Epilogue

Demon -- One Month Later

In my absence, Badger and Slash had cleaned house. All the club whores were gone and a new set had moved in. I'd made it clear to them exactly what their place was in the club. If they so much as disrespected an old lady, or refused to back down if a brother said no, they wouldn't just be out of here, I'd make a painful example of them. Each of them paled every time I entered the clubhouse, which made me smile. Yeah, I was a sick asshole for enjoying their fear, but it meant I didn't have to worry about them trying to fuck me.

Only woman I wanted was at home. In my bed. And carrying my kid.

As much as I wanted to know what we were having, Stitches assured me it was too soon to know. Farrah was roughly two months along. We wouldn't know for certain until she met with the OB-GYN, but she had an appointment coming up. I'd already promised to be by her side every step of the way, holding her hand through all of it.

I'd gotten word from Kraken that MaryAnne had been found. He wouldn't say much beyond that and I worried about the poor girl. I had no doubt she was in good hands and knew that Hades Abyss would treat her right. I only hoped she'd be able to get past whatever Darius had done to her.

Rooster and Lynx had both received open invitations to visit whenever they wanted. I'd never known I had brothers, and even though Darius was gone, I looked forward to getting to know Rooster better. Things were awkward at best between me and Rooster, especially since he'd wanted my woman for himself. Lynx, however, seemed to settle right into the lives of his family. Even after all that happened, Farrah still enjoyed speaking to him and looked forward to any future visits. I was a little more reserved since his stupid plan to use her as bait had nearly gotten the both of us killed.

I sipped my beer and leaned back on the couch, kicking my feet up on the table. Farrah narrowed her eyes at me as she came into the room carrying a plate of cookies. Since she'd learned to cook, she'd been working on fattening me up. Couldn't really complain. Best damn meals and desserts I'd ever had.

"Tables aren't for feet, Cody," she said.

"My table, right? I'll put my feet there if I want."

She set the cookies down and put her hands on her hips. "Is that so? Your table? I guess this is *your* house too?"

I slowly pulled my feet back and stared at her, wondering if she was about to have one of those hormonal meltdowns I'd witnessed several times now. "Nope. Yours too."

"Are you sure? I'm just a lowly servant in your house. Have to do as you say, when you say it."

"Farrah."

She lifted her chin a notch. "Maybe I don't want to marry you after all."

I stood and set my beer down. "Look here, you little brat. You accepted my ring. Carry my kid. You're damn sure going to marry me. Soon."

"Why should I? What do I get from the arrangement? More orders?"

I grinned. "Oh, I'll give you orders all right."

Before she could run from the room, I grabbed her around the waist and hauled her up against me. Her eyes dilated and her lips parted. I'd tried to be more careful with her, not wanting to hurt the baby.

After all the stress she'd been under, I worried she'd not make it past the first trimester.

I kissed her hard, then softer. "You'll take my orders. Know why?"

She shook her head.

"Because you like it. My naughty little girl likes getting tied up, spanked, and told what to do. If I told you to drop to your knees and suck my cock right this very second, you'd do it. And you'd fucking like it."

"Cody." She was breathless, pressing tighter to me.

"My fierce little warrior need something?"

"Yes. You know I do."

I rubbed her breast through her top, her nipples already hard and poking through the material. I'd convinced her to wear knit dresses around the house because it made it easier to fuck her whenever I wanted. I gathered the skirt in my hand and lifted it, growling when I realized she wasn't wearing panties.

"Very naughty. No panties, Farrah?"

"No. I haven't worn them all day."

I worked my hand between her legs and stroked her clit. She gasped and her body went tight. *Fuck me.*

"Holy shit! Did you just come?" I asked.

Her cheeks turned bright pink and it was answer enough, along with the wetness coating my fingers. Being pregnant had made her want my cock all damn day, and I was loving it. I just had to hold back a bit. Not only did I worry about the pregnancy, but she'd been sliced up like a damn Christmas goose. The wounds had healed and left pink scars behind. Seeing them always reminded me of how I'd felt, seeing her tied to the chair, bleeding.

Someone knocked at the door, and I would have ignored it, but Farrah pulled away, settling her dress back around her knees and rushed off. With a groan, I hoped like hell she didn't let whoever it was into the house. The excited bark made me smile and a moment later, Victoria raced into the room as fast as her short little legs would carry her. Trigger lumbered in from the kitchen, his ears perked forward.

"Rachel dropped Victoria off for a playdate with Trigger," Farrah said, coming back into the room. Thankfully alone.

"You set up a playdate. For the dogs."

She nodded, looking down at them fondly. The little pug had met Trigger shortly after we returned from Oklahoma and the two loved to romp and play together. Seeing Victoria try to keep up with Trigger was fucking hilarious, but they seemed to have a good time.

I'd installed a doggy door off the kitchen so Trigger could let himself out into the newly fenced backyard. I made sure it wasn't locked, then took Farrah's hand and led her to the bedroom, shutting the dogs out.

"If Trigger gets to play with his girlfriend, I think I should get to play with mine."

She smiled softly, her cheeks turning pink again. "I like it when you play with me."

I shrugged off my cut and started removing my clothes. When Farrah reached for the hem of her dress, I stopped her with a shake of my head. Once I'd taken off the last of my clothing, I reached for her, pulling the stretchy top of her dress down and baring her breasts.

"No bra either?" I asked.

"Nope."

I leaned down, taking a nipple into my mouth and sucked on it long and hard. She moaned and wrapped her fingers around the back of my neck, holding me to her. I licked the hard bud, then gently bit down, making her cry out in pleasure. Lifting the hem of her dress, I walked her back to the bed. We tumbled onto the mattress and I wasted no time sliding into her wet heat.

"Fuck me, Farrah. You feel so Goddamn amazing. I'll never get enough of you."

She wrapped her legs around my waist. "Good. I need you just as much."

I reached between us, working her clit as I thrust into her. It didn't take much to get her off again. Twice. Taking her faster, driving into her tight little pussy, I knew there was nowhere I'd rather be than right here with her. I filled her up with my cum and kissed her deeply.

"I love you," I murmured against her lips.

"Love you too."

"Then marry me, damn it."

She smiled. "Soon."

Impudent little wench. "You're a brat."

"Yes," she agreed. "But I'm *your* brat. If I changed, you wouldn't know what to do. You'd have no reason to punish me anymore."

I gripped her wrists in one hand and pinned them over her head before I started fucking her again. "Can't have that. You know how much I love spanking your ass."

She leaned up and nipped my lower lip. "I'm still waiting on the day you follow through on your threats and fuck it."

Everything in me went hot at the mere thought, but I'd already decided it wasn't something I'd try until after the baby arrived and she felt up to it. I might be an asshole, and depraved at times, but there were lines even I wouldn't cross.

Whatever brought her to Blackwood Falls -- a deity or Fate -- I would thank them every day for the rest of my life. With her by my side, I knew there would never be a dull moment. She'd keep me on my toes, make me laugh, and give me a reason to live every day to the fullest until I drew my last breath.

"My love." I kissed her. "My life." Another soft kiss. "My everything."

She kissed me back, not letting either of us up for air. With her, I could be gentle, but she also handled the darkness in me, relished it, and for that alone, I knew I'd love her until the day I died.

Harley Wylde

Harley Wylde is the International Bestselling Author of the Dixie Reapers MC, Devil's Boneyard MC, and Hades Abyss MC series.

When Harley's writing, her motto is the hotter the better – off-the-charts sex, commanding men, and the women who can't deny them. If you want men who talk dirty, are sexy as hell, and take what they want, then you've come to the right place. She doesn't shy away from the dangers and nastiness in the world, bringing those realities to the pages of her books, but always gives her characters a happily-ever-after and makes sure the bad guys get what they deserve.

The times Harley isn't writing, she's thinking up naughty things to do to her husband, drinking copious amounts of Starbucks, and reading. She loves to read and devours a book a day, sometimes more. She's also fond of TV shows and movies from the 1980s, as well as paranormal shows from the 1990s to today, even though she'd much rather be reading or writing.

Harley at Changeling: changelingpress.com/harley-wylde-a-196

Changeling Press E-Books

More Sci-Fi, Fantasy, Paranormal, and BDSM adventures available in e-book format for immediate download at ChangelingPress.com -- Werewolves, Vampires, Dragons, Shapeshifters and more -- Erotic Tales from the edge of your imagination.

What are E-Books?

E-books, or electronic books, are books designed to be read in digital format -- on your desktop or laptop computer, notebook, tablet, Smart Phone, or any electronic e-book reader.

Where can I get Changeling Press E-Books?

Changeling Press e-books are available at ChangelingPress.com, Amazon, Apple Books, Barnes & Noble, and Kobo/Walmart.

ChangelingPress.com

Printed in Great Britain
by Amazon